LONELINESS

Books by
Award Winning Author Jay Carp

The Gift of Ruth   2003

The Gift of Ruth—Large print   2008

Cold War Confessions   2007
USA Best Books of 2007 Award Winner

The Patriots of Foxboro   2009

Loneliness   2011

Jay Carp Fish Tales   2011

LONELINESS

JAY CARP

River Pointe Publications
Milan, Michigan, USA

Loneliness
© 2011 by Jay Carp, first edition

Published by
River Pointe Publications
Milan, Michigan 48160
734-439-8031

ISBN: 978-0-9817258-3-3

This is a work of fiction. Names, places, and incidents
either are the product of the author's imagination or are used
fictitiously. Any resemblance to persons, living or dead,
events or locales are entirely coincidental.

Interior design and composition by Sans Serif Inc.
Cover design by Barb Gunia

Printed in USA

Prologue

Loneliness is a haunting, hurting emotion that isolates each infected victim from all thoughts of happiness. It is like an oil spill; it is pervasive and sullen and it destroys beauty. The joy that people feel from being alive is degraded by loneliness. There is no human being who wants to be a prisoner inside this empty and useless obsession.

Yet, there are certain periods in our lives when we all are susceptible to feeling lonely. Among the most vulnerable are those who, for whatever reason, have lost their partner. Whether through divorce, death, separation, or indifference, the loss of a lover, mate, or partner leaves the survivor defenseless against loneliness. Its onslaught usually begins after the partner finally comes to the realization that their other half will never ever again be a part of their life. As the reality of being without a mate sets in, the road to loneliness becomes inviting to travel.

Some partners immediately realize that they are lonely and that they are mired in a bog of unhappiness. They don't seem to be able to cope with their sorrow and, as a result, they become angrier and more bitter. They feel deprived and their outlook on life becomes narrow. They live mostly in the past without seeing any chance for happiness in their future. They are already infected with loneliness.

Other partners fight their loneliness by forcing themselves to be totally busy with frenetic activity. They work extra hard at their businesses or their charities or they micromanage their immediate families. What they accomplish is that they delay the onslaught of loneliness until they slow down to catch their breath. Once they finally do, then they also become infected.

What no one realizes when their life is shattered, is that there is a path that can lead them through their grief. The ability to love, be loved, or even to return love will overcome the deep hurt and pain that locks them in their self built prison. To love again is to inoculate yourself against loneliness.

We never forget the people who were our past loves, but, by learning to renew our capability for love, we become better and richer individuals. Loneliness holds no sway over those who have learned to love again.

This story is about two such people who meet sometime after the end of World War II.

FRESHMEN

1

Benito Da Vinci did not consider himself lonely. Even though his wife, Esther, had been dead for over nine years, such a thought had never once crossed his mind. He would have felt that he was disloyal to both her memory and their three children if an idea such as that had even occurred to him.

"Ben," as he insisted everyone call him because he didn't like his christened name, and Esther had been deeply in love with each other and their children. When she developed breast cancer and died within two years of her diagnosis, Ben was devastated. He went through every negative emotion that ravages partners and lovers after the loss of their mates. Grief, pain, and sorrow at Esther's death, total rage at his fate, and even occasional anger at her for leaving him, were familiar emotions to Ben. The process of reconciling himself to life while his beloved wife was no longer with him, was long, hard and painful.

What made it even harder was that he had to control the boiling volcano of his emotions because of his three children. He had two boys and a girl. At the time their mother first got sick, Greg had been six, Billy had been five and Alice had been three. From that time on,

Ben's duties had expanded from not only being the breadwinner, but also being the lighthouse of love and comfort for his family.

After Esther's passing, Ben had a difficult time trying to explain to his children something he couldn't fully understand himself; why their mother was no longer with them. Children do not grasp logic or death; they only feel emotion. He was forced to muzzle and hide his personal feelings and become the family shepherd for his motherless children. He performed these responsibilities willingly, without complaint, and to the best of his abilities, even while he ached with the same pain that wracked his three children. Almost all of his daily life was spent working for a living and raising his family.

During the week, Monday through Saturday, he put in long hours in his barber shop to support himself and his family. A six day work week was not uncommon for Ben. At the same time, he was conscious of his responsibilities in raising his children. They received every ounce of his love and attention. He was as focused on them as a microscope on a microbe. Ben spent little time thinking of himself. This kept him busy and far away from the waterfall of loneliness as long as he continued to swim upstream.

Sundays were different for him. Ben was thankful that someone in the ancient world had set this one day aside from the rest of the week. He took full advantage of the custom. Sunday was his personal day; he could concentrate on the things that he himself wanted, or needed, to do. It became the linchpin from which he planned the rest of his week. His Sundays were not given over to leisure; as a first generation American of Italian heritage, he had been taught that idleness was akin to deviltry. As a result, Sundays were spent working hard at whatever he enjoyed. To him, doing something different was the definition of rest.

And Sundays always began with him taking his family to church. As practicing Catholics, he and his children went, every Sunday morning, to the early mass at Sacred Hearts Church, in Malden, Massachusetts.

Before his marriage, he had fallen away from the rule that his mother had taught him both as a child and as a young man; attend church regularly. After years of backsliding, he had begun to attend every Sunday after Esther became pregnant with the first of their three children. They both had agreed that religion, for the well being of children's souls, was as beneficial as vitamin pills were for the body. His attendance later became even more important when his wife was diagnosed with cancer. After Esther's death, Ben continued going to Sunday mass with his family; the rituals of the service helped all of them cope with their pain.

However, Ben was more religious by repetition than by philosophy. He had never questioned any of the Catholic tenets such as birth control, priestly celibacy or the ordination of women. What was important to him was that he was at ease with the formalities of the services; they comforted him. He would go to church, keep his pledge up to date, take communion, pass the peace, and enjoy the calm.

The family routine, on a late spring Sunday, was the same as it always had been. It was a pattern that Ben looked forward to. After church, they drove through Malden Square to a diner on Centre Street where they stopped for Sunday breakfast. As they entered, they were greeted by several of the other diners who were also regular Sunday customers. One or two of the men, who frequented his barbershop, called out a greeting to him. He and his family went to a booth near the back and sat down to eat a leisurely breakfast. After their orders were given, but before they were served, Ben's children, Greg, Billy, and Alice, started their Sunday ritual of ragging on each other.

Alice, from the heights of just graduating from Beebe Junior High, began by saying, "Billy, I'll bet you didn't get a thing out of going to church today. I saw you sleeping during the sermon."

"I wasn't sleeping," he replied.

Alice almost snorted her reply, "Yes, you were. Your head was sunk on your chest."

"That's because I was praying that my nosey sister would learn to mind her own business."

Alice pointed her finger at Billy as she answered, "You would be much better off praying for yourself than pretending to pray for your almost completely perfect sister."

Greg joined the fray for the first time, "Listen, you two are giving me a headache. Since you both spent all your time checking on each other, neither of you really heard the sermon. I listened and you both missed out. As a result, I'm the only one full of the spirit."

Billy sputtered, "You're full of something, all right. I'm just not sure what I would call it."

Alice chimed in, "Greg, if anyone needed a sermon, it would be you."

He laughed and answered, "I might need a sermon but certainly not from either of you."

Alice fanned the palm of her right hand at both of her brothers and said, "Both of you are ninny hammers!"

That stopped the conversation for a while because neither of them had ever heard those words before and they didn't want to ask Alice what they meant. For the last few months she had been prone to looking new words up and throwing them at her brothers to purposely confuse them. Shortly though, their conversation picked up on different topics with the three of them constantly splitting into two against one, rotating allies.

Ben sat there listening to his children. On Sundays he never joined in their breakfast discussions. He likened their exchanges to bear cubs boxing and rolling on the ground. Even if they occasionally went beyond the bounds of good taste, he let them work out their differences. At his present age of forty-five, time had finally rewarded him with his doctorate degree in parenting and he was pleased with his abilities and with his children.

When they were very young he was much more of an authoritarian. He would brush aside any complaints with the statement that his own father used, "A family is not a democracy." But, as his children got older and became more independent, they rebelled against his decisions and he found himself constantly fighting with them. He didn't like that; it didn't seem as though that was the way to raise a family. He remembered what he had thought when his father had handed down his arbitrary decisions to him.

Ben began to wonder whether or not his edicts were correct when his other two children began to defend the child with whom he was having problems. Because of that, he started to listen and talk to his children before he made a decision; and it worked out very well. The line between the parent and the children was still there but the boundary was not a wall blocking the trust and love that has to flow both ways. He had taken them from frightened children to maturing adults who were beginning to bloom into their full capabilities. He felt sure that Esther would have been proud of all four of them.

Greg had finished his junior year at Malden High School. Physically, he was much different than everyone else in his family.

He stood six feet two inches tall, much bigger than Ben's five foot eight, and he was wide. He had large shoulders, a barrel chest, and a short neck. Despite his size, he was extremely agile, having what his football coach called "cat quickness." By the end of his junior season, he was already receiving offers of football scholarships from colleges across the country. His head coach was helping him examine the offers and offering advice on which college would best fit his needs. He wanted a career, such as a sports reporter or sports broadcaster, that utilized his athletic background.

Having physical skills and strengths were not his only assets. He was intelligent and had a quiet sense of humor. He appreciated the hard work his father had put in to raise their family and it kept his own life balanced. Because he regarded a football scholarship as the way to get his education, he was as organized as any mature teenager could be and he had inherited his father's capacity for work.

Billy had completed his sophomore year. He was a little shorter and much slimmer than Greg and his personality was different than his older brother. He was more mercurial. He made his mind up faster and he could laugh or lose his temper quicker. He was not as athletic as Greg and he had no specific career in mind and he was in no particular hurry to find one. From the time he was a youngster, he had been interested in art and history. He just cruised through all of his his classes, enjoying what he liked and enduring what he didn't. From that point of view, he was much more of a typical teenager than his older brother.

Alice, would be starting as a freshman at Malden High in the fall. Being the youngest in the family and being the only female, she was spoiled by her brothers. She was tall and slender, with long, auburn hair, and she had a happy personality. Her disposition, her intelligence, and the fact that she was attractive, helped her when she said outrageous things, which she fairly often did. She would say whatever was on her mind and she felt sure that she was always correct; a lot of the time, she was. Being fourteen, she sometimes was brash; however, she would learn to become more cautious and less judgmental as she got older. Maturity would begin when she entered high school; until then, most of her pronouncements were wrapped in baby fat. Which is why her brothers would tease her but they hardly ever would argue with her.

However, the three of them were very close; they had to cling to each other as they grew. They needed the comfort and love of the other two to help overcome the loss of their mother. Both Billy and Alice regarded Greg, their older brother, with his quiet, steady ways, as their leader and they relied on his strength to guide them. He tried hard not to fail them.

When Ben finished eating, and his children stopped chewing on each other, they left the diner and drove home. The house was on Hawthorne Street, a quiet, suburban street located in one of the older neighborhoods of Malden. Both sides of the street were lined with large, two story, wooden homes on big lots. Every house was different, in design and in shape, from its neighbor. The two car garages of each home were separate, wooden structures at the back edge of each property. Ben's house had four bed rooms and was painted white. A first floor porch went around the front and down the side of the house facing the driveway; the porch railings and the roof eaves were decorated with Victorian scrollwork.

After they got home, his three children went their separate ways. Greg went jogging, Billy went to study with a classmate and Alice changed her clothes and rode her bike over to her best friend's house to play tennis. Ben did a few things around the house, put on some work clothes, and went out to clear the patch of land he used for his vegetable garden. It was located in the back, beside the garage, and he referred to it as his "farm."

May was almost over and he wanted to have the soil ready to plant right after Memorial Day. There was a lot to do. He had decided to enlarge his "farm" and plant more vegetables for himself and his neighbors. That meant turning over new soil as well as clearing last year's plot, with all of its old growth, and putting fertilizer down. He worked the earth using a pitchfork and a spade. The sky was cloudless and the sun, at first, warmed him and then made him sweat. It was hard work and he began to take more and more breaks to rest and drink water from the garden hose. He was completely unaware of it, but the more he worked the more he talked to Esther. He told her what he was doing and why he was doing it. Lately, without realizing it, he had begun discussing events with her.

By late afternoon, he was dirty and tired but he had accomplished his goal; his "farm" was ready for planting. He rinsed his face and hands and drank from the hose. He sat and relaxed on the side steps for a few minutes before going in for a shower. He aimed his face at the sun, closed his eyes, and relished the warmth. His thoughts turned to his children and it suddenly came to him that he was home by himself. They would return shortly to fix supper; however, this was one of the few times that all three of them were gone at once.

He was alone. It dawned on him that, in a few years, they would not be coming home; they would be going their own ways. Then, he would be alone, really alone. What would he do? What should he do? For a few seconds he was frightened but he made himself change the subject. Nothing was going to happen for a while so why worry?

He slowly arose, went into the house, and put all his thoughts aside as he showered.

****

Ben was not aware of it but, while he was sitting on the side steps with his eyes closed, a black Mercedes Benz drove by his house. Three houses down, on the opposite side of Hawthorne Street, the car pulled into the driveway. The driver, a woman in her early forties, shut off the motor and spoke to the other occupant, a young boy in his teens, "We shouldn't be too long looking around. Then, you and I will go for some Chinese food."

His response was, "Mom, I don't know why we're here, but Chinese food sounds good to me."

"Jeffrey, I told you why we're here. I'm thinking of buying your Grandfather's house. It has been years since I lived in it and I want to check the condition of the appliances and see what needs to be done. If I buy it we'll be moving into it."

Jeffrey pouted and then said, "It's going to be kind of strange living in Grandpa's old house. Besides, Dad doesn't think this is such a good idea."

His mother answered, "Well, it might seem to be a little strange at first, but it will work out very well. You've been here many times and you have slept over a lot. The only difference is that, now, this will be our home since I'll be the new owner."

His answer was a negative response, which she expected and which annoyed her. "Yuh, Mom, that's true but I only visited before. Now, I'm going to be living here; and this town, Malden, Massachusetts, is the pits. It's nothing like living in the city of Worcester."

His mother kept her frustration out of her voice as she slowly replied, "Jeffrey, first of all Malden is not a town, it is a city. It has its own history. Second, and more important, Malden is not the pit of anything. Where did you get the notion that Worcester is any better than Malden?"

"That's what Dad told me. He said that Malden wouldn't exist if it didn't have the overflow of people and the sewage from Boston. He said that Worcester is a city that stands alone and does not need Boston."

Myrna Cabot froze as she heard her son speak. His words framed almost all of her problems and the reasons she wanted to buy her father's house. Jeffrey's Dad and she had divorced ten years ago but he continually tried to intrude on her life and manipulate their only child, Jeffrey. Their divorce had been bitterly contested and Myrna had been so disillusioned by her marital experience that she had even gone back to using her maiden name. She wanted nothing from her ex-husband, Samuel Skinner, but his attitude was entirely different.

By law, he was out of her life; by character, he absolutely needed to get even. Samuel Skinner was bound and determined to prove to her that she made a mistake in leaving him. At first, he would call Myrna three or four times a week on the phone. Even though his calls were obtrusive and unpleasant, she had been able to handle them.

Although he was awarded visitation rights he never used them until Jeffrey was about ten, five years after the divorce. It was after he started to spend time with Jeffrey that her problems began to be even larger. He began to use these visits to turn Jeffrey against his mother. He would shower Jeffrey with presents and money and question him about what his mother was doing and saying. He particularly wanted to know about her social life. Skinner would always give Jeffrey helpful hints on how to get whatever he wanted or needed out of his mother.

When Jeffrey first started seeing his father on a regular basis, Myrna never asked him about his visits. She believed them to be a private time between her son and her ex-husband and she wanted to respect that. However, Jeffrey's questions to her and his attitude towards her when he came back from seeing his father, soon made her believe that Skinner was taking advantage of their son. Shortly, she was questioning him almost as much as his father was.

In the beginning, Jeffrey had no idea that he was caught in the middle of his parents' war. However, as he got older, he began to sense that he was being fought over. He was overwhelmed by all the money, the gifts and the "suggestions" his father showered on him.

His confusion began to show in his daily attitude. Sometimes, he was hard to handle. He went from a serene child to one who could become very argumentative. In school, his grades began to slip. Even though he knew nothing at all about what his father was like, Jeffrey would boast to his school mates about how rich, famous and important his Dad was. He carried a picture of his father in his wallet and would show everyone his "rich" father who never lost a case.

Myrna decided that Jeffrey needed a more wholesome influence than his father. She wanted to change the impact her ex-husband was having on their son. It was not jealousy on her part; she thought her son was not receiving honest or moral guidance from her divorced partner. His school grades were not very good and he had no really close friends. She believed that, for Jeffrey's own well being, changes had to be made. He needed to have a role model, not a manipulator.

Her mother had passed away when Jeffrey was quite young and her brother had moved to Oregon shortly thereafter. Her father and her brother were the remaining living members of her family and her father was the only one she could turn to. He was retired and lived in Malden. Her father had been against her marriage to Skinner from the very first but he loved his grandson and the two of them got along very well. Myrna began to drive her son to Malden for weekend visits; her father also drove to Worcester during the week to be with them. Jeffrey quickly warmed up to his grandfather.

His grandfather was a gruff old man but he treated Jeffrey as an adult. They went to movies, walked, fished, and spent time together. There were no expensive gifts, no suggestions, and no money, just talk and companionship. Her son loved his grandfather and he enjoyed being with him. He started to return to his childhood calmness again.

It was at this critical juncture of her son's life that his grandfather passed away. His death hurt Jeffrey because no child understands what death really means and no child realizes how it unbalances their tranquility. After his grandfather's funeral, the only male family member around Jeffrey was his father. As a result, Jeffrey inherently again moved even closer to Skinner; he needed guidance even if it came from a conniver.

Her father's passing also had a devastating effect on Myrna. It was completely unexpected. He had had a physical examination a month before his death and he had been pronounced healthy. The shock and grief of her father's passing, along with her mother's death so many years ago, wore heavily on her; she felt that her family roots were being dissolved.

There was another personal feature of her father's death that Myrna had not planned for or even realized. She was a lawyer and her father had asked her to handle his personal affairs. She had reluctantly agreed and now she was enmeshed in the details of his past life;

settling her father's complicated business affairs. Each dry financial transaction she tracked became an emotional upheaval for her. That, plus all of her personal problems with her ex-husband and her son made it a grim year for her.

As she finished the details of her father's estate, Myrna took a week's vacation from work to rethink what was happening to both herself and Jeffrey. After reviewing what she had been through and where she wanted to go, she decided that she had to make some changes in her life. She needed to get Jeffrey out of the war zone he was in and give him a chance to mature at his own pace. This would be a good time for a change for him as he was ready to start high school next fall.

She also wanted a chance to bring some happiness back to her own daily grind. The decision to change her life style completely was the reason Myrna returned to Malden to examine her father's house. She would not move into it unless it was in good condition; if it weren't she would sell it and make other arrangements.

Myrna sat in the driver's seat staring at the house and thinking about Jeffrey's stupid comment concerning the relationship of Malden and Boston. She was not going to try to convince her son that he was wrong. That would put him in the middle of another squabble between his father and his mother. Letting him learn to sort out the truth for himself was more important than correcting him. When she did speak, her remarks were limited to the errand they were on. "Come on, let's take a quick look, both inside and out. Then, on to a good Chinese restaurant."

The house was a little smaller than the other houses on Hawthorne Street. It was a tan saltbox, set back from the street, with large lilac bushes around the sides of the house and a huge thicket of them in the back yard. When she was young, she would take cookies and a book and hide inside her thicket and read. Myrna could remember the smell of the flowers she had enjoyed during all of her childhood. She almost believed that she could smell them now.

She and her son circled the outside of the house and then they inspected the inside. Every room they entered flooded her mind with many memories of her childhood and youth; most were happy, some were bittersweet. All of them made her yearn to return to her past happiness.

Myrna was surprised and pleased to find that the house was in good condition. Repainting, inside and out, along with a few inside alterations, was all that needed to be done to make the house livable. What she saw made up her mind.

"Come on, Jeffrey, we're going to celebrate. This is our new home. You will like living and going to school in Malden; you really will. In the meantime, Egg Foo Young, here we come."

On Monday, she called her brother and, after reaching a financial agreement with him, she bought their father's house on Hawthorne Street. When all the paperwork was finished, she handed in her resignation at her law firm and told her boss that she was going to open her own practice in Malden. The law firm did everything it could do to keep her from leaving because she had been so valuable to them. However, she had made up her mind; the slow, sad merry-go-round she was riding had to be brought to a halt. She wanted a new tune and a new tempo.

She couldn't stop Skinner from visiting Jeffrey but she wanted to limit his casual contacts; and, to some degree, her plan worked. She and Jeffrey moved to Malden a few weeks before school began in the fall. The results of the move appeared to prove Myrna's ideas. It seemed as if the will it took to visit with his son lessened as the distance between them increased. Jeffrey, at fifty miles away, was not as precious to Skinner as Jeffrey, a few blocks away. He didn't visit his son very often.

To compensate for not seeing him much, Skinner spent a great deal of time talking to Jeffrey over the phone. He was afraid of losing contact and thus losing control of his son. To make sure that didn't happen, Skinner tried using the phone instead of his car. The calls were frequent and long. However, they began to slow down in number and in length as soon as Skinner realized that he could easily contact Jeffrey any time he wanted. He was sure that he could exert his authority without even seeing his son. After school started, Skinner occasionally didn't even show up for his court appointed visitation times.

But, the wear and tear on the personalities of both Jeffrey and his mother had already been established. The Jeffrey who moved into the house on Hawthorne Street was a truculent, unhappy fourteen year old; his mother was a chilled woman filled with bitterness and loneliness.

2

Benito Da Vinci was an American citizen born of Italian immigrants. His mother and father were married in Milan and immediately migrated to Boston where they settled in the North End. At that time, the population of the North End was almost completely made up of Italian immigrants, so his parents felt at ease living in their new enclave in their new country. It was almost as if they had never left Italy. English was more of a second language than Italian and visitors could walk for blocks without hearing a single spoken word of English.

His parents moved into a small apartment and started the slow process of adapting to their American life. They both began to learn their new language but neither of them ever lost their heavy Italian accents. They wanted to become naturalized American citizens just as soon as they could so they went to night school in order to learn the language and the history of their new land.

His father opened a barber shop and, as an Italian born business owner, he considered a twelve hour day, six day week, as a normal business schedule. He made a comfortable living and, as the head of his household, he didn't want his wife to work. Benito's mother had been an elementary school teacher in Milan, but in Boston, her Italian accent would make it almost impossible for her to get a teaching job. So, like a dutiful Italian wife, she obeyed her husband's wishes and, instead of teaching, she did a great deal of charity work.

In about a year, his mother became pregnant and, ironically, as his mother often reminded him, he was born on Saint Patrick's Day. Benito, as he was christened, never wondered why, unlike almost all of the other Italian families, he didn't have any brothers or sisters. It was a fact that he just accepted. It wasn't until just before he married Esther, while going through some old family papers, he discovered that, in birthing him, his mother lost her ability to have any other children. This new fact saddened him and deepened the love he held for the memory of his mother.

With his father working long hours, his mother had almost complete control of his formative years. Along with his public school teachers, she was able to give him a love of reading and learning; he had a very gentle upbringing. He developed into a shy child who didn't like confrontations. As he grew older, he was required to work in his father's barber shop. He would sweep the floor, wash the windows, strop the straight edged razors, gather the used linens, and help his father in any way he could. It was a barber shop that never had a female customer and where English was almost never spoken. Benito never gave a thought as to whether or not his childhood was normal; he just dutifully lived it.

When he turned sixteen, his mother passed away, and all that was sweet for him turned sour. His father became an alcoholic and living at home became hell. On his eighteenth birthday he enlisted in the Army to get out of the house. After finishing basic training, he was sent to artillery school and spent his entire Army career at Fort Sill, Oklahoma.

While he was stationed there, he bought scissors, trimmers and enough barbering equipment to earn pocket money by giving haircuts after hours. He eventually built up a large clientele of English speaking Army males of all ranks.

When Benito was discharged, he returned to Boston and lived with his father, who had become a shell of a human. Within three months of his return, his father died and it was during that time that Benito started to reflect on his own life. Like every other child ever born, the only experience he really ever knew about was his own upbringing. He would only be able to compare his childhood to other people's upbringings when he had outgrown his own and could look backwards. And now, that time had arrived.

Until he enlisted, his entire world had been focused around his family and his neighborhood. Traveling across America and seeing diverse life styles, other ethnic groups, and different geographic areas gave him another picture. He started to see a broader America than just his ethnic childhood experience. He began to feel a little sensitive about having such a deep Italian heritage; anyone who spoke with a foreign accent made him feel embarrassed because it reminded him of his father. He decided that it was time for him to leave the North End.

He went to barbering school and earned his license to be a barber. After that, he took all his savings and bought his first barber shop, a small one chair store on Washington Street in Malden. He named it "Ben's Barber Shop" and he hoped that it would attract the local inhabitants of the Malden and Melrose area. He had planned it to be a community barber shop catering to the growing families around that location. What surprised him was that his barbershop attracted a lot of the older Italian males who lived in the general neighborhood. They could talk to him in the language they were comfortable with; they referred to his barbershop simply as "Benito's." He considered it ironic that he was making a good living doing exactly what he had purposely tried to avoid.

He lived in a rented room and worked the same long hours as his father had. He knew of no other way to run a barber shop. Within a relatively short period, he built himself a very good business. During this time, he dated occasionally and had two affairs that didn't last long. He never seemed to be able to strike a balance between his work and his personal life.

That was until he met Esther. One Tuesday afternoon, Ben was invited, by one of his customers, to attend a local Order Sons of Italy in America social. He automatically, out of hand, rejected the invitation; his Italian heritage was still a bit sensitive to him. However, that Friday night, on a complete whim, he changed his mind. When he first arrived at the social, he was sorry he hadn't kept to his original plan of not attending. The room was too small for the number of people packed into it; the whole affair was hot, noisy, smoky and loud. Dancing was almost impossible, couples just held each other tightly and swayed back and forth. There was no footwork. They seemed to be practicing for their own intimate after-the-dance dance steps.

Ben was thinking of leaving when he saw a girl drinking a cup of punch and standing by herself at the refreshment table. She was a petite, slim brunette and she seemed to be amused at the group and grope activities taking place on the dance floor. Ben poured himself a glass of punch and walked over to her; he was struck by her attractive face and her pleasant expression. She looked at him and smiled as he approached. He said, "I'd ask you to dance, but it doesn't look like there's much room out there."

"I'd accept your offer if I weren't afraid of getting bruised. It looks more like a game of tag football than a dance floor."

They both decided to get some fresh air and have a cigarette. They introduced themselves and they eagerly told each other about themselves. Ben learned that Esther had three sisters, one of whom had come with her to the dance. She told him that she worked as a private secretary to a bank president and that she had lived in Malden all of her life. They talked so long that they were surprised to see that the dance was breaking up even though they hadn't finished chatting. Esther's sister was impatiently waiting for her, so Ben got Esther's phone number and she left to go home.

That started their magic interlude together. The bond that attracts opposite sexes to each other was enhanced by their personalities, which complimented each other. There was a sweet, innocent intimacy that was shared between them. They got married shortly after they met and they both relished their marriage; it was truly one of partnership and mutual give and take. Shortly after the wedding, Ben sold his barber shop and bought the house on Hawthorne Street and opened a new barber shop on Summer Street. He bought the house because he and Esther were planning on a large family; he bought the shop because he was planning on a large business.

However, after eight years of marriage, Esther contracted breast cancer and died. Their marriage had had only two unwritten rules. The first was never to go to bed angry. The second was always to say, "I love you," before going to sleep.

****

As a child, Myrna had known no other home than her father's house on Hawthorne Street. From the time she was born, until she first went to college, her mother, father, older brother and she had lived in that house. Her father had it built as a wedding present for her mother. He was a successful business man and real estate agent who made money on almost every venture he attempted. Myrna's childhood memories were bright and cheerful, without any dark overtones.

She and her brother grew up in a household where her mother and the family maids were always ready to assist and shelter them. The cotton batting of their love and care protected her from any bruises until she began working for a living. After Malden High School, she graduated from Wheaton College in Norton, Massachusetts, and then went on to graduate from Cornell Law School.

Each degree she received was won with the highest possible honors, a tribute to her intelligence and her diligence. Despite her affluent upbringing, and the fact that her family would have given her almost anything she wanted, Myrna grew up to be a very competitive person. Whether it was because she was slightly taller than most women or because she believed that women were discriminated against, the fact remained that she wanted to do better than anyone else. She refused to be second in anything she attempted. She took a job with a large law firm in Worcester where she specialized in corporate law.

About a year after she started working, she met the man she would eventually marry. One morning, on her way to the office, she saw an automobile run a red light and hit a bus filled with commuters. Somehow, one of the attorneys involved in the messy litigation that followed found out that she had been on the scene and called her as a witness. He phoned her, introduced himself, explained what he wanted, and asked for a meeting. She arranged to be deposed at her law firm, reserving a small meeting room for the deposition.

Myrna met Samuel Skinner at the front desk and, even before they shook hands, his appearance confirmed her initial thoughts about him. She had been favorably impressed with his deep, resonant voice when they talked on the phone and seeing him in person made her wonder if he were a movie star instead of a lawyer. She immediately decided that he was handsome in a debonair way. Skinner was tall, lean and tanned. He had brown, wavy hair with flecks of gray in his sideburns. She judged that he was about fifteen to twenty years older than she was. His clothes were tailor made to enhance his slim frame. They were expensive and gave the impression of not daring to wrinkle without getting Skinner's permission. He had an aura of culture and wealth about him. Without realizing it, Myrna became infatuated.

For Myrna, the major result of the deposition was that Skinner asked her to join him for dinner the very next evening. On that date, because she wanted to make a good impression, Myrna acted much differently from her normal, quiet self; she absolutely couldn't stop talking. It was as if she needed to tell Skinner all about herself. He would ask her a general question and she would answer in almost total detail. She poured herself out to him like a waterfall in spring time. Myrna told Skinner about her childhood, her family, her education, and even her love affairs. By the end of the evening, there wasn't much that she had left hidden.

By contrast, all that she learned about Skinner was that he was divorced, that his marriage had been bad, and that his life was very lonely. These sparse descriptions made him even more appealing to Myrna.

As Skinner was walking with Myrna back to her apartment she

invited him over for dinner that Saturday. When he left her at the entrance to the building, he accepted her invitation and he said that he had enjoyed the evening very much. They did not hug or kiss.

That Saturday, Myrna spent all day preparing for her date. She thoroughly cleaned her apartment which was immaculate even before she began duplicating clean with even more clean. She spent a long time shopping for the ingredients for her meal and she fussed over the food preparation. Skinner arrived with a large bouquet of flowers and a bottle of wine. They spent a cozy evening leisurely eating and drinking and, this time, Skinner did most of the talking. He elaborated, slightly, on his unhappy marriage and admitted to bearing some of the responsibility for the breakup. His remorse convinced Myrna that she had found a beautiful man with a loving personality. She fell completely in love with Samuel Skinner. Myra was so overwhelmed that Skinner didn't even have to carry out his plans to seduce her, she just followed him into her bedroom.

Skinner moved in with Myrna the following Tuesday. He brought no furniture, just a lot of clothes and a briefcase full of his work. That began the happiest period of her young life. She was working at a job she enjoyed, her employers were well pleased with her, and she was sharing her life with the man of her dreams. There were absolutely no clouds on her horizon as they started living together.

However, from that Wednesday morning on, until she moved back into the house on Hawthorne Street, her life slowly became an emotional roller coaster. Many times, she ranged from happiness to despair, from love to hate, and finally, from heat to ice. That can always happen in relationships that are good; it inevitably happens in relationships that are flawed.

Myrna wanted to share her happiness with her family so, as soon as she and Skinner established a togetherness pattern, she introduced him to her mother and father. Over the next few months, she had her parents come to Worcester to visit her and the four of them would go out to dinner. She also brought Skinner to their home in Malden to meet her brother, when he arrived home for a visit. He had studied forestry at Michigan State University and was living and working in Oregon.

She was surprised, and disappointed that her family, with the exception of her brother, were not as pleased about Skinner as she was. They were not rude or impolite, they just didn't warm up to him as she had expected. Their reasons were never discussed openly but her mother intimated that she wanted Myrna to be legally married; her father suggested that living with an older, divorced man was not really a smart idea. The only family member who was enthusiastic about her relationship was her brother who thought that Skinner was an ideal partner. Myrna assumed that, as her mother and father got to know more about Skinner, they would change their minds, so she kept hoping for a better future.

She also would have preferred that the two of them were married but, since Skinner never brought the subject up, she didn't mention it either. She was happy just to be living with him so she made no demands and went out of her way to please him. As a result, she learned very little about him; he rarely talked about himself, his family or his background. Outside of his large wardrobe of suits and his heavy briefcase, which he constantly carried, he brought no history, no furniture, and no personal belongings.

It was a partnership in which she contributed much more than Skinner; and, at first, Myrna never noticed the difference. She had a hard time gaging the depth and breadth of Skinner as a person because he avoided personal discussions about himself. However, she quickly did notice some of the individual quirks that her partner had. Skinner was vain; he spent more time getting ready in the morning than she did. Skinner was boastful; he would always managed to have whomever he was talking with look at his wristwatch. It was a Rolex. Skinner was secretive; he would avoid discussing either his business or his personal life. What surprised her the most was that Skinner was rarely without his bulging, untidy briefcase which he guarded zealously. Still, Myrna was completely content with their relationship.

Almost a year after Skinner moved in, Myrna was given a promotion within her law firm. Two nights after she told Skinner her good news, they went out to celebrate and Skinner asked her to marry him. She promptly accepted. The wedding was a small affair with Myrna's immediate family and a few friends from her office in attendance. Skinner invited only his law partner and one friend to the wedding; he told Myrna that he had no immediate relatives and that he was not friendly with any of his distant family. They left, following the ceremony, for a honeymoon in Montreal and it was during this trip that her son was conceived.

When they returned, there was a flurry of paperwork as they combined their individual checking and savings accounts into joint accounts. Skinner said that it would make their finances easier to monitor and that he would keep track of all the accounts and let her know of any changes. Myrna went back to work with a zeal and passion that surprised her bosses and coworkers.

As the years passed, Myrna's goals altered without her even being aware of any differences. Jeffrey's birth, and his upbringing during his younger years, and her fierce devotion to her work altered her relationship with Skinner. He no longer was her single source of light, her only sun; he had now become one of a trinity. She began to look at him and see him as others saw him, not as she had envisioned him. She unconsciously began to unwind her tight devotion to him.

She found out that Skinner was a man who practiced law aggressively, close to the border of illegality. Browbeating and intimidation were his favorite tools and he showed no compulsion to follow strict, legal channels in his zeal to win lawsuits. He preferred to call himself a "personal injuries attorney" but he was regarded as an "ambulance chaser" by members of both the American Bar Association and the American Medical Association. Myrna was aware of the way Skinner performed his business and, although she did not like it, she had to accept it as a fact.

When Jeffrey was six, Myrna's mother passed away. Her profound grief caused her to look at her personal life in a different perspective. Her son was growing, her father was beginning to slow down, and she and Skinner were no longer close. The differences in their personalities and their ethics made her realize why her family had originally raised doubts about him. While her professional life was rising, her private life was slowly sinking.

It hit rock bottom one afternoon when her boss called her into his office, shut the door, and told her that her husband had just been arrested and charged with jury tampering and drug smuggling. He offered Myrna his sympathy and they discussed her problems for over an hour. He thought that the charges against Skinner might not hold up, depending upon the evidence; but that resolution would come later. What he was more interested in, at present, was Myrna's well being. He made it clear to Myrna that he, and everyone else in the firm, were at her disposal for whatever she wanted or needed. She could also have as much time off as she requested with absolutely no questions asked.

When he told Myrna that she had everyone's backing and loyalty, she did something that she had never done before. She sat there in her chair, in front of her boss, and cried.

The next few months were a nightmare for Myrna. The charges against Skinner were finally dismissed but not before she found out some facts about him that he had never bothered to tell her; and the truth infuriated her. He had lied to her on at least two important matters. She was stunned when she discovered that she was his fourth wife; he had been divorced three times before. Skinner also had a large, separate bank account that she had known nothing about and, looking at the dates of the deposits, it was reasonable to assume that a lot of her income had undoubtedly been transferred into it.

After examining her heart and soul, Myrna filed for divorce. It turned into a bitter contest as Skinner fought for custody of their son employing every legal tactic he could come up with. Eventually, all the legal hurdles got sorted out and corrected, but Myrna had paid a high personal price for her original infatuation.

****

The move from Worcester to Malden, although well planned, contained a few surprises, both good and bad, for Myrna. They began when she ran into unexpected problems. The contractor she hired to do the painting, both inside and out, was supposed to finish his job before the furniture arrived. He had painted the outside of the house because the weather was good but he had misunderstood her moving date and started the inside later than he should have. The first week or two after she moved, the furniture had to be moved around and covered with drop cloths to paint the rooms; the mess and the smell of fresh paint made living difficult. The other problem was that she learned she needed a new furnace and a new hot water heater. Those fiascos were minor inconveniences, but they were annoying to Myrna. She was never pleased when anything she planned didn't go the way she intended.

The day after she moved in, Myrna got one of her nicest surprises. Her doorbell rang at 8:30 AM and when she opened the door she saw an elderly woman, holding a plate containing a freshly baked coffee cake. She was a small, stoop shouldered lady, ruddy cheeked, her gray hair was wound in a bun and she was wearing rimless glasses. Seeing her visitor standing there caused Myrna's past to hit her like a tsunami.

She almost screamed with joy as she said, "Oh my goodness, Mrs. Bradford. Come in, come in." She took the plate with one hand and, with her free arm, squeezed the woman in a tight hug. "It is so good to see you. I didn't know you still lived next door."

"Myrna," she said, "I couldn't believe my eyes when I saw you yesterday. It brought back so many memories. I will have to call Doris and tell her that you are living next to me."

Lydia Bradford, her husband, Frank, and her daughter, Doris, had lived in the house next to Myrna's family for as long as Myrna could remember. Doris was the only child of the Bradfords and she was the same age as Myrna. They had been the best of friends starting with their meeting in grade school. They had lost contact with each other when they went to different colleges. Over the years, the memories had faded; however, opening the door and seeing Mrs. Bradford brought happy scenes back to life, even if only for a little while.

"Where is Doris? How is she?"

Mrs. Bradford smiled as she replied, "Doris is fine. She is married, has two girls, and has been living in France, near Paris, for the last six years."

Myrna and her visitor sat in the kitchen talking and drinking coffee for over two hours. Myrna was so grateful and pleased to be able to make a connection with her past.

After she and Jeffrey got settled, she found that many of the other old neighbors were no longer living in the neighborhood. Time had put new families into most of the houses around her. The neighbors who did come over to introduce themselves were complete strangers to her, although many of them knew her father and a few remembered her mother. She knew that life brought changes but she had hoped that some of her friends from her childhood memories would still live on Hawthorne Street.

On the other hand, some of her plans turned out to be easier to accomplish than she had anticipated. Two months before moving her household, she found an office layout for her new practice that suited her plans almost perfectly. It was located in Malden Square, on the second floor, over one of the retail stores. It was not too sparse or too ornate, and it was almost completely furnished. A lawyer had previously rented it but he had drunk his clients' trust away and he was glad to get rid of his office; it was draining him financially.

Myrna originally had worries about what Jeffrey would do until school started. Those concerns about her son's activities proved to be unnecessary. Jeffrey easily learned to adjust to his new home and his new city. He earned his allowance by working around the house in the morning; and it was not just a paper listing of make-do jobs. His mother intended to keep him fully and gainfully employed. There were boxes to be unpacked, bushes and trees to be pruned, floors to be scrubbed along with his regular household duties.

It was while her son was carrying out his chores that Myrna got one of her most pleasant surprises. Jeffrey was taking some cardboard boxes up to the attic which was supposed to be empty. However, while looking around, he noticed an old, wooden box tucked away, under the eaves, and not easily visible. It was the kind used for picking apples. It must have been stored there for decades and then forgotten. When he hauled the box out and examined the contents, he found some pictures of Malden Square taken late in the nineteenth and early into the twentieth centuries. He also discovered an old brass inkwell and a nib pen made out of ivory. His grandfather must have used it when he first started in business. He showed his mother their new found treasures and his mother was extremely pleased. She had the photographs carefully cleaned and framed and she put them on the walls in her office. Her father's inkwell she proudly displayed on her desk. It made her feel comfortable to have some personal touches with her past in her new office.

Jeffrey was so pleased with his mother's response to his discovery that for the next few weeks he scoured the cellar, garage and attic for more hidden treasures. He was sure that there were no more riches to be found but knowing that didn't stop him from looking; by nature, teenagers are optimists. Treasure hunting, along with his regular tasks, kept him busy. Mrs. Bradford was there for him if he had any problems and, fairly often, she made lunch for him.

In the afternoon, when his chores were finished, he would ride his bike around the neighborhood and stop and talk with any other boys he saw. The first two he met lived across the street from him, a few houses away. They were both working on a junk heap of a car, in their driveway, when he cycled up to them. They were looking under the hood and they both straightened up as he arrived.

"Hi, my name is Jeffrey. My mother and I live three houses down from you. We just moved in and I wanted to say Hello."

Greg wiped the grease off his hands as he replied, "Hello and welcome to the neighborhood. You've moved into the quietest street in Malden. My name is Greg and this is my brother, Billy. We were just going to take a break; would you care for some lemonade?"

Jeffrey nodded, "Yes." Billy went to the porch, brought a pitcher out from the shade, took some ice cubes out of an insulated bucket, and poured drinks into three large glasses. Jeffrey took a long drink, pushed his curly, black hair from his face and asked, "Have you lived here long?"

Greg answered, "Yeh, we've lived in this house for years. The house is close to our father's business. Is that why your family moved into the neighborhood?"

"Kind of. My mother is divorced from my father and she is going to start a law practice here in Malden. What does your father do?"

Greg said, "He is a barber." Then he asked, "So your father didn't move with you?"

Old habits die hard and Jeffrey felt he had to defend his father before anyone discovered that he had once been indicted, "He stayed in Worcester. He has his own law practice. In fact, he is the most famous trial lawyer in Worcester. He owns his own Mercedes and a Bentley although he doesn't have a chauffeur any more."

Billy thought that talking about expensive family cars and family chauffeurs was a bit odd, but he replied in good humor, "Well, my father, who is the most famous barber in Malden, drives only a beat up DeSoto. His customers would complain about his prices if he showed up at work driving an expensive car."

Without thinking, Jeffrey kept the conversation going by saying,

"That shows the difference between being a good barber and being a good lawyer. My father says that his clients would feel cheated if they didn't pay the most famous lawyer in Worcester a large fee; and, believe me, he doesn't want them to feel cheated."

Billy decided that this conversation really didn't interest him in the slightest and that Jeffrey was a bit snobbish. He simply said, "Well, barbers may occasionally need the services of lawyers but remember that all lawyers need the services of barbers."

Jeffrey had to laugh at that and the conversation then turned to more personal information than their fathers' occupations. Jeffrey found out that, together, the brothers had just purchased the car that they were working on. They were hoping that they could get the car ready for inspection in a week or two. Both brothers were going to Malden High and both were working summer construction jobs. Jeffrey was in awe of the size of the older brother and he asked him if he played football for Malden. When he answered "Yes," Jeffrey wondered if the team would go undefeated and he began to feel better about the move from Worcester.

During the next few days, as he continued to peddle through the neighborhood, he met several other students who were already in high school and two others who were starting at Malden for the first time. One of them, Tom Devoe, lived on Dexter Street, one block away from his house. They became friends and they would bicycle over to the Fells Reservoir in the afternoons and sit near the water and talk about whatever came to mind, their families, sports, and girls. It was relaxing and it helped Jeffrey to unwind.

What proved to be the hardest obstacle for Myrna was the process of building a practice. She knew competition would not be welcomed by the local lawyers who had been practicing for years and she realized that competition with them would be fierce. To give herself a head start, she had opened an office more than a month and a half before her move to Malden because she was aware that it would take time to establish her own clientele. What she had underestimated was the amount of time that would be necessary before her practice made her financially self sufficient. There were days when she wasn't sure whether or not there were even hinges on her office door; no one beside herself, ever entered. She was not discouraged but she began to think of alternate ways to introduce herself to the Malden community.

In the meantime, she was still sure that the change would be good for Jeffrey and that she had made the right decision. She was determined that she would make things work correctly.

3

Two weeks before the start of school, Alice's freshman year, Ben and his two sons drove to White River Junction, Vermont. That was their first stop; they went to pick up Alice, who had been enrolled in summer camp for a month.

This was her second year at the camp. Unlike her brothers, she was at odds and ends during her summers away from school. She spent a lot of time reading in the library and Ben decided that she should be outside, breathing fresh air and enjoying the outdoors. At first, when her father suggested that she go to a summer camp, Alice resisted because she didn't want to be parted from her family. However, after a lot of misgivings, she decided to try it for two weeks. Summer camp was a surprise for her; she thoroughly enjoyed the experience.

She had had such a good time last year that this year she hesitantly asked her father if she could go for a month. Ben had no problem with letting her stay that long; he was pleased she wanted to go for an even longer time.

When they arrived at her camp, Alice was delighted to see her family; she had been impatiently waiting for them. She was tanned, packed and ready to go home. Alice hugged and kissed her father and brothers and introduced them to her friends. And, once their initial greetings were over, the three siblings began ragging on each other in their usual manner. After her brothers packed her belongings in the car, Alice and her family thanked the camp staff and then they drove on to the their second stop, a side trip to Hanover, New Hampshire. Greg wanted to see the Dartmouth College campus.

This was not the first campus the family had visited; however, it was the first one that was not near their home in Malden. Greg and his father and sometimes Billy and Alice, depending on their schedules, had been to the campuses of Tufts, Boston College, Brown, Harvard and Boston University. They would walk through the college grounds, look at the libraries, the football stadiums, and the dormitory facilities of each school. Then they would discuss what they had seen and ask Greg for his opinion because he would be the one who would be going to that school. They had been making these trips, on Sundays, all through the spring and summer.

The idea for these visits came from a conversation Greg and his father had had with Greg's football coach, Stanley Melanson, as his junior year ended. Coach Melanson told them that several college coaches had been asking about Greg and that, during his senior year, he would undoubtedly be hearing from a lot more of them. He explained that each coach would tout his own school and tell Greg how wonderful his opportunities would be at his particular college. These coaches would also tell him that no other school would be as good for him as his school.

Coach Melanson then went on to say that Greg's senior year would be exciting, busy and extremely confusing because of all the different stories he would hear. Sorting out what would be best for his own future would be difficult. He strongly advised him to ask a lot of questions and not to rush into any decision. He told Greg, "Don't let anyone pressure you into making a hasty choice. Forget their promises. Select the school you feel will be best for you."

Ben and his son went home and discussed at length what they had heard. Ben had no doubt that the coach was correct in that Greg, and his family, needed to protect his interests. They both decided to start going to some of the local campuses, unannounced and on their own, and take their time looking around; there would be no escorts to rush them or try to influence them. They admitted that they weren't sure if they would learn anything different from a recruiting tour but it was worth a try. So, on several Sunday afternoons, when the weather was pleasant, Ben and his eldest son, sometimes with Alice and Billy, would stroll through the nearby campuses. Although Greg was unaware of it, he began to feel a respect for the traditions associated with each campus even as he tried to decide which college he felt comfortable with. His education was more important to him than the words of the school's fight song. Taking the initiative, as he and his family were doing, would make his decision much easier when he graduated from Malden High.

They arrived home from their trip to Dartmouth late Sunday afternoon. Ben went back to work Monday morning while his children began their preparations for school. The boys were still working and tinkering with their car, trying to get it running and registered; because it was taking them so long, they nicknamed it, Hunkofjunk.

Alice called all of her friends, telling them she was home and sharing with them their summer adventures and misadventures. Then, she got busy until school started. She felt that her family had not kept the house as neat as she would have so she decided on a complete clean up. She also sorted through her clothes, deciding what else to purchase. According to her schedule, she barely finished what she needed to do by the time she entered Malden High.

Late one afternoon, she was on the second floor, in one of the bedrooms that overlooked the driveway, when she saw her brothers, gathered around Hunkofjunk, talking to another boy whom she had never seen before. He was gangly with a shock of black, curly hair and the three of them seemed relaxed. She was surprised that the conversation lasted over an hour because her brothers were really anxious to get their car up and running. She later learned that his name was Jeffrey Cabot.

That night, as they were eating supper, Alice asked them about the boy she had seen. They told her that he was someone new who had just moved into their neighborhood; his house was across the street from theirs. When they first met him they thought that he was a little odd but, the more they talked with him, the more they thought he was friendlier than he originally appeared.

When she heard that, she asked if anyone else that was new had moved in. They said that, two blocks further down on Hawthorne, another boy had moved in and he had been over to check on their job of restoring Hunkofjunk more often than the boy she saw. Both brothers said that they didn't trust the boy who lived further away. They thought that he had swiped some of their tools and supplies when they weren't looking. It took three of his visits before they connected his coming and going to their missing items. After they were sure he was a thief, they told him not to hang around anymore.

It was at this point in their conversation that there was an error of communication. Either Alice mistook who they were talking about or her brothers didn't clearly identify the boy they thought was guilty.

Alice got the impression that it was the boy from across the street, Jeffrey, that her brothers thought was a thief. She carried that misinterpretation all year long in school and it alienated her from Jeffrey. He was in two of her classes and she avoided him completely; she wanted nothing to do with someone her brothers thought was a thief.

****

Almost everyone in Malden was happy when school started that fall. The parents were pleased that their offspring were finished with summer vacation and were headed out of the house. The students were looking forward to seeing the friends they had missed all summer. The teachers were glad to be going back to work. The thoughts of school, in the fall, are always exciting and promising. The reality of what the grind really is doesn't become apparent until much later in the school year.

Greg, Billy and Alice arrived in Hunkofjunk early the first day of school; they climbed the steps in the front of Malden High, and sat down at the top of the stairs, near the front doors. Because Alice was just starting high school she wanted to see everything that was going on. Greg wore his blue athletic sweater with the gold block M on it. Alice sat between her brothers and the three of them greeted their friends and acquaintances as they walked by.

Jeffrey arrived at the bottom of the stairs and, as he walked up, he noticed Alice sitting between Greg and Billy. He knew the brothers, of course, but he had never seen Alice before and he had never even heard of her. Her brothers had not mentioned their sister in any of their conversations. Jeffrey thought she was a very pretty girl and, when he caught Billy's eye, he began to wave. Alice saw him and she wrinkled her nose and froze in distaste, thinking of him as the boy who was the thief.

Because he was staring at Alice as he climbed the steps, Jeffrey didn't watch where he was walking. As a result, he plowed hard into a male student who was coming down the stairs. The young man he bumped into was off balance, in mid stride, and completely caught by surprise; he was spun around and landed on his backside.

Jeffrey immediately knew that it was his fault. He looked down at the person he had knocked over. Sprawled on the ground was a big lad with flaming red hair and he was wearing the same kind of block M sweater that Greg had on. Jeffrey asked the first question that came to his mind, "Are you all right?"

"You stupid son-of-a-bitch," his victim shouted in response, "I wouldn't have tripped if you hadn't blind sided me." The red head got to his feet; he was three inches taller than Jeffrey and at least thirty pounds heavier. His face was twisted in anger and one of his front teeth showed an old battle injury, it was broken in half; that made him even more ferocious looking. "You dumb bastard," he screamed. "Why don't you watch where you're going? I'm going to beat the living shit out of you and maybe you'll learn better the next time."

He stood there a for a second or two, clenching his fists, and then he began to move towards Jeffrey. From out of nowhere, Greg suddenly stepped between the two of them. Jeffrey immediately wondered, "Where did he come from? He must have moved quickly." He was relieved to see him standing there.

Greg quietly said, "Sean, you probably don't want to get into a fight on school grounds. Coach Melanson would be angry if he heard you were in a fist fight and he probably would bench your ass."

The boy he had been talking to, Sean O'Rourke, turned to look at him with his fist raised. Then, as he thought about what Greg had said, he opened his fist and lowered his arm. He pointed to Jeffrey and said, "You son-of-a-bitch, this ain't over. I owe you and I intend to get even." He walked away.

Greg patted Jeffrey on the back as he spoke. "Sean has a temper but he'll cool down. Let's go to school." With that, he went back to where his brother and sister were and the three of them went inside.

Jeffrey stood there, mortified, as the scene around him quickly changed. Everyone began to enter the school doors. He was sure that Greg's sister had seen and heard everything and she must have thought that he was a complete dunce. He felt so small and stupid and the worst thing was that he didn't know what he would have done if O'Rourke had started to punch him. Would he have fought? Would he have run? He felt like such an idiot.

However, his second thoughts were of amazement and joy. Someone had come to his rescue and had stood up for him; actually had defended him. No taunting, no sneering; someone had helped him. That had never before happened to him.

As he registered for his classes, and went to meet his teachers, he found that Greg's sister was in his history and his English classes. Her name was Alice Da Vinci. He was so embarrassed by what he had done, and what she had seen and heard, that he went out of his way to completely avoid her. For Alice, based on what she thought she knew about him, she heartily reciprocated; she would have nothing to do with Jeffrey. It was over a year before they ever spoke to each other.

****

Greg, Billy and Alice, from the beginning of the year, began to thrive in school. It was football season and Malden, like every city, town and hamlet in Massachusetts, concentrated on the fortunes of their football team. High school football was the measuring stick of local patriotism and most regional problems seemed to be eased with a winning football team.

Communities invest excessive pride in their athletic youngsters and all high school football players are regarded as heroes. If they also happen to be good football players, so much the better. Home town rooters consider star defensive players as royalty and star offensive players as heirs to the throne.

Malden was fortunate that season; there were many more Malden victories than defeats. Greg was one of their two best defensive players, the other being a tackle, Sean O'Rourke. Together, they received a lot of publicity and hype. Greg paid little attention to all the hoopla. For more than a year, Coach Melanson had schooled him in what to expect and, for all his life, his father had taught him how to conduct himself. As a result, he went to school, he played football, and he enjoyed himself; for the time being, that's all he needed. He would let the future sort itself out.

Billy, finally, was enjoying all his classes. During the summer he had come to an amazing discovery about himself; he wanted to be an architect. This had come about because of a visit to the Hatch Shell in the Boston Esplanade. The previous summer, he had gone there to hear the Boston Pops in concert. The beauty of the shell structure made him wonder how it was built and he began to examine almost every old building he saw. The more he thought about how they looked, how they were laid out, and how they had been constructed, the more he decided that he wanted to be able to design and build new buildings just like them. He was pleased with himself for finding something that fascinated him. As a result, and he began to study hard in all his classes, not just the classes he liked. He hadn't told anyone yet, not even his family, but he was working his way towards making his announcement. In the meantime, he began to work as hard as his older brother and his father.

For Alice, high school was a revelation of wider horizons and goals than she had never before known. She was immediately reunited with her friends from Beebe Junior High School. However, in her new classes, she also met students from the other junior high schools in Malden and she made new friends.

At first, she gorged on every opportunity and signed up for more extra curricula activities than she could possibly handle. They didn't conflict with each other but she couldn't possibly keep up with all of them. She finally settled for the cheerleading team, the girl's basketball team, the drama group and the high school choral society. Along with her regular duties of household responsibilities and schoolwork, her outside activities completely filled her daily schedule and she enjoyed every minute of her busy schedule.

Her regular classes pleased her. She had no career goals, she just wanted to learn everything. She thoroughly liked the subjects she was studying as well as the teachers who taught them. However, she soon realized that a lot of her new classmates didn't always agree with her conclusions and ideas. For Alice, that was a learning process in itself; thinking things through before coming to any conclusions. It wasn't long before she understood that there were at least two sides to every story.

In spite of his encounter and his humiliation on the first day, Jeffrey soon began to enjoy himself at school; something that had not happened to him in a long time. After he thought about it, he was grateful for the intervention of Greg; he had been rescued from a situation he had had no control over. It made him feel a little better knowing that a relative stranger took an interest in what happened to him. No one had ever bothered to assist him before and that helped ease the pain of the stupid thing he had done; stare at a pretty girl and not watch where he was walking.

More important was the fact that he felt that he no longer had to stand up and defend his father. None of his classmates had ever heard of his father's indictment and they didn't care; he wasn't on the defensive about him. Jeffrey could relax, without boasting, and be accepted, or rejected, for himself. He liked that.

His relationship with his father was also changing. It had never really been as tight as his mother had thought. When he was younger, he had accepted the shower of gifts, money, suggestions and advice without question; he assumed that was what a father and son relationship was supposed to be. Instinctively though, he began to realize that there was no love from his father in their bond. His father's motivation may have been paternal manipulation or it may have been to check on his former wife; whatever it was it wasn't love. Jeffrey subconsciously discovered that his mother and father both dealt with him in different ways and he began to compare their attitudes towards him. He was maturing.

****

While their children were gaining an education and growing up, both Ben and Myrna as parents, seemed to be just marking time. As individuals, they were not learning anything new or different about their own personal lives, and, as parents, they each felt differently about the upcoming school year.

Ben was confident that it would be a good year for the three of his children. He was eager for them to get a better education than he had and he was sure that they would take advantage of their opportunities. He was so proud of them that he paid hardly any attention to himself.

He continued to work long hours and spent his remaining time tending his family. The only major difference in his life was that, since Greg was a senior and a captain, he closed his shop every Saturday while he attended his son's football games. Also, while the football season continued, and even more so afterwards, strangers showed up at his barber shop for haircuts. They stood out from his regular customers simply because they would be neatly dressed in suits and ties. They would usually arrive just before he closed and wait to be his last customer. That would give them a chance to talk with Ben and, after they believed they had established a rapport, they would bring the subject around to football. They each pitched their school and their football team as the only place for his son.

Among his regular customers were three old men who had been coming to Ben since he had opened his first shop. They had known each other in their home town of Naples before they migrated to America and the three had remained close friends all their lives. Now, as they approached their late seventies and their immediate families had gone their own ways, they stubbornly clung to the lifeline of their friendship. They came together, once a month, to Ben's shop to get haircuts and solve all the world's problems, in Italian. They would stay for hours, reminiscing on what had been, and reworking the world from the Pope to the President. Ben enjoyed them; they were senior citizens living out their lives by recalling their pasts.

When Giorgio DeMario, Luigi Bruno and Alberto Previte, the Three Italian Musketeers as Ben called them, found out that recruiters were dropping by "Benito's", they changed their habits. They were very proud of Greg and they were extremely defensive of him. His Italian heritage and their fierce loyalty made them form themselves into a committee dedicated to protecting Benito and his son. They would arrive just after lunch and screen the customers who came in for haircuts. They were able to identify the coaches and recruiters by their dress and their manners. In Italian, they would talk about each individual as he sat waiting. At first, they were cautious with their remarks but they began to lose their sense of discretion as they realized that none of these strangers understood Italian. They referred to them as "allenatori di football americano," football coaches. Their remarks soon got personal as they felt protected. This "allenatore di football americano" needed his shoes shined or that "allenatore di football americano" was fat.

One day a stranger came in, asked for a haircut, and sat down and began to read the *Wall Street Journal*. The Three Italian Musketeers immediately began talking about the fact that he was smaller and younger than the other "allenatori di football americano" and that his ears stuck out. The man continued to read without paying attention or looking up from his paper. When Ben told him it was his turn, he stood up, folded his paper and turned towards the three of them. In fluent Italian he said, "I'm sorry my appearance does not match up to your expectations. Let me assure you, though, that I am an excellent coach. I'm personally inviting you to visit me, at my campus, so that I can show you."

They were completely surprised and embarrassed. They even stopped talking. However, as he sat getting his haircut he joked with them and eased their embarrassment. He coaxed them back to a good humor. From then on, they were extremely careful in what they said until they knew whether or not their visitor understood them.

Ben didn't like having the coaches and recruiters come into his shop to get his help in having Greg enroll in their school. First and foremost was the fact that he didn't know whether the inducements they offered, and there were many, were legal or not. He didn't want to break any laws or rules for his, or Greg's, sake. He also felt that the decision was entirely Greg's to make. He trusted his son enough to know that Greg would think things through and would not jump to any rash decisions. He felt that these scouts should, as a minimum, be talking to both him and Greg at the same time. At first he was uncomfortable listening to these sales pitches, but he soon learned how to handle himself.

Every conversation Ben had with any college representative was immediately relayed to coach Melanson for his evaluation. The coach would point out to Ben what was good, and what was not so good, in each of those discussions. It didn't take long before Ben could tell what were legitimate approaches and what was a little shady. He may not have had the advantage of a formal education but he certainly had his share of common sense.

Myrna, on the other hand, was not only anxious about Jeffrey; she also had her own concerns. Her hope had been that, by removing him from being a pawn in the game of marital chess, he would do better in a different school. He was capable of making better grades but she knew that the turmoil in his life was affecting his attitude. To give him a chance at a more tranquil and normal upbringing, she had changed both their lives by moving back to Malden. It was a gamble that she was willing to take for both of them. However, the success of her plan depended upon Jeffrey and how he reacted to the move.

Because of the divorce, Jeffrey had gone from an open, talkative child to a boy who was quiet and unresponsive. He was not sullen, he was just not very communicative. He would answer her questions but he would not elaborate or go into any detail. She had the feeling that he was either holding back or that he had decided to tell her as little as possible. She did not know if he acted the same when he talked to his father and the thought that Jeffrey might treat her differently than he treated his father bothered her.

He saw less of Skinner but she knew Jeffrey and his father talked on the phone quite a bit. Sometimes their conversations were very short, sometimes they were fairly long; and she had no idea what they talked about. She also was not sure how Jeffrey would react to his new school.

That is why, on the first day of school, she made sure that she was at home when he came back, carrying his books. Much to her surprise, Jeffrey was quite open and willing to talk about his day at school. He told his mother about accidently tripping up one of the football players but he was careful not to mention how it happened. What surprised Myrna was that he didn't dwell on the confrontation as much as he talked about the other football player who stepped in to help him. He told her all about Greg Da Vinci who lived down the street from them. No one had ever come to his defense before and that surprised and pleased him. This was the first time he had talked openly, almost spontaneously, in a long time. Myrna hoped that this was a good beginning for Jeffrey's school year.

At the same time, she was dealing with a problem that she had not thought of or anticipated. She was not earning enough to make a living; she was drawing money out of her savings account to make ends meet. That was her retirement nest egg and she didn't want to spend it. If worst came to worst, she could always go back to work for her old law firm, but that would be admitting defeat and Myrna would not concede.

So, despite the sneers and innuendoes from the established male lawyers in Malden, she started a new business campaign. She made arrangements with two of the busiest restaurants in Malden to meet and talk at their locations with anyone who had a legal problem. On alternate Saturday mornings from 8:00 AM until Noon at one restaurant, and alternate Wednesday afternoons from 4:00 until 8:00 PM at the other, she would consult with anyone for free for fifteen minutes.

At first, hardly anyone appeared for these consultations; people are always leery of free advice from lawyers. However, after helping several individuals solve minor legal problems such as overdue speeding tickets, domestic violence charges, and divorce and inheritance claims, she began to be busy at both locations. Even though many of the people she talked with did not become her clients, they did spread the word that she was an excellent lawyer. Eventually, she had as many clients as she could handle and changed the number of clinics to once a month at either restaurant. Myrna didn't want to give them up because she felt that it was her duty to give back to the community where she lived.

It was a good business decision for her and the restaurants; they both profited. Soon, the sneers of her fellow lawyers turned to grumbles because they themselves had not thought of her idea.

4

If the original Pilgrims returned to the original location of their original Thanksgiving Day celebration, they would be puzzled by today's customs. In Massachusetts, no feasting is begun until their local high schools battle their fiercest town rivals in the final football games of the season. Since 1889, Malden and Medford have fought to determine which is the better city to live in, at least until the next football game. In Greg's last high school game, Malden won, and everyone in the city truly felt thankful.

Ben's emotions that Thursday were different than any he had ever had before. When he awoke he realized that this Thanksgiving was probably the last one where his family would be together. From here on, his children would be going to college and Greg may, or may not, be able to come home. That thought hit him heavily.

Unlike most other parents, Ben didn't place too much importance on wins or losses. His only concerns were that Greg did not get hurt and that his son enjoyed playing the game. Ben did believe that winning was important, but he didn't think that winning was nearly as important as well being. He dismissed his thoughts of the future as he prepared for this day's events.

Greg left early to join his teammates while Alice, Billy and Ben quietly prepared the dinner before the game. When the time came, they went to Medford; it was an away game and they cheered for both the team and their favorite player. After Malden won, they came home to feast and to celebrate. Ben had established one family custom for Thanksgiving. Before eating their meal, he had his three children hold hands with him as each, from the youngest to the oldest, told everyone the one thing that they were most thankful for.

Ben listened, in sombre silence, as his children, with the earnest innocence of youth, each made their Thanks known. Their love for each other, for the world, and their love of life, touched him deeply. He didn't know what to say when his turn came. He stood quietly for a while before he spoke. "Whatever else may have happened to me, my life has been blessed by having three of the finest children a parent could ever have been given. I'm so thankful for the three of you. Your mother would have been as proud of you as I am.

"Now, let's celebrate each other and toast Thanksgiving. Let's eat."

At the same time across the street, Myrna and Jeffrey were celebrating Thanksgiving in their own way. From the time that Lydia Bradford had appeared at her door, Myrna and she had sought each other out in a mother daughter type of relationship. They would meet early every Saturday morning that wasn't a free clinic Saturday in Lydia's kitchen, for long, personal chats. Lydia had been a high school principal for many years and she was as wise as Buddha. They both enjoyed the closeness that talking about personal matters brings.

As a result of this new relationship, the Bradfords, who were going to be alone this Thanksgiving, had invited Myrna and Jeffrey to join them for their Thanksgiving dinner. Myrna accepted the invitation only after she insisted on being able to bring something; she and Mrs. Bradford settled on her baking a lemon meringue pie for dessert. Thursday morning, Myrna got up early to bake her pie; then, she drove Jeffrey to the football game while she went to her office. She worked until Jeffrey got home and called her. She then came back and they both went next door to the Bradford's house with the pie and a bottle of a fine White Zinfandel wine; she knew that both of the Bradfords enjoyed the subtle flavor of a good wine. They stayed and talked until well after 10:00 PM. It was a pleasant day and it was a welcome respite from her latest concerns. Skinner was again trying to make life miserable for Myrna.

She had been having problems with Skinner since school started. He called to complain that she was trying to turn Jeffrey against him. She denied the accusation and pointed out that Skinner was not visiting Jeffrey as much as he had been when Jeffrey was living in Worcester. Skinner admitted that she was correct but he claimed he was very busy and that his visits had nothing to do with her smear campaign against him.

Myrna had never said a word about her ex-husband but, because it was a "he said-she said" situation, she couldn't disprove his allegations. She said nothing to Jeffrey about her arguments with Skinner but she did encourage her son to be more open about his feelings when he talked to his father. However, the wrangling between Myrna and Skinner continued until Myrna proposed a compromise.

Since Skinner did not come to Malden very often to see his son anymore, Myrna wondered if Jeffrey shouldn't go to Worcester and spend part of his Christmas vacation with Skinner and his new lady friend. Skinner liked the idea but, when he first broached the subject to Jeffrey, he protested against it to his mother.

From listening to her son Myrna realized that, among other complaints, Jeffrey did not like Skinner's latest girl friend. However, after much discussion and gentle persuasion, his mother finally got Jeffrey to agree to be with his father over a part of the Christmas holidays. Myrna was almost amused by the thought that she was in the position of sticking up for Skinner but, in so doing, she knew it was the right thing to do and it got her off the hook. He could no longer complain that she was trying to undermine his position with his son.

****

Myrna's mother and Lydia Bradford had been best friends. When Lydia discovered that Myrna had moved back into her childhood home, she couldn't have been more pleased. And, after reuniting and catching up with Myrna's past, she was happy to, once again, have Myrna back in her life. It felt good to be of use to someone she loved rather than being a geriatric ornament, admired but unused. That is why, after thinking long and hard about Myrna's present living arrangements, she decided to try to introduce Myrna to a man of Myrna's own age; Lydia believed that love was the sweetest pleasure of life and Myrna certainly deserved better than she now had.

The only man she knew who might be a candidate was her neighbor, Ben Da Vinci. He was a gentle, nice man who was an excellent father and a widower. Lydia decided to bring the two together and hope for the best; she knew she was meddling, but she wanted every person in her world to be happy.

To disguise her matchmaking activities as much as possible, Lydia decided to have a small New Year's Eve party. She planned on having Myrna and Ben and two married couples from the neighborhood; that would keep the party small and intimate. One of the couples would be Larry and Laura Donnelley. He was a retired district judge and Lydia had known them for years. The other couple was Melvin and Angelina Green; Lydia knew them through her church. They seemed like a pleasant couple; they lived a block away and were about the same age as Myrna and Ben. So, she spun her web, planned for a pleasant evening, and crossed her fingers.

The holidays came, too fast for the adults, not fast enough for their offspring. Christmas turned out to be a happy holiday for both the Da Vinci and the Cabot families. There is nothing more satisfying and warming than to be with family. Cares and concerns slipped into side pockets and the joys of holiday living took center stage.

The day after Christmas Myrna drove Jeffrey to Worcester and left him to be with his father until after the new year. She hoped that he would enjoy his short stay with his father.

The Da Vinci children had their own plans. Last year, after Greg got his driver's license, Alice and her two brothers took a day between Christmas and New Year's Day to be together. They had borrowed their father's car and drove to Cape Ann. It had been such an enjoyable trip that they planned on doing it again this year; each of them looked forward to their small holiday together. The three of them finally managed to get away on December twenty-ninth. Both brothers were proudly wearing the new scarfs that Alice had bought them while she had on an angora sweater that they had bought her.

Their routine was exactly the same as it had been on their first trip. They wandered around Cape Ann. Leaving early, sometime before dawn, they drove to Swampscott to watch the sun rise over the ocean from Red Rock. After that, they meandered along the coastline, through all the old towns and cities on Cape Ann, stopping and looking at whatever caught their interest, old houses, old cemeteries, ocean views and harbors. Because of their rubbernecking, it took them hours to get from Swampscott through Marblehead, Salem, Manchester, Beverly and all the other towns, to Rockport. When they arrived, they entered almost every shop on Bearskin Neck looking at merchandise that ranged from pure, unadulterated schlock to exquisite, handcrafted items.

After that, they drove to Wingaersheek Beach to climb the sand dunes and, finally, they ended up at Woodman's in Essex to stuff themselves on clam balls, steamed clams, fried clams, and lobster rolls. This was their sibling celebration of the new year.

As they sat eating, Alice suddenly asked, "Greg, Billy, what are we going to do about Dad?"

Greg stopped cracking open the clamshell he was holding and replied, "What do you mean, 'What are we going to do about Dad?' I thought we decided to donate him to the Massachusetts Historical Society."

Alice was not amused. "You know very well what I mean, Greg. All of us are going out for New Year's Eve. This year, Dad will be at home alone at midnight unless he goes to that party across the street. I'm not sure he really wants to go. Next year, you will be away at school; Billy and I will be going out on dates. The time is coming when Dad will be alone. Who will Dad have after we're gone?"

Greg knew what Alice meant; so did Billy. Both sons had had fleeting thoughts about it. However, children don't like to think about their parents as human beings with the same thirsts and hungers that they have. Children prefer to picture their parents only as the bannisters on their personal stairwell of life; supplying safety and stability while staying out of the way of their sibling's path. Parents are relegated somewhere above their own children but definitely below God.

Alice continued, "He has raised the three of us and not once have I heard him complain. It's true that we lost our mother, but have either of you ever thought how much it hurt him to lose his wife? He has carried on without ever whimpering. Just think about what his life has been like all these years while he has been there for us. I always wondered if he has ever done anything that he wanted to do for himself without thinking of us first? The three of us have been fortunate to have a father like that."

Greg and Billy were both paying attention now. The levity was gone. They both nodded their heads in agreement.

"All I'm saying is that he has raised us and we will soon be on our own. It's time for us, and for him, to move on to a different chapter in our lives. He really needs a woman as a companion, a soulmate."

Greg was silent; Billy finally said, "I never thought of it that way. Dad's world seems to be centered on us and his work. Isn't that enough? Nothing else, except his garden, seems to interest him. At his age, do you think he would even get any enjoyment in being with a woman?"

Alice looked at Billy as if he were a set of false teeth in the communion chalice. "I can't believe you. You're certainly interested in having a girl friend, aren't you?"

"Yes, but I'm much younger than Dad."

"Of course you are, but he is far from a wheel chair. He is still alive and well. We should be encouraging him to start putting his own interests first and us second in his life."

They sat silently for a while, still chomping on all of the sea food in front of them. Greg spoke up, "Alice, you're absolutely correct and the three of us really forget how lucky we are. We couldn't ask for a better parent than he has been. He deserves a medal for his dedication.

"But what will he do when we are gone? Do you think that Dad will change his focus when we are out of the house?"

"I don't know. But he's certainly going to have to do something. We will be gone, that's a fact. He is going to have to do something. He deserves a mate to share his life with.

"It isn't because he hasn't had opportunities. One of his drawbacks is that he is shy. I've seen some of the women at church try to attract his attention and he has gone out of his way to avoid them. He's not only shy, he is also set in his ways. He may be a saint but he would be classified as a stubborn saint.

"I can only hope that we can convince him to start a new life the same way that we're going to start new lives."

That was the end of discussing their father. They turned back to picking on each other, trading barbs, and, at last, confessing their love. The long drive back to Malden was done with little conversation. They got home just after nine o'clock that evening happy with their day of being together and grateful to have each other.

New Year's Eve is an awkward holiday denoting the end of one calendar year and the beginning of the next. It is an extremely important marker for governments and businesses. However, it comes at a time when there is no change in the long range weather patterns and when people have become weary of their lot. The New Year is heavily advertised as a starting point for a change in one's fortunes. As a result, most people seize the opportunity of a new year to revive their hopes. On the night of December thirty-first many will eat too much, drink too much and smoke too much in the expectation that, at dawn of January first, their luck will be reshaped. It can be a frenzied celebration.

In New England, in the cold of the snow and the ice, almost all of the celebrating has to be done indoors. That means that many neighborhood parties are held in the tight confines of finished basements; compacting all the excesses into a smaller area makes them even more noisy, smoky and rowdy. On January the First, the amount of hangovers, sore throats and sour stomachs from these neighborhood parties is close to one hundred percent.

Greg, Billy and Alice had no such after party problems. Alice went to a chaperoned party held by the parents of one of her girl friends. There were no dates; invitations had been sent to all the boys and girls to come to the party which was held in the living and dining rooms of their huge home. Sandwiches and soft drinks and punch were served and the young couples danced until time to celebrate the New Year. Alice and the girls were either driven or escorted home by one of the chaperones after the party was over. She was in bed and asleep by one-thirty in the morning.

Greg and Billy both had dates and they went to a local restaurant for a dinner dance celebration. Greg drove Hunkofjunk and, despite the fact that they didn't have chaperones, they were well mannered. Three teenage couples went to the party together; they were in the midst of a crowd that was older. Neither Greg or Billy had any hard liquor, although they each had a beer. After the dance, they dropped their dates off, fumbling a little with kisses, hugs, feels and "Happy New Year" statements; they were both in bed by three in the morning.

Their father beat the three of them home and he didn't have nearly as good a time as any one of them had. When he first received the invitation he wasn't sure that he wanted to go. He had his classical re-cords and books to read and it really was just another day to him. But, after thinking it over, he decided that he was being a real stick in the mud and that, since the Bradfords were nice enough to invite him, he should go. Had he known of Lydia Bradford's motive, he would have invented an excuse and stayed home.

Ben had gone across the street to the Bradford house a few minutes earlier than the nine o'clock time Lydia had suggested. As he walked he noted that, even though the temperature was close to zero, the sky was clear and there was not supposed to be any snow falling this night. Since his children would all be on the roads around Malden in auto-mobiles, he felt a little better about the weather report. He went to the dinner party with a bottle of Merlot and a bottle of Champagne.

He was greeted at the front door by both Lydia and Frank Bradford. He had known them for years and Frank was one of his customers. They talked for a while and, soon, Laura and Larry Donnelley showed up. Ben also knew the retired judge and his wife so he still was within his comfort zone. They sat in the living room chatting pleasantly about their hopes for the upcoming year. The phone rang and Lydia answered it and spoke to someone for a few minutes. When she hung up she announced, "That was Myrna. She is going to be a little late. I told her that we would hold dinner until she got here."

A short while later, the doorbell rang and Angelina and Melvin Green arrived. They came in with a thick cardboard box containing eight or ten bottles of liquor. By the tone of their voices they had al-ready sampled each bottle several times before they got to the party. Lydia welcomed them and introduced them to the other guests; neither Ben nor the Donnelleys had met the Greens before. After ten minutes in their presence he wished that his previous luck had continued.

The Greens immediately helped themselves to their own liquor, inviting everyone else to participate, and what had started quietly ended up cockeyed. Either the room was too small or their voices were too loud; their conversation added nothing but noise and nonsense. They dominated and disrupted the discussions with their boozy comments. When it came to interfering with a good time, they made a perfect team.

Melvin had a deep basso voice and he displayed his ignorance with dumb statements that had no basis with facts. Continual correction neither bothered nor slowed his ability for misstatements. Angelina had a high pitched voice that grated on the ears of her listeners. Worse than the tone of her voice was her attitude; she was negative about everything. "Every politician was a crook." "Teachers don't bother to teach any more." "Doctors are in medicine only to make money." "There needs to be more Christians and a lot less fake religions in our country." They both had sound bite solutions for any subject that was brought up.

Lydia had never seen them under the influence of alcohol before and she was completely mortified.

Ben immediately went quiet, he had nothing to say in the face of all the loud braying.

While the Greens were dominating the conversation, Myrna arrived at the kitchen door embarrassed at being late and annoyed with herself. She had come home from work tired and she had decided to take a short nap before attending the party. She overslept. She wasn't too enthusiastic about celebrating New Year's Eve but she didn't want to hurt Lydia's feelings. Had she known of Lydia Bradford's motive, she would have refused the invitation.

She knocked on the door and stepped inside. Lydia, who was appalled at the conduct of the Greens, had retreated to the kitchen to take care of the food. She looked up as Myrna entered and said, "Am I glad to see you."

Myrna replied, "Lydia, I'm so sorry to be late. I apologize. What can I do to help."

"Nothing really, Dear. I was getting ready to put the food on the table. You can help. It won't take any time at all. In the meantime, I want you to come out and meet our guests. I don't think you know all of them."

Within a few minutes the two of them had all of the dishes on the dining room sideboard for a buffet dinner. When everything was in place, Lydia took Myrna by the elbow and escorted her into the living room to introduce her.

Ben was sitting in a high backed chair that was facing away from the dining room. The first he knew of Myrna's presence was when Melvin Green stopped talking in mid sentence and said, even louder, "WOW! Look at this! Who is this gorgeous woman. Are you one of our neighbors? I surely hope so." He rushed over to where she was standing and started to shake her hand and introduce himself.

Ben stood up quickly and looked to see who Green was talking to. He immediately thought, "I'll bet his wife is not happy with an act like that." At first, he couldn't see anyone because Green blocked his view but, after moving to one side, he saw Lydia Bradford standing behind an attractive lady. The woman was about his age, had curly auburn hair and she was wearing a royal blue dress that complimented her figure. At the moment, she was glaring at Green but, when she turned to look at the other guests, she had a pleasant smile on her face. Ben thought that she was beautiful.

As Lydia brought Myrna over to meet him, her first impression of

Ben was not nearly as approving as his. She was almost an inch taller than he was; she had always automatically dismissed men who were shorter than she was. She felt superior to them. In addition, he had a glum look on his face, which was pleasant but not handsome.

Both were preoccupied by the circumstances surrounding them. Ben was unhappy with the loud, drunk couple interrupting the conversation; Myrna was displeased with the way Melvin Green fawned over her when she joined the party. Both were too busy frowning inside to really notice each other.

Lydia broke the ice, "Myrna, this is your neighbor from across the street, Ben Da Vinci."

Myrna was a little surprised. She said. "You're Ben Da Vinci? Your son is Greg and you own the barbershop that my son Jeffrey goes to?"

Green, who was standing around, immediately broke into the conversation. He put one arm around Ben's shoulders and intoned, "Your son is our linebacker? And you own a barbershop? I've been looking for a good barber. We will have to get together and I'll tell you what I want."

Lydia was beside herself. She now could see her matchmaking plan was being shot down in alcoholic rhetoric.

To herself, she muttered, "Shit." To her company, she said, "Dinner is ready. There is a New Year coming and I don't want our food to get cold. Please come in and help yourselves."

At the dining room table that seated eight, Myrna sat on one side, between Ben and Judge Donnelley. Ben was quiet and Myrna, who knew the judge very well, discussed legal procedures with him all during the meal.

It was close to midnight when the dinner was finished. When the

New Year came, everyone toasted its arrival. Shortly thereafter, Ben went home. Myrna stayed a long time helping Lydia clean up her kitchen and straighten out her house.

Myrna got home, thought about the evening for a while, dismissed her meeting with Ben, and went to bed.

Ben got home, thought about how disappointing his evening had been, and went to bed wondering about Myrna. However, just as he fell asleep, his mind burrowed into his past and he ended up with a nightmare that he occasionally had and which always frightened him.

He was in a beautiful pine forest, on a picnic with his three children, and they were off in the distance playing while he was spreading the blanket and preparing the food. Just as he called them to eat, a slight fog began to drift in, and, although he could hear them, they didn't return to the blanket. He decided that he would have to walk over to where they were as the fog was beginning to thicken.

He started to walk around, calling for them and, although he could still hear them, he couldn't see them anymore. That made him panicky and he jogged in the direction of their voices to locate them as the fog got thicker and thicker. Both Esther and his mother suddenly joined him and tried to help him locate the children. The fog made it impossible for him to see anything and he soon lost sight of Esther and his mother; he could still hear the voices of his children. They sounded as if they were playing and waiting for him to come get them.

He started to call them and, frantically, he began running. The forest disappeared and he was running in a white nightmare of fog until he couldn't run any more. He had to stop, put his hands on his knees and gasp for air. He could still hear the children but he couldn't see them. He woke up, startled and fearful for their safety until he realized he had been dreaming. For no reason, those were his last thoughts as he went back to sleep in the early morning hours of the new year.

Over the course of the next few weeks, his memory of his nightmare and his meeting Myrna faded away.

The first attempt at matchmaking had been a dismal failure.

5

Soon after the new year, classes resumed at Malden High School; however, the weather was much different from what it had been at the beginning of the school year. In the fall, the days were cool and crisp, the sun was warm and lazy, and student hopes were high. Since then, the weather had changed; darkness was slyly stealing daylight's time and sunshine was becoming so scarce that it had become precious. Days which once had been smooth were now sullen.

That was because this winter was one of the worst, or best, depending upon one's weather barometer, that Malden had had in twenty years. There were heavy snows in late fall and the temperatures never warmed enough to melt them. Piles of old, dirty snow built up and made the streets ugly; walking was dangerous and driving was hazardous. Temperatures were almost always below freezing and every day brought a small amount of snow, sleet, hale or rain; it was the time of the year that was dreary and depressing.

People also had a different outlook about their lives. The price for the high tide of happiness during the holiday season was the ebb of joy as the tide changed. During these down days, the parents' attitudes toward school had not changed; they were still thankful, now almost grateful, that their children were heading out of their homes and returning to their class rooms. Students and teachers held a much different view.

The teachers were seeing their task of dispensing knowledge as a grim grind until the end of the school year. Their pupils were almost awash in the education that they so far had received and there was not much more that they could swallow. Teaching was not as much fun as it had been at the beginning of the term.

On the other hand, the students almost resented being shoved back into their harnesses and resuming the plodding path of education. Learning was not as much fun as it had been at the beginning of the term. They began to feel that their world of parents and teachers were picking on them.

The entire population of Malden seemed to be side stepping its way towards Spring and better weather. Every one seemed to be waiting for the sun to arrive and, literally, melt their paths. The only exceptions to this suspended animation were Ben and Greg. Both father and son were too busy to pay much attention to the weather. They were trying to decide which college Greg should attend next fall.

Ben's barber shop seemed to become a hangout for "allenatori di football americano." After the football season finally ended, the coaches, their assistants or other staff members came in for haircuts and heart-to-heart talks. Until then, Ben had not realized that coaches needed so much personal grooming; even being bald did not stop a coach from needing a haircut. Because his son was a promising athlete and scholar, Ben began to get clientele from all over the eastern half of the United States.

Ben learned many things that Winter. He learned that there were many more large and small colleges than he had ever before imagined. He learned that some institutions of higher education, along with their athletic departments, had low standards of honesty. He learned that coaches and trainers were, as individuals, no better or worse than he was; some were nice, some were not so nice. And, just as important, he learned how to respond to any and all of these sales pitches. He no longer felt uncomfortable talking to any of the representatives from colleges or universities. After all, he reasoned, they wanted something from his family and not the other way around.

Greg was even more active. There were many schools that showed an interest in him; he and coach Melanson were getting inquiries from Notre Dame, schools in the Big Ten and schools in the Pacific Coast Conference. He was not only talking with the coaches, he was also visiting the campuses that interested him. Each time he returned from a trip he would have a meeting with his father and coach Melanson to discuss his impressions. After one trip to Ohio, where bad weather cancelled his flight home for an extra day, he decided that he would not go on any more long trips; he wanted to go to a college that was close to his home. That decision made it easier for him and his father to sort through the other factors that governed his choice. By early spring, Greg was ready to select his college.

Finally, spring did arrive. One day it was bitterly cold and the next day it was unseasonably warm. The change was so sudden and so dramatic that it had the impact of a sledge hammer hitting a ripe tomato. Everybody and everything responded to the good weather. The sap rose in trees, the birds and bees flaunted themselves at each other and humans felt stirrings of yearnings and emotions as their blood pulsed hotter. Spring brought the city of Malden, and everyone in it, to life.

One Thursday afternoon, during those giddy, heady days, Alice was at her wall locker getting her books when she turned to see Sean O'Rourke watching her. He had one arm resting on the wall high over his head and the other arm was bent akimbo, clearly displaying his letter sweater. He was grinning and his broken front tooth caught her eye.

Alice thought, "He is big and with his red hair he does look cute. I wonder what he wants"

She said, "Hi."

"Hi, there yourself. Has your brother decided on what school he is going to go to?"

"No, he hasn't made his decision yet."

O'Rourke put one hand, opened fingered, on his chest and he proudly patted himself. He said, "Well, I have just accepted a football scholarship to Boston College. Tell your brother that if he wants to team up with one of the best defensive tackles in the country to come to Boston College."

Alice replied, "Why don't you tell him yourself?"

"I just might do that. However, that's not the reason I'm talking to you. I want to invite you to be my date tomorrow night at a beach party I'm having in Revere."

Alice was completely taken by surprise. O'Rourke had a steady girl friend, Louisa Del Gardo, who constantly bragged about their relationship. She asked, "What about Louisa? Why aren't you taking her?"

"Well, that's the thing. I've decided that you are prettier than her."

Alice bridled with anger. She was appalled at his answer and disappointed with his grammar. She was glad that she could respond with the truth. "I am busy tomorrow evening." She and two of her girlfriends had previously made arrangements to go the movies.

He nonchalantly replied, "If it's a date, why don't you break it? When I get to Boston College all the girls will be jealous of you."

She couldn't hide her feelings any longer. "What am I to do when you find a girl prettier than I?" she said, emphasizing the "I" very strongly. "I will become a has been. No thank you, I'll just stick to my original plans. You may want to ask Louisa to take my place."

It began to dawn on O'Rourke that his new, chosen date was not accepting his offer. At first he was puzzled; no girl had ever refused to go out with him, at least the first time he asked. Then his ego kicked in and he was annoyed. "You know, you're kind of snooty like your brother. Well, when I make the headlines at Boston College you'll be sorry but it will be too late.

"You probably wouldn't have put out anyhow. Too bad for you."

With that, he turned and walked away. Alice put the incident behind her, but it didn't end there. O'Rourke was blazing inside; his pride had been punctured. He had never been completely rebuffed by a girl before. To restore his manhood, somebody would have to pay.

The payment took place after school during the last week of classes. It started while Jeffrey and his friend, Tom Devoe, were in the gym shooting basketballs; they were the only people in the room. O'Rourke happened to be walking down the hallway with three of his cronies when he glanced through the small glass window in the door leading to the gym. The second he saw Jeffrey he stopped, and his fury began to rise. He said to his companions, "We're going to have us some fun."

The three boys were hangers-on who didn't have any particular skills or talent; they were normal, slightly sub-par students and athletes who followed O'Rourke around just to be able to say they were friends of a football player. One of them asked, "Why did you stop here?"

O'Rourke pointed to the gym and answered, "Because we are go-ing in there and harass the son-of-a-bitch that purposely tripped me on the steps last fall."

"We're not going to get into trouble, are we?"

O'Rourke regarded him as if he were a fly on a pie. "Come on, would I get you in trouble? All you guys have to do is surround him and follow my lead. We will rough him up a little to teach him better manners. This is going to be fun."

The four of them entered the gym and walked directly towards Jeffrey and Tom. As they got close, O'Rourke pointed to Tom and said, "You. Get the fuck out. Our business is with him."

Tom was absolutely petrified. He looked at Jeffrey for instruction and Jeffrey nodded his head. Tom walked out of the gym puzzled, scared and worried. When Jeffrey saw the four of them he immediate-ly knew that he was in trouble. He was sure that O'Rourke was intent on beating him up and Jeffrey decided not to give him the satisfaction of begging for mercy. He turned to face the basket, bounced the ball on the floor a few times and, even though he was shaking, threw the basket ball up and through the hoop.

O'Rourke walked in front of him while the other three circled be-hind and on both sides. Jeffrey could see O'Rourke stoking his rage. He finally said, "You little son-of-a-bitch, did you think I would forget that you purposely tripped me? Did you really think I'd forget?

"You asshole. No one will ever get the better of me, Sean O'Rourke. Certainly not a shit like you."

With that, O'Rourke put his two hands on Jeffrey's chest and pushed hard, sending Jeffrey flying backwards into the boy stand-ing behind him. O'Rourke looked at him and taunted, "I'm about to teach you some good manners." He reached out and slapped Jeffrey hard. Before O'Rourke could do anything else, Jeffrey slapped him back.

O'Rourke roared, in surprise, "You goddamn cock sucker. I'm going to beat the living shit out of you."

Just as he spoke, the door to the outside of the gym opened and Greg and Billy Da Vinci walked in. They were covered with sweat because they had been outdoors working out. They surprised O'Rourke and, in turn, they were completely taken by surprise.

Greg looked at the four of them around Jeffrey and quietly asked, "What's going on, Sean?"

O'Rourke was quick to reply, "This is really none of your damn business, Da Vinci. This is a personal matter."

Greg walked a little closer and took his time before saying anything; he knew that being calm would upset O'Rourke more than bellowing. "Oh, I don't know about that, Sean. You never know about business. Jeffrey is my neighbor, so of course I am interested in what's going on."

"I tell you it's none of your damn business. He insulted me and now he is going to pay the consequences. As a matter of goddamn fact, you were there when he tripped me. Now, I'm getting even with the little bastard."

Greg smiled at him and shook his head from side to side; he wanted to annoy O'Rourke so he said, "Sean, Sean, Sean, you're right, I was there and I also heard him apologize for bumping into you. That was so long ago. He meant you no harm."

O'Rourke looked at Greg and his brother standing there. He began to get the idea that he might have to confront these two if he wanted to continue picking on Jeffrey. His hatred began to waiver between Jeffrey and Greg; his concentration was also wavering. "I'm the one to decide whether he meant to harm me, not you or anyone else. I'm going to teach him some goddamn manners. You have no right to interfere."

"Sean, you're getting ready to go on to BC; so why not forget it? It's something out of the past, why don't you just forget it?

"Besides, as a neighbor, I have an obligation to help. At odds of four to one he looks as if he needs help."

O'Rourke studied Greg. He was almost sure that he was stronger but he knew for sure that Greg was quicker than he was. If his three friends joined the fight it would be four against three; if they ran away it would be three against him. Even one on one O'Rourke had to admit that Da Vinci might take him. That made him even angrier. "Are you telling me that you are going to stick up for that piece of shit?"

"Sean, I guess you could put it that way. I'm telling you to let him go."

O'Rourke almost grunted in pain. He looked at Greg and then at Jeffrey, shrugged his shoulders, and walked away. As he turned he said, "Da Vinci, fuck you and the horse you rode in on." He swaggered out the gym door followed by his three cronies.

Greg looked at Billy and said, "Well. I guess we'd better go and take a shower."

Jeffrey stood there, he almost couldn't speak. Finally, after trying twice, he blurted out, "Thank you, thank you, he was going to really beat me up. I don't know why he hates me, but I'm so grateful to both of you."

Greg looked at him and, after thinking a while, he replied, "Jeff, I don't believe O'Rourke would have done more than cuff you around. Even he is smart enough to realize that his scholarship at BC would be yanked if he got into trouble. His language is filthy, his temper is short, but he's not foolish; he knows what the outside limits are. I don't know what makes him tick, but I'm almost sure he won't bother you again."

Jeffrey felt his fears subside as he breathed deeply. Once again the Da Vincis had come to his aid. Suddenly, he shook hands with Greg and Billy and walked away without saying a word. He didn't know what to say.

That evening, as his mother and he were eating dinner, she asked him how his day had gone. This was a routine question that she asked at every evening meal and it generally led to a discussion of the day's events. Somehow, though, Jeffrey had been hoping that his mother would not follow their daily routine because he didn't want to tell her about his afternoon's escape from harm. It was not that his mother was hard to talk to anymore, she carefully listened to him. He had gotten into the habit of talking with her a little more and, from their conversations, he began to appreciate how her advice and comments helped him with his daily problems. And he had no wish to hide anything from her; he had seen how half-truths and lies had complicated his family life.

Still, Jeffrey was in the process of maturing and he was trying to work through all of his family problems. He had not told his mother everything that had happened the day he had inadvertently tripped O'Rourke so what happened today would be out of context for her. He remembered her lecturing him when he had problems in his schools in Worcester; he had resented her attitude. This confrontation had been nothing like those others; he had not provoked O'Rourke at all. He was afraid that his mother would misunderstand the circumstances and assume that he was to blame. He did not want a lecture for something that was not his fault.

As a result, when his mother asked Jeffrey how his day had gone, he white-fibbed and said "very well," and the conversation rolled on to a different subject. His mother said that she had a call from her brother who wanted to know if Jeffrey would be interested in coming out to Oregon and visit him as soon as school finished. Jeffrey jumped at this opportunity and his mother suggested that he get in touch with his uncle and arrange the details of the visit himself.

At the Da Vinci household, the afternoon confrontation was discussed in much more detail at the dinner table. Ben had had a long-standing rule that his children and he always ate their evening meal together as a family unit. There was no radio or television allowed, just discussion. Any member was free to pick whatever topic he or she wanted and, most times, the conversations were lively. The subjects ran from the thoughtless to the thoughtful; from how Superman and Batman slipped in and out of their costumes, to politics, religion, or the important teen-age subjects of drinking and sex. The tone of the conversations ran the gamut, from free wheeling, funny and frank to hot and argumentative. Agreement was not a requirement but civility was; no one was allowed to be rude or disagreeable. Respect for each other was an absolute necessity.

The final arbiter on any subject was Ben and he only interfered when the conversation got overheated or someone overstepped the bounds of good taste or someone needed help expressing a thought. He constantly encouraged the three of them to be as precise as they could. The evening meal was a celebration of food, fellowship and family; it was a time that Ben and his three children looked forward to.

Billy began the conversation by blurting out, "Boy, you two should have seen what Greg and I did this afternoon. We came across Sean O'Rourke getting ready to beat up the kid across the street."

He stopped talking, leaving a load of silence sitting there.

Alice impatiently asked, "Well, you dummy, what happened?"

Billy resumed at once, "Greg backed O'Rourke down and everything got quiet in a hurry. We surely saved Jeff's ass."

Alice looked at Billy and said, "You can express yourself less vulgarly than that. I'm sure you saved more than his rear end."

Greg laughed, and spoke for the first time, "Yuh, we did. O'Rourke was carrying a grudge from the past and he wanted to knock Jeff around. Billy and I discouraged him from doing something stupid and he went away unhappy and frustrated. And making him unhappy and frustrated isn't too bad at all. He can be a jerk sometimes."

Alice thought back on her recent conversation with O'Rourke and asked Greg, "You don't like him, do you? Yet, you never said anything when we asked about him before."

"That's true, but he was a team-mate of mine and I wasn't going to say anything bad about a team-mate; so, I didn't say anything. Now he is going one way and I'm going another; that leaves me free to speak my mind and tell you what I think."

Alice listened to Greg and replied, "You just said something I want to check on. But first, I have some other questions. This kid, Jeff, that lives across the street, isn't he the person you told me who stole things from you and Billy last summer?"

Billy piped up, "Oh, no, Alice. Jeff's not the crook. I don't know where you got that idea but it's not right. The crook is that kid who lives up the street, more than two blocks from here. Since we caught him swiping our tools, he has been arrested twice for shoplifting.

"Jeff sometimes has a really odd attitude towards things but he is actually a pretty nice guy."

Alice replied quickly, "Doggone, he is in two of my classes and I have avoided all contact with him because I thought he was the one who stole your tools. That's what I thought you both told me; you have put me in an awkward position. I feel bad that I never spoke to him. I wonder if I will have a chance to talk with him before I leave for camp?

"Anyhow, I have a different question. Greg, you just said that you and O'Rourke are going different ways. Does that mean you have chosen the school you are going to this fall?"

Greg grinned from ear to ear as he answered, "Yes, I haven't told anyone else yet but I notified Dartmouth yesterday that I am accepting their scholarship offer. Coach Melanson likes the coaching staff and their football program; he is pleased at my choice."

Alice and Billy clapped their hands in happiness, Ben smiled as the three of them tried to talk at the same time. Finally, Alice could be heard above the noise, "Oh, Greg, that's great. I liked that campus the best of all I saw. But what made you pick Dartmouth?"

"Many things, I guess. I will get a good education; they have a strong alumni backing, so I will have a chance to get a job when I graduate; it is close to home and many of our games will be played in the New England area, so you guys can can come see a lot of them.

"I don't know, I just liked the feeling of their campus and their Ivy League attitude. I am sure that I made the right decision."

The rest of their dinner conversation was spent talking about Greg's choice of schools and his future at Dartmouth. Alice and Billy were so serious that there were no jibes thrown at each other.

However, that summer, Alice did not get a chance to talk to Jeffrey. Their schedules did not mesh. Last summer, after coming home from camp, Alice found that the time she had left before getting ready for school was not enough. That hurried experience, plus the fact that

Greg would be going away to school in the fall, made this summer different. She felt that their childhood years were passing and she wanted to be around Greg as much as she could before he left. To do that, and not be rushed at the end of summer, she decided, before school ended, to go to her camp in an earlier cycle. By the time she returned from camp, Jeffrey had gone to visit his uncle in Oregon. As a result, when school started for their sophomore year, she still had not had a chance to speak to him.

Until it was time for Alice to leave, the three of them hung out together as much as they could. They each realized that they were beginning to go down divergent paths and they were each coming to grips with that idea. For once, they were not freely discussing their future plans. They were individually weighing, assessing and balancing their thoughts; they were maturing to the point where each of them needed space to grow. That summer, the three of them were more subdued than they usually were.

Alice's father and brothers drove her to camp on Saturday, dropped her off, and drove back to Malden in glum silence knowing that they already missed her. Sunday morning Ben and his sons went to church, had breakfast, and started their individual summer routines. Greg would have the most physical schedule because he wanted to be in good shape for the upcoming football season. His neighbors, his friends and every one of Ben's customers automatically assumed that he would be a star football player but he didn't pay attention to their predictions; he had talked to his coaches at Dartmouth and he was told what his role for the first year would be. He knew that they wanted him to be in good physical condition. That meant jogging or exercising every day and eating sensibly.

His brother, Billy, had a less active schedule because he wasn't in training even though he enjoyed working out with Greg. It was more of a desire to be close with his brother than it was to gain weight or become stronger. He wanted to help Greg reach his goal. His primary goal this summer was to save money for his freshman year at college after he graduated from high school next year. They both were working as laborers for a local construction firm and they both were hoping for a hot, humid summer to keep in shape.

Because Alice was at camp, her father assumed some of her responsibilities. He not only worked long hours at his barber shop, he also had to make sure that the household ran smoothly and that his sons were taken care of. He divided the tasks of cleaning and cooking so everyone contributed and it was his job to check and make sure everything was done correctly. The first few days were a little rocky; everything lurched along until the three of them got used to their individual duties. The result was that Ben's sons did not have as much free time, especially on the weekends, as they had hoped. There was work around the house which took time and prevented them from going swimming in the ocean; they had planned on being at the beach in Revere every Saturday and Sunday. They grumbled about the lack of time they had to just relax but they also were aware that they had as many obligations to their father as he had to them. He certainly worked longer hours than they did so they adjusted their hopes and did their jobs.

Early one Sunday afternoon, after Greg and Billy had finished cleaning both bathrooms and the kitchen, they went outside to throw the football around. They stood at either end of the long driveway and gave hand signals as to where they would throw it. They did this for a while until Greg, who was near the garage, decided to punt the ball. He kicked it and the football arched high in the air, landed in the middle of the road, and bounced out of sight.

Billy shook his head, laughed, and said, "Why did you do that? It wasn't even fourth down. Now, I'll have to find out where the ball went. I think you deserve a fifteen yard penalty."

As Billy finished speaking, Jeffrey, cradling the football, appeared at the end of the driveway. He had on sneakers and was dressed in shorts and a tee shirt. He walked a few steps up the driveway and said, "Hi, Guys." Then, he threw the football, with a perfectly tight spiral, to Greg. Greg caught it, immediately passed it to Billy, who tossed it quickly back to Jeff. They continued this game of throwing, catching and running for almost an hour; when they finished, the three of them were soaked in sweat. Billy went into the house and appeared with a large pitcher of lemonade and three glasses and called the other two over to the porch where they sat down on the steps and began drinking the lemonade.

After a while Jeffrey said, "I'm glad we finally quit; I was getting tired. I was walking over to see the two of you when the football bounced into the street and I caught it."

Billy asked, "Why were you coming here?"

"I'm leaving for Oregon in a little while. Before I go, I wanted to invite both of you out for pizza. You both helped me and I want to show my appreciation. Greg may be gone by the time I get back."

Both brothers looked surprised and both smiled and nodded "Yes."

Greg said, "Thank you. But before we go I have to go to the bathroom. I'll be right back."

When Greg was gone Billy asked, "Where are you going?"

Jeffrey replied, "My uncle lives in Oregon and he has arranged a camping trip for the two of us. I'll be gone until just before school begins. I'm really excited about it."

Jeffrey stopped talking for about ten seconds and then, as if he couldn't keep quiet, he suddenly added, "I just wish my father and mother would quit fighting over my trip. Do you have many arguments in your house, Billy?"

"No, I can't say that we do. We have a lot of discussions and maybe even disagreements but I don't think we argue. I guess my father wouldn't allow us to argue. Do your parents have many?"

"It's never ending. It's like they each need to prove the other is never right. They can't change the past so why do they keep on repeating it?"

Billy didn't reply because he didn't know how to answer and he didn't want to get involved. They sat in silence until Greg came out of the house with the keys to Hunkofjunk and the three of them went to get pizza.

That was the last time Jeffrey was together with both of them until the following summer.

6

Myrna was fighting battles on three fronts.

On her school front, everything seemed to be going pretty well. When Myrna saw Jeffrey's final report card she felt both relieved and vindicated. Jeffrey's grades were not as high as she had wanted but they were much better than they had been in the past. And she had not had to make a trip to his high school to discuss any behavioral problems; he hadn't had any. From what he told her about school, she felt that he was at ease and enjoying himself.

Her home front was better than it had been but not as good as she would wish. Jeffrey was not sullen and uncommunicative but neither was he free flowing with conversation. He was polite, a little reserved and aloof, especially after phone calls or visits with his father. Skinner had changed how he contacted his son and his ex-wife after they moved to Malden. He rarely appeared in person anymore but he did call each of them whenever he decided he had something to say.

Skinner's conversations with her were not pleasant. He rarely talked about Jeffrey and he spent most of the time listing the reasons that made Myrna responsible for the break up of their marriage. That angered her because it was a useless waste of time and her opinion was entirely different from his; they were divorced and he had not been truthful during their marriage. However, since she didn't want to keep Jeffrey in the middle of this battle, she did not respond. As a mother trying to protect her child, she endured much more abuse than she should have. She did learn to protect herself by quietly hanging up on Skinner when he became too nasty. He would call back a few minutes later and he would be almost pleasant.

She didn't know what Jeffrey's meetings and phone calls with his father were like; she assumed that Skinner was pumping Jeffrey about her life and distorting the truth about their former relationship. Her assumption was based on the fact that Jeffrey was usually quiet and tense after having contact with his father. She wanted to ask how they were getting along but she didn't, she didn't want to add to Jeffrey's burdens. Still, Jeffrey was growing into a man and Myrna could see signs that he was maturing. She had hopes for his future.

Her work front was finally busy and successful. The free consultations she held at the various restaurants brought her services to the attention of people in Malden and the surrounding cities. Clients began to come to her and, as her name circulated, her reputation began to rise. That was because she worked tirelessly for each client; she took nothing for granted and spent time discussing their individual problems. The result was that no client got the impression that they had been neglected; each felt that he or she had received the best legal advice they had ever been given.

Myrna, though, paid a price for having a busy practice. When she wasn't at home with Jeffrey she was at work. She had almost no social life; she spent long hours either in court or at her office. Myrna was aware of this imbalance but, at this time, it didn't bother her at all.

Nevertheless, there was one consequence of her dedication to work that she was unaware of. She was so driven to succeed that she didn't realize she was losing her zest for life. Her emotional grasp was shrinking to the point where she was becoming hard headed and almost mean. This was demonstrated by her attitude towards a few of the lawyers she had to deal with.

At the time she opened her practice, many of the lawyers were a little skittish about dealing with a female lawyer; there weren't too many of them. As she proved her skills most of them accepted her as their peer and, to them, she was curt and courteous.

However, there were still a few who went out of their way to address her as "Darling," "Dearie," or "Sweetie." They would also make sexual or indecent suggestions and double entendres. Myrna's sharp tongue would puncture their inflated egos and they soon learned that, if they couldn't treat her as an equal, they had better leave her alone. The result was that she had become suspicious of all men and she treated most of them with disdain.

However, there was one weekly event that Myrna genuinely looked forward to; it was what she called "Our Saturday Bake Off Breakfast" with Lydia Bradford. This custom started when Lydia showed up on her doorstep early Saturday morning with freshly baked pecan rolls. That was on the second day she moved into her house. Myrna invited her in and they had coffee as they devoured the rolls, leaving only enough for Jeffrey who joined them after he woke up. The following Saturday, Myrna baked some Danish pastries and took them over to Lydia's house. From then on, every Saturday, when they were both free, Lydia and Myrna would alternate baking some sort of breakfast pastry, from strudels to muffins to kolaches and coffee cakes. They would bring the pastry over to the other's house and the two of them would sit and visit. Jeffrey, when he awoke, would come in long enough to eat some of the Saturday bake-off and then leave. Their conversations would sometimes last for hours and both ladies derived great satisfaction from sitting and chatting about their pasts and their personal lives.

It was from these discussions that Lydia decided to fix Myrna up with Ben and, after the fiasco of the New Year's Eve party, she bowed out of trying to find a partner for Myrna, almost but not completely. Lydia was wise and she noticed the changes in Myrna's attitude towards men. She didn't approve of Myrna's perspective and, instead of head on statements, Lydia would suggest to Myrna that she ought to go out on dates. Myrna refused to take the bait and would change the subject.

This went on until one Saturday when Myrna mentioned that she had bumped into a former high school friend who was now president of his own manufacturing firm. She had met him at the bank she used in Malden Square. Lydia immediately started asking questions about his personal life; more questions than Myrna could answer. Outside of telling Lydia that his name was Fred Connors she couldn't tell her his marital status, if he had any children or if he would get in touch again. When Lydia persisted in asking questions, Myrna became a little irritable, so Lydia dropped the subject.

Two Saturdays later, Myrna told Lydia that Fred Connors had unexpectedly called her at her office and that she could now answer some of Lydia's questions. He had been divorced for ten years, he had no children and he wanted to take her out. Lydia, of course, wanted her to date him but Myrna was noncommittal; she said that she really wasn't interested.

Just two days after Jeffrey left for Oregon, Myrna began to feel lonely. There was no one to talk to at the end of the day and she missed his presence; she felt isolated. So, when Fred called her at her office, she was in more of a receptive mood to accept his invitation to go out with him. She agreed to go to a Red Sox game with him that Friday.

Fred showed up exactly on time dressed in a plain blue sports coat, gray slacks and loafers. He was a tall, distinguished looking man with a full head of brownish gray hair and an engaging grin. He drove into Boston, parked near Kenmore Square; they both walked to Fenway Park and sat in box seats on the first base side of the diamond. The Red Sox beat the New York Yankees, which pleased them both. Then, they took the subway and went to Locke-Ober, a restaurant that Myrna had heard of but had never been to. She was completely impressed with the food, the decor and the atmosphere. On the drive home she reflected on her evening; Fred had been fun to talk to and he had been a generous host. She felt serene and relaxed for the first time in months.

When they arrived back at her house, Myrna led the way up the stairs and inserted the key in her front door. Just as she did, Fred came up behind her, put his arms around her, cupped both of her breasts in his hands, and pulled her against him. He whispered in her ear, "I've been waiting a long time to do this."

Her shock, followed by a wave of fury, was instantaneous. Myrna squirmed free and hissed, "Take your hands off of me you filthy son of a bitch. You bastard. Get off my front porch or I'll call the police."

Fred looked completely surprised. "Don't tell me you didn't expect a little loving. Why do you think I spent all that money on you? I can tell that you want to screw as much as I do."

Myrna was not only angry she began to feel nauseated. "If you don't get off my porch, I'll scream 'rape.' Then you will be in trouble. Leave me alone. Get out of here."

Her anger, her fear and her humiliation made her tremble. At first, it was hard for Fred to believe that he was being rejected; he couldn't believe his charm and his money wouldn't get him whatever he wanted. Finally, he got the message that Myrna meant what she said. "Well, if you won't put out for me, that's your tough luck. You'll never know what you missed, you stupid bitch." With that, he walked away.

Myrna went in the house and cried most of the night; she was too shaken to do anything but occasionally doze.

That Saturday, it was Lydia's turn to bake and, when she arrived at Myrna's kitchen she saw Myrna sitting on a stool, in her nightgown with her hair uncombed and her eyes were red rimmed from crying.

She cried out, "Myra, what's the matter?" Lydia put her baked goods down and rushed over to Myra. "What's wrong, Dear?"

Myrna leaned from her stool and put her head on Lydia's shoulder and, between sobs, she told her what had happened on her date. She cried hard but, after a while, she stopped and just snuffled and began to hiccup a little.

Lydia did not say a word until Myrna had completely quieted down, Then she spoke. "Myrna, you look like a train wreck. Go wash your face, comb your hair and put some lipstick on. You're not the first woman who had to fight off an unwanted assault.

"I'll make our coffee and then we'll talk. You did nothing wrong except choose to go out with a pig. Go ahead and clean up, my Dear. I love you and I can't bear to see you so unhappy over something that wasn't your fault."

Myrna did as Lydia suggested and under Lydia's calm and wise influence, her horror started to recede. Lydia had Myrna sleep at her house for a few nights and, until Jeffrey returned from Oregon Myrna ate her evening meals with Lydia and her husband, Frank. He was also a tower of strength for her with his quiet humor and his fatherly assessment of her experience. His male presence, smoking a big bowled Meerschaum pipe, and his agreeing with his wife's indignation helped Myrna regain her equilibrium. However, almost every Saturday Bake Off after that, Myrna would bitterly say that men valued their waving third leg more than they respected women. She began to look down on all men as nothing but animals who believed in their salvation through orgasm.

Myrna was heading down the path of life without a partner. Without a change in attitude her horizon would become so narrow that there would be no room for anyone to be at her side. She would reach her final destination alone and lonely.

****

After Alice returned from summer camp, the Da Vinci family started to prepare for Greg's departure to Dartmouth. He would be leaving in a few weeks to begin football practice and he would not be home again until just before Thanksgiving. This was more than just packing clothes in suitcases; the Da Vinci family equation was changing. This would be the first time the family would not be together during the school year. Billy and Alice depended upon Greg for advice when they had problems and his father relied on him for guidance when deciding on family activities.

Ben recognized that the branches of the family tree were blooming and developing their own roots. Sometime in the future, there would be a grove replacing the present single tree; and when there were new woods, his duties would eventually become less. He would automatically be relegated to the position of elder statesman. He was not sure that he liked the thought of mechanically being promoted to such a position but he had no choice. As long as his heart was beating and the metronome of time was ticking, change was inevitable. The present tempo hinted at a lock step march out of the arena of activity towards the lane of loneliness.

Ben sighed, he knew change was coming but he didn't want to think about it.

The week after the Da Vinci family drove to New Hampshire and dropped Greg off at Dartmouth, the atmosphere around their home was subdued. It seemed the three of them were extra polite with each other and they all spoke in hushed voices. Ben went to work and Alice and Billy went through the motions of getting ready for Malden High to open for their sophomore and senior years. However, they both seemed at a loss as to what to do with themselves while they waited for the school year to begin.

That Sunday after church, they were all gathered on their porch. Ben had just finished reading the Sunday paper when he looked up and noticed that Alice and Billy were sitting there hardly saying a word. He knew that they only had a few days before school began but he didn't want them just hanging around, so he asked, "Why don't the two of you go see a movie? You need a change of scenery."

They thought that was a good idea and they began to bicker over which movie to see; Billy wanted a western while Alice preferred a love story. They had almost compromised when, through the house, they heard the door bell ring. Ben said he would answer it.

He walked along the side of the porch and turned towards the front of the house. Standing by the front door was a most attractive female. She was about his height and a few years younger than he. She had flaming red hair, blue eyes and a sweet face that made men stare at her. She was wearing a dress that outlined her full breasts, her thin waist and her curved hips; she was at the suggestive border, extremely close to provocative. She was completely aware of the effect she made and she was proud of it. She waited patiently while Ben enjoyed the opportunity of staring at her. Ben could smell the scent of the perfume she was wearing as he studied her.

Then she said, "Good Afternoon, my name is Barbara Bancroft but my friends call me BeBe. Are you Ben Vinci?"

"No, no. My name is Ben Da Vinci. Is that who you mean?"

She looked a little confused. "I think so, let me check my information." she pulled a stenographer's pad out of her purse and consulted it. "Are you the father of Greg Da Vinci?"

"Yes."

"I guess my informant spelled your name incorrectly. For that, I am sorry."

Ben was pleased with the sound of her voice; it was low, clear and almost sultry. The tone seemed to fit with the appealing vision of the woman, a woman who was aware of her sex and was pleased with it. "No need to apologize, that name gets mangled quite a bit. How can I help you?"

"It's what I can do for you, Mr. Da Vinci. I'm a columnist with the *Daily Record*. Our sports editor has given me a list of high school football stars who are going to college and we are going to be publishing human interest stories about some of them and their families. Your son is among the candidates that we might write about. I would like to talk to you and your family about him.

"May I come in, so that I can discuss this possible article with you?"

"You can but you should know that Greg is not here. He is up at Dartmouth already practicing football."

BeBe smiled as she answered, "Interviewing your son is not a necessity for our article; his athletic abilities are a given. Our story will feature his family, their relationship with him and how they helped him achieve his goals. Our sports editor is looking for human interest stories about the athletes' families, not necessarily the athlete himself."

Although Ben was not sure what he thought of BeBe's ideas, he was sure that he enjoyed studying her. He said, "Come in and tell me more about what you want for your article."

He led her to the porch where Alice and Billy were sitting; they were waiting to say goodbye and leave for the movies. Ben introduced the three of them and they exchanged pleasantries for a few minutes before Alice and Billy excused themselves in order to get to the theatre on time.

When they were gone, Ben offered his guest some refreshments. As BeBe drank Coke and nibbled on a cookie, she explained, in detail, what she and the sports editor were doing. She said that the sports editor, Jack Montgomery, had selected ten to twelve local high school football players who had received football scholarships to different colleges and she was to write human interest stories about them. During the course of the football season, if any of them excelled in any way, the *Daily Record* would print this story along with an accompanying article on his football prowess. She added that Jack, the sports editor, thought that Greg could very well be one of his featured athletes.

After she finished her explanation, BeBe started to question Ben about the details of his family life. She wrote both her questions and his answers in her stenographer's pad. At first, Ben was a little reluctant to respond because he didn't want to reveal any personal secrets. However, he soon found himself so proud of talking about his three children that his answers got longer and kept her scribbling his replies long after he finished speaking.

Ben did not keep track of the time. All he was aware of was that he was enjoying himself in the company of an attractive lady. He was startled when, all of a sudden, BeBe almost yelled, "Holy Cow. I'm late for an appointment. Ben, I have to go."

She put her stenographer's pad into her pocketbook, pulled out a business card and handed it to him. "Listen, would you mind if I called your kids and set up a time to interview them? I'd like to get their perspective on their brother. Do you think they would mind?"

Ben replied, "No, I don't think that they would mind at all. But they will be back in school shortly, so if you are going to talk with them it would be best to do it either Monday or Tuesday of this next week. Can you make it either of those days?"

"Yes, I'll call tomorrow and set up a time. You'll probably be working won't you?"

"Yes."

"Well, you have my card with my phone number on it. If you have any questions don't hesitate to call me.

"I've enjoyed our meeting immensely; now I've got to go."

After Alice and Billy returned, Ben told them who the lady that they met was, why she wanted to talk to them, and what to expect. Monday night, they told their father that they were to be interviewed the next day and that they could hardly wait. Tuesday night, when he arrived home, Alice and Billy couldn't stop talking about how much fun they had being interviewed by a lady reporter. Their experience lasted at the dinner table Tuesday, Wednesday and Thursday evening. By that time, the two of them almost began to believe that the interview, if it ever were to be published, would be mostly about them.

Friday evening, after dinner was over and the kitchen was cleaned, Ben was reading the *Daily Record* when the phone rang. He answered it and was surprised to find that BeBe was on the other end of the line.

"Good evening Ben," she began. "I hope I'm not disturbing you."

"No, not at all. I'm just sitting here reading your newspaper. What did you say the name of your sports editor is?"

She answered, "Jack Montgomery. It should be listed in the masthead."

"It is, I just wasn't sure that I had gotten his name correctly."

"Actually, he is part of the reason I'm calling you. First though, I must tell you that I enjoyed talking to your son and daughter. I can see why you are so proud of them; they are just delightful young people. You have done a good job raising them.

"Now, Jack has asked me to go over a few items with you. Will you be at home this coming Sunday?"

"Surely. Why don't you plan on getting here about the same time you did last Sunday. That will leave plenty of time to go over whatever it is you wish to discuss. Will you be able to stay for supper?"

"Thank you for the invitation, Ben, but I won't be able to take you up on it, there are other errands I have to run. I do appreciate the offer and maybe some other time. I'll see you next Sunday. Take care."

Ben hung the phone up; he was happy but confused. He was pleased that he was going to see BeBe again but, after thinking about it, he wondered what were the few items that the sports editor wanted her to go over. As a parent, he hoped that Alice and Billy had not inadvertently said something wrong during their interview. He didn't think so, but where else could her editor get information that needed clarification?

It didn't matter to Ben, he was going to see BeBe again. From the moment that he saw her on Sunday, when she appeared in a cranberry red dress that fit her like the skin on a grape, until she left, late in the afternoon, he thoroughly enjoyed her visit. Much to his surprise, she didn't mention her editor or any items that needed to be gone over and Ben was content not to ask. As a matter of fact, he didn't have to ask any questions; BeBe seemed to lead the conversation. She asked about his upbringing and then she steered the conversation towards the fact that Ben was a widower raising his family by himself. To his surprise, Ben found himself willing to discuss subjects that he had avoided thinking about for years. There is nothing more interesting to a man than engaging in a conversation with a woman who wants him to tell her about himself.

As she was preparing to leave, BeBe mentioned to Ben that her editor now had all of her interviews and that it was up to him when, and if, they were printed in the paper. She said that Ben should defi-nitely keep in touch with her because she would keep track of all the articles; they maybe could get together sometime in the future. She walked to the door, they shook hands, and she left.

The following Friday, Ben was hoping that he would hear from BeBe; he didn't. Sunday was spent wishing that she would appear at his door; she never arrived. Her total absence made him think about her often and he had almost decided to give her a call when, on the next Friday, his front door bell rang. He answered it and saw

BeBe standing on the porch. A wave of happiness flooded through him.

She pointed a finger at him and said, "Ben Da Vinci, your phone is always busy. It is almost impossible to get through to you." She smiled and added, "If I needed an emergency haircut, I would be in bad shape."

He thought about that a second; she was absolutely right about the phone being in constant use. He answered. "Well, with two teenagers talking their way through high school and one calling from college, the line usually is always busy. I hardly have a chance to make any phone calls myself.

"I would have a difficult time getting the phone away from my kids. Your emergency haircut might have to wait for the Last Rites."

BeBe smiled, "Hanging on the telephone is a teenage illness that they all get infected with. I went through the same thing, years ago. Are they home with you now?"

"No, they've gone to the basketball game."

"Good. My emergency haircut will have to wait because I'm starving. Instead of administering me the Last Rites, you could take me out to eat."

After discussing what restaurant to go to, Ben followed BeBe in his car, to a bar on Salem Road. The building looked beat up from the outside but it specialized in tasty Italian food. They sat in a booth and shared a pizza and draft beer.

BeBe seemed wound up; she carried most of the conversation with Ben asking the questions this time. She told him of her childhood and growing up in Brookline. She went to Holy Cross College in Worcester and then spent years in New York City working at several magazines. She had been married once, divorced, and had no children.

Ben didn't understand what had opened the floodgate of personal information but he was glad to hear about BeBe's life. He had been curious about her background but she had shaped most of the other conversations and he had been busy answering questions instead of asking them.

When she had finished telling him about her past, the conversation seemed to come to a quiet halt. Then BeBe asked Ben about his future plans. He had no immediate answers because he had no immediate plans to discuss. When he asked her about her plans, there seemed to be the same awkward silence. They both seemed to sit there hugging their hopes and dreams to themselves without being able to share their innermost thoughts. After a while, their conversation picked up speed and they chatted amiably until BeBe left to go home. Ben walked her to her automobile. Just before she got in, he kissed her on the cheek. She stared at him for a second and then, without saying a word, drove away.

For days, Ben went over their past conversations in his mind; the reminiscing was pleasant. Soon after, the realities of work and living settled in and he had to pay attention to his daily activities. School had started for Alice and Billy and they also got caught up in their own routine. As a break, they went to Hanover to see the Dartmouth-Cornell game. Greg did not play much and his team lost but the family had a happy weekend together.

It was about a month later, on a Sunday afternoon, as Ben was reading the sports page, it dawned on him again that each member of his family was going their own ways. Although today the three of them had gone to church and had had breakfast together, Greg wasn't with them and Alice and Billy were elsewhere for the afternoon. He was alone in his house. Suddenly, Ben had a longing to talk with someone who was his peer in age, interests and experience; raising a family didn't meet those desires. He wanted the friendship of a female.

BeBe had done something no other woman had accomplished. For the first time in years, Ben could put the past behind him as he thought about a woman. Esther's memories were still with him but they were no longer blocking his path. The part of his life that he had frozen with the death of his wife was beginning to thaw.

BeBe had stirred Ben simply by being a woman who was aware of her sexuality and by getting him to talk about the most important aspect of his present life, his children. These two factors had enabled her to open the door to the cage where he had locked most of his emotions. Ben was completely unaware that his feelings were changing; all he knew was that he wanted to see BeBe, talk with BeBe and be with BeBe.

The thoughts of BeBe in her red outfit, the smell of her perfume and her soft, husky voice made him wish she were here with him. He decided to get in touch with her; after all, he thought, she had often invited him to call her any time.

That Monday about mid morning, Ben put up a "closed" sign in his barbershop window and went home to make a phone call. Like his father, he never had a phone installed at his barber shop; he felt phone calls would be a distraction for him. Alice and Billy were at school so his call would be private. He dialed the number that was on the card that BeBe had given him and, when the *Daily Record* operator answered, he gave her BeBe's extension number. The phone rang six or seven times and Ben was about to hang up when, suddenly, he heard a man's answer and say, "Hello."

"Good Morning. Is Barbara Bancroft there?"

The man replied almost immediately, "BeBe? I'm not sure. My

office is next to hers and I answered because I heard her phone ringing. Hold on and let me find out where she is." Ben heard the noise of the phone being put down and, after a short pause, the phone was picked up again.

The man said, "She's gone on a honeymoon with her husband."

"Husband?"

Emotions exploded inside Ben. A nuclear blast couldn't have vaporized his hopes more. He went completely numb; the questions and the pain, like the radiation and the burns, would come after the shock.

"Husband?"

"Yeh, Jack." The man that Ben was talking to seemed friendly and in no rush to get back to his own desk. "Do you know him?"

"Jack Montgomery, the sports editor? I didn't know that the two of them were married."

"Well, to tell you the truth, they haven't been married very long, maybe two weeks. But their hot and cold affair has been going on for years. All the staff has taken bets on how long they will stay married.

"Did you want to leave a message?"

Ben did not want BeBe to know that he had called. "No, no," he said, "It's nothing important. I'll call back later."

He hung up the phone, took a deep breath, and then the anguish and the questions swept in. They stung like sleet slapping bare skin in a snow storm.

Had BeBe been leading him on? Had he misunderstood what the two of them had said? She had invited his attention, hadn't she? Was there an article about Greg and would it ever be in the paper? The questions, and many variations of these questions, kept spinning through his head. He had no answers, just a sickening feeling that something had gone wrong. He felt that he had been betrayed. He sat by the phone completely wretched and befuddled.

After some time had passed, he realized that he had to get back to work. Reluctantly, he returned to his barber shop where he found that he had a backlog of customers; at least that kept him from dwelling on his carousel of painful questions. Over the next few weeks Ben kept asking himself these same questions again and again. One day he would answer a question one way; the next day his answer would be on the other side of the same question.

What made it more difficult for him was that Alice and Billy would scan the sports page of the *Daily Record* and ask why the article about Greg hadn't been printed. Ben pointed out to them that the articles that did appear were about juniors and seniors; Greg was only a freshman and not playing as often as they had expected. These explanations did not satisfy his children and they said that their father should call and demand an answer. Ordinarily, Ben would have agreed with them; however, there was no way he was going to initiate a contact between either the husband or the wife. He wanted nothing to do with either of them. There was never an article about Greg in the paper and it wasn't until long after the football season ended that the family discussions about the article ended.

Over the next few months Ben's emotions stopped boiling and they started to evaporate; he began to be more objective about BeBe and the never seen football article. After he really thought about it, he had to admit that he was more upset with his own attitude than with anything else that had happened. Whether BeBe had been honest with him or not wasn't even important; he had done something that he had not done before. He had raised his personal emotions over his family duties.

After Esther passed his major goal had been to nurture and raise his family. This was his tribute to his wife and to their marriage. Everything else became secondary and, as his own personal life withered and dried, he worked relentlessly for his children. His enjoyment came almost completely through the lives of his three children.

When BeBe entered his life she began to blur his path by focusing, not directly on him, but on Greg, his oldest child. That lowered his defenses, allowing her beauty and personality to stir his dormant feelings. He began to come alive and respond both as a human and as a male. A perfectly normal reaction but one that took him completely by surprise. He had not finished the stewardship of his family; in fact, he believed the most important part of it lay just ahead of him. His children were all reaching adulthood and, until they were on their own, they would need him.

At first, the fact that BeBe might have used him upset Ben. On the other hand, maybe she didn't use him; she might have been sending him a message when they went out that Friday evening. She might have been waiting for him to make a decision. He could have missed something. Either way, it didn't matter. It was over.

When his embarrassment and anger eased, he told himself that his duty to his children must still be his only priority. He rededicated himself to this task. The fact that the two goals, raising his family and his personal happiness, could be met without excluding each other never entered his thoughts. He had been burned once and he vowed not to let it happen a second time.

Ben was heading down the path of life without a partner. Without a change in attitude his horizon would become so narrow that there would be no room for anyone to be at his side. He would reach his final destination alone and lonely.

SOPHOMORES

7

Jeffrey Cabot's sophomore year was not nearly as successful as was his freshman year. It began quietly but, by the time it ended, he felt that it had been a complete disaster. Although he was personally responsible for some of the chaos, he, like every other teenager, was not in control of his own destiny. He was much more the victim than the perpetrator.

His father was the catalyst for the changes. Samuel Skinner suddenly decided to become more involved with his son, Jeffrey. The decision came after Jeffrey returned from his trip to Oregon and just before school began. The trip ignited the sniping between Skinner and his ex-wife that had otherwise been under a cease fire arrangement. Their volleys turned into barrages and their relationship again became an all out war.

Unfortunately, even though they were shooting at each other, his parents' ultimate target was Jeffrey; and he was hit and wounded often. For him, the motives behind the increase in his father's fatherhood were unclear, and, at first, a little unwelcome. Jeffrey couldn't tell if Skinner wanted to check more closely on his ex-wife, or if Skinner wanted to exert more influence over him, or if Skinner just wanted to brag about himself. What made it more difficult for Jeffrey was that he had no one to really talk with. His mother was frozen silent on the subject of her ex-husband and his father did nothing but snoop around, asking questions about his mother. Jeffrey's emotions were once again spinning and he was losing his equilibrium and stability.

This time however, being a little older and a little craftier, he was able to eke out an advantage from all his new found turmoil. He discovered that he could get his father to shower him with either gifts or money; all Jeffrey had to do was suggest that his mother was thinking about buying him something and Skinner immediately brought out his wallet. It was blackmail and Jeffrey knew it was unethical, but he considered it his right to earn something out of this bitter family feud.

The internal bickering, along with his wrong attitude, began to change his outlook on life. At school, he was no longer a pleasant, affable person and his friends began to leave him alone. He began his false boasting about his father's accomplishments and his father's reservoir of cash. He was, once again, sliding into a protective cocoon.

Just after the Christmas holidays, Jeffrey mentioned to his father that he was going to take the test to get his driver's license. His father promised him that, when he had his license, he would buy him his own car. When his mother heard of this latest promise, she was furious. Skinner and she had many angry words about his offer. She argued that a car would distract Jeffrey from schoolwork and that his grades would suffer. Skinner wanted him to have a car so that they could meet more often whenever and wherever Skinner decided to have a rendezvous.

Jeffrey did get his license, Skinner did buy him a brand new red Cadillac, and Myrna's worst fears were realized. Jeffrey, to show off and to regain the friendships he had lost, spent most of his spare time driving around with new found cronies. His grades slipped, he didn't regain any of his old friends, and he was finally ticketed for speeding. Before the situation got completely out of hand, someone stole his car while he was in school, smashed it into a telephone pole, and completely totaled it. Skinner was furious and refused to replace the car and Myrna was relieved that no one was hurt and that Jeffrey no longer had wheels.

The car, and all the incidents that occurred after the car was demolished, marked the high point of the hot emotions and the bad feelings that pulsed through Skinner, Myrna and Jeffrey. After that, the three of them were emotionally exhausted. Even spouting volcanos have to rest between eruptions. They still sparred with one another but there was a sullen period of quiet and coexistence among the three of them. There was little joy at the Cabot house.

That June, on a Saturday before his school year ended, Jeffrey was riding his bike around the neighborhood when he saw a familiar figure in front of the Da Vinci house. It was Greg who was standing on a small ladder trimming the hedges next to their porch. Jeffrey almost laughed aloud; he was so glad to see someone who brought back pleasant memories. He hadn't seen Greg since he had gone to Dartmouth, almost ten months ago. He peddled up to where Greg was working and stopped his bike.

"Hi Greg, when did you get home?"

Greg stopped clipping and looked at him. "Jeff. I got home a few days ago. I'm back for the summer. How have you been?"

"Not too bad. I haven't seen you for a long time. Malden doesn't finish school until next week."

"Yes, I know. I've been razzing Alice and Billy about that."

Jeffrey changed the subject by asking, "How did your first season go?"

"Not too good. We won five games and I didn't play as much as I had hoped. However, our coach says we are a team on the rise and I believe him. He's optimistic about me and he laid out a whole bunch of instructions I'm supposed to follow this summer."

Jeffrey was curious. "What kind of instructions?"

"Well, I'm too light for my position so, I'm going to do some weight lifting this summer and try to gain ten or fifteen pounds. Billy and I are going to clean out the garage and turn it into what we call 'Hulk Headquarters.'"

Jeffrey eagerly asked, "Can I help clean out the garage and lift weights with you and Billy?"

"Why would you want to do that? This is going to be serious business. I want to be on the starting team. I'm not going to be fooling around."

Jeffrey thought for a second and then said, "Greg, I've had a really shitty year. I've screwed it up. Maybe a routine will help me for next year. If you let me work out with you I'll do whatever you ask. I won't fool around. Honest. I promise you that I won't fool around. If I don't keep my promise you can always tell me to 'fuck off.'

"Besides, I'd be willing to pay you for letting me work out by buying us pizzas, doughnuts, ice cream, anything we want after a workout."

Greg laughed at the suggested bribe; that menu was not exactly what his coach had in mind. "Jeff, I'm not hungry right now so free food doesn't interest me. If you are really willing to work, I'll let you try. But, if you fool around or goof off, I won't stand for it. I'm serious."

Gregg thought for a second and then added, "Tomorrow morning,

Billy and I are going to clean out the garage and start to get every-thing set up. If you want to help, be here by nine o'clock."

Jeffrey rode his bicycle home feeling better about his life than he had in months.

When Billy and Alice returned home from running an errand, Greg told both of them about Jeffrey's request to work out with them, along with his offer to buy all their snacks. He also told Billy that he had decided to let Jeffrey join them.

Billy didn't like the idea and said so in no uncertain terms. "Greg, you are making a big mistake allowing Jeff to work out with us."

"Why do you say that, Billy?"

"You weren't at school this last year. He has changed completely. His father got him a red Cadillac and, until it was stolen, he drove me nuts bragging about that car and how rich his old man is. Can you imagine carrying a picture of his father in his wallet and showing it to everyone? Not a girl friend; a father, his own father. I'm just saying he's weird; I don't want him hanging around all summer. He will hold us back.

"I think you're selling your soul, and mine, for some junk food."

Alice listened to Billy and, when he was finished, she spoke up, "Billy, I agree that Jeff was hard to take this year. I avoided him too because of the crowd he hung around with, but I think you are wrong. He's not weird, he's just mixed up."

Billy was quick to ask, "What's the difference, and what's he got to be mixed up about?"

"The difference, my darling brother, is like night and day. His mother and father are divorced and he is caught in the middle."

Billy crowed, "That's no excuse! Everybody has problems. We have problems."

Alice was not about to concede, "Yes, everybody has problems. But we also have each other. He is a single child with no one on his side. He is a war orphan.

"I'm in his classes, I hear him talk, I see him act. He would do almost anything to have a friend. I'm sure he feels alone.

"I think he carries his father's picture because he is looking for him."

Greg listened patiently to what each of them said, and when Alice had finished he stopped the conversation by saying, "OK. I hear what both of you said. I'm still willing to give Jeff a chance. If he goofs off, I'll kick him out." That ended the discussion.

Sunday morning, only Ben and Alice went to church; Greg and Billy were allowed to stay home to begin setting up "Hulk Headquarters." After church, the two of them went for breakfast. When he and Alice had finished ordering, they sat without saying a word for quite a while.

It was not an uncomfortable interlude; they were both combing through the tangle of their unruly thoughts. It was just a pause in the conversation between a father and his daughter. Each spent the time adding up the positive memories they had in their private thought banks.

His daughter broke the mood by suddenly saying, "Dad, I should hear this week about my application as a camp counsellor; if I do get the job I'll be gone all summer. You will have to get Greg and Billy ready for school this fall. Who will look after you?"

Ben smiled at this sudden role reversal. He was pleased with all of his children, but he especially doted on his daughter. He was so proud, he smiled whenever he thought of her auburn hair, her freckles, and the dimple in each of her cheeks. She was an attractive, healthy teenager, finishing her sophomore year in high school. "Alice, I appreciate your concern, but I think that I will be able to manage. I honestly believe that I did fairly well before you took over."

His daughter got a little exasperated. "Dad, you know what I mean. Greg goes to Dartmouth now, Billy will be leaving for Boston University next fall, and soon I'll be the last one home. When I leave, you'll have finished your job of bringing us up.

"What will you do this summer if I get this job?"

Ben had not said a word about the changes but, of course, the same thoughts had been occurring to him. He had raised his children and, now, as they approached maturity, his task was nearing an end. Lately, he had been recalling how young the three of them had been when their mother had died. He couldn't believe that the time had gone so quickly. He was painfully aware that his quiet work and parental duties would be coming to an end. He had become mindful of that fact long before Alice had mentioned it and he really didn't know how to handle it. He had not yet begun to examine what the changes would mean to him. In a sense, he was shying away from the future. He was beginning to suffer the paternal equivalent of the "empty nest syndrome."

He answered his daughter's question, "I'm pretty sure that you will get an offer to be a counsellor. You've been to that camp as one of their campers before the staff asked you if you would be interested in becoming a counsellor. They know you and you know them; so, I think they will follow through and offer you a job. You will make a good counsellor."

"I hope so, Dad. I remember how I wanted to be treated when I was a camper and I'll treat my girls that way. Some of my counsellors were stupid and didn't care about helping out young kids. They acted as if they were at camp to enjoy themselves; they had no concern about looking after the campers. I don't intend to be like that."

"I have no doubt that you will be one of the best counsellors in that camp."

"Thank you, Dad. But what will you do if I'm away all summer?"

"I haven't thought too much about summer but you are right; this year it will be different. You'll be at girl's camp and Greg and Billy will be working and exercising. This will be the very first summer that I won't be running around doing errands with any of you. I will have time on my hands. I guess I could put in a larger vegetable garden. But, should I really do that? There is less and less family at home to eat my vegetables and that might be a problem. If I have a bumper harvest, I may have to close my barbershop and open a produce stand.

"Seriously, Alice, I haven't given it much thought; obviously I'm going to have to do something. I can't even tell you whether a summer without much activity is what I want or what I don't want. It will be an experience that is new for me just as going to camp as a counsellor will be new for you. You do realize that older people can also have new experiences, don't you? Life isn't strictly limited to you youngsters."

"Oh, Dad, I know that. And I'm hopeful that you will find a new life. You certainly deserve it. You have always been there for us, but who has been there for you?"

She hesitated before continuing, "You need someone to rely on; someone your age that you can share your thoughts with, someone to talk to, someone to be with. You should have a female companion."

The memory of BeBe came and went quickly. Ben felt a little embarrassed about where the conversation was going with his teenage daughter. There was no way in the world that he wanted to discuss his personal life with her. He changed the subject, quickly and awkwardly, by asking what she planned on doing the rest of the day. Her response to his question, and the rest of their conversation, didn't border anywhere near his red zone. After they finished eating, they drove home.

The following Tuesday, Alice got her job offer in the mail. When she read the letter to her brothers both of them hooped and hollered. They walked around the house chanting, "Alice. Alice. Alice."

After their victory chant, they sat on the porch and talked about the upcoming summer. They each realized that they were beginning to go their own ways and that they would not have the nearness that they had enjoyed in the past. Their first major separation was last year when Greg left for Dartmouth and they knew that was just the beginning. There would be more as they each went their own way; so they promised to keep their ties strong because they needed each other.

When Ben came home from work Alice told him she had gotten the job and that she had to be at camp by the end of the week. He was happy for her but not surprised. He told her to pick out a restaurant she liked and he would take the family out to eat. This edict pleased his children because no one had thought of preparing dinner and they were all hungry. They went to a Chinese restaurant and everyone came home stuffed and satisfied. They even brought their extra fortune cookies home with them.

The four of them gathered on the porch on the side of the house. That particular evening the discussion was about the future changes coming to their family; no one wanted them but everyone had to be aware of them. They all had something to say even though no one could be specific about what the changes would be. It was a somber conversation.

Later that evening, Greg called Jeffrey and told him that he was not going to start his exercise routine until the following Monday because the family was going to help Alice get ready for her summer job. For the next few days the three siblings hung out together as much as they could. On Wednesday, Greg proposed that the three of them take another trip to Cape Ann. This idea was greeted enthusiastically and they decided to go the next day, Thursday.

They enjoyed themselves immensely but they were surprised by what they discovered. Cape Ann in the winter is not like Cape Ann the other three seasons of the year. This weathered, old peninsula fronting the Atlantic Ocean just north of Boston has provided a home for many cultures and civilizations for centuries. During the winters it is rich in history and ocean views; during the summers it is rich in history, ocean views and tourists. The narrow lanes, crooked streets and open beaches cannot accommodate the throngs that want to avail themselves of the natural beauties and gift shops unique to Cape Ann. The result, as they found out, was one long traffic jam. That was no problem for them as they weren't in a hurry to go anywhere; it just slowed their movement.

However, they found several advantages. At Red Rock, they could walk out on the rock itself and enjoy the spray of the ocean as the waves detonated themselves on the craggy shoreline. They didn't have to worry about freezing. At Marblehead, they could enjoy the view of the small sailing boats bobbing in the harbor at their leisure. The only time they got irritated was when they ran into an unexplained traffic jam at Prides Crossing. When they broke free and had finally parked at The Fishermen's Memorial Statue in Gloucester, they decided that their tour would have to be shortened if they were going to get home by early evening.

They drove over to Woodman's and ate their fill of lobster and crab while talking about what they had seen and done. They bought some fried clams to take to their father and then headed back to Malden. The day was another bead on their memory rosary.

Alice's father and brothers drove her to camp on the following Saturday, dropped her off, and then drove back to Malden in complete silence. This was the first time Alice would be gone for the entire summer and, already, on the ride home, they began to miss her.

For the rest of the summer, until Greg left for Dartmouth, and Billy went to Boston University, the three young men would lift weights at least once every day. Greg would have preferred to have a fixed schedule but, because he and Billy were part of the "pick and shovel brigade" of their construction company, their work load varied. Sometimes it rained too hard to utilize their skills and sometimes the company schedule could proceed without their services. As a result, on weekdays, their workouts would be early in the morning or, occasionally, they would be late in the afternoon. However, on the weekends, they usually planned on morning workouts.

The only certainty was that Greg planned on training every day. He was determined to gain weight and become a better football player. He was more dedicated than either Billy or Jeffrey because he had more to gain but neither of them missed many training sessions as they worked hard under Greg's urging.

Greg faithfully kept his end of the bargain and he would ask Billy to get in touch with Jeff whenever they had to change the time of their workout. Billy would then call Jeffrey's house and relay the information to either Jeff or his mother. That made for a lot of phone calls but Greg was only responding to the changes imposed on him.

By the same token, Jeffrey kept his promise. He willingly bought whatever he was asked whenever he was asked. At first, Greg had thought that Jeff's promise was humorous but, after the first week, he realized that it was not only a good promise but it was also costing Jeff a lot of money. Greg talked to Billy and they both agreed that they really should split the cost of the large grocery bill. When the brothers told him they felt they should help pay the costs, he felt that he was not keeping his promise. However, after watching how much they all consumed, common sense made him realize that dividing the expenses was only fair.

They had to bring a larger trash barrel into the garage to hold the empty pizza boxes, the hamburger wrappers, the empty paper cups and all the other trash they accumulated. Some of the ten pounds that Greg gained that summer was partially due to the amount of fast food that arrived at "Hulk Headquarters."

They got along well. At first, it was three young men challenging their bodies and sweating in the summer heat. As the brothers learned more about Jeff, and themselves, it became an easy, jocular, masculine relationship. Each of the three were pleased with the agreement and the minor inconvenience of changing times didn't bother them. Their growth was more than just their muscles.

Greg discovered that he not only had physical strength and athleticism, he also found that he could inspire others to work hard; even when they didn't want to. He initially made a mistake by trying to drive Billy and Jeff too quickly and too harshly. He soon became aware of when he should be pushing and when he should be praising. He learned that other peoples' strengths and weaknesses have to be measured by their standards, not his. He would take this knowledge and grow into a smarter person.

Billy learned to think longer and be more patient before judging others. After he and Jeff began confiding in each other he discovered that his original opinion was not always correct. Jeff was neither weird nor shallow. Jeff had the same disadvantage that he and Greg had; he was being raised by a single parent. However, Jeff's experiences were much different and less pleasant. Billy appreciated how lucky he and his brother and sister were to have a father who nurtured them.

Jeff didn't have that advantage. Although he was being raised by a single parent, he was a casualty in a war between his mother and father. He was a tennis ball caught in a volley between two rackets. The result was that Jeff was deprived of the love that parents owe to their children. Billy became more tolerant towards Jeff and he began to enjoy being around him. By the end of summer, Billy liked Jeff.

Jeffrey, without his even being aware of it, was the person who gained the most insight into his own life. Before he began working out with Greg and Billy, he couldn't understand why he had no close friends. He was inside a teen age bubble of inferiority complex, worry, and self pity. At first, Jeffrey wanted to quit because keeping up with Greg was so difficult. Greg was a hard task master both on himself and anyone who worked with him. Jeff thought Greg was giving him more weights and repetitions than he was capable of handling. But he noticed that Billy was having the same problems and, in both cases, Greg was very patient with both of them. He praised them when they succeeded and consoled them when they failed. There was never any ridicule or comparisons to the heavier weights that he could lift; he just constantly urged them to do their best.

Jeffrey stuck with it and, after a while, he was able to lift the heavier weights for more repetitions. This made him feel a lot better about himself and he began to relax and join in on the interplay between Greg and Billy. They laughed a lot. Jeffrey marveled at the informal but courteous way they treated each other. As he began to relax with the two brothers, he became the deciding vote on any discussion or argument they had among themselves. He enjoyed his new role.

For Jeffrey, the best part of summer was yet to come. As he and the brothers got closer, he began to hang around his newly found friends' house. It wasn't long before he was joining them just before they ate dinner or meeting with them on their porch after they finished. That is when he discovered how important a father is in raising his children. He met Ben Da Vinci, not as his barber but as a parent.

Until now, Jeffrey had thought of Mr. Da Vinci only as the person who cut his hair for a fee; the man whose services he utilized when he needed him. Skinner, his father, had given him a snobbish attitude about education; if you didn't have a college degree, you certainly weren't intelligent. And, if you didn't use your brain you had to use your back or your hands. Jeffrey never thought about Skinner's axioms so he accepted them without question, and he had automatically put his barber in the non-intelligent category.

He had no reason to doubt his father's ideas until he spent time around Mr. Da Vinci with his sons. These nightly family discussions, among the father and the two sons, were a revelation. He had never seen how family members interacted with each other to make each individual grow stronger and he envied these relationships. Their father guided the conversations with love and skill in even the most heated discussions. Jeffrey noted that Mr. Da Vinci's common sense and his knowledge made his children think their way through their own convictions.

After he saw how Mr. Da Vinci worked with his children, Jeffrey found himself admiring him. Ben Da Vinci earned Jeffrey's respect by being himself. And, after he began including Jeffrey inside the family circle, Jeffrey found himself liking him. He began to wish that he were a member of the Da Vinci family.

All of this was new to Jeffrey as his own family life was atrophied. He hardly ever discussed anything with his mother. She was usually busy and he had a hard time expressing himself to her because he wanted to avoid any confrontation. His father never listened to him, instead he either questioned Jeffrey about what his mother was doing or he spent his time telling Jeffrey about his own successes and how much money he had made. Jeffrey relished the good will of the Da Vinci family huddles; the health of their family life showed him how unhealthy his own was.

One Monday morning in late summer, Greg informed Jeffrey that the upcoming Friday would be the last day they would be lifting weights. Saturday morning he was going to return to Dartmouth to start practicing for the beginning of football season. Jeffrey was surprised. He had known that, sooner or later, they would be breaking up, but he had not thought about it. After Greg's announcement, Jeffrey realized how treasured this routine had become to him and how much he would miss it. For the first time in his life, he felt sad that something he was doing with his peers was coming to an end.

That entire week, without saying anything, he worked extra hard to please his friends. He came over to the Da Vinci house early Friday evening before supper with four large pizza's; one for each of them. He called it the "Last Supper." There was a lot of joking, kidding, and sadness as they ate and talked. Before Jeffrey left, he gave each one of them a Boston Red Sox baseball cap. They all wished each other well, he shook hands with Greg, Billy and their father and then Jeffrey left.

He got home and went straight to his room without saying a word to his mother.

****

Saturday morning Greg, Billy and their father left early and drove to White River Junction, Vermont, to the camp where Alice was working. After their visit with Alice, Ben had to take Greg to Dartmouth. However, before then, Greg insisted that he wanted to have time to say "Goodbye" to Alice. The three of them spent the rest of the day visiting with her, knowing that she would be home shortly. They stayed overnight at a motel and, the next morning they drove to Hanover. After Greg checked in, and was assigned a room, they again toured the campus, the stadium and the town. They said their "Goodbyes" early so Greg could get his rest before he started working out the next day. Their evening at the motel was somber for Ben and Billy as was their drive home on Monday. The gray mood continued all day.

The two of them ate their evening meal with hardly any conversation between them. Billy finally said, "Boy, it's quiet. I'll be glad when Alice gets back on Thursday and lightens this place up again."

His father replied, "I agree with you."

"Oh, Dad, by the way, tomorrow afternoon I have to go over to BU and get some registration information. I'll be driving Hunkajunk into Boston with a couple of friends and I'll be back but I don't know when. We will probably eat in Boston, so don't count on me for supper."

That was the way it was left. His father took it as an omen of what was going to come. Soon, he was going to be living in a large home all by himself; and even though he didn't want to think about it, change was inevitable.

8

Myrna and Lydia changed their Saturday coffee meeting time that summer. Since Jeffrey was usually over at the Da Vinci house exercising early Saturday morning, he no longer ate with them. Myrna suggested that Lydia ask her husband, Frank, to join them but Lydia said that Frank was a sleepy head and didn't get up as early as she did. However, after a few weeks, they both decided to start an hour later so that Frank could join them.

This proved to be a good move for all of them. For Lydia, it stopped the flow of verbal insults that Myrna constantly was hurling at the masculine half of the world. She was edging on being bitter and she sometimes would go too far with her contempt. Lydia thought she was becoming obsessed and that bothered her. With Frank around, his sense of humor and steadfast good nature not only tempered Myrna's remarks, it forced her to soften her attitude to some degree. Myrna backed away from some of her extreme statements and that pleased Lydia; she thought that there still might be hope for Myrna.

Having Frank at their coffee meeting also was beneficial for Myrna in another way; she learned about the Da Vinci family. The phone calls from Billy and Greg changing exercise times confused her because she didn't understand the reason for them. Jeffrey was not much help in explaining the reasons for the changes; the chain of communications between them was more a thin thread than a husky hawser. All she really knew was that her son was spending a great deal of time over at the Da Vinci house. His being there during the early evening hours was also a concern of her's. She had no real sense of what was going on or even why it was happening.

Frank was able to clarify Myrna's confusion by explaining who both boys were and what they were doing. Because Frank was also a long-time neighbor, friend and customer, he was able to tell her about the family and their father, Ben Da Vinci. He helped answer her questions about the background of the family and told her that Jeffrey couldn't be in better company. She noticed that, as the summer wore on, Jeffrey seemed more relaxed and happy. She was relieved that her son was enjoying his vacation.

Although Jeffrey was having a good summer, he did not tell his mother much about the Da Vincis. His attitude towards the world was loosening up but not yet to the point that he could sit and explore his inner feelings with his mother. It was as if his happiness would melt if he talked about it with anyone. As a result, he did not tell his mother much about the Da Vincis or about when Greg and Billy were leaving for college.

This oversight of not keeping his mother aware of his activities profoundly changed the lives of everyone in both families.

During their last week of working out, Greg had asked Jeffrey to do him a favor. He wanted some books returned to the library, some pieces of equipment moved around, and "hulk headquarters" generally restored as their garage. Jeffrey gladly agreed to Greg's requests. He went over to the Da Vinci house shortly after they left that Saturday and went into the garage through the side door. By the time he finished the sweeping and the cleaning and returned home, his mother had gone. She had left some baked goodies for him to snack on and a note telling him she had errands to run but that she would be back in the early afternoon.

He read the note, threw it back on the table and sat down to eat the freshly baked apricot bread which he ordinarily enjoyed. This morning it didn't taste like it normally did; he didn't eat much. He was in a sour mood as he thought about the fact that his summer interlude was now over. His friends were gone and school was coming and none of his thoughts were at all pleasant.

The phone rang and it jarred him out of his mood and into action. He picked up the receiver and said, without enthusiasm, "Hello."

"Jeffrey. I was hoping to catch you at home." His father's deep voice continued, "I have been meaning to call you. How have you been?"

Jeffrey wasn't exactly thrilled to hear from his father. He hadn't spoken to him all summer and today wasn't a good day to talk to anyone. "Hi, Dad," was all he could muster.

"Well, you don't seem overjoyed to talk with your Old Man," snapped Skinner.

"Sorry, Dad, I have a lot on my mind. How are you doing?"

"I'm doing marvelously well. Superfine. I just made a killing in court; I made one of my biggest settlements in all of my life on a case; I took the other side completely by surprise and slaughtered them. I made them pay through the nose. They won't forget Samuel Skinner for a while.

"That's why I'm calling. I want to see you today."

"Today? Dad, does it have to be today?"

"Yes, today, Saturday. I haven't talked to you in a long time and I'll be busy all this next week. I'm in a good mood and I want to celebrate my victory. We could meet at the Stone Zoo in Stoneham and decide where to go from there."

"Dad, you know that I don't have a car."

"That's no problem. Borrow your mother's car. She'll let you."

Jeffrey hesitated. His mother had begun to let him use her car but only to run errands and never outside of Malden. She certainly would not be pleased to let him have the car to visit his father. Finally, he said, "I don't think Mom would let me have the car to drive out of the city."

His father responded brusquely, "Jeff, grow up. First of all, the Stone Zoo is only a few miles from your house. Second, you don't have to tell her you are taking the car to drive out of town. Just say to her that you are going over to a friend's house on an errand."

Jeffrey didn't want to lie to his mother; it was something he really did not want to do. She had never lied to him and he appreciated that fact. He expected to get a lecture from his father when he replied, "Dad, I can't lie to Mom."

Instead, there was silence for a moment and then, in a sad tone, his father said, "Well, if you don't want to meet me that's your decision. But, one of the things I wanted to talk to you about was me getting you another automobile. I guess you're not interested in that though, are you?"

Jeffrey was hooked; the thought of having another car made the idea of telling his mother an untruth a trivial detail. He arranged a time to meet with his father and hung up the phone.

When his mother came home, Jeffrey hesitated for a while, but he finally worked up enough courage to ask if he could borrow the car on the pretext of going over a friend's house. Taking him at his word, Myrna handed him the keys.

****

The next Tuesday evening, when Ben got home from work, he got a beer out of the refrigerator and sat on the porch; Billy was out somewhere so he was by himself. He drank his beer slowly while reflecting on the fact that none of his three children were home and, sooner or later, it was permanently going to be that way. He drew no conclusions; he was just being reminded that he was entering a new phase of his life.

His thoughts were interrupted by the sharp ring of his front door bell. He put his beer down and opened the door. He opened it, hoping, in the back of his mind that it would be BeBe. Much to his surprise, it was his neighbor who was at Lydia Bradford's New Year's Eve Party. She had lost a little weight and she had a pretty face and lively blue eyes. Dressed in a business suit, with her short, black hair, she looked both the picture of efficiency and attractiveness. The expression on her face was not friendly.

She asked, in a crisp voice, "Mr. Da Vinci?"

He thought to himself, she knows who I am, why the formality? He replied, "Yes."

In a sharper tone she said, "My name is Myrna Cabot. I'm Jeffrey Cabot's mother."

Ben again thought, she knows we met, so why all of this formality? He didn't like the tone of her voice but he gave no indication of his feelings as he answered, "We met at Lydia's New Years Party but

I didn't know that you were Jeffrey's mother. He talks about you all the time. Come in, come in." He shut the front door and led her to the porch. When she was seated, he asked, "Can I get you something?"

Her answer was as cold as her other statements, "Mr. Da Vinci, this is not a social call; it is a personal matter. I need to speak to your son Greg."

Ben did not appear disturbed as he replied, "May I ask why?"

"As his parent, you certainly have the right to ask why. As Jeffrey's parent, I want to know why your son is buying liquor and beer and feeding it to my seventeen year old son."

Ben couldn't believe what he had just heard. His heart began beating faster; the bald accusation angered him. His voice was not cordial as he responded, "I hope you intend to tell me exactly what you think are talking about?"

"I certainly will. Saturday afternoon, Jeffrey asked for my car because he said that he had an errand to run. I didn't use the car until Sunday morning when I discovered empty beer cans and an open bottle of Scotch in the back seat. Of course I confronted him; he finally told me that your son, Greg, had bought it all and they had drunk it together. I want to know why your son gave liquor to my son, who is a minor.

"Of course, you should be present when I do talk to your son."

Ben sat quietly for a few seconds. His anger was rising and he felt cold towards Jeffrey's mother. She was accusing Greg of something he could not possibly have done. She was not asking questions, she was not seeking explanations, all she was doing was making accusations which were false. He would prove her wrong and defend Greg every bit as aggressively as she was attacking him.

He was about to reply when Hunkajunk pulled into the driveway with the car radio blaring loudly. Billy was back from his errand. Ben stood up and waved for Billy to come up on the porch. Billy turned the radio volume down slightly, shut the motor off, got out of the car and bounded up the porch steps. He said, "Hi Dad, I just came home to get my glove. I'm pitching in a softball game in about twenty minutes."

"Billy, this is Jeffrey's mother, Mrs. Cabot."

Billy looked surprised as he said, "Oh, I'm sorry. I didn't see you sitting there. Hello, Mrs. Cabot. Nice to meet you after speaking to you on the phone so many times."

She did not reply but she did nod her head slightly in cool acknowledgement of the fact that they had talked to each other. Ben decided how to shoot down her ridiculous accusations. He spoke to his son. "Billy, tell Mrs. Cabot what we did this last weekend."

"Sure, Dad, but what part of the weekend do you want me to tell Mrs. Cabot about?"

"Start with Friday night. Tell her where we went on Saturday and Sunday; what we did and the times we did it."

"I'll try. Friday night Jeffrey came over with pizzas to say goodbye to Greg and me. Saturday, me and Greg and Dad went to see Alice in Vermont; we left about five in the morning. Then, Sunday, the three of us drove to Dartmouth and we dropped Greg off at his dorm and drove home yesterday. Do you want more details, Dad?"

"No, I think that is good enough."

"OK, then you'll have to excuse me. I've got to go." With that he dashed into the house, appeared a few seconds later with his softball glove, bounced down the stairs, got into the car, and drove off taking the music with him. Everything was still.

Ben's guest sat quietly with her head down. During the time it took for Billy to tell her about the weekend, Myrna Cabot had gone from a ladle of molten metal to a dish of dry ice. She felt totally humiliated; she had never before been so publicly embarrassed. She was so mortified that she wanted to hide. Finally, without looking up, she softly said, "I was totally wrong, I'm sorry."

Ben was no longer angry but he was not in a gracious mood either. He had not forgotten that Mrs. Cabot had accused his son of not only breaking the law but also doing something morally wrong. His answer was with words that were individually spit out like watermelon seeds, " As the mother of a minor, you certainly have the right to protect your son. Where you went wrong was in assuming that my son was guilty of something he didn't do. You should have checked out the facts before believing your son's story and making accusations against my son."

Without another word, Mrs. Cabot rose from her chair, walked to the front door, and left, leaving the door wide open. Ben walked behind her and shut the door after she was gone. It was only then that he began to feel badly that he had spoken so harshly. He wondered why Jeffrey had lied to his mother. He thought, "Jeffrey shouldn't have treated his mother that way." As an afterthought he illogically added, "And she is such an attractive woman."

****

When Ben woke up the next morning, the episode was almost completely put aside as he prepared for work. Depending upon his mood, the weather, and if he had errands to run, he would either walk, bicycle, or drive to his shop which was a few blocks away on Summer Street. His workdays were almost always the same. He would arrive early and enter through the back door. After checking everything, he would don a white jacket, turn on his red and white barber's pole sign, and open for business. Usually, sitting on the two park benches he had outside the front door, there would be several men waiting for him to open.

It was a typically old-fashioned barber shop. Although there were three barber's chairs, Ben had rarely ever hired another barber. He could easily have afforded the cost and sometimes his customers had to wait almost an hour before it was their turn. However, over the years Ben had developed a personal interest in his steady customers. He could sort through the hundreds of stories he heard and remember the details of each man as they sat in his chair. He would almost automatically ask, and care about, the details of the person's life as if the last conversation hadn't been interrupted by weeks of quietly growing hair. One wall of his shop showed his concern for both his customers and his business. Mounted on the wall, in evenly spaced rows and columns, were banks of photographs of children sitting in his barber chair. When a parent brought his or her child in for his first haircut, Ben would take a picture of the event. After the film was developed, he would give a picture to the parent and mount a duplicate of his new client, with the date and the child's name, on the wall. From the time that he opened his door each day, until he closed it at night, he would be busy. It was a robust oasis where men could gather and discuss sports, politics, and joke about sex; it was a hometown barbershop.

His business had served Ben well and afforded him a living. He had bought the building his shop was located in and, over time, he had bought several prime business properties in Malden. He had an income that allowed him to live comfortably and that was enough for him. Accumulating wealth had never been his primary goal.

Over the years, his clientele had changed from almost all older

Italians conversing in Italian to a younger, more ethnically diverse customer. He still had a lot of older Italians but his customer base had shifted to second and third generation English speaking customers. However, his customers still were all men. No woman had ever entered his shop except to accompany a child. He never gave a thought as to why it was that way; his father's barbershop never had had a female customer and neither had his. He would never have refused to give a woman a haircut. Discrimination never entered his mind; it was just that no female had ever asked him to cut her hair. That was the order of things. Ladies went to hair salons; men went to barbershops.

About a week after his confrontation with Mrs Cabot, on a Friday evening, Ben had closed his barbershop and was cleaning up in preparation for Saturday's business when he heard a light knock on the door. It was a while before he opened the door and, when he did, he saw Jeffrey preparing to get on his bike and ride away. Before he could start peddling, Ben sharply called, "Jeff."

That stopped him in his tracks. He put the kickstand down and came over to where Ben was standing. He looked completely pitiful as he asked, "You don't hate me too, do you, Mr. Da Vinci?"

Ben was about to give him a tart response when Jeffrey's word, "too," caught his ear. That, along with his abject appearance, made him change what he was going to say; Jeffrey was suffering. "No, I don't hate you, but I do need to know why you involved Greg in something he didn't do. Why don't you come in?"

They entered the barbershop and Ben locked the door and turned most of the lights off. He sat in his barber's chair and motioned Jeffrey to sit in the one beside him. They sat facing each other for a while before Jeffrey began, "I am so sorry, Mr. Da Vinci. You and Greg and Billy were so good to me this summer. I never meant to harm Greg, I never meant to harm Billy, I never meant to harm you. Everything got out of hand. I'm so sorry, Mr. Da Vinci.

"And now I don't know what to do. Everyone hates me." Jeffrey sat there, confused, upset and alone.

Ben looked at Jeffrey and whatever negative thoughts he had about him melted. He had enjoyed talking with Jeffrey when he had been coming over to his house. Now, he was dealing with a young man who needed guidance more than he needed censure. Ben said to him, "Jeff, why don't you start at the beginning and tell me how you got into this mess?"

"Sure, Mr. Da Vinci. I just backed into it. My father called me on Saturday and said that he wanted to meet with me. We haven't seen each other very often this summer and my visits with him lately haven't been too pleasant. He asks questions about my mother and he is always telling me what I'm doing wrong. But, I hadn't seen him in a while and he promised me that we would talk about maybe him getting me another car. That's what I wanted, another car. But I was also hoping that maybe we would be able to talk like a father to a son.

"Well, I did wrong. I lied to my mother about where I was going. I didn't tell her that I was supposed to meet my father because I knew that she wouldn't let me drive out of Malden, especially to meet him. I used her car and met him at the place he selected, the Stone Zoo.

"When I got there, he was already waiting for me in his car. It was one of the worst visits I have ever had with him. I parked beside his car but he acted as if I hadn't arrived. After a few minutes, I got out of my car and got in on his passenger side of the front seat. He had been drinking and all he wanted to talk about was how he had outsmarted the people he had sued and how much money he had made. He kept it up for a long time until I finally asked him about his promise to talk about getting me another car.

"First, he told me, he wouldn't talk about that until I was man enough to have a beer. After I started drinking a can he said that he hadn't any intentions of buying me a car. I was too gullible and not very smart. And, besides, I wasn't giving him any good information about my mother.

"It was terrible. I said I was going home. I got out of the car and went into the bushes to pee and when I came out he was standing beside my mom's car. That's when he must have put the empty beer cans and the bottle of whiskey in the back seat. I drove home, spoke to my mother from the door of her bedroom so she couldn't smell my breath, and then went to my room.

"My mother found the beer and the whiskey bottle on Sunday and she was as angry as I've ever seen her. At first, she kept asking if there were girls involved in the drinking and then she wanted to know who gave me the liquor. I couldn't tell her that it was my father because I had already lied to her. She was relentless; she kept asking me all day Sunday, Monday, and Tuesday. Finally, I told her Greg had given it to me thinking that she would let it go once I gave her a name. She knew that I had been working out with him all summer and that he was heading back to school but she didn't know when. Instead of forgetting about it, she went ballistic and went storming over to your house.

"When she came back, she was embarrassed and even angrier at me because I had lied. I think she knows who gave me the liquor but now I can't tell her. It doesn't make any difference. I am completely restricted. No car, no going anywhere, nothing but school activities. I just sneaked out to come here. I can understand her anger at being lied to, but I was only trying to do what I thought was right.

"I don't know what to do. My mother is angry and doesn't trust me. I got you and Greg into trouble that you don't deserve. I feel like Hell. I want to run away from home and join the Marines.

"I didn't mean to get Greg into trouble. Mr. Da Vinci, I'm sorry. I don't know what to do."

Ben looked at Jeffrey sitting in a barber's chair about four feet from him. He seemed completely beaten and confused. Ben's negative feelings were swept away by his feelings for what Jeffrey was going through. His first thought was anger at the father, "Where is Jeffrey's Father? His son is catching Hell for trying to protect him. He should step up and be half the man his son is."

After thinking about what Jeffrey had told him, he asked,"Do you really want to join the Marines?"

"I don't know, I don't think so. I don't know what I want, but I know I don't want everybody angry at me."

"I'm not angry at you, Jeffrey. You didn't tell the truth but you didn't mean any harm. I think you are paying too high a price for making the mistake you made." He thought, "And now you're being shredded like a kleenex in a washing machine."

Aloud, he said, "No, I'm not at all angry with you. Do you have any idea what you are you going to do?"

Jeffrey had tears in his eyes as he softly asked, "No, but I need help. Can you help me, Mr. Da Vinci?"

"Well, I'm not sure, but I can try. Let's talk, Jeffrey, and see what can be done. I guess we should start with your mother first. She was completely hurt and humiliated when she found out that you lied to her. Your first lie triggered your second lie. She left my house upset at both of us and, being a parent, I can't blame her. I'm sure that the first thing you must do is show her how sorry you are for what happened."

"You don't mean that I should tell her who put the whiskey and beer cans in the car do you?"

"No, that won't do a bit of good now. The damage has already been done. What you need to do is to start showing her how sorry you are; that will begin to ease her anger and her humiliation."

"How do I do that, Mr. Da Vinci?"

"Now that's where I'm stumped because I don't know a thing about your mother or her habits. Does she have any hobbies?"

"None, Mr. Da Vinci. She does nothing but work and come home. She's kind of grim. She used to like to knit but not lately."

Ben thought that children really don't know parents. His mother probably was grim, but there had to be a reason why she was. Children judge their parents by their own principals and parents never measure up to these younger, more innocent standards. He asked, "Does she like fresh fruits and vegetables?"

"Oh, yes, she is always preaching about eating healthy."

"Well, let's try this. I still have a lot of produce in my garden. Drop by my house after school every day, starting Monday, and I will leave a small package for you to take home. Just put what I give you on the kitchen table for your mother without saying anything. When she finally asks, tell her that I gave them to you to show that I am no longer angry or upset about our confrontation. Let's see if we can get your mother to start talking about what is bothering her. It's worth a try."

Jeffrey asked a few more questions about what he should say and, after a little more coaching from Da Vinci, he left to go home.

He left the barbershop a happier person than when he went in. First, he had made peace with someone he had wronged. Even better, he had found someone who was not angry with him. Second, he no longer had to feel alone; he had an ally. Third, and the most important, he was going to take a positive approach towards solving his problems. Swimming is always better than treading water.

When Myrna got home later that evening, she noticed that her son had set the table and had started to prepare their evening meal. She said nothing but she was puzzled by these actions. Since she had grounded him, there had been almost no small talk between them and they had each turtled into their own personality shell. Jeffrey avoided her and, deep in her mind, she couldn't blame him; she knew that her hurt and her pain had made her an absolute witch.

Saturday and Sunday Jeffrey did all of his household chores before he was asked and even did a few of his mother's, like the vacuuming. By Sunday evening, although there still was little conversation between them, there had been a slight thaw in their frosty attitudes. Jeffrey began to hope that, between them, all was not hopeless.

9

Although Myrna was sure that her move to Malden had been the correct thing to do, she did go through periods of self doubts. There had been unplanned events that she had been forced to handle and they had caused her problems. She had given no thought that her son Jeffrey would mature from a child into a young man and the change took her by surprise. She was spending so much time establishing her practice that, at times, felt that she was neglecting Jeffrey. Although Skinner now saw their son much less often then before, she wasn't sure that Jeffrey's attitude towards her was any better. He still had periods when he seemed remote, far away from her even though he was just across the dinner table.

Adding to her strain was Skinner. He would call, both at home and at her office, saying that he had to talk to her. His excuse was that he wanted information on his son but his questions were as much as about Myrna as about Jeffrey. Was she dating at all? Was she seeing anyone? Was there anyone special in her life? She was uncomfortable with these questions; it was absolutely none of Skinner's business. But she didn't want to alienate him because he still had access to Jeffrey and she knew he would ask his son the same questions. She gave him short, vague answers but she was uncomfortable and on the defensive whenever she spoke to him. Added to her hatred of him was her new disdain for men in general.

She was also bogged down with burdens and doubts that she had not anticipated. She knew that her law practice would not earn her as much money as she had been making so she was prepared to live on a smaller income. However, establishing that practice had not been as easy as she had anticipated; her finances were no burden but they were one more concern.

All these pressures built up inside Myrna until she was ready to explode. She had no idea that her emotions were in the red zone.

The pin that popped her balloon was finding the opened whiskey and beer cans in the back seat of her car. She exploded. Her first thought was that Jeffrey lied to her. Her second thought was that he did that because there were girls involved. What if he had been drinking and having sex in the back seat? Were there any drugs involved? Those thoughts were so uppermost in her mind that she completely forgot about Skinner. She was so worried and concerned about Jeffrey that she made a major mistake; she confronted him. Her anger and rage gave her son no room to explain his actions. The stage was set for the misunderstandings that followed.

And, after Jeffrey lied to his mother and she came back from being humiliated by Da Vinci, the relationship between mother and son was absolutely ice and daggers at close range. Jeffrey was shaken but Myrna cried every night. She was a mother hurt by a son who had not been honest and who could be doing inappropriate things. These last few days had been miserable for Myrna.

As Da Vinci had promised, that Monday afternoon, when Jeffrey walked by his house, he saw a small brown bag on the front steps with his name on it. In it, were some tomatoes and a large cucumber. When his mother arrived from work, she found the table set, the evening meal almost ready, and the sliced, fresh vegetables near her plate. She enjoyed the tomatoes and cucumber but she said nothing about them. Tuesday, there were fresh string beans and tomatoes and his mother still asked nothing about them. Jeffrey began to wonder whether or not he should say something.

Wednesday was different. There not only were fresh tomatoes and cucumbers, but after dinner Jeffrey took a freshly cut musk melon out of the refrigerator and placed one half of the melon in front of his mother. She looked at her son, tasted her melon, and said, "This is absolutely delicious." She took another, larger bite and then asked "Jeffrey, where has all this lovely produce been coming from?"

He answered quickly, "From Mr. Da Vinci."

His mother gasped, "Mr. Da Vinci?"

Her son nodded, "Yes."

"The man who lives three doors away?"

Her son, once again, nodded, "Yes."

She was very puzzled. She asked, "Why would he give you fresh fruits and vegetables?"

"Not me, Mama, us."

Myrna had not forgotten how mortified she felt when she left his house and she was still grappling with the connection between her initial feelings and this sudden cornucopia of produce. "Well, then, why in the world would he bother giving us fresh fruits and vegetables?"

"Mama, I rode my bike over to his barbershop last Friday and talked with him. He told me that he is not angry with me and he feels badly for you. He said that giving us some of his harvest is his way of showing us that he bears us no hard feelings. As a matter of fact, Mr. Da Vinci said that, as a parent himself, he understands that your first concern should be for the well-being of your son."

She sat there for a while, trying to sort through the confusion of her thoughts. She could not get over the shame she felt after Da Vinci had coldly shown her that she was wrong. She knew that she should not have said what she had said but couldn't he have been less arrogant while correcting her? It was much easier to blame Da Vinci for what happened than to take any of the responsibility for making accusations that were out of line.

And now Da Vinci was indicating to both Jeffrey and her that he was willing to overlook what had happened? That didn't make any sense to Myrna.

Could she do the same? Should she do the same? She had avoided asking herself the most obvious question in this whole sorry mess, why had her son lied in the first place? She still had concerns about whether sex and drugs were involved in this episode. There were areas that, as a mother, Myrna felt that unanswered questions remained.

"Jeffrey, why would Da Vinci care about how we felt?"

"Mama, he is really a nice man. I learned that this summer. He is a good father; he really talks and listens to his kids. Even though he has a funny last name, I wish my own father was more like him."

Her son's statement completely surprised her. It also pleased her. She had never heard him say anything, either pro or con, about his father before. She had the sudden hope that there may be less to his relationship with Skinner than she had thought.

Lydia and Frank had told her about Da Vinci's family but she felt the need to ask anyhow. "What about Da Vinci's wife?"

"He has no wife; he has been a widower for a long time. He has raised his family by himself."

"Well, how big is his family and what does he do for a living?"

"He has a barbershop on Summer Street that he has had for years. That's where I've been getting my hair cut since we moved here. He has the two sons who I met and worked out with all summer long. They were nice to me and I really like them. He also has a daughter who was in a couple of my classes. She has been working as a counsellor in a summer camp somewhere in Vermont and I haven't seen her all summer."

"So you get your haircuts from this barber. What does this Mr. Da Vinci want us to do? Pay for his fresh produce?" His mother was being mean spirited because she was taken aback by his attitude and she was not sure how to respond.

"Yes, Mama, I get my hair cut at his barbershop. He never mentioned paying. I don't think he cares about that. I guess he just wants every one to have peace. He always talks about that during his evening discussions with his family."

Although his mother did not reply, she was was still unconvinced and unsure of Da Vinci's motives. In her experience, everyone wanted something for nothing. There must be a reason for this flurry of fruits and vegetables; especially from someone who had shamed her. There had to be something Da Vinci wanted.

****

Thursday brought Jeffrey and his mother tomatoes and zucchini squash; Friday brought tomatoes, cucumbers and a lot more zucchini. By the time she received the second wave of squash, Myrna Cabot's attitude had begun to undergo a change, even though she still kept asking her basic questions, "Why all of this? What does he want?"

Along with asking herself these questions, Myrna began to take the time to evaluate her painful encounter more objectively. After thinking about that ugly meeting, she had to admit that her personal attitude had been wrong from the very start.

Even though she knew that her conduct was her responsibility, she, at first, blamed her son. She had been expecting him to tell the truth. When he lied to her and had named Greg, the boy he had been working out with all summer, she had panicked and jumped to the wrong conclusions. She immediately became frightened that Jeffrey and his friends were drinking alcohol, doing drugs, and having sex. They might have been doing these things all summer inside the Da Vinci garage. The thought that this might not be a one time event was more than she could stand. With these nightmare type of visions in her thoughts, she had completely lost her composure.

She should have approached the problem more discreetly without making any accusations. However, whatever confused and jumbled thoughts she had harbored back then made no difference now. At the present time, she was mortified by her behavior, especially by the thought of how Da Vinci had proven her wrong.

The more she thought about what had happened the more she realized that she should try to make amends. After coming to that conclusion, she sighed and made her plans. Saturday evening Myrna dialed Da Vinci's phone number and, when a female voice answered, she asked, "May I speak with Ben Da Vinci, please?"

The female voice said, "Just a moment." Then she heard her say, "Dad, there's someone on the line to talk to you."

A moment later, Myrna heard Ben's voice say, "Hello."

She drew in her breath and softly said, "Good evening, Mr. Da Vinci."

"I'm sorry, but I can hardly hear you. Can you speak a little louder?"

She tried again with more vigor in her voice, "Can you hear me now?"

"Oh yes, quite plainly."

Myrna did not know what kind of reaction she would get but she continued, "Mr. Da Vinci, this is Myrna Cabot."

There was just a slight pause before he replied, "Oh, Mrs. Cabot. Good evening."

"Mr. Da Vinci, I want to thank you for all the fresh fruits and vegetables you have been sending over to Jeffrey and me." She waited for his response.

"You are more than welcome. I hope you are enjoying them. I have raised so much produce this year that I'm having a hard time finding people to give it to. It really is my pleasure."

Myrna thought to herself, "Now, for the hard part." Summoning her courage, she asked, "Mr. Da Vinci, could you drop by my house tomorrow afternoon? I would like to talk with you." She knew that Jeffrey went to the movies every Sunday afternoon and that would let them talk privately.

He immediately answered, "I would be delighted, Mrs. Cabot. What time would you like me be there?"

Myrna breathed easily, the hard part was over. She replied, "Would three o'clock work for you?"

"Yes. That would work nicely. I'll see you, then."

She hung the phone up with a sense of relief. Da Vinci had been easier to talk to than she had anticipated. So far, so good. For the first time since Myrna found the liquor and beer in her car, she was able to go to sleep without crying and agonizing over what was happening between herself and Jeffrey. She slept peacefully.

****

Every human being is a candidate for loneliness. Being busy does not immunize one from loneliness; it only delays the effect. Both Myrna Cabot and Ben Da Vinci were candidates for loneliness and, of course, neither of them were aware of it. They had avoided its ravages, not only by staying active and working long hours, but also by concentrating on the needs of their children. Any faltering from their obligations and they would become vulnerable to this unsparing sentiment. They were on a tightrope and they needed to change course.

Sunday morning, Myrna made sure that her house was clean and then, on the spur of the moment, she decided to bake some zucchini bread. It occurred to her, that as hostess, it would be a nice thing to do with the produce Da Vinci was providing her and it might help break the ice between them. She was nervous about meeting him face to face. She had no idea how this meeting would go.

As Ben crossed the street to get to Myrna's house he kept practicing what he would say because he was nervous. He wanted the meeting to go well so that Jeffrey and his mother would mend their relationship. Promptly at three that afternoon, he rang her doorbell. When Myrna opened the door, Ben was standing there holding a loaf of bread. He had meant to hand her the bread and say how glad he was to see her. However, he got flustered at the sight of this attractive woman and, instead of speaking, all he did was extend his hand with his loaf of bread towards Myrna. He immediately felt embarrassed.

Myrna looked at Ben and the bread that he was handing her and she giggled a little. Ben looked puzzled. She quickly took his bread and said, "Mr. Da Vinci, please excuse me, I'm not laughing at you. It's just that this morning I baked two loaves of zucchini bread. One was for us to eat while you were here and one was for you to take home. I completely forgot that you undoubtedly have a lot more zucchini than I do."

The small, self conscious faux pas by each of them made it easier for both of them to be at ease. Their hard edge of concern over how to act was blurred by their initial blunders. To compensate for their individual awkwardness, they were more open to reconciliation.

Ben smiled as he replied, "I can't blame you for laughing. Instead of breaking bread, it looks as if we are swapping bread. There seems to be a glut of squash on this street."

"I'd much rather have a neighborhood glut than a famine. Do come in, Mr. Da Vinci." With that, Myrna stepped aside and Ben entered the house.

He walked into the living room, stopped, and then turned completely around. He said, "This room looks different from the last time I was here. Have you done some redecorating?"

Myrna was surprised to discover that Da Vinci had ever been inside her house. "Yes," she replied, "I've had the two small front rooms combined into one and repainted the whole interior. I didn't realize that you had been here before."

"Your father was the real estate agent who sold me my house. I was his barber for many years and he and I were in the same bowling league. As neighbors, we got to know each other and, on occasions, he was over at my house and I was over at his. He used to play with my children. That was quite a few years ago."

"I wonder why I didn't know that?"

"As I remember, you were going to law school and then working in Worcester. Your father would talk about you and your brother. Since both of you were out of your house when we moved in, I knew nothing about either of you."

Myrna sighed. "That was a long time ago. Well, come sit down and we'll have coffee and see which of us is the better baker."

After they sampled both breads and after they admitted they could taste no difference between them, they talked about the weather and local politics for a while. When Myrna felt confident enough to get down to the business at hand, she took a deep breath and said, "Mr. Da Vinci, I need to apologize for the way I acted when I came storming over to your house. I was off base because I was so concerned about Jeffrey.

"However, that is no excuse for my behavior. All I can do is say to you that I am sorry."

Ben could see that Myrna was anxious. He sat for a second, and then answered, "Mrs. Cabot, I was angry with you after you left. You did come on strongly and, I thought, unfairly. Then, as I began to cool down, I was not concerned by your anger as much as I was by your accusations. They bothered me a lot more than your attitude.

"As far as your anger, my first thought was that you were doing what every parent does; that is coming to your child's defense. I probably would have flared up the same way so I could understand your emotions. I didn't agree with them but I could understand them.

"My second thought was more irritating and it stayed with me for a long time. I just couldn't figure out why Jeffrey would tell you that my son bought him the liquor. It didn't make sense. First of all he knew that Greg wasn't in town that weekend. Jeffrey had personally said goodbye to Greg, and wished him luck, the Friday before Greg left for Dartmouth.

"More importantly, your son had been associated with my family almost all summer. He worked out with Greg and Billy and he often ate dinner with us. He sat in on our family talks and took part in many of them. I got the impression that he liked us; I certainly liked him. At first he was quiet, but, after a while, he began to speak up. He has a nice sense of humor. I like him; he is a good boy.

"After seeing him for most of the summer, I kept wondering why he would tell you a lie like he did."

"Did you ever get an answer to that question?"

"As a matter of fact, I did. A week ago last Friday Jeffrey came by my barbershop. He waited outside my shop until I had closed. He had a lot he wanted to get off his mind and he was tightly wound up. He had to talk with someone.

"What he really was looking for was advice."

"Will you tell me what his reason for lying was?"

"Mrs. Cabot, I can't. That would betray Jeffrey's trust. However, I will tell you that when he left my barbershop I felt sorry for him. Your son is a good youngster but, right now, he feels alone. He made a mistake, a bad mistake which he compounded with more lies. He didn't know how but he wanted to put things right with everyone. He wasn't sure how to do it."

Myrna said, "I'm not sure I understand. Why should he have a problem with apologizing if he is truly sorry?"

Ben took his time composing his thoughts. "Mrs. Cabot, it isn't that easy for Jeffrey. As his mother, I'm sure you realize what a war zone he feels he is in. He had no idea that you would follow through once he named a person he had been drinking with. He thought that, by naming someone you didn't know, you wouldn't carry it any further. He hoped that you would discipline him, give him a lecture, and the episode would finally be closed."

Myrna quickly replied, "That's ridiculous. I'm his mother. I won't let any predator prey on my child. Parents have to protect their children."

Ben smiled, "You're preaching to the choir. But let me finish looking at what happened from your son's viewpoint. He lied, not to protect himself, but because he wanted to get you off his back.

"I am sure you realize that he may be fully grown physically but, from an emotional point of view, he still is very young and he has a lot to learn." Ben stopped for a few seconds thinking of his own children, he paused, and then he asked, "Don't all teenagers?"

Myrna smiled ruefully. She asked, "Is that why you sent us those daily CARE packages?"

"No," Ben answered quickly and, after a pause, added, "Only partially for Jeffrey. I felt badly for your son; he didn't intend to either get in trouble or to cause trouble. And once he did both he was in over his head; he didn't know how to get out.

"However, when I started to think of a way for him to redeem himself, it occurred to me that you were having a hard time as well. Believe me, I understand what responsibilities a single parent faces. It is a never ending grind of work and vigilance. I'm not saying it doesn't have its rewards but a single parent is always on duty; it seems like forever. You feel isolated and it has to take a toll. We never have a furlough.

"Mrs. Cabot, sometimes I would make a mistake in dealing with one of my children. I would get angry at something one of them did and I would react without really thinking of what I was doing. Either

I didn't take the time to try to understand the circumstances or I was too harsh. It would take a long time to resolve my error but, at least, I had help. I had two other children who would be advocates for the one in my doghouse. Having only the one child, you don't have the luxury of a jury to help sort things out.

"So, while I was trying to help Jeffrey, I also wanted to let you know that I appreciate what you are going through. Basically, I'm really on the side of the parent. I didn't want to interfere in your family affairs, I was just trying to help.

"In my long winded way, that's what my 'CARE packages,' as you call them, were meant to do."

At first, Myrna didn't know how to reply to Ben. She completely understood what he had said to her and she had to agree with his comments. Being a single parent was a relentless chore and she recognized that she had made a mistake; she had pushed her son too far. When she found the liquor and the beer cans, it flashed through her mind that his father had left them in her car; what she had really wanted was for Jeffrey to admit it. It wouldn't have made any difference but what she was after was the satisfaction of hearing her son tell her that his father had done something wrong. The bond between her ex-husband and Jeffrey was constantly on her mind. Then she mistakenly thought that sex and drugs were involved.

However, by being so insistent, she had unintentionally put her son in the middle of his parents' turmoil. Then, she compounded a bad situation by believing her son's lie; she was completely taken by surprise when her son named Greg Da Vinci as his drinking companion. She had run amok.

Now, talking with the parent of the son she had wrongly confronted, Myrna felt foolish and remorseful for the way she had reacted. Her own responses had blown Jeffrey's lies out of proportion. Mr. Da Vinci had responded better to the situation than she had. In fact, he was not the cold, male bastard she had decided he was; he seemed to be a caring person. Trying to help her son was proof of that. For the first time in weeks, she began to feel peace; it was a good feeling.

She started to say, "Mr. Da Vin . . . ," but she stopped before finishing his name. She began again. "You know, we both have been talking about personal matters, but we have been addressing each other formally. I feel the conversation is a little stilted. Would you mind if we used first names? I would be more comfortable if you would call me 'Myrna,' unless you have any objections."

"I have no objection calling you Myrna as long as you call me Ben."

Myrna answered, "Ben, you are right. I went off the tracks and I've had a hard time trying to get back. I must seem stupid to you; I'm really not."

"I'm sure you're not stupid. Listen, Myrna, don't feel too badly. All parents occasionally get into train wrecks. Their kids have a tendency to do that to them; no mother or father is immune from mistakes. My batting average is not nearly as good as you think it is. As a parent I've done some awfully dumb things.

"But being off the track is not nearly as important as getting back on. Jeffrey needs your love and you need his. He wants to atone for his mistake and you do, too. Keep that in mind and it will be easy for you and him to reconcile."

"Do you really think so?"

"I not only think so, I believe a falling out like this can strengthen the bond between parents and their children. If you handle it honestly, it teaches the responsibilities of parents and children to each other. And responsibilities are the beauty of any relationship."

"Is that your philosophy?"

"Yes, Myrna, that is the way I have raised my children all of their lives."

"Well, I hope you're right; we shall see."

They talked about other subjects for a while, including the fact that Ben's gardening was just about done for this year. After a few more pleasantries, Ben left to go home.

When Myrna was alone, she sat and thought about their conversation. She was pleased that her neighbor had relieved the heavy rock of remorse she had carried because of her treatment of him. She also realized that it was her responsibility to smooth the path between herself and her son. She was eager to do that but, what she was not prepared to do, was to admit to him that she had been wrong to put him in the middle. She was still hurt that her son had lied to her and had made her look foolish in front of a stranger. Her apology would come later, after her anguish finally subsided.

Myrna now felt a sense of joy that she had not had in weeks.

When Jeffrey came home from the movies later in the day, he found a plate of freshly baked brownies sitting on the kitchen table. He sat down and Myrna got him a glass of milk; she had coffee. While they were munching on the brownies she casually said, "Mr Da Vinci dropped by while you were at the movies."

Jeffrey was both surprised and pleased; he had not known that they were getting together. He asked hopefully, "And?"

"We had a long talk. He seems to be a nice man."

"Oh, he is Momma. What did you two talk about?"

"Many things. You, me, his kids, being a parent. We didn't solve any of the world's problems but we did talk about the family situations that single parents have to deal with constantly. In a way, we compared notes."

"And?"

"We both agreed that it is the parent's responsibility to be available to talk with their children at all times.

"And, for your information, he thinks I should have cut you more slack. I guess he's right. When I saw the back seat, I was almost sure that it was your father who left that stuff in the car. There was nothing more to gain by asking you. I should have let it go at that point."

Myrna sat quietly after that last statement. That was all she was prepared to say at this time. Jeffrey waited another few seconds before he spoke up. "Momma, I love you. I never should have lied to you about using the car and I never will lie again. I lied because I needed the car to meet Dad. I didn't know how the stuff got into the back seat but I thought I could get you off my back by giving you the name of someone you never met.

"Momma, I was wrong."

Myrna reached across the table and patted her son's hand. After they finished eating, Jeffrey said, "I've got a book to read for school." He got up, kissed his mother on the top of her head, and left.

****

The simple act of talking bridged the gap between them and it was like a breath of fresh air; and the fresh air slowly wafted in a total climate change into their household. Myrna noticed that his father's influence faded as Jeffrey started to look at his life from his own viewpoint. He was less snobbish in his opinions and more solicitous towards her. He became more independent, even from his mother, and she had no problem with that because their differences were respectful. As her son prepared for his junior year, his mother became satisfied that her decision to move away from her ex-husband was the correct thing to do.

Time and distance had changed Jeffrey. He felt that he was no longer the shuttlecock in the badminton game between his mother and father. At first he blamed his mother for taking him away from his father. However, as their father-son meetings became less frequent, they became more uncomfortable for Jeffrey. His father lectured him more than he talked with him and his father wanted Jeffrey to spy on his mother; neither approach satisfied or supported his son. Jeffrey never again took any money or gifts from his father; nor did he forget the fact that his father did not admit that, for whatever reason, he had been the person who put the liquor in Myrna's car.

Becoming acquainted with the Da Vinci family and the way they lived was an eye opener for Jeffrey. He envied them their rollicking, their disagreements and their sticking up for each other's rights. His father made fun of them as "Dagos" and "Wops" but that didn't matter a bit to Jeffrey. Those characterizations were only ignorant name tags that did not describe his friends; they only showed that his father was rather shallow and prejudiced.

Most of all, Jeffrey was angry at his father for not defending him after his mother found the liquor in the car. All his father had to do was tell his ex-wife that it was his booze and Jeffrey would have been off the hook. Jeffrey felt that he shouldn't tattle on his father but he also felt that his father should have admitted his error.

As a result, the simple knocks that come from maturing into an adult changed Jeffrey. He discovered that his mother was an unheralded hero while his father was not the strong, honest person he blustered he was. Jeffrey could not deny the fact of who his father was, but he also realized that his father wasn't a role model. Thus, as he developed into his own person, his father's influence began to drift into insignificance.

JUNIORS

10

Jeffrey did not see Alice Da Vinci all summer and, when their junior year started at Malden, he avoided her completely. He knew her brothers were now in college, Greg at Dartmouth and Billy at Boston University. However, since he wasn't sure whether or not she knew that he had wrongly accused her brother, he did not want to meet her face to face. Avoiding her was no problem because she was popular with her classmates; she was almost always surrounded by either a gaggle of guys or a giggle of girls. Even though they were both in the same history and English classes he would get to class just as it began and leave just after it ended. He didn't want a confrontation with Alice over a mistake for which he had already paid his penalty.

On the other hand, he had no problems getting along with all his other classmates. He had learned his lesson; this year was different than his last year. He was quiet, making no boasts about how powerful or rich his father was, and he was accepted for who he was. His wallet, with his father's picture, stayed in his pocket. Last year's conduct and the escapades with his car were past and forgotten. In his junior year, he was at peace both at school and at home.

Jeffrey had wanted to let his hair grow longer so it wasn't until a few weeks after school started that he went to the barber shop. While getting his hair cut he asked if Mr. Da Vinci had told his children about the problem he had caused by not being honest with his mother. Da Vinci laughed and reassured Jeffrey that he had not thought the episode important enough to mention to anyone; it was a closed incident. Jeffrey felt relieved. From then on, he felt that he no longer had to leave whenever Alice arrived on the scene. He didn't intrude on her crowd but he didn't hesitate to make his way through her throng to get to where his friends were gathered. He even stopped shying away from making eye contact with her.

One afternoon, he was sitting on the steps outside the high school when Alice came up to him and asked, "You're in my history class aren't you?"

He said, "Yes."

"Did you understand what our new assignment was?"

"I think so."

"Could you explain it to me; I just read what I copied after she wrote the assignment on the black board and I can't make heads or tails out of what I wrote."

It took a while but he clarified what their teacher wanted from them; after that, they chatted for about half an hour. Alice told him that last summer, just before she left for camp, she discovered that she had Jeffrey mixed up with the boy who lived down the street and that her brothers had straightened her out. Jeffrey knew the reputation of the other boy and was pleased that Greg and Billy had taken the time to vindicate him. As they talked, Jeffrey looked at Alice and decided that, with her close cropped auburn hair and freckles, and her lively manner, she was attractive. From then on, they would casually talk to each other when they met but, for the most part, they continued on their separate ways.

One Friday afternoon, the school librarian came up to Alice, who was at a table reading by herself, and asked her if she knew Jeffrey Cabot. Alice told her that she did and that he lived a few houses away from her. The librarian asked her if she would take two books and give them to him. He had left them in the library earlier in the day even though he said that he needed them for a weekend assignment. Alice agreed to deliver the books to him and she added them to her own pile.

After supper that evening, Alice strolled over to Jeffrey's house and rang the doorbell. A woman, whom Alice guessed as about the same age as her father, answered the bell. Alice asked, "Good evening, is Jeffrey home?"

The woman, who was about the same height as Alice, smiled and answered, "No, he is not here right now. He is running an errand for me and won't be back for a while. Is there anything that I can do for you?"

Alice thought that she was an attractive woman. "No, I just wanted to drop off some books that he forgot and left in the library today. The librarian wanted to make sure he got them."

His mother shook her head, "That sounds just like my son. He can be so forgetful some times. Thank you for bringing them over. What is your name?"

"Alice Da Vinci. I live a couple of houses down the street from you."

"You're Alice? I met your father. Won't you come in?"

Alice hesitated for a second. She wasn't sure whether she wanted to or not. But then she thought that this lady seemed so pleasant, why not? She had no plans for this evening; she said, "Yes."

Myrna escorted her into the living room and Alice saw two or three pairs of knitting needles, skeins of yarn, and two pattern books sitting on a small table.

"Can I offer you a cup of tea or coffee?"

"Tea would be nice, thank you."

"I will go make us a pot. Why don't you sit down and make yourself comfortable? It will only take me a second."

"Mrs. Cabot, may I come with you? We are always in the kitchen in my house and that's where I'm most comfortable."

Mrs. Cabot's eyes twinkled as she answered, "Of course, Alice, come along. Kitchens are cozy, I like them, too."

As she prepared the tea, Mrs. Cabot asked Alice about her brothers and Alice replied with long answers and upbeat updates. While they were drinking their tea and nibbling on cookies, they casually talked about Alice's school, the weather, and other general subjects. Alice, as an aside, suddenly asked, "Mrs. Cabot, I saw a lot of knitting needles in your living room. Do you do much knitting?"

"I haven't for a while but I'm getting ready to start again. I used to do a lot of knitting but, when we moved here, I got busy trying to build up my business. I miss knitting, it was relaxing and fun; so, I'm going to get back to it. Do you knit?"

Alice didn't answer her question, she asked another one, "What do you knit?"

Mrs. Cabot replied, "Lots of different things. I knit caps for new born babies; I give those to the hospitals. I knit gloves and scarves for the Veterans Hospital. Occasionally, I'll knit a sweater for either myself or Jeffrey. It keeps my fingers busy and my mind free."

Alice said wistfully, "If I could knit I could make my brothers and my father sweaters for Christmas. That would make my gifts more personal and it would save me a lot of money."

"Alice, I could teach you to knit but your idea for three sweaters is too ambitious. There is not enough time between now and Christmas to learn the skills necessary for three sweaters. If you could be satisfied with something easier, like three scarves, that is a more realistic goal; and it still would give you the satisfaction of doing it yourself and saving money. What a nice surprise that would be for the men in your family. Are you still interested?"

"Oh yes, Mrs. Cabot. I'd work hard and I'd be so grateful. When can we start?"

Myrna got up and went into the living room and, when she returned, she was carrying the pattern books, the yarn and the knitting needles that had been on the table. For about the next hour Myrna began to give instructions and advice to Alice. They pored over the pattern books as Myrna discussed the art of knitting. Alice decided to make a Dartmouth green scarf for Greg since he was going to Dartmouth, a scarlet and white scarf for Billy since he was going to Boston University and a blue and gold scarf for her father.

They were completely unaware of the time until Jeffrey slammed the front door, announced that he was home and appeared in the kitchen. That broke their concentration. The three of them chatted for a while and Alice said that she had to go home. Myrna walked Alice to the door; they set up appointments for both of them to buy their yarn and start their knitting. Alice was pleased; she left feeling that she had discovered a bag full of gold coins.

From that time until close to Christmas, they would meet at least once a week. Their meetings were private; if Jeffrey was around he was told by his mother to disappear. Under Myrna's tutelage, Alice went from clumsy to competent; her work began as skeins of wool and ended as colorful scarves. They were both pleased. Alice had knitted three attractive scarves with only a few dropped stitches. She was proud of her new found ability and Myrna was pleased that she had taught a young woman a useful skill.

For both of them, the meetings had been enjoyable and satisfying. Working so closely together they developed a strong bond based on their individual needs. Myrna didn't have a daughter and she was delighted to find such an intelligent and pleasant a girl as Alice. Many times, she wondered whether or not she had been like Alice at that age when she was young. She hoped she had.

Alice, who really didn't remember much about her mother, welcomed the advice and suggestions of her mentor. Talking with an older woman about nothing, anything and everything fulfilled a need that she didn't know she had. The intimacy they formed was close to a mother-daughter relationship. They both were warmed and pleased with their newly formed family relationship; they provided comfort to each other.

****

As the school year continued on towards the new year, the days began to get short, the nights began to get long as they both got chilly and gray. The sparkling reds and oranges of fall turned to barren trees and stark branches with black outlines. The sun departed for warmer climates taking a lot of gaiety with it. The colder weather forced people to wear heavy clothing and hunker for warmth. These external changes were obvious and evident. What was not noticed during this same time were the internal changes that were taking place within both the Cabot and the Da Vinci families. These were more lasting than the seasonal alterations.

Myrna and her son were now getting along quite well. After years of being in the middle of a split family, Jeffrey was learning right from wrong. He was disappointed that his father had not stepped forward and confessed. He never asked Skinner why he had put the liquor and beer cans in the car; he figured his father owed him an explanation and that he shouldn't have to ask for one. However, the incident and its consequences shook him to his core. He had to stop and think about what he was doing instead of using his feelings as his life's compass.

Because of his new found maturity, he refused all gifts and cash that Skinner wanted to give him and he met with him only when he couldn't avoid it. He moved closer to his mother and began to realize what a strong person and a good parent she really was. His father was losing his dominance as reason and intelligence replaced fantasies and wishful thinking. Jeffrey was growing into manhood.

Myrna, on the other hand, was bearing the brunt of Jeffrey's new attitude. Skinner soon became aware of Jeffrey's coolness and he was determined to take it out on his ex-wife. He called more often and was nasty with his questions and accusations regarding his son and his ex-wife. She coped with him by either hanging up on him more often or by just laying the phone down and walking away. Still, the idea of putting up with more abuse from her ex-husband made her even colder on the outside. Even the new warmth on the inside, from Jeffrey's love, couldn't quite take the chill off her outside attitude.

Alice started school feeling alone. She was the only one left at home, both her brothers were away and she missed them. Billy would come home occasionally during the week and sometimes for a weekend but that wasn't the same as being home full time. She could tell that her father, while he didn't say so, also missed them. Their supper conversations were more subdued and quieter than they were when her brothers participated. And, after supper, her father would spend more time reading his books and listening to his music. He seemed less upbeat. His children were spreading their wings and Alice felt that her father would be left alone in the empty nest. She decided that she needed to talk this over with her brothers.

And, between Christmas and New Year's Eve, on their annual tour of Cape Ann, she did. They had explored some different winding lanes and had ended up at the Clam Box, in Ipswich, for their late afternoon lunch. They trooped in with Greg and Billy proudly showing off their hand knit scarves and Alice wearing a Dartmouth Big Green sweatshirt. After getting their fill of fried clams and lobster rolls, Alice interrupted the frivolous conversation with the same question she always asked, "What are we going to do about Dad?"

Greg sat there for a while before he spoke. "Alice, you've been asking us that question every year we come up to Cape Ann. This time I have watched Dad because I wondered whether you were right or wrong. He hasn't changed much in looks but he does seem to have slowed down a little. Is that my imagination?"

Alice replied, "No, it's not your imagination. I'm home with him now and I see him daily. He's OK right now but, after next year, I'll be going to school and he will be alone. After all these years the shepherd will have no sheep. We need to find him someone to have and to hold."

Billy finally spoke, "How do we do that, Alice? He is shy; we just can't spray him with perfume and put him up for sale. He has to show some interest himself in finding this 'someone' you refer to."

The three of them discussed the issue for a long time and came to no conclusions. They agreed that the family was growing away from its fledgling home and shelter. They were not concerned about what their relationship with each other would be but they wondered what their father would do when they were gone. They agreed that there probably would come a time when they would have to take care of their father.

From the day after the outing with her brothers until she returned to school at the end of the Christmas break, Alice gave a lot of thought to her father's welfare. She knew better than her brothers that without their activities and their noise around him he would be lonely. A home that echoes only with silence is not a happy home. Her father should have, and was deserving of, fun, love, and companionship. She decided that he needed more than a companion, he needed a mate. Alice was totally convinced of that. She made her plans.

The day that Alice got back to school, she went looking for Jeffrey Cabot. They had become friends as a result of her coming over to his house to work with his mother. They didn't date, but they occasionally met after their classes to chat. Now, she needed to tell him her plan and get his opinion. She found him sitting on the floor in front of his locker.

She asked, "Jeff, what are you doing down there?"

He grinned as he answered, "I'm not shining shoes, I'm waiting for Jenny."

"Jenny?"

"Yes, Jennifer Fleck, Jenny. We've been dating about a month. Do you know her?"

"I certainly do," thought Alice. She did not like Jenny, and it was not because of any jealousy. They were both on the cheerleaders team and Alice had noticed Jenny's behavior from the time that she had joined. Jenny was now a sophomore and was extremely attractive, slightly shorter than average height, with the face of a porcelain doll and beautiful green eyes. Jenny had the tight, lush body of a teenager and she was fully aware of her physical attributes and she put them on display for everyone to see. Her father owned a large automobile dealership and his financial success allowed Jenny to assume regal airs, which she did.

Alice's opinion was that Jenny cared for no one but herself. Alice thought of her as full from the neck down and empty from the neck up. She had watched Jenny try to vamp several football players away from their girlfriends. She was afraid that Jenny would dump Jeffrey as soon as someone else caught her attention. Alice was sure that, sooner or later, Jeffrey was going to have his feelings hurt. She shrugged and thought, "That's life." There was nothing she could do about it.

She sat down beside him and got to the subject at hand. "Jeff, what did your mother do over Christmas and New Year's Eve?"

"Nothing, really."

"Didn't she go out or celebrate?"

"No. Christmas we exchanged gifts and had a small dinner; after that, I took Jenny skating. New Year's Eve Jenny and I went dancing and my mother stayed home and read. Why?"

"Well, my father read seed catalogues and listened to music by himself on New Year's Eve. That seems kind of lonely for both of them, don't you think?"

"I guess it is."

Alice looked squarely at Jeffrey. "I would like to fix my father up with your mother."

His reaction was one of compete surprise. He said, "My father is not going to like that."

"Do you give a damn?"

"Not even half a damn. He doesn't care for anyone but himself. My mother deserves a better life than she has now. What made you think of fixing the two of them up?"

Alice thought for a moment and then answered, "Well, when you're a single parent, like my father and your mother, there comes a time when you need more in life. Why shouldn't my father and your mother enjoy themselves?"

"You're right. Your father is a good guy; he has been awfully nice to me. They would go well together. How are you going to manage this? What do you want me to do?"

Alice waved her hand in the air and said, "There is not much we can do directly. I will ask my father to talk to your mother, maybe invite her over to dinner. Something like that. He is the male so it should be up to him to make the first move. All you can do is suggest to your mother that she encourage my father when she hears from him."

"Do you think we can get them together? You know they met once and nothing became of it. They just went their own ways."

"Jeff, I'm not sure we can get them together. Both of them are hard to move. There's that old adage about bringing a horse to water. We'll just have to wait and see if we can get them out of their present ruts. I'll keep you informed and you do the same.

"One thing is the most important of all. Whatever you do, or say, don't mention me or that we are in cahoots. If either your mother or my father think we have collaborated they will bolt in the opposite direction. They both can be very stubborn"

Jeffrey wholeheartedly agreed to work on his mother and Alice started her campaign almost immediately. During dinner that evening she said, "Dad, I'd like us to do more entertaining this year."

Her father looked at her curiously and smiled. He wondered if this was another one of her schemes. "What type of entertaining do you have in mind, Alice?"

"Next year, at this time, I'll be in college somewhere and everything will be changed. I'll start being a stranger in my own neighborhood. I don't want that; I want all of our neighbors to remember me. To make sure that I don't lose touch I'd like to start having some of the neighbors over for dinner."

"That doesn't sound too unreasonable. Who were you thinking of?"

"Well, there are the Owens across the street. They looked after me when I was young and I have baby sat their grandchildren. Also the Bradfords and the Schindlers. Then, there are the Cabots, Jeffrey and his mother."

Ben looked at his daughter; he couldn't tell what was motivating her suggestion. Her request was certainly not out of line. She had known all of their older neighbors for years and Alice was fond of them; even though she saw a lot less of them these last few years. However, the Cabots seemed a little different. She saw Jeffrey in school every day and she had been going over to Mrs. Cabot's house frequently. He even had a handsome scarf that he got out of their collaboration. His answer reflected his hesitation. "Alice, your request is not unreasonable. You should say 'Goodbye' personally to all of our neighbors. The problems are that I work long hours and, right now, it's still winter. I get home later than most people and we would be eating after normal dinner times. Let's wait until the weather is better and you're closer to graduating and, on the days we have people over, I'll cut back on my hours."

The truth really was that Da Vinci was afraid of Myrna Cabot. He had not forgotten that she had paid no attention to him at the New

Year's Eve party they had both attended. And he was not sure that she appreciated his advice when she had him over to apologize.

He was wary. Even older people do not like to be rebuffed and he was almost sure that's what would happen to him. He had nothing to offer a lady like her. His looks, at best, could be described as average. What did he have to interest an attractive woman who went to college and had at least two degrees? He was a man who did not have a college education and who earned his living by trimming hair and shaving other men. He certainly couldn't hold her interest by telling her stories about his trade. Outside of the Army, he had never travelled anywhere except in New England itself.

On the other hand, Mrs. Cabot was a good looking woman who dressed with a flair; she was always well groomed. She had travelled extensively around the world. She was educated, urbane, and articulate and probably made a lot more money than he did. He would never be able to hold up his end of any partnership. Da Vinci thought that it was better to hide than to be humiliated.

In the past, each time he was supposed to make a personal commitment, he was also ready to delay doing so. His method for avoiding choices was to put off any immediate decisions. Da Vinci used his responsibilities as a single working parent to block all other avenues of life. There was some truth in his promise to reconsider Alice's request when the weather turned better, but not much.

At the same time, Jeffrey was having no better luck with his mother than Alice was having with her father. He approached the problem more directly than Alice. At dinner, He asked his mother if she would be interested in going out with Mr. Da Vinci. She told him, quickly and firmly, "No."

It was a simple word but a complex answer. She had rational

reasons for her feelings. Her disappointing marriage and the disastrous aftermath of that marriage had blown her life apart. She had left behind a good job to start over and the wounds from her years of struggle were still raw. She felt betrayed by men and she was wary of any personal involvements. This attitude of distrust had been strengthened by her unfortunate groping experience; she considered herself an active, card carrying man hater.

However, there was also a strong, irrational response. She had wondered about Da Vinci very briefly after she had apologized to him. He seemed like a gentle, intelligent person, but he was shorter than she was. Even though she despised her divorced husband, Skinner, she immediately wondered what he would say if he, and everyone at her old law firm, knew she was seeing Da Vinci. Her first thought was, "How can a lawyer go out with someone who is only a barber."

That upset her. She had never thought of herself as being a snob until that moment. After thinking about it she was not pleased with her reaction; it was stupid and childish, unworthy of her and contemptuous of Da Vinci. But the idea of Skinner's scorn bothered her and influenced her decisions. She made no attempt to change her mind.

The discouraged co-conspirators got together to compare notes and both were bewildered by their parents' lack of enthusiasm. When they did meet Alice said, "I don't understand my father's attitude. He knows his children are going their own ways. By the end of next year he will be alone and he's not doing anything about it. My father's no dummy; I wonder why he is not preparing for his future?

"Does getting older prevent you from moving rapidly? I'll have to figure out something else to do."

Jeffrey thought about the conversation he had with his mother and replied, "Alice, I'm not sure we should do anything else. I can look at your problems and solve them to my satisfaction; you can look at my problems and solve them to your satisfaction. However, neither outside solution solves the real problem. The truth is that I have to solve my problems by myself and you have to solve your problems by yourself.

"You and I must be overlooking something because our parents are neither stupid nor slow. Both of them are being held back from reaching out; maybe it is something from their past. Until they clear their own roadblocks I think we should butt out. At least I am going to leave my mother alone; absolutely no more suggestions for a while. I think you'd be better served to do the same thing."

Jeffrey's statement surprised Alice. Until now, he had been a compliant ally in her scheme. Now, he was speaking out in protest. She liked that; he was more resolute than she had previously thought. And, actually, what he said made sense, they had moved neither parent into action. There was really nothing they could do. Reluctantly, Alice stopped trying to be a matchmaker. At least, for the time being.

11

Until Christmas, all of the meetings between Myrna and Alice had been for one purpose; the knitting of scarves for presents. While they knitted, they talked endlessly, they talked breathlessly, they talked continuously. Their conversations were honest and open and ranged from trite to timely. Their needles pointed their stitches to individual scarves; their thoughts pointed their words to distinct personalities. Myrna knitted two sweaters for her son and found a young woman she wished were her daughter. Alice knitted three scarves for her two brothers and her father and found an older woman she wished were her mother. Myrna's responses to Alice's personality represented the first warming of her frozen feelings.

After Christmas, even though their knitting was finished, they continued to get together. The first few times they would bake, go shopping or take in a movie but, soon, their conversations led to a more serious purpose. That came about when Myrna casually started to ask Alice about what she was going to do after her graduation. Much to Myrna's chagrin, Alice had no firm plans for her own future that she could talk about.

Alice had been thinking about the same question and she had not been able to come up with any answers. She jokingly told her friends that she wanted to be a either a cook on a cattle roundup or a deep sea diver; the truth was that she had no idea of what she wanted to do. A lot of jobs interested her but not to the point that she wanted to spend her life doing any of them. Not many high school seniors have any real idea of what their future should be because realization comes only with maturity; and that doesn't usually happen until after graduation. Her own inability to select a career bothered Alice because she considered herself a very organized person. Because of her uncertainty she welcomed Mrs. Cabot's interest in trying to help her. She completely trusted the older woman's experience and intelligence.

Myrna easily could remember her own personal confusion when she was Alice's age. Her father had assumed that she would join him in his real estate business and that had no appeal to her at all. She was miserable during her freshman year at Wheaton because she didn't know what she wanted to do while her father kept talking about his plans for her at his office. It was not until one of her professors took the time to talk with her that she decided to go to law school.

Because of her own experience, Myrna decided to try to guide Alice along a path that would let her make her own decision. Myrna wanted Alice to choose a job that would be satisfying and fulfilling during her working life. To that end, the two of them started talking about different career paths. The one thing that Myrna was extremely careful about was not to talk about the law profession. She would be delighted if Alice chose that field but Myrna didn't want to influence her one way or the other. Alice had to decide what was best for herself by herself. If Alice didn't ask about becoming a lawyer, Myrna was not going to bring the subject up.

That began a process of discussing almost every other profession and job available to a high school graduate. Teacher, writer, architect, accountant, nurse, plumber, welder, airline pilot, nothing was below or above talking about as a career. Alice summarily dismissed a lot of the proposed subjects; she had no interest in any field that required either math or science. Those that she thought she would like were examined more closely, including looking at their educational requirements.

Myrna played devil's advocate in these discussions because she wanted Alice to make a wise choice; it was important to her that Alice be happy in her chosen field. In that role of asking questions, Myrna began to learn a lot more of Alice's life as she was growing up. Alice spoke honestly of how lonely and scared she was at the loss of her mother and of how her father had comforted her and and her brothers and had been their shield. She recounted the numerous times her father had performed little kindnesses and gestures for her and her brothers without him ever complaining or saying anything negative. Myrna didn't say much but she began to be impressed with the man she had thought of as "only a barber"; her negative veneer towards him began to crack.

As she and Mrs. Cabot worked together, Alice kept wondering when Mrs. Cabot was going to bring up her profession as a possible career field. Her continued silence on that subject began to intrigue Alice. One day, she artlessly blurted out her concern, "Mrs. Cabot, how come you have never suggested that I become a lawyer? Don't you like your profession?"

Myrna smiled. She was always tickled by Alice's direct approach to any subject she wanted to know about. "Alice, as an attorney, I have been involved in several different areas of law and I have enjoyed each of them. I wanted you to look at all of your possibilities before you made any decision. If you want to talk about the law as a profession, nothing would give me more pleasure than to discuss it with you."

So began a conversation that started slowly but gathered momentum as Myrna talked and Alice questioned; she found herself interested in what her opportunities would be with a law degree. For Alice, it opened up a way of earning a living and being a responsible citizen. Soon, as she became more interested in seeing how lawyers functioned, she began accompanying Myrna on some of her routine tasks of registering deeds and appearances in court. Alice, with Myrna's help, had found a career field that she thought she would enjoy.

****

Until they had joined forces to try to bring his father and her mother together, Jeffrey and Alice had been going their separate ways. They each knew of the other but circumstances and choice kept them from getting together. Even when Alice came over to his home to meet with his mother, Jeffrey was not a part of their meetings; they were work sessions and not socials. That didn't upset him because he wasn't interested in what they were doing and he had his own activities and circle of friends.

Since they both knew the other's family and had tried, and failed, to get their parents together, they began to consider themselves as friends and collaborators. After Cupid's arrows fell short of smiting their parents, they began to meet once a week to chat and commiserate with each other. They felt that they should get together away from both school and home, and talk freely with no restrictions. They chose to meet at Russo's, an ice cream parlor in downtown Malden Square.

They would each order a hot fudge sundae and sit in a back booth and talk about their activities.

Jeffrey would often tell Alice how lucky this year had been for him. He had told her that it had started off with his mother being angry with him but he would not elaborate; no details were ever revealed. The fact that he had gotten into trouble with a lie and that Alice's father had helped him out was a secret Jeffrey never shared with Alice. He would skip over that episode and tell Alice that after a bad start, his year had completely changed. He enjoyed school, he was beginning to think of what to do after graduation, and he had the nicest girl friend in the world. Occasionally, he would even talk about his disenchantment with his father. Jeffrey was becoming his own man.

One weekend near the end of the school's first term, Jeffrey's smooth sailing foundered on the rock of unhappiness. To his complete surprise, he found himself jilted by Jenny Fleck. There had been no advanced warning from Jenny and she gave him no explanation whatsoever. He had gone to her house to pick her up on a Friday evening, as he usually did. Her mother answered the doorbell and, when he asked for Jenny, her mother replied, "I'm sorry Jeffrey, she left for the movies about a half hour ago with Jimmy Verrengia." He was totally mortified; crushed. He mumbled something and slunk back to his house. He spent the entire weekend blaming himself for something that he could not even understand.

The following Monday, Jenny came up to him as he stood by his locker, and said, "I've decided to start dating Jimmy." Then, she walked away.

He asked Alice to meet him at Russo's that afternoon and he came over to the booth where she was sitting; he had not ordered any ice cream. He sat down without saying a word. He felt sick.

Alice patted his hand and said, "I'm sorry to hear about you and Jenny."

Jeffrey couldn't believe it; did everyone in school know that he had been dumped? Did everyone blame him? What had he done wrong? He asked, "How do you know about me and Jenny?"

Alice answered, "The girls on the cheerleaders' team thought Jenny would break up with you about two weeks ago."

Jeffrey was hurt and angered by that reply. He thought, "Two weeks ago? How could they have known two weeks ago when I only found out last Friday? What is going on?" He loudly said, "Goddamit! How could you know about this two weeks ago?"

Alice patted his arm. "Relax Jeffrey, none of this is your fault. About two weeks ago Jimmy Verrengia found out that he was going to receive a football scholarship to Boston College. The cheerleaders figured that Jenny would probably break up with you and invite Jimmy to be her new boyfriend."

"But I don't understand. We got along so well. I thought that she liked me. What happened? What could I have done differently?"

"There is nothing you could have done differently because this has nothing to do with you. It all has to do with Jenny. She is thinking of herself and planning ahead for the football weekends she will have at Boston College. Believe me, if she meets someone who will be an All American football player, Jimmy Verrengia will be the next boyfriend to receive a pink slip. Jenny insists on nothing but the very best for Jenny."

Jeffrey heard Alice. He listened to what she said and, logically, he understood what she said; emotionally, it didn't make him feel any better. He had been dumped, brutally dumped like garbage over a ship's rail, and that hurt him. To be socially shamed was a scathing experience for him and it would take time before his pride began to heal. He would think about his rebuff many times before he would be able to dismiss it and start to feel good about himself. He would eventually become a better person but only after his psyche healed and that was no comfort to him now.

Although Jeffrey believed he had been deeply struck, it really was a flesh wound and he soon began to heal. His breakup didn't stop him from thinking of what he wanted do after he graduated. He completely discarded what his father wanted, which was to go to law school and become partners together. He had an easier time sorting through his possibilities than Alice did because he had found a profession he liked. The idea of becoming a reporter interested him. He joined the staff of the school newspaper, the *Blue And Gold,* and thoroughly enjoyed the work and the atmosphere.

Once he made this decision, he began to clear away some of the clutter that he had been carrying in his mind. Because he now regarded his father entirely differently than he had before he started this year, he began to automatically reject his father's plans and suggestions. Although he would apply to Dartmouth, he would not go there unless that was the only school that accepted him. He knew his father would be angry but Jeffrey didn't care; he would make his own decisions. He preferred Brandeis, Tufts, Bowdoin, or Brown over Dartmouth; he would have to wait and see what his choice would be. He finally knew what he wanted even if he wasn't sure of the path he would have to take to get there.

****

The summer before Alice and Jeffrey started their final year at Malden High School was a good summer for them. By the time school had let out, her brothers were home. Billy finished at BU first and had started to set up Hulk Headquarters again in the garage. Greg came home from Dartmouth pleased with his grades and in excellent physical shape. He and Billy were going back to work for the same construction company they worked for last year. Both of them were upbeat about their futures. Alice had decided not to return as a counselor at her summer camp and had notified them early enough for them to find a replacement. Instead, she got a job as a waitress at Russo's because she wanted to be near her family and Mrs. Cabot this summer.

Jeffrey worked mowing lawns, trimming bushes and doing odd jobs in the neighborhood; he almost had more customers than he could handle. The first time he saw Billy and later, Greg, he was hesitant to speak to them. If they knew about his lie they would angry with him. However, each seemed glad to see him and included him in their weight lifting plans; their casualness put him at ease.

Although their jobs were important to each one of them, they were not as interesting as their activities at Hulk Headquarters. Working out at least once a day during the week and twice a day on the weekends was what they hoped to do. Since their jobs were weather dependent, their exercising schedule became weather dependent. There were many phone calls and trips between the two houses changing times and insuring that everyone knew what was going on.

Alice loved Mrs. Cabot; she considered her as the mother she never knew. That was one of the reasons she gave up her job as a camp counselor; she did not want to lose contact with her adopted "mom." She had never called her "mom" but that is how she thought of her.

Alice tried to avoid working on the weekends so that she would be available for any plans her brothers had in mind.

That summer, while life was flexible and busy for the Da Vinci and the Cabot offspring, their parents were equally as busy, but not nearly as flexible. Myrna and Ben had their normal, long working hours and their commitments didn't allow them to change their schedules just because of the weather. They both soldiered on while they were aware of what their children were doing.

For Ben, their antics and activities were no surprise as Jeffrey had been over at his house quite a bit the year before. The rushing around, the change of plans, the quick comings and goings, were routine events and he considered the hubbub as normal teenage traffic.

However, for Myrna, getting to know Alice's brothers was a complete revelation. She met them after her son asked her to bake some brownies for all of them; he was trying to save some of his money. She was happy to please and she began to supply all kinds of homemade pies and cakes for them. Greg and Billy got in the habit of coming over to personally thank her and find out if there was anything else to eat. She was pleased with their manners and, as she got to know them, by their intelligence and their sense of humor.

In their Saturday morning bake offs Myrna and Lydia had always confided in each other. For Myrna, especially, her talks with Lydia relieved her tensions and helped to cope with her problems. Lydia was as neutral as the walls of a hand ball court; she would absorb the energy of an idea and bounce it back to Myrna at exactly the same angle. Lydia rarely offered advice; her job was to listen with love and care.

From the time that Myrna was groped, she had shared her feelings with Lydia. Myrna had explained the confrontation she had had with Ben Da Vinci and how she had apologized. She casually told Lydia about meeting Alice and helping her learn to knit. As the relationship between the two of them deepened, Lydia thought that Myrna sounded almost like Alice's mother when she talked of Alice. Lydia smiled to herself at how Myrna was softening her attitude towards the world.

After Myrna met Alice's brothers, she began telling Lydia about them. Greg and Billy were polite, never interrupting, always respectful, and were delightful teenagers. Like their sister, they could make her smile and laugh. Lydia reminded Myrna that she knew all about them because she had seen them grow from young children to young adults; that surprised Myrna. She thought about the Da Vinci children and, after a while, she began to ask more questions about their father.

Lydia was sure that Myrna was subconsciously changing her attitude towards men. She was beginning to talk about their positive traits as well as their negative ones. Nothing would please Lydia more than having Myrna open her heart to the world around her. Maybe there was hope.

It was a slow, sweet summer with no anxieties and no concerns for anyone. Ben planted and distributed enough produce to feed the entire block. His children worked, helped him with his gardening, and, in turn, they also ripened to full maturity. Myrna became aware that life was more than a gray treadmill and Jeffrey was delighted that his mother was relaxed and beginning to enjoy herself.

SENIORS

12

A student's senior year of high school is the final step to the top of the educational pyramid. He or she has worked all the way from kindergarten through the eleventh grade studying and learning enough to be promoted each year. As a reward for diligence, the student's senior year is usually considered as the most satisfying and the easiest. By then, almost all the academic battles have been fought and, win, lose or draw, the outcome of graduation has been decided. For the little while that they are high school seniors they still have a shelter of serenity. When a student walks out of their high school door for the final time, that student is facing his or her personal future. There is no returning to school for more education.

True, there are more battles and decisions to be made but they are off in the distance. Once they have their diplomas they will have to come to grips with reality and decide on their futures. They will go on to other schools or institutions, look for jobs, join the military, or, do whatever it takes to begin a new life. The student has transitioned from a child seeking an education to a young person starting his or her life's work.

The summer had been good for the soon to be seniors, Alice and Jeffrey. Being close with her brothers gave the Da Vinci's the opportunity to reassure themselves that they were not drifting apart even though they were going their separate ways. This was important to Alice.

Jeffrey learned more about the dignity of family life as he came in contact with the rough and tumble antics of the Da Vincis. He tried to apply their guidelines to himself and to his mother with immediate results. They began to enjoy each other.

Alice and Jeffrey started into their senior year enthusiastically. Each enjoyed their classes, each cheerfully joined in student activities, and each dutifully applied for admission to several colleges and universities. They both savored their senior year.

In the meantime, Alice had been giving a lot of thought as to what her father would do when all three of his children were gone. The more time she spent with Mrs. Cabot the more she believed that the two single parents should get together. However, she decided to again discuss her ideas with Jeffrey and get his opinion; he certainly was involved in this equation.

They had been meeting almost every Thursday afternoon at Russo's to talk over their business. That included who they were dating, what schools they had applied to, and what was going on within their families. Jeffrey had reached the point where he would even talk about his feelings for his father. They were comfortable with each other. This one Thursday, as they were eating their hot fudge sundaes, Alice suddenly said, "Jeff, I have an idea that I want to run past you."

Jeffrey groaned and replied, "The last time you got an idea I was given two hours of detention for trying to help you. Is it absolutely necessary for you to have an idea?"

"Yes, it is. Definitely. And this time you won't get detention; you will get satisfaction. Your help will be necessary. I have figured out a way to get your mother and my father together."

Jeffrey groaned again. "Didn't we try this once before?"

"Yes, we tried but we didn't succeed. This time we can't fail. I love your mother as much as I love my father. I tell you, they belong together. We need to act."

"Listen, Alice, I have great deal of respect for you, your father and your brothers and I would like it if they would get together. But, it may be like trying to get two water soaked logs to kindle a flame. There may be nothing there to catch fire and burn."

Alice tossed her head and answered, "What a horrible thing to say. They both are very much alive and well. Neither of them is water logged. We just have to find a way for them to show themselves to each other; and that's what I just figured out how to do."

"I think I'm afraid to ask. How do you plan on bringing them together?"

"It's really simple. I'm going to ask my father to invite you and your mother over to our house for Thanksgiving."

Jeffrey toyed with the maraschino cherry that was on the top of his sundae before he replied, "That sounds like a good idea, but you haven't really asked him yet, have you?"

"No."

"And you haven't asked my mother yet?"

"No."

"What about your brothers?"

"Jeff, you are the first person I've talked to about it. I wanted your comments before I went any further."

Jeffrey smiled as he said, "I like it. It's a good idea. It is simple enough to work.

"When are you going to blow the whistle to start the game?"

"Next Sunday, after church, when we go to breakfast, I'll bring it up with my father. He's usually more receptive on Sunday than during the week.

"I've never thought about that before; I wonder why that is?"

"I don't know. I guess maybe church makes him happy. In any case, I'm not saying a word to my mother until I hear from you.

"Good luck."

Sunday, while Alice was eating breakfast, she took a deep breath and spoke slowly, "Dad, I would like to make a suggestion about our Thanksgiving Day dinner."

Ben looked at his daughter with a tolerant smile and asked, "Alice, what do you have up your sleeve this time?"

"Honestly, nothing Dad. It's just that I would like to invite Jeffrey and Mrs. Cabot over to our house to join us." Alice stopped, not knowing how her father would take this suggestion. She was half expecting a negative reply.

Ben sat still for a moment and then he asked, "You realize that the Bradfords usually have them over? Have you thought of that?"

Alice winced at her dumb mistake. She had not considered that fact. She had to own up to her oversight. "No, Dad, I was thinking of the boys and me and Jeffrey and how much more fun it would be for us to have a crowd over at the house. I guess I didn't think; I'm sorry." She was crestfallen; she expected her father to tell her that the idea was not practical and to forget it.

Ben was still sitting quietly. He had grown fond of Jeffrey and he was fully aware that his mother was a pretty woman. Then, unexpectedly, he said, "You have nothing to be sorry about. It's a good idea. Thanksgiving is a time to celebrate friends as well as family. You kids have as much right to have friends as your parents do. I like Frank and Lydia. Why not invite the Bradfords along with the Cabots?"

Alice couldn't believe it. Her father was actually joining in on her conspiracy. She leaned across the table to pat his hand. "Thanks, Dad. This will be one of the best Thanksgivings we have ever had."

And it was. Alice and Jeffrey went to the Bradford's house together and invited them first. When the Bradfords realized that Myrna and Jeffrey would also be at the Da Vinci's they quickly agreed. Especially Lydia, she was hoping for a status change between her neighbors. Jeffrey's mother also accepted the invitation; she had to admit that she didn't have much in the way of an alternative.

Greg and Billy arrived home a day or two before Thanksgiving and Alice and her brothers went shopping and bought enough food to fatten every resident who lived in Malden. Thanksgiving Day, Frank, Lydia, Myrna and Jeffrey descended upon the Da Vinci house early in the day. The four younger ones went to the Malden/Medford football game while their parents were in the kitchen fixing dinner. It was a scene to behold. They all had wine. Frank sat at the kitchen table doing whatever he was told to do by the other three as they rushed around the kitchen. He chopped vegetables, made hors d'oeuvres, counted out silverware and napkins; he was a bulwark of calm in a whirlpool of noisy activity. The three cooks drank wine, prepared food and checked each others' work. They enjoyed themselves and they finally did make progress in getting their dinner cooked.

When the youngsters returned they were subdued, Malden had been badly beaten. They were assigned the job of setting the table in the dining room.

When everything was ready, Ben asked his guests to stand behind their chairs. He looked at them and said, "Before we sit down and enjoy this meal together, I'd like to explain something. We Da Vincis have a Thanksgiving ceremony that is simple. We all hold hands and each of us tells the one thing that we are most thankful for.

"It is not mandatory or required, so if anyone wants to pass that is all they have to say is 'Pass.' If you will please hold hands Alice will speak for all of us Da Vincis."

Everyone reached out, held hands and bowed their heads; they formed a circle of humans around the table. Alice waited a second and then, in a faltering voice, she said, "I'm thankful for the love given me by my family and my friends."

The Bradfords were next. Frank spoke quietly. "I'm thankful for the forty-six years of marriage given to both me and Lydia."

Jeffrey, who wasn't aware of this tradition and hadn't expected a flood of emotion said, "I pass to my Mother."

Myrna had been taken completely by surprise. She had never witnessed anything like his before and, although she liked the idea of giving thanks, she didn't know exactly what to say. After a pause, she began, "I'm new at giving thanks in front of everyone and I'm a little scared. However, I do give thanks for neighbors who care about Jeffrey and me. It is comforting to know you are not alone."

With that, all solemnity was thrown aside and the food was literally attacked from all four sides of the table. The talking and feasting went on for hours and, after that, the talking and cleanup went on for hours more. The spirit of the day was truly of thanks for the good things in their lives. It was late at night before anyone left to go home.

Alice went to bed pleased and happy; she had her holidays mixed though because, that night, dreams of the sugar plumb fairy danced through her head.

****

The following Saturday was a bake off Saturday and Myrna appeared at Lydia's door with a freshly baked roll of monkey bread. After she put the platter on the kitchen counter she hugged Frank and Lydia. Myrna said, "I was so happy and thrilled for both of you. Married for forty-six years? I envy you."

Lydia smiled, poured coffee, and cut slices of monkey bread for everyone. Then she asked, "Wasn't that a marvelous Thanksgiving? It wasn't solemn but it was touching. What did you think of it, Myrna."

"I'm not sure I can describe my feelings. But I do agree with you, that was one of the best Thanksgivings I've ever had. We had so much fun in the kitchen and then the emotions at the table. I'm stunned."

Lydia was pleased to hear what Myrna said. She was back to match making and, this time, she was determined to get it right. She led into the subject by casually asking, "What did you think of the Da Vinci family? That was the first time you saw all of them together."

Myrna answered, "They are so close. They have been taught the value of love and respect. Ben has been a good father to them; he must have worked hard."

Lydia kept the discussion headed in the direction she wanted it to go. She said, "He is a wonderful person. There's a lot more to him than you think."

"You are probably right. I wonder why he never married again?"

Lydia continued, "My guess is that he was busy raising his three children. Plus the fact that he is kind of shy and private.

"Listen, I'm planning on writing him a thank you note for inviting Frank and me over for Thanksgiving. I'm also planning on inviting him over here for a New Year's Eve party. What do you think of that?"

A vision of the last New Year's Eve party, with the loud drunk couple dominating the conversation flashed through Myrna's mind. She asked, "Will Ben even accept after the last party you had?"

"He will," Lydia replied. "He will feel he can't refuse me after I thank him for his being such a good host. And this party is going to be entirely different. There are only going to be four people at that party and, right now, I'm talking to three of them."

Myrna realized that Lydia was sending her a challenge. She sat there a second, wondering whether she should or shouldn't refuse to come. Then, she decided; it was only a social get together. She loved Alice and was becoming intrigued with the family. What the Hell? "OK, if you can get Ben to come I will too."

Lydia beamed; things were beginning to take the shape she wanted them to take. "But, you are not to say a word to Ben. He will not know who is, or isn't, going to be here and I don't want him to know it is to be a small party. If he feels that someone is trying to fix him up he may not come. Sometimes I get the feeling that part of his family devotion is because he is afraid to search for a new life."

Myrna didn't reply because she had no way of knowing whether that was true or not and she didn't want to apply that yardstick to herself.

Thank You cards were set from Myrna and Lydia to Ben and the arrangements for New Year's Eve were sent up and then put aside as the Christmas season took central stage. Greg and Billy came home from school and began their plans, along with Alice, for the Da Vinci family Christmas. It was while they were deciding which day to take their trip to Cape Ann that Billy, surprisingly, asked if Jeffrey could come along with them.

Greg looked at him as if he had been caught goosing his grandmother. He asked, "What brought this up?"

Billy answered defiantly, "Nothing, really. I saw him downtown a couple of days ago and we got to talking." He nodded to Greg. "You and he got along all summer; and I like him. If you don't want him with us just say so."

Greg replied, "I don't mind, I was just surprised. Alice, what do you say? Have you and he ever dated? Do you mind if he came with us?"

Alice answered, "Jeff and I have not dated; his mother and I are very close. He and I are friends. I hadn't thought about it before but I think having him with us might be fun. He's got a good sense of humor and we have worked in the past to get his mother and Dad together. It's OK with me."

The three of them decided that the best day to go would be two days after Christmas and they invited Jeffrey. He was happy to be asked and immediately accepted their invitation. Jeffrey told his mother about joining the Da Vinci children on their jaunt; the Da Vinci kids did not mention anything about Jeffrey to their father. He had never been directly involved in their past trips so they assumed it wouldn't make any difference to him if, this time, a friend came along.

Lydia Bradford's match making activities were finally beginning to align themselves with reality. Alice loved Mrs. Cabot, Jeffrey respected Mr. Da Vinci, and the four offspring got along well. Ben was attending a New Year's Eve party not knowing that Myrna was also going to be there. They would both be alone on the twenty seventh while their offspring were out celebrating together. The time was right for the parents to finally move to assert themselves and change their lives.

The week before Christmas Ben went to the post office to buy some stamps. He stood in a long line of people carrying presents they wanted to mail. After waiting a while, he got frustrated at the delay and started looking around; that's when he noticed Myrna in line behind him. She was juggling five or six small packages. Ben immediately dropped back to be with her and he said, "Hello, Myrna. Can I give you a hand with your load?"

Myrna answered, "They are not heavy but it would be easier for me if you could hold a couple of them. I never expected such a long line. I guess everybody did what I do, wait until the last minute."

They stood in line together making small talk until Myrna casually said, "Jeffrey is really looking forward to going with your children on their trip to Cape Ann."

That caught Ben's attention. "I didn't know that Jeff was going with them. They didn't mention it to me."

Myrna said, "I'm sorry, I didn't know. I hope I didn't let the cat out of the bag."

Ben quickly responded, "That's no problem. It's their outing and they handle it themselves. I'm glad they have included Jeff. He's a nice young man.

"If they follow their usual routine, they will be gone almost all day until some time in the evening."

That was news to Myrna. "I didn't know that. Well, it will give me a day of rest to clean the house."

The line kept working its way forward. Shortly, Ben bought his stamps, put Myrna's packages on the counter, wished her a "Merry Christmas," and left.

He was outside the post office when he stopped and thought, "Her kid will be gone and your kids will be gone. Why not ask her to do something with you? Even if she refuses, what do you have to lose. Why not?"

Myrna was surprised to see Ben when she came out. She said, "Hi, again."

"Hi. Listen, I've been thinking. Our kids won't be home that day. If you have nothing planned, we could go for a drive ourselves. The ocean is big enough for two trips."

"You mean to Cape Ann?"

Ben smiled a little relieved. At least he wasn't being immediately turned down. "No, that's the last place I would go on that day. I wouldn't want to bump into my own children. No. I meant in the opposite direction; we would head for Cape Cod."

Myrna was taken aback. She thought, "That's a good idea. Why be alone that day? Why not?"

She replied, "Ben, that sounds like a lovely suggestion. I'd be happy to go with you."

The two of them settled on their plans to meet that day. They again wished each other a Merry Christmas and went their separate ways. Because of the prior pressure from their children, Ben and Myrna independently decided not to tell them about their trip.

Christmas was merry for both families. Within each household there were many decorations, many wrappings, too many gifts, too much food, and an overload of happiness. No cares were big enough to trip the joy of the day.

And that spirit carried over to the time that the young adults left for Cape Ann. They were no sooner on their way when Ben came over to Myrna's house and they left for their own day trip. First, they went to the diner where Ben took his family after church and had breakfast. While they were eating, Myrna said, "Ben, I have been wanting to ask you something and this is the first time I've had a chance. Your Thanksgiving Day prayer, when you had everyone hold hands and say their most important thanks, was so impressive. I almost cried because it made me think of what was really important to me. Anyhow, where did you get the idea for that? I had never thought of it before and now I intend to do it every Thanksgiving. Was that a tradition from your family?"

Ben sat quietly for a second before answering. "No, my family never had many traditions. That idea came from Esther just after we were married. I forgot about it when the kids were very young but I realized how important it was to teach them to appreciate what they have. So, I started having them say their most important blessing out loud. That cuts their speech down to the very essence of Thanksgiving."

"And that makes it very moving."

"Yes, it does."

It was with that open discussion that Myrna and Ben were able to take off their masks of manners and engage in direct conversation. They soon found themselves chatting comfortably with each other.

They drove on to Cape Cod and meandered around Falmouth. They stopped at several small bookstores and looked at the beautiful, imported Christmas cards from Germany and England; even at half price they were very expensive. Myrna bought two or three boxes of them for next year. Then they drove to Woods Hole, briefly discussed taking a ferry to Martha's Vineyard, discarded the idea, and meandered over to Hyannis, where they rubbernecked at the small town and again shopped for Christmas cards. They had bowls of steaming clam chowder for lunch and, as they were eating Myrna asked, "You seem very familiar wandering around Cape Cod; you have done this before?"

Ben said, "Yes. Esther and I used to come here the day after Christmas to relax and enjoy ourselves. That's how we would unwind. She would buy the imported Christmas cards because they were always half price the day after Christmas. It was our time to be together."

Myrna became quiet for a while as she thought about the devotion of this couple. They continued to East Orleans where they got out of the car and walked along the sandy beach. It was a cold, gray winter's day with a high, gusty wind that blew salt spray into their faces. As they walked on the deserted beach, the plaintive cry of the seagulls rang in their ears. The salty, marsh smell of the beach and the cold spray from the Atlantic chilled them both, but it also exhilarated them.

When they got back into the car, Myrna said, "Oh my God, I'm frozen stiff; I'm absolutely soaked. That was absolutely beautiful. I haven't had so much fun in years."

Ben was pleased at her remark. He said, "We will defrost when we get to Provincetown. We will be eating dinner indoors and that should help your icy condition."

They dined in a restaurant in which there were few customers; they sat in a corner and had almost complete privacy. As Myrna drank her wine, while they waited for their food, she said, "I have forgotten how much beauty there is in this world. A day like this reminds me of what life should be like. Ben, I'm having a wonderful time. I thank you"

"You are welcome, Myrna. But your comment does go both ways. I'm also having a good time."

Myrna didn't say anything while they ate their broiled lobsters. When the meal was finished and they were drinking more wine, she asked, "Are you really having a good time?"

"Oh, yes. Why do you ask?"

"You came to the cape for years with someone you loved, your wife. Now, you're back with someone you don't know very well, your neighbor. I hope the difference doesn't bother you."

Ben looked at Myrna for a while. Then he smiled a little as he replied, "Thank you for your concern, but all my ghosts were laid to rest years ago. I loved Esther when she was alive and I love her memory now that she is dead. That was a part of my life that is over; it will never happen again. It is not what I wanted but I wasn't consulted. I was not given a choice but I have had to live with the consequences."

He paused before he continued. "We both knew she was dying. Esther talked at great length about what she wanted for me and the kids after she was gone. She was good at giving directions. She told me what she expected from me and I have done almost everything she asked."

Myrna was listening intently. Automatically, she asked, "What haven't you done?"

"Esther wanted me to have a normal life. She wanted me to raise the kids and get married again. She was insistent that I not live alone."

"Why didn't you do as she asked?"

"I think I trapped myself. First of all, I know this sounds stupid, but I was angry with Esther for leaving me. I grieved for her but I was mad at her at the same time. That doesn't make sense but that's what I felt.

"It took a long time for me to realize that what had been was no more. I'm not very clever when it comes to dealing with ladies so I concentrated on being a parent and hid from Esther's request by raising my kids.

"Now, here I am on the verge of being a single parent in an empty house.

"My question to you is, have you laid all of your ghosts?"

Myrna shook her head negatively. "Ben, I haven't been as successful as you; my ghosts still haunt me. I have a very contentious life."

It was now Ben who listened intensely. "In what respect?"

"My ex-husband and I hate each other. I used to be so afraid that he'd corrupt Jeffrey into doing bad things. That was the reason I was so wrong the first time we met. Jeffrey used to be caught in the middle between us but lately, he seems to be maturing."

Myrna stopped talking for a second and Ben spoke up. "Listen Myrna, from what I've seen of Jeff you have no worries at all with him. He is a fine boy. You should be proud of him.

"Hopefully with a new year coming, both your luck and your life will begin to change. Maybe that will happen for both of us."

They finished dining and made the long drive back to Malden thinking about their day. They arrived home well after midnight. When Ben stopped the car, in front of Myrna's house, she put her hand on his arm and said, "Ben, thank you for inviting me today. I have enjoyed myself and, because of you, I had a day that I will treasure for a long time.

"Don't bother getting out of the car. I'm sure that the minute I get to the steps Jeffrey will pop out of the house wanting to know where I've been so late. You may find yourself facing a homecoming posse wanting to know the same thing when you get home."

Myrna was correct on both counts.

****

Lydia and Myrna were not in touch with each other between Christmas and New Year's Eve. As a result, Lydia did not know if

Myrna had had a good time when she and Ben went to the cape and she was anxious to find out what happened. Myrna came into Lydia's kitchen carrying a platter of cheeses for their party and Lydia immediately asked, "Well?"

Myrna put the platter on the counter, kissed Lydia on the cheek and playfully answered, "Well, what?"

"Don't play games with me, young lady, you know perfectly well what my 'Well' means. Are you going to tell me or should I ask Ben how the two of you got along?"

"Don't ask him, I'm not sure how he would answer. For me though, I haven't had such a good time in years. He is certainly easy to talk to and he has a good sense of humor. I felt more relaxed than I have in a long time. I didn't have to be careful about what I said or how I said it; I just had fun. To answer your question, I got along well with Ben and I enjoyed our date.

"But I'm not sure about Ben. He used to make that trip every year with Esther until she passed away; it was their tradition after the holiday. Now, he does the same thing with a neighbor, whom he doesn't know very well. In a way, I was asked to take the place of his wife.

"I think he enjoyed our time together but I haven't heard from him since we went to the Cape. I do know that I see him in a much different light than the first time I barged into his house. He has raised three really nice children and, after I came to know Alice, I realized there is more to him than I had thought.

"I like him but, I'm ashamed to say, that his being shorter than I am still bothers me a little."

Lydia laughed at Myrna's last statement and replied, "You are beginning to make some progress. You are not faulting him for being a barber or not having a formal education. He is well read, intelligent, and expresses himself well. As for his height, you certainly don't tower over him; you are probably the only one who even bothers to think about the difference in height.

"Let me ask you if having a husband like Skinner, who was taller than you, made for a better marriage?"

Myrna shook her head, "You know the answer to that question."

"Precisely my point. I love you as much as my daughter, but you, my Dear, are stuck in your own past and you are going to have to change."

Myrna didn't reply for a few minutes and then she began, "You're right. I have hated my ex-husband so much that I keep trying to picture what I do through his eyes. There's no happiness in living like that. I don't need to avoid his disapproval. I need an attitude adjustment towards running my own life.

"Why use yesterday's poisons to fertilize tomorrow's hopes?"

She leaned over and patted Lydia's hand and smiled at her, "Thank you for being my friend and my mother, Lydia. I'm so glad that you are here for me."

With that, the two of them began the preparations for the party. After preparing the food, they began moving everything into the dining room. Frank came downstairs when he was ready and he lit a fire in their huge fireplace. They sat around the fireplace chatting and waiting for Ben to arrive; he had said that he would arrive about 8:00 PM.

That time passed without Ben, so did 8:30 and 8:45. Lydia became a little restless because Ben was usually prompt. Just before 9:00 Ben rang the front door bell and Frank let him in and fixed him a drink. When he was settled in a chair by the fire, Lydia said, "We were a bit concerned about you."

Ben sipped on his drink and looked around. "I'm sorry to be late. I would have called if I had known this was to be a small gathering. I thought you were going to have a party like you did last year and that I wouldn't be missed by anyone.

"What kept me was that Alice wanted to introduce her new boyfriend to me. All three of my kids are going to be at the same party for the first time ever but she didn't want me to be concerned about drinking so she wanted me to meet her date. I hope I didn't keep any of you from starting to celebrate."

Frank laughed and replied, "No chance of that happening. No, this year we are not going to have the hats and horns of last year but we will undoubtedly have a lot more fun."

With that, they sat at the dining room table and ate and drank leisurely. Afterwards, they returned to the fire, and as midnight began to approach Lydia said, "Frank and I will tell you what we hope for us in this coming New Year and then we want Ben and Myrna to tell us their hopes.

"Frank and I are considering becoming snowbirds and going to a warmer climate next winter. That is what we are looking forward to next year."

Ben smiled and said, "Make sure you have a spare bedroom. In the meantime, my hopes will be different this year than ever before. My kids will all be in school, out of the house, and my life will be different. I'll be able to do things that I haven't done in the past. I'm excited about the possibilities of traveling, taking cooking courses, doing whatever comes to mind. This may sound a little selfish but I think of next year as the Year of Ben."

Myrna immediately spoke up, "You have just touched on something I have been avoiding. I'm going to be in the same position as you. Jeffrey will be out of the house and my role as a parent will begin to be less. I need to alter my pattern of living, so if you don't mind, I'll call my upcoming year the Year of Myrna."

As midnight approached, Frank opened the bottle of Champagne that Ben had brought, poured the contents into four glasses, and handed them out to everyone. Lydia asked Ben to make a toast just before midnight. He thought for a second and then said, "Let each of us think about our past memories, our present joys and our future health and happiness. For each of you, my neighbors, with all of my heart, I wish you a Happy New Year."

They celebrated the entrance of the New Year by hugging and kissing. Shortly after 1:00 AM Myrna left and Ben walked out with her. They were both surprised at how mild the weather was; the pavements were dry, the air was cool and pleasant with a slight fog which made the street lights seem to be candle lit, not a harsh electric light. As they reached the street they both inhaled the fresh air deeply. Myrna said, "Ben, that was a very touching toast you proposed. Did you make it up?"

"Oh yes, I'm good at that. I sometimes think that I could have made a fortune writing sayings for fortune cookies."

"Listen, that's not funny. You shouldn't downplay your abilities. Your daughter is quite proud of you and she has a right to be. You have set her a good example. You are a good man.

"I have to go in now, Ben. Happy New Year. Let me know if you take any cooking courses, I might be interested."

Ben walked Myrna up the steps and waited until she had unlocked her door before he said good night and left. He didn't know it but, in his act of doing nothing, he had just purged her memory of her groping nightmare.

13

The personal warmth of the holiday season was completely blown away by the harshness of the winter weather that swept in after the beginning of the new year. Snow, hail and sleet fell daily and was whirled into huge drifts by high winds that gusted and moaned as they scoured the streets, sweeping away all pedestrians. The temperature dropped to below zero and the thermometers froze at that reading while ice coated every surface that it touched. Just keeping alive was a daily struggle. Normal routines were difficult under abnormal, dangerous conditions. Ordinary living was hard to sustain as everyone hid in their own social igloo.

No new shoots of romance could survive such frigid conditions. Both Ben and Myrna were caught in the chill. The warmth of their Christmas and New Year's Eve contacts faded as each remained inside their individual work schedules. Their routines began to become a rut that bordered on being a trench; the daily grind of making a living under harsh conditions became their major concern.

As a result of their lack of contact, whatever thoughts each had for the other were overtaken by their self doubts. Ben decided that Myrna was not interested in him; Myrna decided that Ben was not interested in her. The deadlock between them continued.

Alice and Jeffrey kept up their weekly meetings at Russo's. The weather didn't bother them and they enjoyed talking with each other about their own problems as well as conspiring to bring their parents together. In their naïveté they were trying to bring happiness to the two people they loved the most. They were not making much progress.

When they got together for their first meeting after the start of the new year they were both excited. Each talked about their own New Year's Eve dates and parties until they almost ran out of breath. Then they turned their attention to their parents.

Alice said that she had quizzed her father at great length and, although he didn't go into any detail, he seemed to have enjoyed being with Mrs. Cabot both times they were together. Alice believed that her father would keep in touch with Jeffrey's mother.

Jeffrey said that his mother seemed more forthcoming in talking about Alice's father. She not only said that she had enjoyed his company, she had asked Jeffrey questions about what he thought of Mr. Da Vinci. Jeffrey believed that his mother hoped Alice's father would be in touch.

Throughout the winter, Alice and Jeffrey continued to meet at Russo's every week. They were close friends who used each other as a sounding board for their troubles; they also considered themselves allies in a lost cause. They had hoped their parents would turn towards each other and find their happiness together. When that did not happen Alice and Jeffrey went from being annoyed to being vexed, to a state of frustration. Alice tried to prompt her father several times into taking the initiative but she was rebuffed and she almost gave up. The emotional inertia of their parents was too much for their offspring to overcome.

As spring started to kitty claw its way through winter's harsh domain, Alice and Jeffrey began to come up with scenarios to get their parents to pay attention to each other. Their plans were far fetched ranging from staged kidnappings to intentional fender benders; they soon realized the absurdities of their schemes and talked about abandoning their efforts.

However, when the weather finally turned better and the soft air began to melt the snow and flow the spirits, Alice suddenly came up with a new approach. She would combine two of her goals into one campaign; she would roll matchmaking and college selection together.

She had applied to many colleges for admission and, in her mind, she had already made a list of which schools she would attend, depending upon which schools admitted her. After thinking about it she decided to try another approach.

"I made a mistake to pre-select any school," she explained to Jeffrey over their hot fudge Sundaes. "I am going to visit every college that sends me an acceptance letter."

Jeffrey shook his head in bewilderment, "I don't get it. Where are you going with this?"

"Hah, Jeff, you have no imagination. Listen, my father is going to have to pay for all the costs not covered by scholarships; he should accompany me and help me choose. He did that for Greg and Billy. By the same token your mother helped me select my goal to be a lawyer; she should accompany me to help me select the right college to lead me to law school. See how simple and beautiful this idea is."

Jeffrey stared at her. "Wait a minute, I'm still missing something. Your father works six days a week. Are you going to these schools only on Sundays? The staff and faculty won't be available on Sundays."

"You're being hard to get along with. Of course, we won't be going on Sundays. Right now, my father does work six days but, for a long time, he has been talking of cutting back on his work schedule. I'm hoping that he finally does something about what he has been thinking. He closed the shop on Saturdays to see Greg play football. He has thought of either closing his shop on Wednesdays or hiring one or two more barbers. He really should see the campuses I visit.

"I need both him and your mother in my life. I just wish we could get them to be side by side.

"That's why I want your help. As soon as I get your agreement on this arrangement, I want you to come with us when we start visiting these campuses."

"Why would you want me to tag along? I'm not going to any of those schools and I'd just be excess baggage. If you're trying to get two lovebirds to bill and coo, the less offspring around the better for the lovebirds."

Alice laughed, "Even if you're right, I'll need you to fill up space, at least to begin with. My father will drive and I want your mother to sit in front beside him so that they can talk. If we pull up in front of your house she might get in back and then there would never be any 'billing and cooing.'"

Now it was Jeffrey's turn to laugh. "Alice, you may be right about the big picture but you are getting the details confused. If you get out of the car when you get to our house you can move to the back seat. My mother is not going to sit beside you and leave your father up front as the chauffeur. After the first time, everybody will automatically sit in their places."

Alice thought about that for a while and then she grinned and thumbed her nose at him. "Smarty Pants, this time you happen to be correct. But it still would be more fun if you came along."

Alice had no trouble convincing both her father and Mrs. Cabot that she wanted their opinions about the colleges in which she was interested. She appealed to their strongest asset and their weakest link, their parental responsibility; it worked perfectly. They were engaged in helping her while she became engaged in helping them.

***

Love is a force that is impossible to describe. It can't be weighed, it can't be tasted, it can't be smelled, it can't be heard, it can't be seen. Yet, it is the most overpowering emotion that life has to offer. Love is to the soul what food is to the body; we must have it if we are to survive. Humans crave it; we chase after it all of our lives. It is the one feeling that distinguishes us from all the other species on earth. Love can make a sane person insane or an insane person sane; it impartially works both ways. Love is luscious.

And it works in mysterious ways. Love strikes younger people without warning like a bolt of lightning. It is more powerful and awesome than lightning. Property can be protected from lightning bolts with lightning rods but people cannot be protected from love bolts. They transmute people for better or worse.

As humans mature, they are no less immune to the power of love; they just take longer to feel the effects. Age tempers the elasticity of youth. A more mature person has the history of his or her prior emotions; and this history insulates instantaneous reaction. It can only delay love, it cannot stop it. In addition, the fear of making a mistake can rule a mature persons' emotions for a while. But the need to love, and be loved, is too powerful for humans to resist. Every individual on this planet needs a companion to share the sorrows and joys of life. If love is available, people will find it.

Alice believed that her father and Myrna Cabot were meant for each other. She realized that her father had loved his wife and that Mrs. Cabot had had a bad marriage but those events had taken place years ago. She thought their lives were changing and that they should face the future together and be happy. She was determined to cut the umbilicals to their pasts.

As a start, Alice talked with her father about her visits to the schools that she was interested in. She told him that, unlike Greg, she did not play football and was not particularly interested in their stadium or how their campuses looked; she wanted to talk to the school's administrators and faculty. On that basis, Ben agreed to close his shop on any Wednesday that Alice selected as a visitation day. Next, Alice asked Myrna about rearranging her schedule so that she would also be able to accompany Alice when she made these visits. She told Alice that she would try to change her appointments but that might not always be possible; but give her as much lead time as possible.

With those provisos in mind, Alice chose Brown University, in Rhode Island, as the first school to visit. Going to Brown would require being together in the car for almost two hours each way and it also meant stopping for a meal sometime during the day. That was just what Alice wanted.

So, on a designated Wednesday morning, the three of them departed for Brown University. Alice sat in the back seat nervously monitoring every silence and every spoken word between her father and Myrna. She did not know what to expect but she was hoping for the best. As a start, she wanted them to knit their loose relationship into a strong friendship. From there, she was sure an affair would blossom.

For Alice, the day turned out to be interesting and puzzling. She found that the mechanics of formal education and loan applications were complicated. She took all of that in stride. What she could not tell was what her father and Mrs. Cabot thought of each other. They were compatible talking with each other but they didn't appear to get intimate. They were polite but not animated. She had to find out.

The next day, Thursday, Alice met Jeffrey in the one class they had together and she told him to hurry over to Russo's right after school because she had to talk with him. Her brusque manner made Jeffrey smile but he knew that she hadn't intended to be rude; what she wanted was to hear if his mother had said anything to him about her trip.

When he arrived at Russo's, Alice was already eating a hot fudge sundae while she waited for him. He got one for himself and then sat opposite her in a booth. "Well, at least I don't have to pay for your sundae," he said.

"You hardly ever do anyhow," she replied. "But, that's not important. What did your mother say about our trip?"

"Not much, she said that you had a good visit and that she learned that colleges handle things differently than when she went to school."

"No, no. I don't mean about me. What did she say about my father?"

"Nothing at all."

Alice got a little annoyed. She said, "She must have said something. Why didn't you ask?"

"Alice, you're nuts. What am I to ask my mother? 'Did you and Alice's father fall in love?' I can't ask my mother anything like that. Did you ask your father if he was in love?"

Alice toyed with her sundae for a minute or two and then sighed as she answered, "Maybe you're right. But, I don't understand. I know that they enjoyed each other yesterday. I know it."

"Really? Just how do you know it?"

"Listen, I watched them carefully. At first, their conversations were a little formal. By lunchtime they were talking freely and what they were telling each other about was their children. My father talked about us and your mother talked about you. When two parents chat, in detail, about their families you can be absolutely sure that they are comfortable with each other."

Now it was Jeffrey's turn to play with his ice cream. After a while he said, "OK, that's a valid observation. That doesn't mean they have to fall into each other's arms immediately does it?"

"Maybe not. However, I saw them and I know they are attracted to each other. They need more time together. I'm convinced that we are going to become brother and sister."

Jeffrey shook his head negatively as he laughed and said, "What did I do to deserve that? You may be right but there is one thing I think that you are overlooking. They need conversations between themselves; they won't speak freely when any of their children are listening to their conversations. Children and Cupid are not compatible."

"Jeff, you are absolutely right. I hadn't thought about that. They need privacy just like we do. What can we do?"

"Absolutely nothing. They have to give signals to each other. If they can't figure it out we can't do anything for them."

Alice continued her school visitations and asked Myrna to accompany her. Myrna did, when she could, but she was only able to be at two others. Those that she did attend she seemed to enjoy. She and Alice's father got along but Alice didn't have the feeling that their conversations were getting any more intimate. She felt sure that if they were alone, they could be more open with each other.

Alice felt frustrated. She wanted her father and Myrna to get together; she could not understand why they didn't. After this latest attempt to bring them heart to heart, she started to wonder if she shouldn't just butt out of the match making business.

****

Parents do not talk about their private lives with their children. Their personal emotions, their bodily functions, their past loves, their adult life, aside from parenting, has no connection to the raising of their kids. So, that life is kept separate from the discussions parents have as their children grow. That is a major reason that a parent is such a mystery and a deity to their offspring.

Alice was correct about her father and Myrna, but she didn't know it. The social stockades that Ben and Myrna had spent years building to protect themselves were still there but they were beginning to crumble. Since their walls were high, it would take some time before the breach would become evident. Neither Ben nor Myrna realized that their bastions had been compromised. After all, who can tell which snowflake in the blizzard is the snowflake that caused the roof to collapse?

Ben was the first to feel the effects of change. He did not have to change his attitude as much as Myrna. He had been a fountain of love for his children and had not closed himself off from part of society as Myrna had. He had avoided personal involvement with women but that was because he was shy and he was dedicated to his children; he did not have a grudge against females. It was not that he was impervious to the charm and beauty of Myrna; it was more that he was afraid of being rejected. As his emotions melted into an increasing desire for love, he was bothered with his own shortcomings. He felt that Myrna would snicker at his lack of formal education, his lowly profession, and even his ethnic background. He wanted to lower his shield and get closer to Myrna but, after his encounter with BeBe, he was afraid to even try.

Myrna, on the other hand, had an entirely different set of problems. First, was the hatred she felt for her ex-husband. She had been shrouded in that emotion for so long that it tarnished almost all of her thoughts. Added to that was her disdain for men due to the sexual bias she had to overcome in order to earn her living. It would take her longer to lower her shield than it took Ben. But it was happening. During her Saturday morning breakfasts with Lydia, she began praising him; she even began to forget the slight difference in height between the two of them. Lydia recognized the change and began to smile.

The warmer weather melted the snow and raised hopes that winter was coming to an end. The air carried the fragrant smell of fertility for gardens, for animals, and for human hopes. Spring finally stood its ground and ordered winter away. No one was more pleased at the change than Ben. He prepared his garden for planting as soon as he could. The following week saw clear skies, sunshine and the promise of glorious warm weather.

That Sunday, he sat on his side porch alone; Alice had gone to the movies with a friend and the boys were still in school. He had open catalogues of fruits and flowers on his lap but he really was not paying attention to them. He was restless and he didn't know exactly why. He paced up and down for a while and, all of a sudden, he said, "To Hell with it."

He went into the house, dialed a number, and then almost hung up before the call was connected. When the person on the other end said, "Hello," he took a deep breath before he spoke.

He responded. "Myrna, this is Ben Da Vinci, are you busy right now?"

"No, Ben, as a matter of fact I'm sitting here reading the *Boston Globe.*"

"I'm going to go for a walk at Breakheart Reservation. The weather is too pleasant to stay indoors. Would you be interested in coming along?" He held his breath not knowing how Myrna would reply.

"That sounds like a wonderful idea. If you can give me ten minutes to do a couple of things here, I'll be ready."

Ben almost sang he was so happy. When he picked Myrna up she got into the car and said, "Thank you for inviting me. What a wonderful idea. I was just sitting around wasting time. Jeffrey has gone off with his friends to play basketball. I had to leave him a note."

"How is he doing in picking a school to go to?"

"He's narrowed his choices to either Brown or Bowdoin. He seems so relaxed and mature lately; I used to worry so about him." Then, she thought a second and added, "I haven't heard from Alice in a while. Is she doing well?"

"Oh yes, she'll be over to see you shortly. She thinks she is leaning towards Smith College but not without first talking to you. She has a great deal of faith in you."

"And I think she is a lovely girl. She has to be the apple of your eye; you should be quite proud of her."

They drove the rest of the way making comfortable small talk. They walked along Ridge Trail and both Myrna and Ben seemed to come alive as they strolled through the innocence of nature's beauty.

As they neared the end of their walk, Ben said, "I'm glad you were able to come with me. I used to come here with my kids when they were very young. I have nothing but happy memories of this place."

Myrna stopped and smiled at Ben. "I have fond memories also. My father used to bring me here when I was a child. We both appreciated this place. I thank you for rescuing me from a solitary afternoon. I have enjoyed the day."

Their conversation, on the way home, was much more lively. When the car stopped in front of Myrna's house, she said, "Ben, if you do this again I hope you'll ask me to join you. I truly enjoyed our walk." With that she got out of the car and went into her house.

When Ben entered his house, Alice was sitting at the kitchen table reading a book. "Dad, where have you been? You left no note and I wasn't sure where you had gone. I didn't prepare anything for supper because I didn't know what time you would be back."

Ben came over to where she was sitting and kissed her on the top of her head. "Don't even be concerned about supper. Where have I been? Well let me tell you and you will be pleased.

"I finally did what you have been urging me to do. I was with Myrna Cabot all afternoon. We went walking in Breakheart and we both enjoyed ourselves.

"Now, what do you have to say?"

Alice jumped up squealing with delight. "Oh, Dad, I'm so happy. I knew it would turn out happily for both of you. When are you going to see her again?"

"I'm not sure. In the meantime she wants you to let her know how you are coming along with picking a school.

"I'm hungry. Come on, let's go out and get a hamburger."

The following Saturday, Ben called Myrna and made arrangements to pick her up again early Sunday afternoon. They planned to go to Breakheart again but the weather didn't cooperate, it rained hard. Instead, they went into Boston and visited the Museum of Fine Arts. As they wandered through the exhibitions, Myrna said, "My father would take my brother and me here once or twice a year."

Ben chuckled and answered, "When I was very young, my mother and I came here almost every week. She knew almost every guard by name; she taught me a lot about painting."

That caught Myrna by surprise. "I didn't know that. Was your mother an artist?"

Ben replied, "She had had a little training. My mother was a lovely woman. She received a classical education in Italy but, because of her accent, she couldn't get a job in this country. She spent a lot of time making sure I was exposed to music, art and literature. I never realized the gifts she gave me until I had my own children. That is why I tried to pass her love of the arts on to my kids. I wish she had lived long enough to have met her grandkids."

Both of them remained quiet after that remark. They softly spoke as they pointed out paintings or details to each other. After a few hours, when they left the museum, Ben suggested that they drive down town and eat at Durgin-Park.

As they were eating, Ben said, "That museum holds so much beauty and love. I tell my three that life would be so much easier if everyone in the world would go to a museum and let it speak to them."

Myrna answered, "You may be right. I've never thought about it before." Then she remembered his reference to his mother. "Your mother must have loved life very much to have pass these values on to you."

Ben felt a little uncomfortable talking about himself so much, so, to change the subject, he said clumsily, "As the weather gets warmer, I will be busy working on Sundays on my 'farm.'"

Myrna, noticing the change and recalling how much she had enjoyed the harvest of his fruits and vegetables, asked, "Can I get a job as a farm hand? If you hire me I'll work cheaply and I'll be there every Sunday. Scout's Honor."

Ben laughed and replied, "Your application will be considered and, if you are hired, the 'farm' will supply the necessary tools." He didn't believe Myrna was serious and the exchange turned to other topics.

The following Sunday, after church, Ben was completely surprised when, as he turned the car into the driveway, he and Alice saw Myrna sitting on the porch steps, dressed in blue jeans.

Alice was pleased to see her. She leaped from the car, hugged her, and said, "Mrs. Cabot, I'm surprised you're here. Are you waiting for us?"

"Yes, Alice, your father has hired me to help him on the 'farm.' Didn't he tell you?"

Alice was tickled that both parents were becoming aware of each other. "No, he sometimes forgets to inform me of the important things. I'm glad you are going to help him; I have a tennis match to play."

Ben changed into work clothes and they spent the afternoon getting his garden ready for planting. As they worked and sweated they began to loosen up and talk more directly about themselves.

And this became the pattern for the following Sundays even when Ben's two sons came home. The four offspring always found important errands they had to run; they left their parents alone hoping they would discover each other in what the four of them now called "the Malden Garden of Eden."

Myrna and Ben talked as they worked, planting, fertilizing, water-

ing, and harvesting their garden. Episodes from their pasts were revealed for each of them to share with the other. There was no shame or
cringing from the truth in any of their conversations.

Once Myrna began talking, it was like opening a sluice gate into
her past. The hatred she had for her ex-husband and the distrust she
felt for all men washed through the gate and started to dissipate. The
poison in her system was replaced with the serenity of cheerfulness.
She began to be a happier and better person.

The identical process was happening with Ben. He began to talk
about his mother and her gentle influence much more than his father's
influence and his discipline. His uneasiness about his Italian background and upbringing began to ease and he felt more self confident
about himself. He began to be a better and happier person. In his
thoughts, Myrna was becoming his intimate companion and friend.

Like the plants they were gardening, their shoots were growing
and vining towards each other.

****

Lydia was the first to notice the change in Myrna. During their
Saturday morning coffee meetings, Myrna seemed more relaxed; she
laughed a lot and her comments about all men was less vitriolic. She
never mentioned her ex-husband and rarely said anything about Ben.
However, there was a lot of talk about Alice and the Da Vinci family.
When Greg and Billy came home for the summer, Myrna spent a long
time describing the noise and the bedlam that now filled their house.
"When we were growing up, my brother and I never made nearly as
much noise as that family does."

Lydia asked, "Is it offensive? Does it bother you?"

"Oh no, it never gets out of control. It's just that they have so much fun it can get boisterous. They are well mannered and Ben keeps them under control."

"And what does Jeffrey make of all of this?"

"He seems to fit right in with the boys. They are on their summer schedules and the boys seem to be over my house as much as they are over at their own house."

Lydia giggled, then she smiled as she asked, "Do you know what I think, my Dear?"

"No."

"I think that you have fallen in love."

"That's ridiculous. With whom?"

Lydia giggled again and wagged a finger at Myrna, "Quit being coy with me, Missy. You know who I mean. The post man."

"Lydia, I'm too old to fall in love. I'll admit that lately everything about life seems nicer. And for some reason, I feel clean and I enjoy doing things I used to consider a chore. But that's not love." She hesitated for a second and then added in a soft voice, "I don't think it's love. I'm just too damn old."

Lydia shook her head and had the final word, "I'm not going to press the point. I'm the one who's really old; you're not. You'll find out for yourself what I'm talking about. I couldn't be happier for the both of you."

Myrna was a little frightened by Lydia's observation so she tried to bury it in her subconscious; however, it wouldn't stay there. The thought that Lydia said she was in love kept popping into her mind and she would quickly replant it.

A few weeks later, New England was hit by a bad storm. A nor'easter, came ashore on a weekend and deluged the area with heavy rains and howling winds. That Sunday, Myrna assumed that there would be no outside activities so she settled down to do some household chores. Her phone rang and it was Ben who spoke, "Are you busy this afternoon?"

"No, not really, but you're not thinking of gardening in weather like this are you?"

"I hadn't thought of it. No, I want to take you somewhere and show you something. I think you will enjoy yourself."

"A mystery trip?"

"Not really. It's a place I like and haven't been to in years. It's a place that I think you'll enjoy."

"That sounds like an offer I can't refuse."

"Myrna, dress warmly and put on a raincoat. I'll be over to pick you up in a few minutes."

As Ben drove he explained to Myrna, "We are going to go to Red Rock. It is a huge rock that sticks out from the shore. I used to take my kids there and they have fallen in love with it. Did you ever go to Swampscott and see it?"

"No, I never have. What is there?"

"Nothing but the ocean, the Atlantic Ocean. It should be fierce in this storm."

It was. The wind howled so badly Myrna and Ben had to yell to be heard. The rain came down in sheets almost forcing them to shut their eyes. The wind blew the tops off the waves as the tons of water relentlessly pounded the rocks and destroyed themselves in explosions of salty, white, high rising foam. The roar of the wind and the ocean surge almost hurt their ears. It was nature showing her power and her disdain for the two humans clutching hard to the metal guard rails as they watched her fury. Myrna was so excited by the anger of the storm that she kept pounding Ben on the back of his shoulder and screaming words at him; he couldn't make out what she was saying.

When they got back in the car, which was parked on the causeway, Ben handed Myrna a towel and she wiped the streaming water from her face. The wind rocked the car as they sat. Ben turned the heater on and tuned the radio to WGBH; Brahms third symphony was being played.

Myrna gasped, "My God, I've never experienced anything like that in my entire life. That was thrilling; I'm shaking I was so scared. How magnificent, how beautiful.

"Thank you, for inviting me, Ben. It is something I'll remember my entire life."

They sat in the car marveling at what they were seeing. Finally, Myrna said, "I'm getting hungry. Let's get a pizza and I'm buying today. I know a place that makes really good pizza."

The restaurant she picked happened to be the same one that Ben and BeBe had been in the night they parted. As they walked in Ben said to himself, "If you live long enough, you certainly do meet the ghosts of your past." Then he thought no more about it.

As they ate their pizza and drank their beer, Myrna asked, "You said that you took your children to Red Rock?"

"Yes, many times when they were growing up. We certainly never went in weather like we had today."

Myrna hesitated before asking her next question, "Did you and Esther go there often?"

Ben replied quietly, "Oh no, I never took Esther to Red Rock. Don't forget that our kids were very young when she died. I only started taking them places after she passed because I was trying to make up to them for their loss. I wanted to be a good father and they were so little and bewildered."

Her next question was asked in such a low tone that Ben hardly heard her, "Do you miss Esther very much?"

Ben put his slice of pizza down and looked Myrna squarely in the eyes. He could see the beginning of wrinkles near her eyes and her mouth but he thought that she was still a beautiful woman. He didn't know why he made that observation just as he was trying to answer her question. "Myrna, when I married Esther we were madly in love. She died; but my love didn't disappear. It never should. The living would dishonor the memories of those we loved if it did.

"However, my marriage ended a long time ago. It took me years to reconcile myself to the fact that it is over, but it is. My marriage is history, cherished, but still history. Esther insisted that I go on living and loving and I should do both out of respect for her memories and for myself. I am just beginning to realize that she was correct; life and love have to continue.

"The answer to your question is that I miss her but I'm not frozen to the past. I miss everyone I have ever loved. I miss my parents. Let me ask you, don't you miss your mother and father?"

"Of course I do and I understand what you are saying. Love is a sacred torch whose flame should never die. I'm sorry that I even asked you those questions; I'm not sure why I did. I was out of bounds and I apologize."

Ben opened his mouth to say something and then stopped without uttering a sound. They drove home and then, instead of stopping in front of Myrna's house and letting her out, Ben parked the car in his own driveway. The rain had stopped and the wind had died down but water was still dripping off of everything. He said, "Come on, I'll walk you home."

When they reached Myrna's house Ben followed Myrna up the

stairs to her porch. He asked her to sit in one of the rocking chairs and he sat beside her. With no preamble he said, "Myrna, I love you."

Myrna put her hand on his forearm. "Ben, please don't say that unless you really mean it. I made a wrong decision years ago and I have paid a bitter price. I don't want to be hurt again. I don't want you to be hurt. I do care for you, very much."

She paused briefly and began again. "I guess I sound all mixed up. I don't mean to be. I'm just trying to be careful."

Ben took her hands in his and spoke softly. It was hard for him to tell Myrna of his feelings when he was mired in his own self doubts. "I'm not much as a person; I'm not famous or talented, but I do love you deeply. I have for a long time. From the very first time you came storming into my house I have admired you not only for your beauty but for your courage. You make my days sweet and my dreams happy. I just can't stand not telling you how I feel.

"I have felt this way for a long time. I have to tell you what is in my heart even if I don't know what's in your heart. Myrna, I love you, I need you, I want to marry you."

Myrna's eyes filled with tears. "Oh Ben, I'm so happy. I do love you. I should have known that I love you and I didn't. Two weeks ago, Lydia told me I was in love and I told her 'No.' She is so wise.

"You have no idea how much I love you. If you ask me to marry you, I will say 'Yes' before you finish speaking.

"Oh my God, I'm in love."

They stood up and kissed fiercely, tongue to tongue. After a few minutes Myrna pushed away almost gasping for breath. "Listen," she said. "I will marry you but, for now, I don't want our children or any-one else to know about us."

Ben hugged her and laughed as he said, "I'm sure that it won't take long for them to figure it out. Alice has been pushing me in your direction for a long time and she watches me like a hawk. I'm not good at keeping secrets so I'm sure Alice will discover what is going on between us almost as soon as I get home. But why should we hide the way we feel?"

Myrna nuzzled against Ben. "I love you, Ben Da Vinci. I'm not trying to hide anything. I can admit to it; I couldn't before. I just want to enjoy this feeling that is between you and me. We have to make plans but I don't want to think about them, at least not yet. I want to bathe in my own private pool of happiness.

"You're correct. It won't take long for our nosy kids to ferret out our intentions. Even if it's only fifteen minutes, I would like to have the joy of a secret. I know it's silly, but I'm giddy. I'm in love."

Ben massaged her back as he answered, "You're not the only one either giddy or in love. I'm walking on stilts. I want to marry you as soon as we can. We have a lot to planning to do."

"You're right. Let's get married quickly. I hope you want the same thing I want, a small, private ceremony. We need to think the details through but I want us to do it together.

"Oh Ben, I can't get over the fact that you have changed my life. I can't get over the fact that Lydia was right. I can't get over the fact that I didn't know I was in love. I'm so happy I can't get over anything. That nor'easter was my engagement party. I can't get over it. I'm so happy.

"Oh my God, I'm in love."

14

Samuel Skinner was angry. He slammed the phone down on its cradle and pounded the side of his fist on the top of the desk. "SON-OF-A-BITCH," he yelled. He had just been talking to his ex-wife, Myrna Cabot, and he had been unable to provoke her; she had been as uncooperative as she always was but he could not arouse her fear or her anger.

That bothered him. For years he had been able to manipulate her moods with his threats or his bullying. For the last few months she had shown no concern for whatever he said or did. There was something going on that made her unafraid of him and he did not like that. It was bad enough that she had divorced him; the thought that he could be losing control was unacceptable. Something had to be done.

In the past, he had been able to work on his son, Jeffrey, and find out whatever he wanted to know. However, after his scheme to get his wife in trouble by having her teenage son caught driving with open liquor bottles in the car didn't work, Jeffrey seemed more sullen than ever. It had been a good scheme but Jeffrey had gotten home and parked the vehicle before Skinner was able to notify the police.

Whether he was unwilling to talk or not, Skinner should be able to get whatever information he needed out of his son. After all, he was an experienced attorney who could easily sift the wheat from the chaff.

So Skinner, based on his needs as a concerned and loving parent, made arrangements to meet Jeffrey for lunch at a local restaurant in Malden. It was on a Friday and he arrived early. As his son came to join him, his thoughts were on how best to get what he wanted to know out of him. As they ate, Skinner asked Jeffrey what he was doing this summer.

Guilelessly, Jeffrey told him about Greg and Billy and the weight-lifting and the big garden that Mr. Da Vinci was working with his mother. Skinner changed the direction of his questions and started to ask about the father of his friends, Billy and Greg.

After he had pumped Jeffrey enough to give him a picture of what was going on, he leaned forward and asked, "How long has your mother been seeing your friend's father?"

Jeffrey seemed surprised at the question and he replied without thinking, "All summer, I guess. They both started working in Mr. Da Vinci's garden last spring and things just worked out from there."

Skinner kept his composure but he was furious. She was the only woman who had broken up with him; he was the one who had always dumped his partners. Since Myrna had had the nerve to get rid him he never wanted her to remarry; that would close off his chances to get even.

Then he made a monumental blunder. Without understanding that Jeffrey's loyalties would be completely with his mother and his friends, Skinner tried to enlist him to help break up the relationship between Myrna and Ben.

"Listen son," Skinner began, "this man Da Vinci is only a barber and he is not worthy of your mother and you. We have to do something to keep your mother from making a grave mistake."

For the first time in his life, Jeffrey openly disagreed with his father. "Dad, I don't think you understand. Mr. Da Vinci is an outstanding person no matter how he earns his living. Mom has never been happier and I'm all for him."

"He is a foreigner, a Wop, A Dago. Probably second or third generation. I see these kind all the time; I make my living defending these uneducated immigrants. Surely, you don't want your mother subjected to these kind of people."

There was no way that Jeffrey was going to let his father insult his friends. Thoughts of Greg and Alice and Billy flashed through his mind. Jeffrey replied angrily, "You don't know anything about the Da Vincis. You've never met them. If you had, you would throw your cookbook ideas about them away.

"I'm proud to be their friend and Mr. Da Vinci will probably be a better husband for my mother than my father ever was."

With that, Jeffrey got up from the table and walked out of the restaurant without a backward glance. Skinner sat there for a while, payed the bill, and left. He was both stunned by Jeffrey's statements and more angry than ever. Skinner was determined to show Myrna that he was a better man than this ignorant, Italian bastard barber. He was absolutely sure that he was.

When Myrna got home from work later that day she found Jeffrey sitting on the steps waiting for her. She guessed that he might want to talk about his visit with his father, so she sat beside him. "I'm sorry, Mom, but I messed up today." With that, he told her in detailed description about his luncheon meeting with Skinner. He finished by saying, "Mom, I didn't mean to tell him about you and Mr. Da Vinci.

He just drew it out of me before I knew it. Now, I've gotten you into trouble again."

"Honey, don't be concerned. You did nothing wrong and whether Skinner knows about Ben or not doesn't make one bit of difference. In one way, I'm glad that he does know; you and I and the Da Vincis have nothing to hide from him or from anyone else. Don't be concerned. I'm certainly not."

"Well, if you're not worried, then I'm not either. But shouldn't you go ahead and tell Mr. Da Vinci about this meeting? Dad may try to do something."

"Jeffrey, I'd be surprised if he doesn't try to meddle in some way. But he won't try anything without first calling me to try to bully me. When that happens I will talk to Ben; until then, we don't know very much. So, let's not say anything for a while."

The next morning, at 7:30, Myrna began to learn about Skinner's mood. He called, and in his best baritone voice he began, "What in the Hell are you thinking about by going out with a Wop barber? How could you have sunk so low?"

In the past, she would be cowed by such an onslaught. Either the fear of their past relationship or her concern that he would turn Jeffrey against her would have put her on the defensive. She heard his words but they went only as far as her ears; they did not enter her mind. "Skinner, I'm telling you right now I'll hang up if you don't change your tone. What I do is my business, not yours."

He caught his breath. His ex-wife had never said anything like that before. He decided on a different tactic. "You may be right about that but I'm concerned for my son's welfare. He should not be exposed to ignorant people who have no right to be in this country. He should meet only people with high principles."

Myrna was furious. She was not going to let Skinner slander Ben or his family. She recklessly said, "You should have considered your son's well being before you went whoring around and stole my money without my permission."

Skinner immediately snapped back, "It's not my fault that I married an inadequate woman. Since I couldn't get it at home, I got it wherever I could."

Myrna hung up without saying a word. She was shaking. Nastiness is like a putrid smell; even when the air clears, the memory of the stink remains. She wanted to rush into Ben's arms for reassurance so she called him. He came over immediately and she clung to him for support; she needed reassurance from the new love of her life.

Myrna told him everything that had happened from the time that Jeffrey had lunch with Skinner up through Skinner's spiteful phone call to her. Then, she started to cry. "Love, what are we going to do? Why is my past always coming back to trip me up? Why won't it go away?"

Ben patted Myrna on her back as he held her. He said, "Ladylove, we are molded by our past. That's how we know who we are; that's how we learn. My past has taught me that I love you. I adore you. We are together and you have nothing to fear. We will work our way through this.

"Please don't cry, Ladylove. I'll do anything to help. We will straighten this out. We will be together and live happily ever after. I want to marry you, we should marry. You are more necessary for me than the air I breathe; you are my life."

Myrna snuffled for a while and then pulled away from Ben. She smiled weakly and then put her head back on his shoulder. "I didn't know I needed anyone as much as I need you at this moment. You are my heartbeat, Ben. My dearest, I only wish I had met you earlier.

"What are we going to do about Skinner?"

Then she thought a second and added, "It's Saturday. Don't you have to go to work?"

Ben quietly replied, "Work is no problem. I can have one of the kids go down to the shop and hang a 'closed' sign on the door. It will do until I get there.

"As for us, there's a lot we can do. We know the future, so what happened in the past is not that important. First, let's have a cup of coffee, take a deep breath and talk. I want you in my life, so let's talk about getting married and getting married quickly.

"We will plan our wedding from the bottom up and there are a lot of details to take care of. What we tell our children, what we do about our houses, when we have the ceremony; there are lots of things to decide. When we finish, the path will be easier to follow. When we finish, you will not be looking at the past over your shoulder.

"And tomorrow night, let's have a big dinner and sit down with our kids and tell them what our plans are. They already know about us and it won't come as a surprise; more like a 'What took the two of you so long?' We have each other and that's what is most important. What do you think?"

Myrna agreed and they spent their time discussing and deciding until eventually, between them, they laid out a schedule of what had to be done. All of a sudden, they both felt an urgency to speed up their schedules; nature was beginning to rouse their passions.

Their first decision was when they would wed; they selected a date close to the time that the four of their children left for college. They then decided that, since Ben's house had more bedrooms than Myrna's, she would move in with Ben. She would decide later when, and if, to sell her home. They agreed to tell their children about their plans; they picked Sunday as the time to notify both families that all their scheming finally worked.

When they were through with their planning, Ben went to work and Myrna went shopping for food for tomorrow's dinner. That evening Ben announced to his children that Sunday evening, at 6:00, there was to be a dinner at which they were all to attend without any of their friends; it was for family alone and attendance was mandatory. He would not say another word about the reason for this extraordinary dinner but he could see the smirks on each of his children's faces the rest of the evening.

On Sunday, after he returned from church, he shooed everyone out of the house, refusing their help and telling them not to return until it was time to eat. They left and Myrna came over and they began to prepare their announcement meal. They cooked enough ham, fried chicken, mashed potatoes, lima beans, lasagna, corn on the cob, and cakes and desserts for an entire football team. They were so busy preparing their meal and setting their table that here was little time to smooch and celebrate their feelings for each other.

At 6:00PM, the table was loaded with food and wine and Ben, his three children, and Myrna and her son and two guests, Lydia and Frank Bradford were seated. Ben rose to his feet, lifted a glass of wine and began the ceremonies. "Welcome everyone. For those of you who think you know the reason for this celebration let me tell you that you are wrong; I'm not planning on joining the priesthood.

"Instead, I want to tell you that Myrna Cabot has consented to marry me and I'm bursting with happiness. This news is no shock to my children, Alice has been dragging me towards the altar for years. Until I met Myrna I was reluctant to head in that direction. That certainly has changed.

"I don't display my feelings easily, but this summer we have found each other and our love has brought us together and made our lives as sweet as maple syrup.

"So to my friends, Lydia and Frank, and to my family, let peace and friendship reign at this table. Welcome to all of you and, above all, welcome to my heart my beloved fiancee, Myrna, whom I adore.

"Salud."

With that, Ben raised his glass of wine towards Myrna, whose happiness enhanced her beauty and her demeanor, and he invited everyone to drink. The initial noise level that arose from such a small group was unbelievable. When the din subsided, Greg stood up, refilled his glass, and said, "My first statement is from the three of us, our father's children. We want him to know that it took us a long time to get him started in the right direction. We have done our job correctly and he is now no longer our responsibility.

"My next statement is from the four of us, Jeff, Alice, Billy and me. All of us may be too young to be drinking this wine legally, but that doesn't matter because each of us is old enough to understand and appreciate the sacrifices the two of you made to raise us."

Greg paused because he was choked up. Then he again began, "I won't go into that. What I will say is that the four of us couldn't be happier. Each one of us gain a new parent, either a new mother or a new father.

"So, the four of us, as your children, say to each of you, we love both of you, and we are glad to be part of this new family."

The hugging, kissing and eating that followed would have been shameful if it hadn't been so sincere. It lasted until everyone was exhausted and stuffed. Frank and Lydia left about ten; both were a little tipsy and a lot happy. They had helped match up two of their favorite people. By midnight, what was left of the food had been put away and the house had been cleaned and straightened up and everyone had kissed everyone else goodnight. Myrna and Jeffrey went home and everyone fell into their own deep, dreamless sleep.

GRADUATION

15

Love is a volatile explosive made up of carnal desires and spiritual feelings. Its formula is different for each human being in the world and it is buried deeply within each individual's psyche. Until a man and woman with the identical formula meet, it remains inert. Once triggered, the awesome power of love changes lives forever. That is the mechanism that insures the human race perpetuates its species.

In the beginning, when societies were not as stratified and religions were not as codified, living was much simpler than in our modern world. On every continent on our globe there were diverse groups of humans each with their own divergent societies and religions. Their customs and rules were made for the sole purpose of making life easier for their people and these rules were not as complicated as are ours.

Myrna and Ben were about to find out how complex our society has become.

Ben had made an immediate appointment with the Pastor of Sacred Hearts Church. He wanted Father Dante to meet Myrna and help guide them both through the rules and regulations necessary for a Catholic wedding. When he introduced her to the priest, it was simply as, "Myrna Cabot."

Father Dante was a tall, older man who had soldiered for God for almost fifty years. He was gray headed and stoop shouldered from his battles but, when he smiled, which was rarely, his inner peace showed and he looked almost saintly. They had coffee and chatted. He told Myrna that Ben and his family had been faithful parishioners for years and, while making small talk, he was surprised to find that Myrna had lived much of her life in Malden.

Finally, he said, "Ben, what was it that you wanted to talk to me about?"

"Father Dante, Myrna and I want to get married."

His face lit up with pleasure, "I was hoping that was what this meeting was about."

Ben continued, "However, Myrna is divorced."

"That presents a problem. He looked at Myrna as he spoke, "You will have to file a petition to ask that your marriage be annulled."

Myrna was disturbed by this news and she asked sharply, "I don't understand. My wedding was not in a Catholic church and my divorce was finalized over ten years ago. What does that have to do with Ben and me getting married in this church now?"

Father Dante raised both of his palms near his shoulders. "Mrs. Cabot, please listen to me. I understand what you are saying and I respect your feelings. This is a difficult, emotional subject and it will not be easy for you. I don't want you angry at the Catholic Church and I certainly don't want you upset with me. I will always be here to help you in any way I can.

"Let me explain the importance the church places on annulments.

If I'm not clear in my explanation, you will ask me questions, won't you? I really want to help."

Myrna smiled at him and softened her tone, "Father Dante, I promise I won't shoot the messenger."

"Good. The Catholic Church believes that marriage between a man and a woman is sacred; we consider it binding in the eyes of God. That sacredness is for all marriages not just for Catholics. It makes no difference as to the faith of the partners or if the service was a civil ceremony; every marriage is regarded as sacred. The Catholic Church believes that marriages bind spouses together for their entire lives. When a marriage fails the Church has to examine the marriage to determine if it was valid from the beginning. If the marriage was not valid, the Church can issue a declaration of nullity.

"A divorced person cannot remarry in a Catholic Church unless that person has had the previous marriage annulled."

Myrna was puzzled and asked, "Even if the person has a divorce?"

Father Dante replied, "That is considered a civil law that separates partners legally. The Catholic Church does not accept a divorce as church law. An annulment examines the marriage to see if, for any reason, the marriage did not meet the required church values. If the marriage did not, an annulment declares the marriage invalid and you will be free to marry in a Catholic Church."

"Are you saying that, until I receive an annulment, Ben and I cannot be married in a Catholic Church?"

Father Dante simply said, "Yes."

"How long does it take to get an annulment?"

"I would say between twelve and eighteen months. The average is probably close to sixteen months."

Ben was the one to ask the next question, "We are expected to wait all of that time before we get married?"

"Ben, I know that this is a bitter pill for you and Mrs. Cabot to swallow. I could tell you that the waiting period for an annulment proves your love for each other. However, you are both mature, intelligent adults and will decide what you want. I can't tell you what to do. The only thing that I can tell you is that you will need an annulment if you wish to be married in a Catholic church."

The conversation continued for over an hour longer as Father Dante asked Myrna about her previous marriage and explained how to file for a declaration of nullity. He also explained how a diosecan Tribunal reviews the marriage and how their opinion is forwarded to another Tribunal for review, and agreement, before the declaration is issued.

At the end of the discussion, he saw them both out of the building and, as he said goodbye, he said, "Ben and Myrna, I know that you are both upset by our talk. I feel sorry that both of you are unhappy. Please, please, contact me if I can be of any help to you."

Ben and Myrna sat in gloomy silence after they got into her car. Then, she said, "I like Father Dante. I do not like his message."

"I'm disappointed. Myrna, you're not the guilty party and you deserve better. I understand why the Church has its annulment procedure but you've been through enough. I don't think it is fair to ask you to open up old wounds and wait a year while the Church ponders our future.

"Boys and girls have been pairing off since Adam and Eve and they had no religious procedures getting in their way. I think we should look to see what our alternatives are."

That evening they held a family conference at Ben's house where they explained, in detail, their meeting with Father Dante and their disappointment at the outcome. Alice was the first to react. She moved to the sofa where Myrna was sitting with Jeffrey and she sat down beside Myrna.

She put her arm around her shoulder and said, "That's not fair to Mrs. Cabot. They have no right to treat her like that. I'm not sure that I want to stay in that church if that's the way they treat decent people."

Despite the uncertainties that he and Myrna were facing, Ben had to smile. He said, "Alice, you are free to go to any Church you want, or even not to go to any Church you want. Even though I don't like the decision, the Catholic Church has every right to make the decision it did. Myrna and I will just have to move on from here."

Greg spoke up and asked, "Dad, if you marry outside of the church could you be excommunicated?"

Ben answered, "That is a good question and I'm not sure I know the answer. We didn't get into anything else besides talking about annulment.

"I don't think I'd be excommunicated but I don't know about taking Communion. I think I would still be allowed to take communion. Myrna couldn't take communion because she is not a Catholic; but that's the way it is now. It looks as if she and I still have many questions we need to have answered. The only thing I can say is that we are going to marry when we want. Any other consideration, at this time, is not important to either of us."

Later that evening when Ben and Myrna were sitting on the porch, Ben asked, "You really don't want to wait over a year to get married do you?"

"No. Do you?"

"Absolutely not, but I do have questions. I'll tell you what, let's go back tomorrow and ask Father Dante. Talking with him again will probably help us decide what to do."

The next morning they went to see Father Dante. He listened to their questions and answered them all. No, Ben would not be excommunicated if he married outside of the Catholic Church but he probably should not take Communion. However, he would be encouraged to attend Mass every Sunday to benefit from God's Words. They also talked more about obtaining an annulment and Ben and Myrna found out, to their complete surprise, that the process would continue even if they were not married in a Catholic church. They left knowing a lot more and feeling a lot better.

When they met with their children that evening the family atmosphere was more upbeat than their last meeting. Ben explained that he and Myrna had decided to marry as soon as their arrangements could be made and that the wedding would take place at Myrna's Church. When the annulment was announced they would examine their options and decide what to do.

After the discussion was over, ice cream and brownies were served and everyone was as pleased as if they were at a birthday party.

****

The next morning Myrna arrived at her office early feeling rested and content; she was even humming as she unlocked her door. As she started to enter Skinner came into view. He was carrying a big bouquet of dark, red roses. There was a snap to her voice as she asked. "What are you doing here?"

"I may have overstepped the bounds of good taste during our last phone conversation," Skinner said in his honey-speaking voice. "I would like to smoke the pipe of peace with you."

Myrna didn't answer at first, she kept walking into her office and sat at her desk. Skinner followed her, holding his bouquet in his right hand. "I'm due in court shortly, Skinner. I don't know that we have anything to say to each other. What is this pipe of peace you are talking about?"

"Myrna, Dear, I want to apologize to you; I don't want you hating me."

She looked at him a few seconds before she replied, "Skinner, I don't hate you anymore. This summer I have found a better way to live. I've met someone who has changed my life. Right now, if I had to tell the truth, I would say that I almost feel sorry for you."

Although Skinner's expression didn't change, he still kept his professional smile, he became so enraged that he curled his toes inside his shoes. "Myrna, I'm glad that you don't hate me. Tell me about your new boy friend."

She was not sure about Skinner. That was always the way he began, friendly and innocently. He could get nasty very quickly if it suited his purpose. Until she knew what he was up to, Myrna decided to keep him at arm's length. "He is not a 'boy friend'. We are going to set a date to get married."

This was the second piece of bad news for Skinner but he was not going to show his inner reaction. He smiled and waved a hand in salute. "And just when is your wedding planned?"

Myrna became cautious. She was wary of Skinner and his motives. She replied, "Depending upon the church's schedule, we would like to get married before our kids leave for school. That is probably no longer than a month from now."

In a warm, sincere tone of voice, Skinner asked, "Are you sure that you are doing the right thing?"

Myrna was sure he was fishing. She answered, "After years of being single and fighting with my ex-husband? Yes, I'm sure."

"He must be quite a person to make you feel that way despite his background and his deficiencies. You are very fortunate."

Myrna felt intrigued. She was curious about the picture Skinner had of Ben and she was confident that she could stand up to Skinner when it came to cross examinations. "Since you know so much, tell me, just what is his background and what are his deficiencies?"

"Well, coming from poor Italian immigrants, and being only a barber, I'm not sure he has money enough to support you in a comfortable manner."

Myrna interrupted Skinner with a spontaneous laugh. "Come off it, Skinner. First of all, if you check the public records you will see that he is one of the biggest property owners of commercial real estate in Malden. He has more money than you and I put together and doubled. Making money is not what motivates him.

"We are going to share expenses, but not in the way that you and I once did. Actually, our arrangements are none of your business."

Skinner did not like the way this interview was going, but he was determined not to give up; he had to find a way to spoil her happiness. "But what about his lack of education? What does a barber know about culture or good taste? You'd almost be better off marrying an Italian brick layer; that way you could get things done around the house if something broke and he still would be able to satisfy you when you wanted it."

Myrna didn't change her expression at Skinner's coarseness. She was every bit as good a lawyer as Skinner and she knew enough not to lose her temper or at least not to show that she had lost her temper. "Skinner, this conversation is over. You don't know a damn thing about my fiancee except that he has put you out of my life. You aren't worth the hair that falls on the floor of his barber shop.

"You are much more interested in a smoke screen than in a peace pipe. You go your way and I'll go mine.

"By the way, take your roses with you. You and I are finished. Get out and shut the door behind you."

Skinner stood up and, without saying a word, he left with her bouquet still in his hand.

16

As Skinner left Myrna's office, he was a seething volcano of hate and anger. He flung his roses into the first trash barrel he came across. His thoughts shot from him as fast and as maliciously as machine gun bullets. "Who the Hell was she to dismiss him like a school boy?" "This wasn't the first time that she had tried to dismiss him." "Who was this Wop bastard anyhow?" "How could she prefer a Dago barber over me?" "How could a Guinea son-of-a-bitch turn my own son against me?"

He wanted a drink, in fact several of them, but it was too early for the bars to be open and he was too far from the flask in his car. Instead, he crossed the street and entered Russo's for a cup of coffee; he needed time to think. And plan. Myrna had been the only woman who had left him on her own terms. That had gnawed at him ever since and he was determined to make her pay. The fact that he had character defects meant nothing to his ego; Myrna had dumped him and she deserved to be punished.

As he sat in a booth drinking what he considered tasteless coffee, his fury slowly shifted between Myrna and Ben. It struck him that she was now out from under his control. He could no longer influence her or affect her thinking. Her relationship with Ben was to blame for her new independence so Ben was the person he wanted to get even with the most. But how?

At first, he thought of doing physical harm to either Ben or his property, such as having Ben beaten up or torching his barber shop. He fantasized that he himself was the perpetrator doing either job but he came to the conclusion that he shouldn't be directly involved. It was too risky; he had seen too many people caught because of unplanned coincidences. He had his reputation to uphold so he shouldn't be connected to any crime. He knew enough criminal characters so that he could hire one to do whatever he paid him to do. On further reflection, though, he admitted to himself that was also a bad idea. They would take his money and do his dirty work but, sooner or later, they would attempt to blackmail him. Reluctantly, he conceded that he would have to give up the idea of violence. He needed to select another option and there wasn't much time left for him to disrupt Myrna's and Ben's wedding plans.

Skinner started to concentrate on what he believed to be Da Vinci's personality. He was a barber and barbers were quiet, docile types; they did not have the same dynamic personality that he had. Also, Da Vinci was the son of an immigrant and had not gone to college. Skinner wasn't sure if he even had a high school education. All indications led Skinner to believe that he could bully Da Vinci into a rift with Myrna. But time was not on his side; he would have to act quickly if he wanted to prevent their wedding.

He left Russo's, went home, and started to write a series of letters that he would mail to Da Vinci. He outlined five of them and then started to compose each one. His plan was to mail one of them daily to Da Vinci and, the following day, he would mail the same letter to Myrna so she could see what he had written. Skinner figured that five letters would be enough to get them angry at, and embarrassed with, each other. It wasn't a perfect plan but it was the best he could do. He was hopeful that it would work.

The first letter came for Ben on the following Wednesday. Alice always put his mail beside his plate at the dinner table and he looked at it before eating. He would sort out the junk mail and go through what was left. This particular letter had no return address and his name was typed on the front of the envelope. It was postmarked from Worcester, which seemed strange to him. He opened it and read:

"Da Vinci, I wonder if you are even literate enough to read this you ignorant son of a bitch. Almost all of you Wops have trouble with big words so I will stick with language even you can understand. You may think you are going to be happy marrying my cast off bitch but I doubt it. Bad as she is at screwing, even she is too good for a dumb Dago like you.

However, I'm willing to try and help by explaining to you the few things she does fairly well. I'll tell you all about them and make some suggestions on things I have tried.

Maybe you can get her to be better at screwing and sucking than I ever could.

More tomorrow."

The letter was unsigned. Ben stared at the letter so long that, when he looked up, his children were watching him. He asked quietly, "This was in today's mail?"

Billy replied, "Yes, Dad."

Ben folded the letter, put it back into the envelope, and stood up. "I'm not hungry. Excuse me." He then walked out of the kitchen, went to the porch, and sat by himself. His children looked at each other in surprise; their father had never left them at the table until everyone had finished eating. Ben did not talk very much the rest of the evening, answering all questions in short sentences, and he went to bed early.

Thursday evening, when Ben arrived home, there was another letter, postmarked from Worcester, beside his plate. This time, Greg, Billy, and Alice watched him as he picked up the envelope, inspected it, and finally opened it. It read:

"Even a dumb Dago like you should have known that a bitch like the one I'm throwing to you couldn't be faithful. While she has been love talking you she has been screwing with me. We have laughed many times over just how ignorant you really are.

You are an ignorant asshole Guinea and you deserve a lying whore like her.

Be my guest

I'll fill you in on our exploits tomorrow"

Ben did not even bother to excuse himself. He just went out on the porch and sat down; the letter and the envelope were in his right hand. Alice motioned Greg and Billy to come close and, when they did, she whispered, "What is going on? Something bad is bothering Dad and it has to do with those letters. Do either of you know anything about those letters?"

Her brothers agreed with her that the letters were upsetting their father but they knew nothing about them; they were as puzzled and concerned as she was.

An unhealthy air of complete gloom and unhappiness surrounded the Da Vinci household. And the atmosphere only got worse when another letter, postmarked from Worcester and without a return address, was delivered in Friday's mail. When Ben saw it next to his plate he didn't bother to open it. He picked the envelope up by one corner and tapped it on the table.

Greg finally asked, "Dad, what's the matter? Those letters have been upsetting you. Is there anything we can do to help?"

Ben looked at his children and shook his head. "What makes you think anything is bothering me?"

Greg replied, "Come off it, Dad. Ever since those letters started arriving you've been different. You haven't spoken to us or eaten with us in three days. You've been on your own planet. I'll bet you haven't talked to Mrs. Cabot, have you?"

"No, you're right about that; I haven't been in touch with Myrna. Yes, I'm having problems that I have to work through. That's all I want to say for the time being.

"I appreciate your concern and I love all of you but no one can help me sort this out. I need time to think."

****

While the Da Vinci's were bewildered, the Cabot's were almost dysfunctional. Myrna got the same letters one day later than Ben. The only difference was that typed on the top of each of her letters was the line, "Hi Myrna, here is a copy of what I mailed to your Dago bastard boy friend yesterday."

As she read each letter she squirmed in shame and then became furious; Skinner was attempting to cheapen her with lies and distortions. She wanted Ben to call and console her, but he didn't. She believed that Ben was hurt by the letters and disgusted with her. How else could he react when he read what Skinner claimed the two of them did?

She worried that not hearing from him meant that he was through with her. Each letter along with the ensuing silence from Ben, unsettled her all the more. She was battered and overcome with huge waves of negative emotions and she had no idea of whether she was swimming or drowning. Myrna was falling apart.

Saturday morning, she brought the letters with her when she went over Lydia's house for coffee. She handed them to Lydia without saying a word. After Lydia read them, Myrna said, "I don't know what to do. I haven't heard from Ben. I'm ashamed. I'm frightened. I think Ben is going to leave me. I can't bear the thought. Why hasn't he called? Why hasn't he called?

"Lydia, what can I do?" Myrna sat there with tears streaming down her face.

Lydia held her and comforted her with soothing words until Myrna had regained her composure. Then, Lydia said, "Darling, your ex-husband is as nasty and mean a human as I've ever encountered. He has thrown so much hate into his letters that I don't know how Ben is going to react. I'm not sure if he knows either, which is probably the reason he hasn't called.

"However, I do know this; your stewing and fretting is not doing you any good. What you need to do is call Ben and have him come over to your house. You both absolutely need to talk this out and come to some decision.

"You can survive with decisions; you will rot into pulp on hesitation."

Myrna sat quietly for a while. Then, in a soft voice, she replied, "You're right, of course, Lydia. I have been so scared of the answer that I haven't wanted to ask the question. But I must; not knowing is killing me.

"Skinner had no need to humiliate me. I think he has ruined my future just as much as he has my past. I finally found a true partner and, now, I'm afraid I have lost him.

"Ben is at work now so, tomorrow I'll get in touch with him and we will see from there. I don't know what I will do if I lose Ben. Oh Lydia, please pray for the both of us."

Myrna went home and discovered that Jeffrey had already gone out. She left him a note telling him what time she would be home and then she went to her office.

Jeffrey was the one who gathered the mail when he got home from school and he had noticed the letters and had seen the postmarks. He was almost positive they were from his father. He saw what the letters were doing to his mother and he was scared for her and Mr. Da Vinci. So, after his mother left for Lydia's house, he picked up the phone and dialed the Da Vinci's phone number. Billy answered. "Hi Billy, this is Jeffrey. Are the three of you home right now?"

"Sure. Why?"

"I need to talk to you guys. My mother has been receiving letters from.."

He got no further in his explanation. Billy immediately bellowed into the phone, "My father has been getting letters too."

Jeffrey groaned out loud, "Oh shit. This is terrible."

He was about to speak when Alice came on the line and said, "Jeff, you had better come over so we can compare what's happening and try to make some sense out of this."

When Jeffrey got to their house, the four of them sat down and shared their worries. The Da Vincis told Jeffrey that their father had been extremely upset over the arrival of "those letters," as they referred to them, but Greg, Alice and Billy had no idea what the letters were about. Jeffrey said that his mother also had been receiving letters and that he also didn't know what was in them. However, when he told them that he was now sure that the letters were coming from his father, things began to fall into a logical perspective. They agreed that Jeffrey's father was trying to meddle with their parents' affairs; they had no idea what, if anything, they could do about it.

Alice wanted the four of them to drive to Worcester, have Jeffrey point out Skinner and, then, confront him and tell him to butt out of their business. Billy suggested almost the same thing except that he would have had Greg rough him up a little. Jeffrey listened to them while this discussion took place. After Alice and Billy finished speaking, they waited for Greg who had not said a word while they talked. Finally, he spoke, "It seems to me that you both are asking for too much. You want Jeff to point out his own father so that we can confront him. Would you do the same thing to our father? That's demanding an awful lot from Jeff, isn't it?

"Second, we each have our notions of what is in those letters but none of us knows for sure. We could be making matters worse by butting in without knowing what we are talking about.

"Listen, although I love Dad and Mrs. Cabot, I think the best thing we can do is stand by and support them. We shouldn't interfere. This is something that the two of them will have to work out by themselves. They are mature and we should leave them alone. What do you think of that idea?"

Although Alice, Billy and Jeffrey weren't happy, they all agreed that to do nothing was their best course of action. Alice asked, "Greg, do you think they will?"

"I don't know. If they are honest with each other they should be able to sort through their problems, whatever they are. But, who knows?"

Sunday morning, Myrna relaxed in bed listening to the birds chatter near her window. Talking with Lydia on Saturday had calmed her nerves and she knew exactly what she had to do. This was going to be a big day for her; she desperately wanted Ben's love but she knew that she might have to resolve herself to a life without him. She couldn't stand the thought of that happening so she stopped thinking about it; she would have her answer by nightfall.

She hopped out of bed, showered, and looked at her naked body in the bathroom mirror. "Still attractive," she thought, "But I'm definitely not young any more. I'm beginning to sag. Where has all the time gone?"

She fixed a huge breakfast for herself and Jeffrey and then got him out of bed. He was going with friends to a Red Sox game and needed to leave early. While they ate, she chatted away and he was surprised at her gaiety; she had been so closed mouth and upset the past few days. As he was getting ready to go she hugged him and said, "Jeffrey, I'm sorry if I have been short tempered with you. I'm trying to work out a personal problem and I'm not doing a very good job. I'm sure that I have been hard to live with. I've been a real bitch.

"I know I've been short with you and I apologize. I've been taking my problem out on you. I want you to know that I am proud of you and that you are the nicest son any mother can have. I do love you."

Her son replied, "Mom, you don't need to apologize. I don't know what the problems are between you and Mr. Da Vinci. I can only hope they can be solved. You deserve the very best and he sure is that. I love you very much, Mom. Good luck."

After he had gone, Myrna took her time dressing as carefully as she could; she wanted to look her very best when she met Ben. Then, she began to rehearse what she was going to say. She certainly was not going to surrender her future without a fight, a good fight. She tried to anticipate all of the things Ben might say and how she could reply to them. Finally, after debating with herself, she gave up. It was too confusing to try and plan ahead of time. She would just have to play it by ear, something she knew that she was very good at.

Myrna kept looking out the window and she soon saw Ben's car pull into his driveway; he was home from church. She looked at herself again in the mirror, took a deep breath, thought, "Let the fun begin, and, Oh God, please let me be happy." She headed for the front door. As she passed the table right next to the door, she was surprised to see that she had left Skinner's letters lying there after she read them this morning. She picked them up and was wondering where she could hide them when her doorbell rang.

She was so startled, she jumped. She had been concentrating on where to put the letters and the outside noise shattered her thoughts. Her reaction was to simply open the door. Ben stood there carrying a bottle of wine and a large musk melon from his garden. Myrna's first fleeting hope was, "Oh thank God, he's on a peace mission." They stared at each other for a moment. Ben spoke first and what he said was not what he had practiced, "What are those papers?

"Are they letters? Did you got letters too?"

"The same ones you did only a day after yours."

Ben exploded, "That filthy God-damn-son-of-a-bitch."

Myrna had never heard Ben swear before and it unnerved her.

Their conversation took a path that neither of their ploys nor their practices had anticipated. She said simply, "After I got the letters I felt so dirty, so ashamed, I wanted to curl up and die. I have been waiting for you to comfort me, Ben. Where were you? Why didn't you come?" With that said, large tears began to flow down her face.

Ben put his presents down and held her close. "Please don't cry, Myrna. I can't stand the thought of you being unhappy." He stopped, and then his voice cracked as he began again, "I didn't know, until now, that that bastard was mailing you the same letters. I swear I didn't.

"All this time, I was wrestling with my own pain. I knew nothing about yours."

Myrna knew immediately that Ben was telling the truth. She recognized that she had spent so much time concerned with her own emotions that she had not given Ben enough credit. He had to be going through his own personal Hell like she was and she had assumed that, as a man, he was disgusted with her.

Without thinking of the consequences Myrna blurted out, "My love, I'm so sorry for the pain I've caused you. I never expected anything like this in our lives. I'm so ashamed. I love you more than life itself, but if you leave me, I would understand.

"Those letters are filled with lies. Please don't leave me." With that, her tears increased even more.

Ben started to weep, his eyes filled with tears. "Myrna, I'm not going anywhere. I love you. You owe me no apologies.

"That first letter paralyzed me. I had so much pain I almost stopped breathing. My pride was slashed. He had spit on me and the woman I intend to marry. He tried to make me feel inferior to him. I hate Skinner; for a brief second, I hated you. Never, in my entire life, have I hated a man as I hate Skinner.

" I certainly didn't know that he had also sent you those letters. That only shows how rotten he is. Since I didn't know you were reading the same letters, I never once considered you or your feelings. I thought I was alone in my agony.

"After my pain and shock, I began to realize something. Sex only becomes dirty when a pig like Skinner roots in it. You did no more than Esther and I did after we were married. That's part of the vow of matrimony.

"I wish I hadn't read a word of those letters. However, your life before we met is your business and you owe me no apology. Nor do I need to apologize for being married before I met you.

"I was hurt, I am hurt, but my ego will survive. What is more important to me is that I love you. My life would be empty if you weren't in it. I want to marry you and live with you until my dying day. Ladylove, will you still consider marrying me?"

Myrna almost stopped breathing while he was talking. She had never paid as much attention to each word as carefully as she did listening to Ben. Tears of happiness now replaced tears of sorrow. She looked at Ben and replied, "I accept your proposal with all of my heart, my darling. You have no idea how miserable I've been without you. I want to be your wife." And then, she added mischievously, "For life."

They came together to hug each other and celebrate the fact that they were still going to marry. At first, it was a tender salute but, as their tongues touched, passion and years of self denial soon had both of them squirming in anticipation of more intimacy. They went upstairs to Myrna's bedroom and selected a variety of sweets from the candy store of sex.

****

That evening, Ben had his children come over to eat at Myrna's house. When Myrna and Ben and their four children were seated at the dinner table, Ben said, "Myrna and I want you to know that our wedding will go on as scheduled. We both realize that you have been worried about us and that's why we are having dinner together. We have resolved our problems and we are committed to each other. Now, any questions from any of you?"

Alice got up and kissed Myrna on the cheek. "I'm so happy Mrs. Cabot for you and my father. I need you as my Mom."

Myrna thought, "I hope I can get her to start calling me 'Mom' soon. I want no barriers between me and these young people. I'm looking forward to being the 'Grandma' for the four of our children."

Billy interrupted her thoughts by asking, "Dad what was in those letters that started the problems?"

"Billy, that is something that you will never know."

Billy persisted, "But those letters were what caused all the trouble between you and Mrs. Cabot, weren't they?"

"Yes, they were Billy."

"Well, why shouldn't we know what the problem was about?"

Just as he was about to answer, Jeffrey spoke up and asked, "Mr. Da Vinci, may I say something?"

"Jeffrey, you are as much a part of this group as everyone else. If you have anything to say, put it on the table and we will talk about it."

"Well, I was going to say that the four of us are aware that those letters were sent by my father to you and my mother. I guess that they were meant to cause trouble, which they did for a while. Since they didn't accomplish what they were supposed to, why should we bother to try to find out what was in them? I'm not sure we really need to know. The only thing I'm interested in is that they didn't do what they were designed to do. And I am thankful for that.

"I haven't said this before but I'm delighted that you and my Mom are going to get married. You have given me better advice than I ever received from my own father. You helped me when I needed it the most. I have been thinking of asking my mother what it would take to get my last name changed to Da Vinci."

Alice giggled and then blurted out, "Jeff, you can't be serious. You don't even know how to speak Italian and you want to take our family name of Da Vinci?"

Ben spoke up, quietly but forcefully, "Alice, I'm willing to bet that you don't know too many words yourself. Besides, you are not listening to what he said.

"What he is doing is bringing both families together just as his mother is. Jeffrey I am pleased that you would think of adopting our name. I don't know the legal procedure but, with or without a name change, you are most welcome into our family. I'm sure that Greg, Billy and Alice feel the same way."

They applauded and shouted their approval and, after the noise subsided, Alice spoke again. "Jeff, you are really welcome; that was a poor attempt at a joke on my part. I apologize to you. Your mother has helped me every bit as much as my father has helped you. I want to clarify my stupid attempt at humor because I don't want any more clouds hanging over this marriage."

Nobody could disagree with her sentiments.

****

Myrna and Ben both wanted to get back to their candy store but they had few opportunities. Their biggest problem was not that their wedding was so close; it was that they had so little chance at any privacy. They didn't want to reveal their new relationship to their children so finding a time when they could secretly get together was difficult. The thought that their offspring would discover that their parents were having sex before their marriage bothered both of them. As a result, they listened to their kid's plans and tried to arrange their trysts at Myrna's house accordingly. Even though they only had two more visits to the candy store, they almost got caught once when Jeffrey suddenly returned to pick up something he had forgotten.

They would have been embarrassed had they realized that their children knew what was going on. Hiding sex from the teenagers who were responsible for bringing their parents together was impossible. What Ben and Myrna never discovered was that their children were mature enough to allow their parents to think that they had succeeded in hiding their new relationship.

They both accepted their few moments of intimacy knowing that, after the wedding, they wouldn't have to hide their passion. They were impatient about having to wait for sex, but in its own way, it brought them even closer. They were together as often as they could be and, when they weren't together, they were on the phone with each other. So much so, that their children threatened to take away their parents' phone privileges in order for them to talk to their own friends.

One result of their new relationship was that, as they spent more time together and talked continuously, they got to understand each other's childhood and background better. Myrna learned how Ben's upbringing had made him appear almost backwards until he taught himself to speak up when he had to. Ben learned how hateful Myrna's marriage had made her towards men and how she had feared becoming a victim again. When he understood the background of her concerns, Ben opened up his finances for her complete examination.

These physical, emotional and personal intimacies allowed the two of them to blend together as closely as any man and woman could. They began to talk about their life together and lay out their future without fear.

Even before the wedding they had become partners.

17

Skinner was pleased with himself the way he had crafted his letters to Ben and Myrna. As he chose his words of hate carefully he wondered if he shouldn't have spent more time on a writing career. He was sure that the letters would be hurtful and break up their wedding plans.

However, by the time the last letter was delivered, Skinner was a little nervous and irritable. He had no direct way of knowing how much damage he had done and this bothered him. He wanted more information on how successful he was and he was getting impatient.

He could wait no longer. He called Jeffrey and when he had him on the line, he was all sugar and honey. "Jeffrey, my son, I'm delighted to talk to you. How are you doing?"

Jeffrey ignored the salutation; he was intent on guarding his mother. "Dad, why did you send letters to Mr. Da Vinci and, a day later, send the same ones to Mom?"

Skinner quickly assumed that, if his son was so concerned, he must have hit his mark. He decided to gamble and try to find out more. "Do you know what I wrote in the letters?"

"No."

"Well then, you shouldn't judge what I do."

"Dad, I'm not going to get into a peeing contest with you. You are out to hurt Mom and you don't have the balls to confront Mr. Da Vinci head on. Just leave my mother alone."

With that, he hung up the phone. Skinner was stung that his own son would turn on him like that. Then, he felt much better when he assumed that he had caused some real friction between Myrna and the Wop. But how much? Enough to stop their marriage plans he hoped? He had to find out. But how?

After thinking it over, Skinner decided that he would get his hair trimmed by the Dago himself. That way, after looking and listening to that Bastard, he could judge for himself if there were problems. After all, he reasoned, the barbershop was open to the public so he would be perfectly safe. The Wop had never been introduced to him and there were no pictures of him in Myrna's house so Dago Bastard Barber wouldn't know who he was. He could walk into the barber shop as a complete stranger. Skinner thought he might even tell the Wop who he was as he walked out the door without tipping him. The more he thought of his plan the more he thought of himself as clever and the more the idea appealed to him. He wore his arrogance the same way the Emperor wore his new clothes.

****

Alice considered herself the godmother of her father's upcoming wedding; and she truly was. She had labored long and hard to get her father and Myrna Cabot to recognize their need for each other. And once they reached her conclusion, Alice was impatient for them to fin-ish their journey together.

She was not pleased that they could not get married immediately in Sacred Heart Church. At first, she accepted that fact because alternate plans were swiftly made for the marriage to take place at Myrna Cabot's church, First Parish in Malden Universalist. Until the letters from Worcester began arriving, Alice paid little attention to the change in plans; she was content knowing that the wedding would happen.

However, after the problem caused by the letters was resolved, Alice began to pay more attention to the details surrounding the marriage. The mechanics associated with the preparations began to interest her. As she thought back on the reason for the change of churches she began to be annoyed. She decided to find out for herself why her father and Myrna were not being allowed to marry in her father's own church. It was the only one Alice had ever known.

To that end, she made an appointment to talk with Father Dante and, on a day when she was not working, she drove over to his office. After they were comfortably seated, Alice began by saying, "Father Dante, why couldn't my father and Mrs. Cabot get married immediately in our church?"

"Didn't your father discuss this with you, Alice?" he asked.

"Yes, he did Father but it didn't make sense to me."

"What doesn't make sense, Alice?"

Alice said, in a rush, "Father, I was baptized and raised in this church. My father has been a parish member in good standing and he is an outstanding citizen as well as a marvelous parent. I think he should have been allowed to marry this lovely woman in the church he has supported for many years."

The Father was surprised by the depth of her emotions. "Alice, you do know that Mrs. Cabot is a divorced woman."

"Of course I know that. But, I also know that she is one of the finest, sweetest women I have ever met in my life. She is divorced, her past is behind her. Why can't the church let them marry?"

"We can, Alice, but the union that Mrs. Cabot had with her previous husband has to be annulled first.

"Surely you understand that a civil divorce is not recognized by the Catholic Church as dissolving a marriage. A tribunal has to examine the marriage and acknowledge that it was not valid. Once the marriage is declared invalid, your father and Mrs. Cabot are welcome to marry in Sacred Heart. From the little I know of her marriage, Mrs. Cabot had every right to file for a divorce.

"So, all it takes is time."

"But Father, that would be a whole year wasted."

"No, Alice, not wasted. It is a year, if it takes that long, for reflection and meditation."

Alice was getting a little exasperated. "Father Dante, at the risk of disagreeing with you, it is not a year of reflection and meditation. The church is plowing through an extremely brutal period of her life. She will be concerned each day on when, and what, the tribunal will rule.

"And, what will be the outcome? If they rule in her favor, which they will, she and my father will have wasted a year. If they rule against her, they will marry in another church after wasting a year. This case looks open and shut to me."

Father Dante sat there quietly. He had heard these impassioned arguments many times before. Youth was always in a rush. "Alice, if it were up to me as we sit in this office, I would perform the wedding service tomorrow. However, as a member of the Catholic Church, I am bound to see that the covenant of marriage is not violated. That is what the tribunal examines. Your personal feelings, or mine for that matter, can never take precedent over Church policy. I hope you understand that."

Alice replied, "I do understand that but I have a lot of thinking to do." Then, as if another subject came to her mind, she asked, "Father, are you familiar with The First Parish in Malden Universalist church?"

"Oh yes, I know the Pastor, Bill Frieland, very well."

"Will you be in attendance when he marries my father and Mrs. Cabot?"

"Alice, I can't even if I wanted to. Mrs. Cabot is a divorced woman and the Bishop would never give me permission to attend her wedding."

Alice was crestfallen. From her youthful outlook she thought that both her father and Myrna Cabot deserved much better treatment from the church he had been so faithful to for all these years. She understood the church's attitude but she didn't agree with it. These were almost perfect people in her eyes and she felt that the church was letting them down. She was not a happy person when she left Sacred Heart Church.

After dinner that evening Alice went across the street to visit Mrs. Cabot. When Myrna came to the door she was pleased to see her visitor. "Come in, my Dear, we haven't gotten together for a while."

"I know and it's mostly my fault. They have increased my hours at Russo's and I'm working as much as I can to save money for school.

"Am I interrupting you or Jeff?"

"No, he's out on a date and I was just getting ready to do some baking. Help me out and we can talk while we work."

As they measured, poured, sifted, and chopped Alice went into detail about her meeting with Father Dante. Myrna asked her to set the temperature to three hundred fifty degrees and, by the time she finished her narrative, the cake was ready for the oven.

As they cleaned the kitchen, Alice added, "I just don't think that's fair. You and my father deserve kinder treatment."

"Alice, your father and I will be fine. We will be married in the Church I have belonged to for many years. I know that he was unhappy when he realized what a long path we would have to follow to be married in Sacred Heart Church. Your father soon got over it; the most important thing to remember is that we will very shortly be married. When the declaration of nullity is announced, we will probably remarry. That would please your father."

Alice appreciated Myrna's open mindedness and that made her happy. "Yes, but what are you and he going to do each Sunday? We won't be able to go to church as a family any more."

"That's true. Remember, though, that after this summer you all will be in school and you will be gone for the majority of the year. I will certainly encourage all of you to go to church when you are home."

Alice replied, "I know you will.

"New subject. Is there anything I can do for the wedding? I will be glad to take time off from work if you want me to."

"Thank you, Alice, but that won't be necessary. Everything is on automatic pilot and there is almost nothing left to do."

They sat around chatting as the kitchen filled with the pleasant aroma of fresh baking. However, when the time was up and Myrna checked, the cake was ruined. It had risen on one side and fallen on the other. She pulled it out of the oven, set it on the stove top, and looked it over.

"Why did it do that?" she asked. "Alice, did you set the temperature to three fifty?"

"I think so. Let me check." She looked at the temperature dial and gasped, "Mrs. Cabot, I'm so sorry. I don't know why but I set the temperature at four hundred. This is my fault. I'm such a klutz. I have done nothing to help you with your wedding and, now, I ruined your cake.

"I am so sorry."

Myrna looked at Alice who was close to tears. "Alice, don't be so concerned. Everyone can make a mistake. In half an hour we can have another cake ready for the oven. It is no big thing.

"As far as the wedding, don't forget that it was you who brought your father and me together. Cheer up and help me dispose of this mess and we will set things right."

Myrna was correct. In short order they had another cake baking in the oven at the correct temperature. As they sat drinking tea, Alice said, "Mrs. Cabot, after you and my father are married, what should I call you? I certainly don't want to call you what I do now."

"How about using my first name of Myrna?"

"No, using your first name does not show the respect I feel for you. I'm kind of stuck."

Myrna looked directly at Alice and quietly asked, "Well, do you have any suggestions?"

Alice hesitated before replying, "You didn't give birth to me but you have given me as much love and guidance as any mother ever gave to a daughter.

"Would you object if I called you 'Mom'?"

Myrna couldn't contain her happiness. Her eyes welled with tears as she patted Alice's hand. "Object? Alice, I'm flattered and pleased. You will be the daughter I never had and I will be the mother you never had.

"Life has a funny way of fulfilling people's dreams. I never thought that I would ever fall in love again and now, the more I give away, the more I get back. Life has so much meaning for me now. Love has no equation, it is infinity itself."

When the cake was finished, they each had a slice to celebrate their relationship with each other.

****

Skinner was still determined to see for himself how much damage his letters had inflicted on Ben. However, he wanted to be prepared for any possibility before he entered Ben's barber shop. Even though there wasn't much time before the wedding he drove by for a few days to scout the territory; he noticed that, later in the day, the shop was almost empty. So, late on a Thursday afternoon, some two and a half weeks before the wedding, Skinner parked his car almost directly in front of Ben's barber shop, folded his suit jacket on the back seat, entered the shop and sat down to wait his turn. The thought that a lowly barber could outwit someone as clever as he was never entered his mind.

He picked up the daily *Boston Globe* and sat back pretending to read but really was observing what was going on. There were two old men waiting while a third old man was sitting in the barber chair. They were wearing worn, clean work clothes. All three of them were jabbering in Italian and the barber bastard was replying in the same language. Skinner couldn't understand a word that was being said. That annoyed him; this was America and why didn't they speak English. He thought, "Look at them. Damn them. Those three jabbering apes are old, wrinkled and hairy eared. Why don't they speak our language in our country?"

The Wop barber was shaving the customer sitting in his chair. He stopped spitting Italian long enough to tell Skinner, "There is only one man ahead of you." Skinner peered over the paper and watched Ben intently; after all, he had come here specifically to study this man. Skinner had made it his mission to stop this marriage.

What he saw was reassuring to him. Ben was slim, not muscular and only of average build. He was not handsome nor would he be noticed in a crowd. Coupled with what Skinner thought was his personality, he didn't appear to be a formidable person. Skinner was more than ever convinced that his letters had damaged the relationship between the Dago and his ex- wife. He was also positive that he had arrived at Ben's barber shop totally unnoticed and unrecognized by anyone.

Skinner was wrong on both counts.

Skinner himself had unknowingly guaranteed that he would be noticed by parking his expensive foreign car right in front of the barbershop window. As he stepped out of his new, fire engine red Mercedes-Benz and folded his jacket, he was in plain sight of everyone inside. It immediately begged the question why a man who could afford such an expensive car and was so particular with his clothes would bother coming to a local barbershop?

His second mistake was assuming that he would go unrecognized. He hadn't realized that Jeffrey had shown the wallet sized picture of his father to Ben and the Da Vinci family almost a dozen times. The minute Skinner entered his shop, Ben knew who he was.

When Skinner had first entered the door, Ben had looked at him, grunted, and jumped. He almost choked in shock. Giorgio, the man he was shaving, said in Italian, "Be careful where you are waving that razor. I don't want to lose the family jewels."

Ben apologized, in Italian, and went about his business as he continued shaving Giorgio. However, he slowed his actions down so he could think. His mind was racing and his emotions were raging. "What was Myrna's ex-husband doing in his shop? Why was he here? What am I going to do about it?"

It was when Ben got to the last question that his emotions began to rise. Anger, which was a rare emotion for him, almost made his hands tremble. He thought about the anguish this man had put Myrna and him through and he was almost blinded by hatred. His thoughts screamed, "REVENGE!"

Ben decided what he was going to do. He stepped away from Giorgio, cleaned his razor, and began stropping it. While he was methodically sharpening the razor he said slowly, in Italian, "Listen, you three old buzzards. I need to talk privately with this man who just came in. So, even though Luigi is supposed to be next I want the three of you to leave after I finish Giorgio. If all of you leave, I will give the three of you free haircuts and shaves next month. Do you agree?"

The three of them agreed quickly, and gratefully, in Italian. Something free always appealed to these older people who had lived through the Depression.

Ben continued the discussion in the same language. "OK. Here's what I want you to do. After I finish Giorgio, all of you stay around until my friend sits in the chair. When I put the sheet over his shoulders I want you to leave quietly. I want you to change my sign to show "closed" and I want you to throw the bolt on the door so that the door will lock when you are gone. If the three of you can remember to do all that then you will get your free haircuts and shaves next time you come."

The three of them hooted and claimed that they never had to work so hard for so little. With that, Ben's plan began to take shape.

While these discussions were going on, Skinner pretended to read the newspaper but he watched and listened, trying to make sense out of what he was witnessing. It seemed like utter and trivial noise and nonsense and it offended him. He thought, "Inferior people speaking an inferior language."

His thoughts were interrupted when he saw the old man who was in the barber chair stand up and walk over to where his companions were seated. The Wop barber looked at him and said, "Your turn is now."

This puzzled Skinner. He asked, "I thought you said that there was someone ahead of me?"

Ben answered, "I did. However, my friends have decided to let you go ahead of them. They are older than you and they are in no rush; they think that you seem to be too important to have to wait."

Skinner couldn't argue with that statement so he got into the barber chair and Ben flapped his sheet high in the air and settled it around Skinner's neck. When he had tucked it in place, Ben turned to face Skinner who, because he was seated, had to look up to see him. In a soft voice Ben asked, "How are things in Worcester?"

Skinner was completely caught off guard. He replied, "What are you talking about?"

"Come off of it, Skinner. You know perfectly well what I'm talking about."

Skinner was no fool. He knew that he had been found out and that he had to change tactics. So, to gain time until he could figure out what was going on, he asked, "How did you guess who I was?"

Ben was not about to give him a shred of information; he answered, "It was not a guess." Then he changed subjects, "What are you doing in my shop?"

"This place is open to the public. I have a perfect right to be here."

Ben was beginning to feel good about jousting with this person he hated so much. "It is open to the public during business hours. We are closed and, therefore, Skinner. You are trespassing on my property."

Skinner looked around and for the first time realized that there were only the two of them in the shop. He yelped, "Where are your other customers?"

"Skinner, I told you that it is after hours and we are closed."

For the first time, Skinner had a foreboding that he was in trouble. He said, "You closed in a hurry. I think I had better go."

As he put his hands on the arms of the barber chair to help himself get up, Ben picked up his straight edged barber's razor and waved it close to Skinner's face. Skinner recoiled into the chair and gasped, "You crazy son of a bitch, what do you think you are doing?"

Suddenly, Ben stopped waving the razor and thrust it even closer to Skinner's eyes. He held it there and let Skinner stare at it. Skinner recoiled even further in the chair. Both men froze in that position.

The pressure of his hate began to build inside of Ben like steam in a teakettle. He felt hot and he was now breathing heavily through his mouth. As if anticipating Skinner's next move, he snarled, "Don't even think of trying to grab me, you bastard. Your face will be sliced before your arms are raised above your shoulders." His face was so contorted with anger that he was almost unrecognizable.

Skinner was frightened; he knew he was in danger. He softly repeated his question, "What are you doing?"

"What am I doing? What am I doing? I don't even know yet. That depends on you, you son of a bitch. You are a rotten, evil person. You caused me pain. You caused Myrna pain. I have never hated anyone as much as I hate you.

"I don't know why you were dumb enough to come into my shop but you did. We are going to talk and what I am going to do depends on our conversation. I will be asking the questions; you will only reply to my questions. Nothing more. Be warned that I'm not going to take any bullshit from you. Do you understand?" He was so angry he was trembling.

He slapped Skinner on the cheek with the side of the razor, taking care to keep the sharp edge away from his skin. It was a hard slap and the noise and the proximity of the blade to his eyes scared Skinner even more.

"Yes," he croaked.

"Good. Now we can begin." With that, some of the insanity that was boiling through Ben subsided into a calm craftiness. He decided to make it difficult for Skinner to get away; he needed to discourage Skinner from trying to bolt for the door. "First, I want you to undo your belt, unzip your pants and pull them down to your ankles."

"Why do you want me to do that?" Skinner asked.

Ben was infuriated. "God Damn It, I don't want you speaking until I tell you to. I told you that I would ask the questions. You broke my rules. Now, you will pay.

He brandished his razor close to Skinner's eyes, he slowly waved it as he whispered, "Stick out your tongue!"

When Skinner did, Ben took his razor and quickly and deftly tapped the end of it into Skinner's tongue. The razor penetrated only enough to draw a little blood. Ben then commanded, "Stick your tongue back."

He waited a little while Skinner tasted his own blood; he began to tremble a little. Ben waited another second before he began, in a soft tone of voice that was almost a song, "You see how sharp my razor is? This razor is one of my favorites; it holds an extremely sharp edge. As a Dago Bastard Barber I've been doing this many, many years. Your ear would come off easily if I wanted it to. Now, please don't question me and do as I ask. Pull your pants down around your ankles."

When he had complied, Ben said, "Good. Now, I will put a sheet over your legs; I don't want you to catch cold. We have a lot to talk about." As Ben turned to reach for something, Skinner started to lean forward as if he were going to rise out of the chair. Ben got excited and again slapped Skinner across his cheek with the razor. Skinner slumped back without saying a word. What little fight he had to this point was completely replaced by his fright.

Ben had also changed. He was almost out of his mind with his passions. His anger, his rage and his lust for revenge were driving him past his boundaries of decency. He was in an area of emotions he had never been before. He had no idea of what he was doing or where he was going.

Ben pulled a stool up and sat beside his barber chair, close to Skinner. "Now that we are both comfortable, let us chat. First of all Skinner, I want to know why you came into my shop." Ben stopped, thought a second, and then added, "Hold on. Before you answer, I think that Skinner is too formal. I think that I will call you Sammy. That's more informal, more intimate. Now, why did you come into my shop, Sammy?"

Skinner replied, in a low voice, "I don't know."

"Sammy, you are fibbing to me. I'm not pleased with your answer. You undoubtedly came here to try to cause me more trouble. How? I really don't know; but I'm sure you didn't stop by to congratulate me. I don't care why you came; it is not important. You are here, and now we are sitting and talking, almost like old friends. That's really nice, don't you think?

"No, you probably don't think it's nice. But, be aware that, even though I didn't like your answer, I'll let it go this time. But I want more honesty from you.

"Now, why do you hate Wops?"

"I don't."

Ben sighed. "Sammy, didn't I tell you that I wanted more honesty. You are not being forthright; you are being evasive. Do you want me to ask you to stick your tongue out again?"

Skinner shuddered, "No, please no."

Ben hissed, "Then answer my question. Why do you hate Wops."

This time, Skinner answered quickly, "Because they don't belong in this country. They weren't here when this country was founded and they are noisy and different." Then he added, "They don't speak English."

Ben spoke up. "Of course, being of Italian heritage, I strongly disagree with you. You know, I read some of the letters you wrote me. I could overlook what you said about me but when I thought of how my mother had raised me, you made me angry, very, very angry.

"I only read the first three though because they were so filled with hate for us Wops that you became boring. Your idea of what Italians have done for our country is not correct; but at least you did tell me why you hate Italians.

"This isn't a debate so I will consider that you answered my question even if I didn't like the answer. Let me say, however, that I'm glad you are not the head of Immigration Service.

"Now, for the record, I would like to know why you put the liquor in the back seat of Myrna's car and got your son into trouble?"

Skinner's fear had subsided a little so he could answer without hesitation, "I love my son. I certainly would never do anything to get him in hot water directly. My plan was to get the police to stop him with an open liquor bottle in the car. They could find Myrna an unfit mother who couldn't control her son."

Skinner didn't realize what that statement would do to Ben. That reply infuriated him even more. He sat quietly for a while thinking about what he had just heard. Skinner had gone out of his way to get both his son and Myrna into trouble. He wouldn't stand for that. He decided he would prod Skinner just to get even for Myrna. In the worst way, he wanted revenge.

"Sammy, that is absolutely despicable. That could have gotten her censured if not disbarred. What good would that have done you? Absolutely no good. What am I going to do about that? I have no idea right now. However, what I will do, in the meantime, is give you a shave, free of charge. I want you to feel close to my razor while we continue our discussion. You have done a lot of terrible things that brought trouble to a lot of people.

"Don't you dare go away," he said laughing unpleasantly.

With that, he lowered the back of the barber chair until Skinner's body was almost horizontal. Then he pumped the chair higher off the ground so that he would be comfortable and not bent over while he shaved Skinner. He held the razor close to Skinner's face while he talked. Skinner couldn't take his eyes off that lethal, shining piece of sharpened steel. "Sammy, I don't know what to do about your hair. It is so well coifed. Should I leave it alone? Shave it off? Give you a buzz cut? What do you think?"

Skinner was hoping that he might be able to get out of his predicament. He still couldn't bring himself to accept Ben as an equal when he said, "Da Vinci, let's talk business. I'm willing to write you a check for a couple of thousand dollars if you let me out of this chair right now."

Ben went ballistic; he was first angered by Skinner's admission of trying to frame Myrna. Now, with Skinner's attempt to buy his way out, Ben became completely irrational. He grabbed Skinner's ear and pulled it hard. "You son of a bitch, open your mouth and stick your tongue out or I'll slice your ear off right now."

When Skinner did as he was told, Ben inflicted another cut to his tongue. Skinner began to realize how deranged Ben was and fear began to overpower any other of his emotions. Ben took two or three deep breathes and seemed to regain some of his composure. He wagged his razor at Skinner and said. "Sammy, you don't understand your situation. This has nothing to do with money. I can probably buy and sell you three times over.

"What this is is that you are on trial and I am the judge, jury, and prosecuting attorney. I already think that you are guilty but I will let you plead your case. Now do you understand?"

Skinner neither spoke nor moved. By this time, he was so frightened he could barely breathe let alone respond. Ben said nothing about Skinner's silence as he applied lather to his face. He slowly and meticulously shaved Skinner as he talked. "Now, Sammy, we come to the heart of our discussion. Namely the vicious accusations you made towards Myrna. Why would you write such things?"

Skinner did not reply. He was like a mouse in a corner trying to avoid an alley cat. Ben spoke harshly, "I'm getting angry, Sammy. Speak up or I'll have to make you stick your tongue out."

After a few seconds, Skinner managed to say, "I was jealous. I didn't want to lose her."

Ben nodded his head up and down; he liked that answer. It was truthful. He asked, "Does that mean you admit that you were wrong to write the things what you wrote about her?"

Tears began to fall from Skinner's eyes as he hoarsely said, "Yes."

Ben leaned closely to Skinner's face and sternly said, "Speak up, Sammy. I want to hear you apologize again. Now that your pants are down I may look at that tool you seem to be so proud of; you told me how you used it so often. I may decide to trim it to half of its size. My next plans will depend on what you say to me."

Skinner was almost sobbing. "I lied about her. I didn't want to lose her. She was the best thing that ever happened to me. I didn't know that until she left me. I shouldn't have written what I did. I'm sorry.

"Please don't hurt me. Please, please, don't touch my pecker. I beg you for the love of Christ, leave it alone.

"Please. Have mercy on me."

Ben heard every word that Skinner spoke. He understood what Skinner was going through but he felt no remorse at all. His rage was gone but his thirst for revenge had not been slaked. He was still unhinged and he wanted Skinner to suffer at least as much as he and Myrna had. He sat beside Skinner, wiping his razor clean. He was almost in a dream as he tried to decide what to do next. He had run out of plans and ideas.

Just then there was a sharp tapping on the glass door. The noise startled him so much that he almost jumped off his stool. He looked over to the door and saw a man standing there with a bunch of keys tapping on the glass. Ben, quickly put the back of the razor against Skinner's windpipe and said, "Don't say a word!"

Skinner shivered in fright.

The man tapped a few more times and then yelled, "Can you open up and give me a haircut?"

Ben shouted back, "No, I'm closed for the day. You'll have to come back tomorrow."

"Are you sure?"

"Yes, I'm closed until tomorrow. This is my last customer."

The man muttered, "Damn, just my luck," and walked away.

As he watched the man leave, Ben smelled a fetid odor. He wrinkled his nose in revulsion at the foul stench. It was poop. He quickly looked at Skinner, who was lying there with the back of the razor against his throat. Skinner was crying and trembling. "I've shit my pants. I've peed my pants. I'm scared. Please don't slit my throat. Don't kill me. I beg you for my life, I beg for your mercy. Please. Please."

Ben looked at Skinner lying there, trembling and pleading for his life. Then, for the first time, Ben understood what the words meant. No matter what Ben felt, or thought, Skinner was a human being and Ben had no right to decide his life or death.

Ben felt disgusted. Not with the smell, not with the evil person he had in his control, but with himself. He thought, "I'm no better than Skinner. I am torturing a person because he hurt me. That's for revenge. I've never done that before.

"That makes me no better than he is. Is that what I really want? Is that who I really am?"

Suddenly, Ben felt tired. He was completely ashamed of himself. He sat back on his stool and said, "Skinner, go home."

Skinner stopped crying but he didn't move. Ben lowered the height of the barber chair and slowly and loudly repeated what he had just said, "Skinner, go home."

After a pause, Skinner began to stir. He slowly brought his reclined body to the seated position, took off the sheet that had covered his legs, and pulled his pants up. He got out of the chair and, holding his pants up with both of his hands, he started to walk. He shuffled each foot, without bending his knees, and he kept his legs straddled. When he got to the door, he twisted the deadbolt lock with one hand and then opened the door with the same hand. He needed one hand to hold his pants up. Then, he continued his stiff legged shuffling to his car. Skinner got into his beautiful red car and drove away with the sheet that Ben had tucked around his neck still in place.

Ben sat on his stool feeling weary and dirty. He couldn't believe how evil his actions had been. Finally, he stood up, locked the door, shut out the lights and went through the back door. When he was standing in the alley, he realized that he still was wearing his barber's coat. He took it off, placed it on a hook on the outside wall and sat on a crate he occasionally used as a chair. He put his hands up to his face and began to sob. His remorse was a deeper feeling than his hate had been and his conscience was bothering him. After almost ten minutes of crying, he reached for his barber's coat, wiped his face and blew his nose on it, and, then, dropped it on the ground.

He went home and spent almost a half hour scrubbing himself in a hot shower.

18

The next morning, when his children came down for breakfast, Ben was sitting at the table waiting for them. That wasn't unusual; what was different was that he had prepared an elaborate morning meal and he wasn't dressed for work. Greg, Billy and Alice dug into the fruit salad, egg omelet, home fried potatoes, bacon, and sausage with gusto before they decided to quiz their father. In the morning, teenagers are more hungry than they are inquisitive.

After he emptied his plate for the first time, Greg asked, "Dad, is this your new career?"

Ben had expected their comments and knew that there were a lot more questions to come. So, he replied with a question of his own, "Is that a complaint about the service you are receiving?"

Billy joined in, "Not from me, it isn't; but I noticed that you're not dressed for work. Does that mean you are not opening your shop today?"

"Yes." Ben did not elaborate.

After awhile Billy continued, "OK. Now that you have cooked a big breakfast for us, aren't you going to tell your family the rest of the story?"

"Yes, but I wanted you well fed before I started. I'm going to take time off before the wedding to make sure everything stays on track. Myrna is busy putting her business affairs in order. I said that I would make our honeymoon arrangements and surprise her. I haven't done anything about that yet and I have to. I also have to take care of my business properties. I am planning on closing my barber shop.

"The fact is that, after Myrna and I are married, we want to be able to travel and enjoy our lives. We have both been planning on lessening our work loads and now is as good a time for me to start as any. After we come back from our honeymoon, we are going to sit down and change our schedules and our priorities."

Alice whistled and then she asked, "Does Mom agree with you? I know, after following her around, that she has worked hard to build her practice. Has she agreed to cut back on her work schedule?"

"Yes, Alice, you may not believe this but she was the first to bring the subject up. We have talked about our future and we want to be close to each other. The four of you will all be in school by the time we get back from our honeymoon and there will be just the two of us.

"Myrna and I have come to realize that the most important possession that anyone can ever have in life is a partner.

"At any rate, to answer your question, yes, we have both agreed to cut back on our work schedules. We both want the same thing. We will enjoy life until we become grandparents and then we will enjoy our lives even more."

Alice was impressed. She said, "Wow, both of you have certainly changed; and for the better. Until now, you have been working machines; hopefully, you now will be pleasure machines. I'm pleased for you and Mom."

Greg, Billy and Alice finished their breakfasts and left the house for their jobs and their personal errands.

Ben had not lied to his children but he had not been totally honest. In not telling them about his encounter with Skinner he had been a bit devious. He also did not mention that it was only this morning that he had decided to close his barber shop. He would never give another person a haircut or a shave.

He had not slept much last evening. He was totally stunned by what he had done and how he had done it. The depth of his hate and revenge shook him to his core. He never realized that he was capable of such negative emotions. His attitude towards the tools of his trade had completely changed; he didn't ever want to touch them again.

Myrna had previously suggested that he get a real estate broker's license. Using his business acumen along with handling of all his own commercial properties himself, made her sure that he could make a comfortable living. Up until yesterday he hadn't given her suggestion much thought. This morning he knew he would never pick up a straight-edged razor again and, after the Hell of last evening, the thought did not bother him in the slightest.

After he cleaned the kitchen, he poured himself a cup of coffee and went out on the porch. He wanted to sort out what he had to do from what he wanted to do. He had a lot on his mind and he had decisions to make. His actions of last night still pressed heavily on his mind but he didn't linger too long on what had taken place; he had done what he felt was necessary to protect Myrna. That was his consolation.

His big question was whether he should tell her what happened immediately or should he wait? After thinking about it, he decided that, no matter the reason, he had no right to hide information from her. He would tell her some time this weekend.

With his personal concerns taken care of he thought about what else had to be done before the wedding. He decided where to go for their honeymoon and he also planned a surprise for Myrna over the last weekend before the wedding. He laid out the list of phone calls that he would have to make; then he picked up the phone.

The first call was to Myrna to tell her of his decision to close his barber shop. Ben didn't tell her the reason and she automatically assumed it was because of the discussions they had about a broker's license. Myrna told Ben that she was glad of his decision.

He then phoned the building firm that he hired for any construction project on his properties. He had used them for years and was comfortable doing business with them. He gave them explicit directions on cleaning and renovating the barber shop. All his equipment was to be put into storage and the space would be made into an office for his new business. The contractor told him that he would start the renovations sometime in the next three weeks and that the work would be finished before he got back from his honeymoon. They discussed a new sign but Ben decided to wait until after he talked to Myrna. Setting out a new path made Ben feel better.

Ben called a customer of his who ran a travel agency and booked his honeymoon along with a weekend stay at a bed and breakfast in Lenox; he also reserved tickets for the Friday, Saturday and Sunday performances at the Tanglewood Music Festival.

After he made a few more phone calls concerning his business and his upcoming wedding, he left the house to run an errand. He needed to locate Giorgio, Luigi and Alberto and talk to them. He knew that they would be unhappy when they found that his barbershop, their meeting place, was going to close and he wanted to speak to them personally. He didn't know their home addresses, as they moved occasionally from relative to relative, but he knew the two or three places they occasionally stopped for coffee. They weren't anywhere to be found.

On a hunch, he drove to his barber shop and saw them sitting on one of the two benches he had provided on the front sidewalk. He parked his car and walked over to them; they immediately greeted him, in Italian, with jeers of "Sleepyhead" and "Lazybones."

He laughed and, in the same language, he told them that he could have them arrested for loitering on his property. After a few boisterous minutes of bantering, Luigi asked Ben if he and his friend had had a pleasant visit the evening before. Ben was taken aback until he remembered that his three customers had been in the shop when Skinner first arrived. After he recovered his train of thought, he told the three of them that he was closing his barber shop and, since he had promised them free haircuts and shaves, he was inviting them to his wedding instead. They joked amongst themselves for a while, pretending to balance the price of barbering against what the cost of feeding them would be. They decided that they were better off going to the wedding. They were really not talking costs, they were talking companionship. They knew that they would be surrounded by people in a happy environment and elderly people need social warmth as much as their bodies need sweaters. They also understood that they had just received a much better offer and they gratefully accepted the invitation, but not without raising a friendly fuss. Then, they got into an argument about which of them was going to be the first to kiss the bride.

Ben went home feeling better about not leaving his long time customers in the lurch. He added their names to his guest list, and went out on the porch to relax and drink some lemonade. There was one more goal that he had in mind but he needed to think about it. After a while, he changed into his work clothes and went to the "farm" to pick vegetables for the family supper.

The next morning, Saturday, Myrna came over early to work in the garden and be with Ben. After he greeted her, he showed her the guest list and when she saw the three new names, she asked Ben about them. He told her that they were three old customers to whom he had promised free shaves and haircuts. Since he was closing without keeping his promise, he wanted to invite them to the wedding. Even though his narrow version of the story was true, Ben felt guilty about not telling her the entire background. Of course, Myrna had no objections and the matter was dropped.

It was a hot, late summer day and they worked for hours weeding, pruning and gathering their harvest. Myrna noticed that Ben was not very communicative and, finally, she said, "Ben, I need a break. You have hardly said a word to me all morning. Is something wrong?"

Ben looked at her and smiled. "You are right, we need a break. No, there is nothing wrong but I do have to talk with you. So, go sit on the porch and I'll bring out some refreshments."

Myrna rinsed her hands and face with the garden hose and sat at the table on the porch. Ben came out of the house with fresh lemonade and sugar cookies; she noticed that he had also cleaned up. They were careful not to touch each other; they knew where that would lead. Having been to the candy store, they were aware that they wouldn't be able to control themselves if they started shopping again. With their families lurking in the background, they didn't dare to begin to make any selections. So, they carefully tried not to get excited; the result was that they acted as if they were in a Victorian comedy.

After Ben brought out refreshments, Myrna sipped her drink and asked, "My Dear, what is it that you want to talk with me about but that has kept you quiet all morning?"

Ben laughed as he answered, "Ladylove, you make it sound worse than it is. I'm not tongue-tied, it's just that I'm not sure how to begin. I have three subjects I want to tell you about and one of them is difficult for me and it is blocking the other two."

"Start with the difficult one, Dear, and it will get your concerns out of the way."

And he did. Ben told her, in great detail, how Skinner had come into his barber shop and what had taken place from the moment he entered until he got into his car and left. He described his emotions from his surprise at seeing him, to his anger at him smearing Myrna, and how he wanted to revenge himself on Skinner. Then, he told her how disgusted he was that he had almost stooped to Skinner's level.

When he finished his story his face was moist with sweat; he had rekindled all the emotions he had described as he talked about them. He stared at Myrna who hadn't said a word during his narrative.

Ben stared at her for a few seconds and then asked, "Well, what do you think of that?"

Myrna got out of her chair, walked around the table and kissed Ben on the top of his head. "I think you are my hero and I love you. That's what I think."

"You don't think that I acted like that scumbag?"

Myrna shook her head from side to side and kissed his head again. "Honey, you're not even close. You had evil thoughts and intentions. At times, every person does; but, you didn't carry them out. You didn't follow through on your bad instincts. You were human enough to let someone you detested go free. That shows what type of person you are. Skinner never did a kind thing for anyone.

"I love you because you are so kind. I am so glad that I know you, but to tell you the truth, I sometimes lie in bed and wish that we had met years ago."

Ben had been expecting a lecture on good versus evil and he was surprised at what Myrna said. After thinking about it, he realized that she had been fighting Skinner's attempts to dominate and disparage her for years; as a victim, she would have little compunction for her tormenter. Her attitude, about what he had done, would be more forgiving than his. He was happy to be able to substitute her judgement for his own.

"Myrna, I love you. I acted on impulse because of what he had done to you. Then, I got worried about what you would think of me for doing what I did, so I needed to tell you. I just had to. If love isn't truthful it isn't pure. I was afraid of what you would think of me; I don't ever want to lose you.

"Ladylove, I feel better now that you know. I can breathe happily again. I'll be much happier after our marriage.

"Now, I'm ready to discuss my second subject if you are."

"And what is this second subject about?"

"Our honeymoon."

"Ah, you have decided on where we are going and how long we will be staying?"

"Yes, we will be going to Italy for three weeks."

"We're going to Italy? I've never been there. What made you pick Italy? I thought you were sensitive about your Italian heritage."

"I guess I was for a long time but I've come to realize I don't have to apologize for my upbringing. Lately, I've been thinking of my mother and what she went through coming to America. She did not have an easy time of it. I want to see the town she and my father were born and raised in. So, we will fly to Milan and I'll try to find my relatives. Then, we will tour the rest of Italy. You don't think the Pope will be disappointed if we don't get to visit him?"

"Italy? What a surprise. I'm so excited. Oh my God, I can hardly wait. The Pope will just have to get over his disappointment. Love, thank you for our honeymoon; it will be so beautiful."

Ben felt like a robin chick who had just pecked himself out of his shell; he was chirping with happiness. He said, "The third subject is something that needs your approval. We will be married two weeks from today. We have no time for ourselves and I can't wait. Next weekend, I've booked us into a bed and breakfast in Lenox. We can go to Tanglewood and there will be no families, no distractions; we will be by ourselves.

"What do you think of that?"

"You're spoiling me. Our own weekend alone? And at Tanglewood? I can't wait; I'll be a nervous wreck all this week. I adore you, Ben Da Vinci and I thank you from the bottom of my heart."

She thought for a while and then she asked, "I wonder what our kids will think when we tell them we are going away for a weekend together?"

Ben chuckled, and answered, "I'd be very surprised if they are at all surprised. I'm sure that they know about us and are just being polite."

Myrna agreed, "Yes, of course they know. I'll bet they were surprised to find out that their parents could be horny. So be it. I'm looking forward to our next weekend.

"The only problem I will have is that I will have to rearrange my schedule so that I'll be free to leave on Friday. That's no biggy but it will keep me busy all next week. Oh, Ben, I have so much to look forward to."

Sunday evening, as Ben and Myrna had dinner with their "new family," as all six now referred to themselves, they broke the news about their honeymoon plans and their plans for the weekend at Lenox. Their four children took the news with smiles and nods and none of them made any remarks. They were not as shocked as they were pleased; each of them privately cheered.

The weekend in Lenox was idyllic. The bed and breakfast was a large house set on the top of one of the beautiful hills that New Englanders think are mountains. Their hosts were generous, friendly and asked Ben and Myrna no questions. They ate well both before and after the three concerts they attended and they had desert at their candy store. It was a tranquil holiday which calmed their nerves and stoked their expectations; they felt that they would be on their tiptoes until their wedding day.

Sunday evening, after the last concert which had featured the Franck symphony, they were sitting on the porch of their lodging. They were by themselves, drinking coffee and looking at the moonlit mountains and forest. Myrna was humming one of the melodies she had heard when Ben softly said, "Ladylove, I have a question to ask you and I need you to be completely honest in your answer."

Myrna stopped humming and replied, "You are interrupting the second movement but, if it is honesty you want, go right ahead."

Ben took a deep breath and then continued, "I want to write a letter to Esther. If I did that would it hurt your feelings?"

"Why should my feelings be hurt?"

"Well, it's a little strange for a man who is about to be remarried to write a letter to his dead wife, isn't it?"

Myrna was quiet for a long time before she replied. "Honey, it is different but it is not strange; it is typically something that you would do. As you yourself told me, we each had a history before we met. Yours was a happy one and you want to make sure you are not dishonoring its memories as you move on.

"No, my feelings are not hurt. On the contrary, I feel proud to be loved by a caring, thoughtful partner. Write your letter to Esther with my best wishes and blessings."

"Ladylove, thank you for your understanding. Esther was my wife many years ago and we were in love and she died. Our relationship is over, it has been over for years, but it was part of my past life. I want to move on to a new life with you, but I believe that I have to close the first chapter. That's why I want to write a letter.

"This is the last night of our vacation. Let's make the most of it."

And they did; they went to bed.

They got back to Malden early Monday afternoon; on the drive they discussed what each of them had to do before the wedding. After laying out their plans, Ben suggested that Myrna and Jeffrey come to dinner, over at his house, during the next week. That would enable them to make sure nothing was overlooked and they would be together. When they got home, they immediately got on board their individual merry-go-rounds.

Myrna unpacked and found a note from Jeffrey welcoming her back and saying that he would be working until supper time. She went to her office to check on her case load and her clients. She wanted to insure everything was in order before Friday.

Ben and Alice arrived home at the same time. She had just gotten off work from Russo's; she hugged him and asked if he and mom had had a good time. After he told her about the concerts, they planned the meals for the rest of the week. Then he made some phone calls to check on his own business interests.

Tuesday evening, before Myrna and Jeffrey joined them for their evening meal, Ben sat down with Greg, Billy and Alice and had a family meeting. They talked about closing the house while he was in Italy and they were in school. He asked what they needed before school began. They laid out emergency plans and how to contact each other. As they were finishing their discussion Ben mentioned that Friday morning he was going to place flowers on their mother's grave. He was surprised when none of his children offered any comment. He was about to say something when Myrna and Jeffrey arrived and that ended the meeting.

Thursday evening, after dinner was over and their kids were cleaning up the kitchen, Ben asked Myrna to sit on the porch; he had something he wanted her to read. When she was seated in one of the rocking chairs, he gave her the letter he had written. She read it twice, dropped it in her lap, and sat without saying a word.

Finally, Ben asked timidly, "Are you offended?"

"Offended? Why should I be offended? No, I was just thinking of Esther. She must have been a very sweet person. She would be easy to love. I know that, had I ever met her, I would have liked her very much.

"Ben, it is a beautiful letter. I hope Esther hears it when you read it to her."

****

Friday morning, after his children had gone to work and he finished cleaning the kitchen, Ben paid bills, made phone calls and checked on the wedding arrangements for the last time. In mid-afternoon he shaved, showered and dressed even more carefully than he usually did. He stopped at a florist and bought two dozen long stemmed red roses and then drove to Holy Cross cemetery. He parked his car and walked down the long row of graves until he was standing before Esther's grave.

He was surprised to see a huge bouquet of pink carnations laid in front of her headstone. He thought, "The children must have come to visit their mother." Tears fell down his cheeks. He knelt and laid his roses next to the carnations. Ben could feel the dampness of the grass wetting the knees of his pants but that meant nothing to him. He sat back on his heels, reached into the inside pocket of his suit jacket, and brought out his letter. He read it aloud. There were times when he had to stop because he was so overcome with emotion. It took him a while to read:

Dearest Esther,

Until I started adding up our time together, I had lost track of the simple fact that our lives have been intertwined for over twenty-five years. Actually, it has been almost twenty-seven years since we met, married, and had our three children. We were so happy; even now, I don't understand why it had to end. However, it did finish and it was extremely hard for me to reconcile myself to your passing. It's strange but, for years, one of my most piercing regrets was that you and I never had the chance to celebrate our tenth wedding anniversary together. It was something I was looking forward to. I don't know why not having that anniversary with you bothered me so much, but it did.

Before you left, you asked me to make you two promises. The first, was that I would raise our children with patience and dignity.

That has been a labor of love and I have tried very hard to set a good example for them. All of our children, Greg, Billy and Alice will be in college this fall. They are fledglings who would make their mother bird proud. They are intelligent, honest and good children who will grow into leaders in their communities. I look at them and I see some of you in each one.

Your second promise, for me to find another partner to share my life with, was a hard promise for me to fulfill. Until now. Esther, near the end, you kept telling me that, "The temple of love has many altars. Each is different from the other and all are sacred and beautiful."

All the years, since you were gone, I found that hard to believe. I was numb and refused to think that I could ever have a happy relationship again. However, I have finally met a woman who has rekindled my interest in life. And, you were right. My falling in love again does not demean what you and I had for so long. Nothing can ever tarnish our time together. Loving you has helped me raise our children while your wisdom has made me a better person than I ever was before.

I will carry your lessons with me for the rest of my life. As I look forward to standing in front of a new altar in the temple of love, I thank you, with all my heart, for the life and love that I was fortunate enough to share with you at our own special altar.

Love,

Ben

****

Ben remained in front of Esther's headstone for a long time. Finally, he got to his feet, got into the car, and drove home. He was surprised to see Hunkajunk parked in the driveway and equally amazed to find that his children were waiting for him on the porch. All three were dressed as if they were ready for a party. Ben looked at them and said, "I thought the wedding was tomorrow. What are you dressed for now?"

Greg replied, "Well, first of all, we wanted to be here when you got back from the cemetery. We didn't want you to feel alone."

Ben was touched. "That was nice of you. I don't feel alone; I'm sad and happy at the same time. That's hard to explain but I went to your mother's grave to honor her memory. I read her a letter that I had written."

Alice said, "Dad, that's how I felt when we were at the grave yesterday. Sad and happy. I stood by Mom's headstone and I wished that I had gotten to know my birth mother. I was so young when she passed. That makes me more determined to love and honor my new mother. Sad and happy is such a good description. I'm so excited about tomorrow."

Billy finally entered the conversation, "Dad, if you wrote Mom a letter, what did you do with it? Did you leave it at the grave site?"

"No Billy, I have it here," and he patted his suit jacket. "It is a personal letter from me to your mother. If I left it there anyone could have read it; that's not what I want. I will keep it among my possessions and, after I'm gone, you can see what I wrote."

Ben thought for a second and asked, "You three are home early today aren't you? And, again, I ask why are you all gussied up?"

This time, Alice spoke up for them, "Dad, we have decided to throw a stag party for you."

"A what?"

"A stag party," she continued as she laughed, "We want to follow all the rules for a happy marriage. The four of us, and that includes

Jeff, are taking you and Mom out to eat at an elegant restaurant. This is our stag party for you."

"Does Myrna know about this stag party?"

"Jeff just told her and she is getting ready as we speak."

Greg spoke up, "Dad, this is our treat to both you and Mom. Tomorrow we start a new family and the four of us couldn't be happier about it. This stag party is our way of celebrating. We are going to Swampscott to Anthony's. After that, we will make sure you and Mom get to bed early and are in good shape for tomorrow. We offspring have a lot invested in tomorrow's activities."

It was not a wild stag party with nubile young ladies jumping out of cakes but neither was it dull and boring like a proxy meeting. It was a fitting, happy tribute marking the end of one era and the beginning of another.

19

Saturday morning arrived in Malden the way mornings always have. The light sneaked in from the east while the dark skulked out to the west. The birds awoke and began their singing and their searching for food. People began to stir as they needed to arise and, softly, the city began to come awake. The pace was slow and steady, except for the two households.

Although the wedding was scheduled for late in the afternoon, there was nothing to prevent panic from rising the minute everyone woke up at the Da vinci and the Cabot houses. The panic began, actually, because there really was nothing to do until the ceremony and there was too much time to do it in.

At the Da Vinci home, the family ate a leisurely breakfast. Then Alice, wanting to be with Myrna to help her, started the confusion by immediately scheduling everybody's shower and dressing arrangements. That began a period of people rushing up and down halls, doors slamming, people yelling, and useless pandemonium. All the while the phone was in constant use with incoming or outgoing messages that only deepened the disarray. Alice would call the Cabot house and give directions to Jeffrey who would call back five minutes later for confirmation or clarification. If Greg or Billy answered the phone, the messages got even more mangled. By the time Alice went over to help Myrna, it was just after noon and Greg and Billy were dressed and ready but they had nothing to do but sit and wait. Ben had been wise enough to sidestep the whirlwind of turbulence by slipping out the door and working on his "farm."

Myrna's household was seeing the same surge of activity but the tide had not risen as high as the Da Vinci flood. Myrna was a little nervous but Lydia Bradford came over early and was a calming presence. When Alice arrived with her "get ready immediately" attitude, the tempo changed a little. Jeffrey was given a list of things to do and the phone became clogged with messages. Myrna finally escaped by going to Donna, her hairdresser, and getting her hair styled; she had scheduled the appointment for that day. She took Alice with her and insisted that she also get her hair styled. That not only pleased Alice, it settled her down.

Time passes whether people are active or inactive. So, slowly, the clock ticked and everyone got ready and appeared at the church when they were supposed to. The church was full because both Ben and Myrna had many friends. It was a simple, short ceremony and, afterwards, they held a reception dinner at the caterer's hall.

It was a merry time. Their guests enjoyed eating their food, drinking their drinks and constantly tapping on their water glasses with their forks. Myrna almost cried when three older men, all dressed in black suits that didn't quite fit them, came up to her and shyly gave her a copper tea kettle that they had pooled their money to buy. She hugged each man hard, gave him a kiss, and thanked him for coming to her wedding. The three of them left her talking amongst themselves in Italian and beaming from ear to ear.

Just before Ben and Myrna were driven to Logan Airport to leave for Italy, Ben got to his feet and addressed his guests. "To each of you who can't understand why such a beautiful, talented woman would choose me for her husband, let me tell you what is true; love is blind. For that, I am most thankful."

He motioned for Myrna to join him and he put his arm around her before he continued. "Myrna and I want to tell all of you that we both feel fortunate. We both are blessed. Before we met we each had been through our own good times and our own bad times. We believed that laughter and joy were behind us. But both of us are survivors and, somehow or other, we have been given another chance at life and at love.

"We are both smart enough to recognize how lucky we are. We intend to seize the opportunity to enjoy our life together as man and wife.

"That word 'together' is almost sacred to both of us.

"We only hope that all of you can feel as happy and as fortunate as we do on our wedding day. God bless us all."

They walked out of the hall and went outside. Myrna and Ben kissed and hugged all four of their children and then Greg drove them to the airport. Their life together had just begun.

Epilogue

There are only two ways that people can look at happiness and/or loneliness. Optimists see happiness as an oasis in the desert of loneliness; pessimists see loneliness as their homeport on the island of happiness. In either case, only conscious action will ever change a person's condition; inactivity is the strait jacket of progress. People either swim in the stream of life or they are swept away by it.

Myrna and Ben were both survivors who seized their opportunity for happiness and, in so doing, they not only achieved their goal, they also showed their children how to enjoy their lives.

After they returned from Italy, Myrna moved into Ben's house and sold hers. Ben became a real estate agent and made a lot more money working a lot less hours than he did as a barber. It wasn't long before their combined income became so high that they cut back on their work loads and spent more time taking trips and involving themselves in local charitable activities.

The declaration of nullity was rendered in Myrna's favor fifteen months after they married. They waited two years before making any decisions but, when they heard that Father Dante was going to retire, they asked him to marry them in Sacred Heart Church. That was his last official responsibility before he retired.

Over the years, they settled into a comfortable living routine while anxiously awaiting to become grandparents. Ben was patient and said nothing about the subject but Myrna would occasionally drop discrete, and not so discrete, hints to their four children. When she finally had their four children meeting her expectations, she began to think in terms of great grandchildren.

Billy was the first to get married. After he graduated and started working as an architect in a Boston firm he met a young, lady architect and they became engaged. She was Japanese and it took a while for her to understand the boisterous Da Vinci family. Their two daughters were delicate models of both cultures.

Greg married shortly after Billy. He was named All Ivy linebacker in his senior year but he was not interested in trying out for a professional football team. He changed his major and became a medical doctor. He met the girl he was to marry on a blind date. They settled in Hanover with their four boys and he kept in close touch with the rest of the family.

Jeffrey was the one who became the best known. He became a sports writer and then wrote several murder mysteries that earned him both fame and fortune. He married his secretary and, since they couldn't have children, they adopted a boy and a girl. He had always said that he would never have just a single child; he was a devoted father.

Alice was the last to marry and contribute to Myrna's pool of grandchildren. She took her time and went through several candidates before selecting a stockbroker as her husband. In between her career as a lawyer she had three boys and a girl. Myrna and she were in almost daily contact with each other over whatever came to their attention.

As a contrast to the joy of life that throbbed through the entire

Da Vinci family, was the fate of Samuel Skinner. Jeffrey found out about him, entirely by chance, on one of his book signing tours. Over drinks, he was talking to a Chicago detective about odd criminal characters when the detective said that he had just finished a case where the criminal came from the same area where Jeffrey lived. The culprit was a lawyer who had bilked several older women out of thousands of dollars. He was sentenced to prison for at least ten years. When the detective told Jeffrey the name of the swindler, he decided that it would do no good to go see his father.

After he got home he told the rest of the family about what he had discovered. The news saddened Myrna and Ben; they both had put their anger at him aside a long time ago. They preferred smiling to grumbling. However, they realized that some people, like vultures, enjoy preying on the weak. There was nothing they could do. They shrugged their shoulders and went about their business of being kind to the world.

That is because they had learned that the most powerful force on the face of this earth is neither man made nor negative. It is positive and it has the capability of changing the world. It is the power of love that wells up in each individual and it is available to mankind whenever mankind chooses to use it.

Acknowledgements

Behind every book there is always a list of innocent people who are guilty of nothing more than helping the author express himself. This author is no different; there was a group that tried (and the emphasis is on tried) their best not to have me display my ignorance. There is nothing more humbling than to have innocents and editors show an author just how illiterate and ignorant he really is.

Among the most innocent of the guilty parties are the following:

Father Dennis Dillon	St. Mary Student Parish, Ann Arbor, MI
Donna (Mancusi-Ungaro) Hart, PhD	University of Michigan
Judy Beam	Editor without Equal
Donald Proctor	Punctuation Prodigy

Among the most guilty of the innocent parties is the following:

Hazel Proctor	My wife who mistakenly believes that I am William Shakespeare

daybook, *n.* a book
in which the events
of the day are
recorded; *specif.* a
journal or diary

DAYBOOK
. . . .
of Critical Reading and Writing

AUTHOR

VICKI SPANDEL

CONSULTING AUTHORS

RUTH NATHAN

LAURA ROBB

Great Source Education Group
a Houghton Mifflin Company
Wilmington, Massachusetts

A u t h o r

VICKI SPANDEL, director of Write Traits, provides training to writing teachers both nationally and internationally. A former teacher and journalist, Vicki is author of more than twenty books, including the new third edition of **Creating Writers.**

C o n s u l t i n g   A u t h o r s

RUTH NATHAN, one of the authors of **Writers Express** and **Write Away,** is the author of many professional books and articles on literacy. She currently teaches in third grade as well as consults with numerous schools and organizations on reading.

LAURA ROBB, author of **Reading Strategies That Work** and **Teaching Reading in Middle School,** has taught language arts at Powhatan School in Boyce, Virginia, for more than thirty years. She also mentors and coaches teachers in Virginia public schools and speaks at conferences throughout the country.

Book Design: Christine Ronan and Sean O'Neill, Ronan Design

Developed by Nieman Inc.

Printed in the United States of America

International Standard Book Number: 0-669-48039-8

2 3 4 5 6 7 8 9 10 - POO - 09 08 07 06 05 04 03 02 01

Readers

Great Source wishes to acknowledge the many insights and improvements made to the Daybooks *thanks to the work of the following teachers and educators.*

Madeline Andrews
North Londonderry Elementary School
Londonderry, New Hampshire

Linda Cooper
North Londonderry Elementary School
Londonderry, New Hampshire

Janel de Boer
Stonewall Elementary School
Nicholas, Kentucky

Candy Hernandez
Dike-Newell Elementary School
Bath, Maine

Judy Hughes
Panama City, Florida

Cindy Hutchins
Fisher Mitchell Elementary School
Bath, Maine

Liz Johnson
Lincoln Elementary School
Mount Vernon, Washington

Lois Johnson
Cedar Grove Elementary School
Panama City, Florida

Deb Larson
Berryton Elementary School
Berryton, Kansas

Emily Luke
Patronis Elementary School
Panama City, Florida

Judith P. McAllister
Fisher Mitchell Elementary School
Bath, Maine

Arlene Moore
Lincoln Elementary School
Mount Vernon, Washington

Cathy Paquette
Dike-Newell Elementary School
Bath, Maine

Kim Prater
Cedar Grove Elementary School
Panama City, Florida

Barbara Pringle
South Elementary School
Londonderry, New Hampshire

Patty Roberts
Mark Twain Elementary School
Littleton, Colorado

Beth Schmar
Emporia State University
Emporia, Kansas

Jean Smith
Depaul University
Chicago, Illinois

Lucy Smith
Patronis Elementary School
Panama City, Florida

Table of Contents

Table of Contents (cont.)

Pupil's Skills and Strategies

WRITING	FOCUS
story ending	As you read, ask yourself: What do I think will happen next?
paragraph (main idea)	When you read, look for the most important idea. This is called the main idea.
rewrite from a different point of view	When the point of view changes, the story changes too.
journal entry	As you read, look for character clues. Pay attention to what the characters say and do.
setting sketch	When you read a book or story, look for clues about setting.
summarize and review a story	Plot is what happens in the beginning, middle, and end of a story.
use rhythm and rhyme to write a poem	Rhythm and rhyme make poems enjoyable to read.
paragraph	Sometimes writers choose words in order to help readers form pictures in their minds.
paragraph	Look for clues when you come to words you don't know.
character sketch	When you read, think about how characters look and act and what their lives are like.
schedule	Part of an author's style is the way he or she uses details to paint a picture in the reader's mind.
begin a story	Writers use their own experiences to create realistic characters, settings, and situations in stories.

LESSON TITLE	LITERATURE	AUTHOR	RESPONSE STRATEGY	CRITICAL READING SKILL
Unit 5: Reading Well				
Why an Author Writes	from *Fables*	Arnold Lobel	ask questions	author's purpose
What's It All About?	from *Fireflies in the Night*	Judy Hawes	mark up the text (clarify)	main idea
Using What You Know	from *Real Live Monsters!*	Ellen Schecter	ask questions	prior knowledge
Unit 6: Reading Nonfiction				
Sum It Up	from *Safari*	Robert Bateman	mark up the text (clarify)	summarize
Tracking the Order of Events	from *A Picture Book of Helen Keller*	David A. Adler	mark up the text	sequence
Reading Maps, Charts, and Graphs	from *Hottest, Coldest, Highest, Deepest*	Steve Jenkins	visualize	graphic aids
Unit 7: Understanding Language				
Hey, Reader—Are Your Senses Awake?	"Great Crystal Bear"	Carolyn Lesser	visualize	sensory details
Understanding Similes	from *Angels in the Dust*	Margot Theis Raven	highlight	simile
When Animals Talk	from *Desert Voices*	Byrd Baylor	predict	personification
Unit 8: Reading Authors				
Characters Make the Story	"Monday" from *Ma Dear*	Patricia McKissack	mark up the text (clarify)	character
What's My Purpose?	Author's Note from *Ma Dear*	Patricia McKissack	highlight	author's purpose
An Author's Language	from *Mirandy and Brother Wind*	Patricia McKissack	mark up the text (clarify)	author's style

WRITING	FOCUS STATEMENT
questions for interview	As you read, ask yourself, "Why did the author write this?"
main idea paragraph	When you read, look for the most important idea.
"what I learned" paragraph	Before you read, ask yourself: "What do I already know about this subject? What do I want to know?"
summary	A summary tells the most important ideas.
paragraph that shows sequence	Understanding sequence helps you keep track of events.
create a graphic aid	When you read nonfiction, use the graphic aids to help you picture ideas.
descriptive paragraph	Sensory details help the reader imagine what the writer describes.
simile sketches	Similes make meaning clear by showing how one thing is like another.
personification paragraph	Writers make stories come to life by giving animals and objects human qualities.
journal entry	Interesting characters talk, act, and feel like real people.
tribute to a special person	When you know a writer's purpose, it can help you make sense of what you read.
write a dialogue	Good writers make their characters sound like real people.

Correlation to Write on Track, ©1996

Daybook Lesson	Writing Activity	*Write on Track,* ©1996
Reading Well		
1. What Will Happen Next?	write ending to story	45, 113, 149
2. What's the Big Idea?	write a paragraph	55-57, 59, 60, 62, 63
3. My Side of the Story	rewrite a fairy tale	59, 166, 167
Reading Fiction		
1. Character Clues	write a journal entry	77-81
2. Where Am I?	drawing activity	
3. What's Happening Here?	write short book review	116-121
Understanding Language		
1. Listening to a Poem	write a poem	177-189
2. Word Magic	write a paragraph	55-57, 59, 60, 62, 63
3. What's the Word?	use a made-up word in paragraph	55-63
Reading Authors		
1. Finding Out About Characters	write a character sketch	55-57, 59, 60, 62-63
2. How an Author Writes	write descriptive sentences	38-39, 69-73, 324-327
3. Writing About Real Life	write beginning of story	41, 45, 55-60, 62-63, 149, 153
Reading Well		
1. Why an Author Writes	write a list of interview questions	252-253
2. What's It All About?	write a paragraph	55-63
3. Using What You Know	write a paragraph	55-57, 60, 62-63

Daybook Lesson	Writing Activity	*Write on Track,* ©1996
Reading Nonfiction		
1. Sum It Up	write a summary	64-67
2. Tracking the Order of Events	describe activity	55-57, 59, 62-63
3. Reading Maps, Charts, and Graphs	create a bar graph	
Understanding Language		
1. Hey, Reader—Are Your Senses Awake?	write descriptive paragraph using sensory details	38-39, 55-57, 59, 62-63
2. Understanding Similies	write a description and use a simile	55-57, 59, 62-63, 183
3. When Animals Talk	write a paragraph	55-59, 62-63
Reading Authors		
1. Characters Make the Story	write a journal entry	77-81
2. What's My Purpose?	write a tribute	
3. An Author's Language	write a dialogue	174

Overview

What is a *Daybook*? Why do I need one? How do I use it? These questions come up almost immediately among teachers when they first see a *Daybook*.

Purpose

A *Daybook* is a keepable, journal-like book designed to improve students' reading and writing. Its purpose is to engage students in brief, integrated reading and writing activities daily or at least weekly. By asking students regularly to read good literature and write about it, students will become better readers and writers.

Lessons

Each lesson is a brief, highly focused activity that concentrates on one aspect of critical reading. By focusing on a single skill, students can see how to do critical reading. The lessons include models showing how to respond actively to literature in the Response Notes. Each *Daybook* even begins with an introductory "Active Reading" unit to show students some of the ways to respond actively to literature. Then, in the lessons, students respond creatively to the literature through writing descriptions, journal entries, narrative paragraphs, and many other kinds of writing—all in response to great literature.

Literature

The literature included in this *Daybook* came from suggestions teachers made. More than sixty master teachers recommended their favorite books and authors, and from these came the quality selections included here. Each selection was reviewed for its appropriateness and for its illustration of the critical reading skill at the heart of the lesson. In addition, a blend of traditional and non-traditional authors, fiction and nonfiction, and different genres were considered. At each step, teachers from the appropriate grade level commented upon the literature, readability, appropriateness of the activities, and critical reading skill.

Goals

The final result can be seen in the *Daybook*, where each individual lesson has been crafted to fit in the reading and writing curricula of elementary teachers. The goals of the *Daybook* are reflected in the headings of the units:
- to teach students how to read actively
- to build the essential skills (such as summarizing and finding the main idea) for reading well
- to develop an appreciation for the elements of fiction, poetry, and nonfiction
- to create a love and appreciation of language
- to introduce students to and foster an appreciation of fine authors and great literature

Uses for *Daybooks*

Teachers suggested numerous ways to use the *Daybook*, from introducing author studies to reinforcing key reading and writing skills. It can serve as a portfolio of daily reading and writing practice or as a guide to introducing key skills. How you use the *Daybook* ultimately depends upon you. No matter how you use it, the *Daybook* can become a powerful tool to help create better, more confident readers and writers.

Who Is This Book For?

The immediate response to the question "Who is this book for?" is that the audience is average, ordinary students. The *Daybook* targets everyday students in grades 3–5. Because of their intensive work on reading and writing, the *Daybooks* can help all students, but they are aimed at neither the best nor the worst, just average students.

What's Average?

The question about the audience for the *Daybook* comes up when considering how the literature was chosen, how its readability was gauged, what assignments were chosen, and how much readiness or scaffolding is needed in each lesson. But even average students vary widely and respond much differently to individual lessons.

For example, in "Hey, Reader—Are Your Senses Awake?" in grade 3, students read "Great Crystal Bear" by Carolyn Lesser. For students in predominately warm climates, polar bears do not represent everyday experience. Teachers there will need to build some readiness about these strange, magnificent creatures. In one state, students may be tested on writing descriptive paragraphs in the state assessment exams, and thus practice writing descriptions regularly; but, in another state, descriptive paragraphs may just be starting to be introduced. To establish what would work on average, then, state standards as well as the appropriate on-grade-level texts were referenced. (Writing assignments, for example, were matched to expectations in such appropriate grade-level texts as *Write on Track*, *Writers Express*, and so forth. The same is true of the reading skills.) Current practices and materials provided reference points to check assumptions about what's average.

Why Use These Authors?

Likewise, selecting specific authors to feature at specific grade levels seems somewhat arbitrary. What makes Julius Lester a fourth-grade author and Patricia McKissack a third-grade one? Here teachers guided the selection of which literature and which authors to use. Asking sixty master teachers to recommend literature and authors hardly approaches scientific reliability, but it is a useful touchstone. The intent is not to limit authors or a piece of literature to a specific grade level as much as it is to offer a rich, broad variety of literature at each grade level.

What's the Readability?

For teachers in the elementary grades, helping students find materials at their specific reading level is a major challenge. Each student is different, and the right reading level for one student poses insuperable challenges for the next student. The readability of selections in the *Daybook* will change from lesson to lesson. The entire notion of "readability level" depends, among other elements, on word choice, sentence length and complexity, and subject matter. As in the case of the "Great Crystal Bear," such words as *polar, winter solstice*, and *winter* may have different levels of familiarity to students who live in different parts of the world. Readability can vary from student to student.

If one selection seems too easy or too hard for your students, realize that the selections and "readability" changes throughout the *Daybook*. Lessons are organized by the critical reading skills taught, not by the reading "level" of the selection.

How Will I Know?

Is this *Daybook* right for my students? As teachers, you routinely ask this question—about the *Daybook* and all of the other books in your classroom. You want assurance that the selections will match the reading abilities of your students. One obvious answer is simply to try some lessons with your students. The experience of other teachers has been that those who get started and work through some lessons with students find a way to make the fit between the materials and the students. Each lesson in this teacher's guide includes a Vocabulary Activity and a Prereading Activity to improve students' readiness for the selection. Such supporting activities can help students with more challenging selections.

In the end, the best guide will be your own experience and instincts as a teacher. Try a number of lessons with students. Encourage them, challenge them, and evaluate them. Let your students be your guide in whether or not the *Daybook* is right for your classroom.

How to Use the Daybook

The *Daybook* is a tool. Like any tool, such as a hammer or screwdriver, the *Daybook* can have one purpose or many, depending on the ingenuity of the user. Teachers who reviewed the *Daybook* lessons suggested any number of ways they would use them.

1. In the Reading Period

Reviewers of the *Daybook*s often introduced *Daybook* lessons to students during part of their reading period. Whether they were using thematically linked trade books or anthologies, teachers saw the *Daybook*s' focused lessons as helpful ways to reinforce (or introduce) key skills and bring more good literature into their classrooms.

*Daybook*s also served as ways to kick off author studies or a series of reading skills lessons. Other teachers preferred to introduce an author or a skill, such as prediction, on their own and then complement their lessons with ones from the *Daybook*.

2. In the Language Arts Period

Because each lesson begins with great literature, teachers like launching writing activities with *Daybook* lessons. Each lesson gives students literature to which they respond as well as a series of scaffolded assignments to help students get ready to write. Because the *Daybook* includes so many strong writing assignments (summaries, descriptive paragraphs, narrative paragraphs, journal entries, and so on), teachers like the clear, efficient ways the *Daybook* draws students into writing. The daily writing in the *Daybook*s appealed to many reviewers facing state tests, because their students would be able to practice regularly and build confidence as writers before test day.

3. In Reading and Writing Workshops

Numerous teachers use reading and writing workshops each week in their classrooms, and they found the integrated nature of the *Daybook* lessons to be a perfect fit for what they were trying to accomplish. The goals of their workshops and the *Daybook* lessons matched up almost exactly. Each lesson leads students from literature directly into writing, helping students to see the connections between what they read and what they write.

4. In Alternative Settings

As after-school tutorials and summer sessions become more common, teachers are looking for ways to reinforce key reading and writing skills. The brief, efficient lessons in the *Daybook*s fit well with the brief sessions in after-school and summer school programs. Teachers also pick and choose among the lessons in these alternative settings, focusing on areas where students need the greatest help. Here the flexibility of individual lessons that integrate reading and writing becomes valuable, because each lesson weaves together so many elements: fine literature, active reading, critical reading skills, and creative writing.

The uses of the *Daybook*s are limited only by the teachers using them. Laura Robb's article "Ten Ways to Effectively Use Daybooks" on pages 26–28 suggests a number of additional ways to use *Daybook*s. However you choose to use them, keep in mind that the original intent behind the *Daybook*s was to create a flexible tool for teachers to help them give students meaningful reading and writing activities, day after day, in their classrooms.

Frequently Asked Questions

Reviewers raised a number of questions during the development of the *Daybook* manuscript that might be useful to teachers using the series for the first time.

1. Why is it called a *Daybook*?

A *Daybook* traditionally is "a book in which daily transactions are recorded," but nowadays it is being used to mean "a journal." The name connotes "daily work," which is the intent behind the *Daybook*, as well as the idea of "journal," because a *Daybook* does become a place where students can record their work and ideas.

2. Can students write in the *Daybooks?*

Absolutely! In fact, that is the purpose behind this format. By writing in the book— their book—students begin to "own" the book. It records their work and their ideas. It becomes a personal record of their creative efforts, a portfolio of sorts of their development as readers and writers. One of the strongest elements of the *Daybook*s comes in allowing students to mark in the text, highlighting, underscoring, circling, and writing notes. Reading and writing in the same book creates the seamless integration that makes the *Daybook* work.

3. Can I photocopy these pages?

No, photocopying the pages in the *Daybook* is prohibited. It violates copyright laws that protect the authors' rights to their work and the publishers' rights to the product. Besides, the effect of working on a few loose-leaf sheets of paper or of working in a *Daybook* of one's own is very different. So, not only is copying unlawful, but it fails as a teaching practice.

4. Can I skip around, picking and choosing the lessons?

Yes, you can pick and choose the lessons you want to teach. One strong feature of the *Daybook* is its incredible flexibility, making it a perfect tool for teachers who want to interweave *Daybook* lessons into a crowded language arts or reading class period. The lessons in the *Daybook* have been organized into units with a logic and continuity that make sense; but other organizations of the lessons or individual lessons may well fit better with the specific needs of your classroom, and you should feel free to take advantage of the *Daybook*s lessons' flexibility.

5. What if my students are not active readers and need more help in learning how to mark up a text?

Begin with the Active Reading unit that introduces students to the most common ways of marking up a text. That's the obvious starting point, but it's only a start. Not every child will, in a few quick lessons, "get it." That's what the *Daybook* is for. Through repeated practice, students will "get it" and learn how to become active readers.

6. How were the literature selections chosen?

First, we asked approximately sixty master teachers what sort of literature they wanted to see, and they listed their favorite authors. With that background, the individual selections were evaluated on several criteria—the author, interest and accessibility of the selection, fit with the critical reading skill and writing skill, and overall balance of genre, sex, race, and ethnicity. But, first and foremost, the mandate from reviewers was good literature by good authors, and that ultimately guided selection of every piece.

7. How do I assess students' work?

Assessment looms as an issue for almost any classroom practice, including the *Daybooks*. How you "grade" them is an individual decision. Most teachers who have used *Daybooks* at the upper grades collect them periodically and mark in them. They may make an encouraging comment, check off that work was completed, and acknowledge the hard work and creativity students have poured into their *Daybooks*. Vicki Spandel addresses this issue of assessment more thoroughly in an article in this teacher's guide on pages 29–31. The important issue is that you assess students as active readers and as writers and that you take into account that students' writings in the *Daybooks* are responses to literature more than finished, published compositions.

Organization of the Daybooks

The units and lessons follow an organization designed to offer you the greatest flexibility in using the *Daybooks*.

Unit Organization

Throughout the *Daybooks*, three or four lessons are organized into a unit. This gives you a concentration of lessons on a general idea. For example, Reading Fiction allows you to introduce all of the key skills (plot, setting, characters) at one time. The units are focused on a few broad areas:

Introduction: Active Reading
- introduces the fundamentals of marking up texts, such as highlighting, underlining, questioning, predicting, and visualizing

Reading Well
- looks at basic reading skills, such as prediction, main idea, and making inferences

Reading Fiction or Nonfiction
- focuses on reading related to a genre, such as sequence, setting, characters, and so forth

Understanding Language
- highlights appreciation of words, sensory images, similes, and metaphors, with a focus on poetry

Reading Authors
- studies individual authors, their ideas, and skills related to their writing

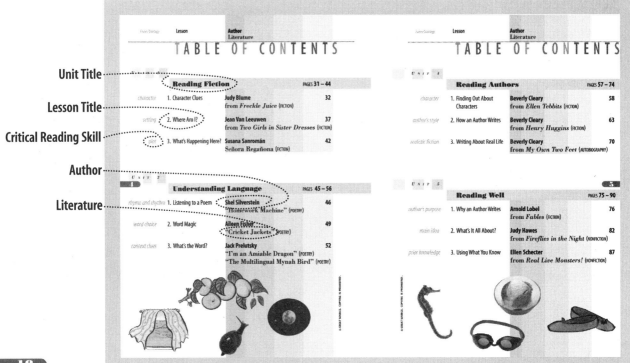

Lesson Organization

Each lesson also follows a simple, flexible organization. A typical lesson begins with a few sentences that introduce a critical reading skill. Just before reading the selection, the lesson gives the response strategy that tells students what to look for and how to mark up the text in the Response Notes. The "response" strategies given here pick up the active reading strategies introduced in the first unit, **Introduction: Active Reading.**

The literature selection follows, after which—in most cases—students have an initial activity that invites them simply to respond to the selection. This initial activity asks for their thoughts, feelings, or first impressions. Then one or more activities prepare students to write a longer assignment.

focus on critical reading

initial "response" activity

running head with unit title

lesson title

"response" or active reading strategy

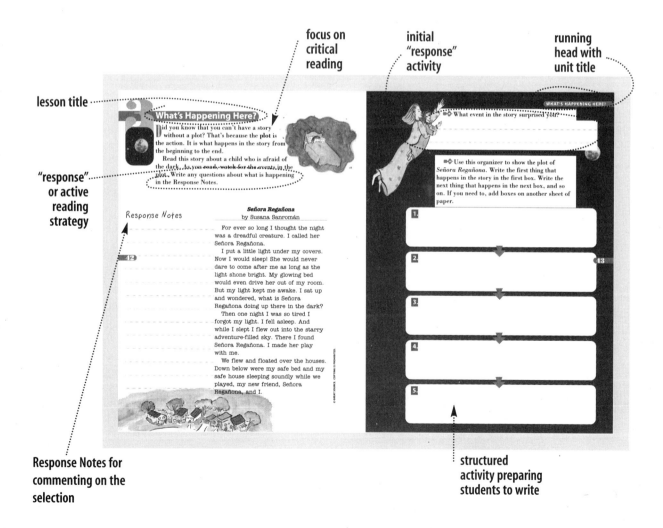

Response Notes for commenting on the selection

structured activity preparing students to write

The last writing activity culminates the lesson and asks for a writing product, such as a descriptive paragraph, summary, review, character sketch, or the like. The lesson then ends with a summary statement that restates the critical reading idea.

culminating writing activity ·······························▶

➥◇ Write a short book review of *Señora Regañona*. Use the notes from your organizer to help you describe what happened in the story. Then tell why you liked or did not like the story.

Book Review: <u>Señora Regañona</u>

<u>Señora Regañona</u>, by Susana Sanromán, is about _____

This is how I felt about this story: _____

focus or summary statement at the end
of the lesson ····························▶
Plot is what happens in the beginning, middle, and end of a story.

T e a c h e r ' s   G u i d e

Because of a strong emphasis on reading, the *Daybook Teacher's Guide* includes more than just resources for each lesson. Teachers encouraged the authors to offer more help in improving reading instruction in the classroom, and the *Daybooks* attempt to do that in several ways:

1. Program Resources
• Skills and Strategies overview
• Correlation to *Write on Track*

2. Professional Articles
• Ruth Nathan on "Building Better Readers"
• Laura Robb on "Ten Ways to Effectively Use the *Daybooks*"
• Vicki Spandel on "Assessment of Writing—Some Guidelines"

3. Reading Workshop
• workshop on key reading skills and strategies
• do-it-yourself blackline masters to implement the strategies

4. Lesson Resources
• prereading, vocabulary, critical reading, response, and rereading skills and strategies for each lesson
• prewriting and writing activities for each lesson

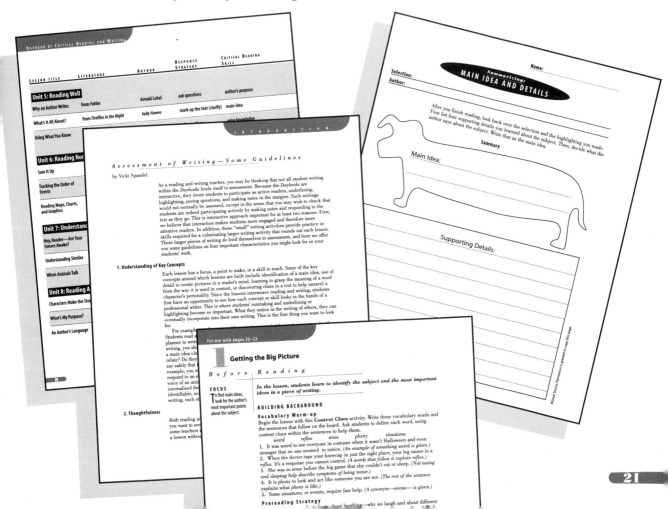

Lesson Resources

The first part of each lesson in the *Teacher's Guide* helps briefly to prepare students for the selection, providing background and introducing new or difficult words. Then each lesson discusses the response strategy, critical reading skill, and a rereading suggestion.

Focus statement is restated.

Vocabulary Warm-up introduces new words in the selection.

Prereading Strategy builds background and readiness for the selection.

Model for active reading shown

Main critical reading focus taught and explained

Rereading Strategy encourages students to go back into the selection and improve comprehension.

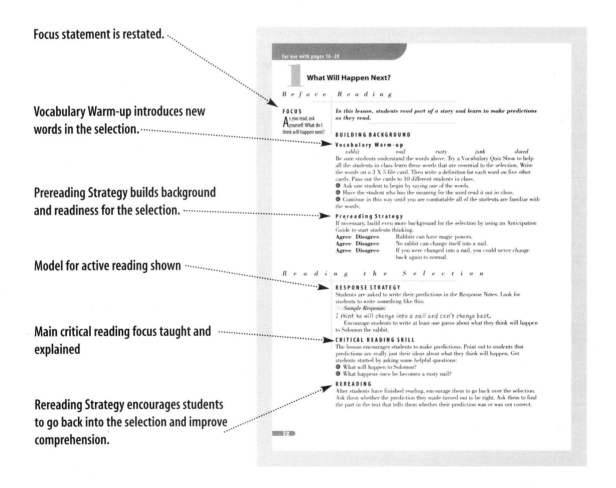

For use with pages 16–20

What Will Happen Next?

Before Reading

FOCUS
As you read, ask yourself: What do I think will happen next?

In this lesson, students read part of a story and learn to make predictions as they read.

BUILDING BACKGROUND

Vocabulary Warm-up

    rabbit   nail   rusty   junk   dared

Be sure students understand the words above. Try a Vocabulary Quiz Show to help all the students in class learn these words that are essential to the selection. Write the words on a 3 X 5 file card. Then write a definition for each word on five other cards. Pass out the cards to 10 different students in class.
❶ Ask one student to begin by saying one of the words.
❷ Have the student who has the meaning for the word read it out in class.
❸ Continue in this way until you are comfortable all of the students are familiar with the words.

Prereading Strategy

If necessary, build even more background for the selection by using an Anticipation Guide to start students thinking.

Agree Disagree   Rabbits can have magic powers.
Agree Disagree   No rabbit can change itself into a nail.
Agree Disagree   If you were changed into a nail, you could never change back again to normal.

Reading the Selection

RESPONSE STRATEGY

Students are asked to write their predictions in the Response Notes. Look for students to write something like this:

    Sample Response:
I think he will change into a nail and can't change back.
    Encourage students to write at least one guess about what they think will happen to Solomon the rabbit.

CRITICAL READING SKILL

The lesson encourages students to make predictions. Point out to students that predictions are really just their ideas about what they think will happen. Get students started by asking some helpful questions:
❶ What will happen to Solomon?
❷ What happens once he becomes a rusty nail?

REREADING

After students have finished reading, encourage them to go back over the selection. Ask them whether the prediction they made turned out to be right. Ask them to find the part in the text that tells them whether their prediction was or was not correct.

22

The second half of every *Teacher's Guide* lesson concentrates on the writing portion of the lesson. Sample responses are indicated for each activity, not to indicate right answers but rather to suggest the way students might respond. Then writing suggestions are included for helping students as they write, and quick assessment criteria are suggested for each lesson.

Quick Assess gives rubric for assessment.

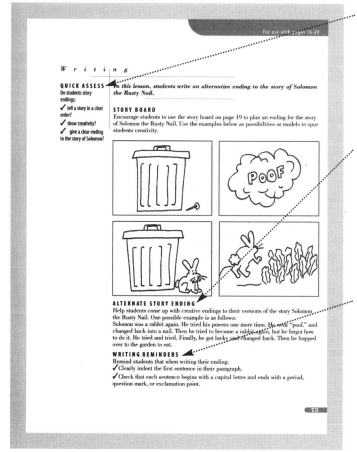

Writing Activities are noted and explained, with sample responses indicated.

Writing Reminders provide some additional help for students as they write.

Building Better Readers

by Ruth Nathan

Introduction

Today we know enough about the teaching of reading to insure that all students become competent, life-long readers. The past half-century of research has shed light on what skilled readers know and can do as they read, and on what skilled teachers do to enhance the reading success of all their students. The creators of the *Daybooks* kept this research in mind as they developed the series.

What do skilled readers know and do as they read?

Thoughtful, active, and proficient readers think about their own thinking during reading: they are "metacognitive." For example, good readers know what and when they are comprehending, and when they are not comprehending they use a variety of strategies to solve their problems. They also know how to deepen understanding by summarizing as they read, seeking clarification of unknown terms or concepts, questioning the author, using what they know to make inferences, and predicting upcoming events or concepts. Simply put, proficient readers monitor their comprehension actively. Before they read, they prepare in various ways. They might look at how texts are structured to get the "big picture," review graphics, predict what will be covered or what will happen, or bring forward relevant background knowledge. After reading, thoughtful readers reflect in a variety of ways, from discussing what they've read with friends or classmates to actively summarizing, outlining, or creating graphic organizers. Young, skilled readers tend to read widely and often. They see reading as one way into both joyful times and a successful school year.

How do skilled teachers enhance reading success for all?

Among the many features of effective instruction that successful schools use, four features stand out relative to learning to read. First, students learn strategies for doing their work. Effective teachers guide students through strategies step-by-step, giving them tips on how to read as well as how to think about their reading. Second, teachers help students make connections across instruction, curriculum, and life. They weave a web of connections within and across lessons, as well as to students' lives in and out of school. Third, students learn skills and knowledge in multiple lesson types. This means, for example, that a skill might be highlighted out of context and then reintroduced within a more natural reading experience. And, fourth, students are expected to be generative thinkers. For example, students might be asked to compare the treatment of an issue in a piece of literature with other pieces they have read or with their own life.

Building Better Readers: The *Daybook* Connection

The *Daybook* Series has brought what we know about skilled readers and skilled teaching together in one student-friendly paperback. The stories are, first and foremost, readable. The literature excerpts, all written by widely known and beloved children's authors, are varied and have been leveled in difficulty such that students are reading stories and essays at their ever-changing instructional/independent level.

With pencil in hand, students actively read by marking up the text. Children highlight and underline, draw pictures, and respond in margins as they predict, question, visualize, and think about new words during reading. By guiding students through comprehension strategies step-by-step, the *Daybook* teaches and reinforces the critical skills of finding the main idea, summarizing, making inferences, and other aspects of active and successful reading. Embedded in the *Daybooks* are strategies for monitoring comprehension, including rereading the text. Each lesson in the *Daybook* begins with activating students' prior knowledge and is followed by writing opportunities that connect the selection to other texts and students' lives. Each lesson ends with valuable writing activities, all designed to help students feel comfortable with writing as well as reading. Taken together, the approach used and strategies selected in the *Daybook* mirror current research findings. These books will encourage students to become active, engaged, and comfortable readers.

Ten Ways to Effectively Use Daybooks

by Laura Robb

"I'm such a slow reader. I don't enjoy reading."
"Reading is boring; it's just words, words, words."

These comments, spoken by middle-grade readers, reflect youngsters who are not actively involved with making meaning. The challenge we teachers face is to help every child develop that intense I-can't-put-that-book-down-feeling that motivates engaged readers to turn to books for entertainment and to learn new information. Allocating ample time each day for independent reading and ensuring that students are actively engaged in reading during that time are among teachers' most important tasks in comprehension instruction. The lessons in the *Daybooks* can transform children into active readers who connect their lives and experiences to the the finest poets and authors of fiction and nonfiction.

Research has demonstrated that the more time children read and write in authentic ways, the greater their progress in reading and writing. When children read and write at school for twenty to thirty minutes each day, they are developing their minds and imaginations in ways similar to athletes training for a sport—where daily practice is the key to progress and developing expertise. Whether a basal anthology or children's literature is the core of your literacy program, the *Daybooks* can enhance the reading and writing power of every child.

"Each of my third graders loves having their own *Daybook*—they can create a unique set of responses to the literature, and I love the extra time they spend reading, writing, and thinking." These words, spoken by a teacher required to cover a third grade anthology, illustrate the versatility of the *Daybook's* reading and writing experiences. I have identified ten ways to integrate the *Daybooks* into your reading program—ten top-notch ways that can move your students forward.

1. Introduce Students to Reading/Writing Strategies

In the *Daybook*, students practice active reading strategies such as marking a text, jotting notes while reading, predicting and questioning, and pinpointing the key details in nonfiction and fiction. Short selections are ideal for students to practice and apply the reading strategies that proficient readers use to construct meaning and link what they know to new information. The writing students complete grows out of their reading and provides opportunities to plan writing and to explore different genres, such as persuasive, informative, and descriptive paragraphs, writing dialogues, summaries, and narratives.

2. Become the Core of a Literature-based Program

As the centerpiece of your reading program, the *Daybook's* reading and writing skills (summarized in the strategy grid on pages 6–9) become the guide for your reading and writing program. All the skills and strategies that students practice are those third graders need to improve comprehension and recall and to develop test-taking skills. With the *Daybook* as the core of your reading program, it's easy to extend students' reading experiences for you can:

- Offer students the book from which they read a selected passage.
- Conduct an author study and have students read other books by a *Daybook* author.
- Invite students to read books and materials that relate to a theme in the *Daybook*.
- Ask students to read many books in a genre that the *Daybook* introduces.

3. Enrich Your Basal Program

I view the stories in basal anthologies as one part of a reading program. To progress, students must read widely and reflect on their reading. With the *Daybooks,* you can extend students' reading experiences and involve them in thinking and writing activities that grow out of the reading selections. Moreover, you can use selections from the *Daybook* to reteach strategies and skills, offering students the additional practice they require to deepen their understanding of pinpointing the main idea or figuring out the meaning of new words using context clues.

4. Guide New Teachers and Teachers Making the Transition to a Literature-based Program

As you read and study the *Daybook*'s *Teacher's Guide*, you'll explore tried-and-true suggestions that model and explain how to effectively introduce each selection. During the year, as your students complete the *Daybook* lessons, they'll access research-tested reading strategies that can deepen their involvement with fiction, nonfiction, and poetry.

5. Introduce Children to Fine Authors and Literary Genres

I want all students to read literature that they will enjoy rereading and that is worth thinking about and discussing. That's why we've spent months carefully selecting pieces by such award winning authors as Beverly Clearly, Patricia McKissack, and Jon Scieszka, while still always being careful to maintain a cultural and gender balance. Equally as important, the authors in the *Daybooks* are favorites of children and teachers. To link reading and writing, we've invited students to experience and study a genre, then to try their hand at writing in that genre.

6. Reinforce Specific Reading/Writing Strategies

Use the *Daybook* to offer students additional practice and/or review of reading strategies and writing techniques. As students revisit and review, they deepen their understanding of how these skills and strategies work and develop the problem-solving tools that readers and writers use.

7. Works Perfectly for Small Group Instruction Led by the Teacher

The short selections in the *Daybook* are ideal for organizing small group instruction that focuses on a reading strategy, such as stating the main idea or a writing technique, such as planning a piece. You can abandon those time-consuming searches for short, grade-level pieces; instead choose a selection and follow-up writing activity from the *Daybook*.

8. Encourage Students to Work Independently

We've designed the *Daybook*s so students can successfully complete lessons on their own or while working with a partner or small group. While students independently read and write, you're free to support students who need scaffolding.

9. Individualize Instruction

If the students in your classes are like the groups I teach, then you'll be supporting students with a wide range of reading and writing abilities. *Daybooks* simplify individualizing instruction because students can complete each lesson independently. Have grade level readers work in the third grade *Daybook*. Those reading above grade level can complete the *Daybooks* for grades four, five, or six. By individualizing instruction, you enable every child to start at his or her independent reading level and slowly move forward.

10. Save Teachers Time

The hours you set aside to rummage through stacks of books and magazines searching for literature for your students can now be used for responding to students' written work. When you include the *Daybooks* in your curriculum, you have a collection of the finest literature as well as reading, writing, and vocabulary skills and strategies that relate to each selection—and it's all there in one ready-to-use book!

Assessment of Writing—Some Guidelines

by Vicki Spandel

As a reading and writing teacher, you may be thinking that not all student writing within the *Daybooks* lends itself to assessment. Because the *Daybooks* are interactive, they invite students to participate as active readers, underlining, highlighting, posing questions, and making notes in the margins. Such writings would not normally be assessed, except in the sense that you may wish to check that students are indeed participating actively by making notes and responding to the text as they go. This interactive approach is important for at least two reasons. First, we believe that interaction makes students more engaged and therefore more attentive readers. In addition, these "small" writing activities provide practice in skills required for a culminating larger writing activity that rounds out each lesson. These larger pieces of writing *do* lend themselves to assessment, and here we offer you some guidelines on four important characteristics you might look for in your students' work.

1. Understanding of Key Concepts

Each lesson has a focus, a point to make, or a skill to teach. Some of the key concepts around which lessons are built include identification of a main idea, use of detail to create pictures in a reader's mind, learning to grasp the meaning of a word from the way it is used in context, or discovering clues in a text to help unravel a character's personality. Since the lessons interweave reading and writing, students first have an opportunity to see how each concept or skill looks in the hands of a professional writer. This is where students' notetaking and underlining or highlighting become so important. What they notice in the writing of others, they can eventually incorporate into their own writing. This is the first thing you want to look for.

For example, one lesson provides practice on main idea and supporting details. Students read about a subject such as fireflies and make notes, then use a main idea planner to write a paragraph of their own. As you look at your students' original writing, you should look for a reflection of the lesson learned: using details to make a main idea clear. Is there a main idea? Is it easy for you to identify? Do the details relate? Do they help make the main idea clear? If these things are true, then you can say safely that the student has internalized the point of the lesson. As a second example, you might look at a lesson on personification. Students first read and respond to an example of personification. Then, students are asked to adopt the voice of an animal and write from this unique perspective. Those who have internalized the concept of personification will show this in their writing through an identifiable, accurate voice that comes from this new perspective. Through the writing, each student will "become" the animal character he or she is portraying.

2. Thoughtfulness

Both reading and writing are thoughtful, reflective activities. In students' writing, you want to see evidence of this reflection and thoughtfulness—a characteristic some teachers might call "depth." It is quite possible for students to breeze through a lesson without really asking, "Which words create meaning? Which passages are memorable enough to underline? Which phrases give me important clues about the point this author is trying to make?" Students who read this way, however, will have difficulty projecting much thoughtfulness in their own writing—simply because they have not taken time to notice what skilled writers do to create meaning.

For example, in another lesson students read and consider two fables and are asked to identify the author's purpose. A surface sort of response might be "to tell a story." While this is true on a literal level, it does not reveal much probing into the real reasons authors write, and more specifically, the reasons authors write fables. More thoughtful responses might be—"to make readers think," "to teach readers about life," "to show what people are like," "to make us laugh at ourselves," or "to teach lessons." Reflective responses are often striking, surprising, and even provocative. They may raise questions in your own mind—or push you to a new level of thought. They may make you see a piece of literature in a way you had not anticipated. Look for writing that shows insight, in-depth understanding, a willingness to question, or an unusual point of view; any of these will tell you, "This was a student who put real thought into his or her writing." Appreciate the student who does not settle for an obvious answer, but who tosses a question around in his or her head for a time and insists on responding in an original way.

3. Attention to Detail

Young reader-writers reflect attention to detail in a number of ways. One is through the ability to make connections to their own lives and experiences. Writers such as Beverly Cleary are famous for their perception and sensitivity to the details around them. When we share their literature, we invite students to share in this perception, too—to tune into their own world (using Cleary or another author as a model) and note the details they might otherwise have missed. In "Reading Authors," students have several opportunities to make connections between the readings and the events or images from their own experience. The power of these connections depends largely on attention to detail.

For instance, in a lesson "Finding Out About Characters," students read about a third grader named Ellen Tebbits. Readers who are inexperienced in looking for detail may simply see Ellen as a young girl on the way to her dance lesson. They may not notice that Ellen is lonely, that she hurries because she is shy and does not want to speak to anyone, or that she feels relieved to be the first one to arrive at dance class so that no one can stare at her as she walks in. Perceptive readers will pick up these little details and clues. When they write a character sketch, it will go beyond a description of Ellen's appearance (thin, scraggly brown hair), and will touch on her inner self: her motivations, fears, hopes, thoughts, and wishes. Detailed writing is thorough and satisfying; it digs beneath the obvious. It holds your attention. It paints a picture in your mind, and often evokes feelings as well. These are the things you should look for in your students' writing.

In addition, writers who read for detail find it easy to summarize what they have learned. In a lesson "Using What You Know," readers are asked to read not just for pleasure but also to gain information. Those students with a strong sense of detail will look for the unusual or intriguing as they read, and then create writing that is both accurate and attention-getting. First, they will capture details correctly. But in addition, like all good nonfiction writers, they will grab and hold your interest by using details you can't ignore. In students' nonfiction writing, look for accuracy and detail that counts.

4. Growth as Readers and Writers

As students record their thoughts and reactions in the *Daybook*, they create a kind of portfolio. Like all portfolios kept over time, this one will show growth—one of the most important qualities you can look for in your students' work. What does growth look like? How will you recognize it?

First, you may simply see an expanding fluency, a willingness to write more text and to include more detail, more opinion, more personal observation. In addition, you may sense that your young writers are writing with more ease, that writing is becoming a natural and comfortable thing to do. You are likely to see more marginal notes, more sensitive and thoughtful questions, more text everywhere—and less hesitancy to share personal thoughts and feelings, even when others may not agree.

Second, you may find that your students are more creative, adventurous, and experimental in their writing. Their sense of voice may grow stronger, so that the text takes on the power that comes from expressiveness, individuality, and confidence. You may not work your way through these lessons exactly in the order they're presented, of course, but let's say you did. You might then make some comparisons by looking at early writing, then later pieces, to see how voice and confidence have grown. An early lesson in *Daybook* 3 presents students with an excerpt from Jon Scieszka's *The True Story of the Three Little Pigs by A. Wolf.* Students are then asked to come up with a "true story" of their own, based on another fairy tale, such as "Cinderella." Their responses may be very lively and filled with voice—or they may be slightly more restrained and tentative. After all, this may be one of their first attempts at this kind of writing. How much will this early voice grow? You can tell by comparing this writing with later pieces. It is likely that you will hear an emerging personal voice that reveals both a strong sense of self and an awareness of an audience. Strong writers never forget that they are writing to someone; in fact, every sample in this *Daybook* was chosen because it revealed that audience awareness. When you see and hear awareness of audience in your students' writing, you know the voice is strong.

Third, expect growth in the amount and quality of detail you see within their text. In one lesson, readers focus on sensory detail, first noticing the detail-rich text, then creating a sensory passage of their own, bringing an animal to life through sights, sounds, smells, and feelings. Compare the detail of this text with that of earlier writings. Is it more vivid? Are the words more precise? Is the picture more clear in your mind than those created much earlier? If so, then the writer has grown both as an observer and as a recorder of detail.

You may also see growth in such things as vocabulary (a willingness to stretch and use new words and an ability to use new words accurately), sentence fluency (longer sentences, more variety, a more natural flow), and control of conventions (spelling, punctuation, grammar, capitalization). No one thing should be the focus of your measure of growth; but together these many qualities of writing give a full picture of how a student is gaining in confidence and control.

Once students have worked with the *Daybook* for a time, you can look inside and see, through their comments and their writings, that they have traveled on a journey of understanding as readers and writers. The final, most significant assessment is this: Have they taken the best of what they have observed in the writing of others and woven it into their own text? This noticing, borrowing, and interweaving is what the *Daybook* journey is all about.

The *Daybook* attempts to build better readers—ones that read actively, marking up the text, highlighting, questioning, predicting, and visualizing. The numerous, brief selections give students many opportunities to become more fluent, more active readers.

But the many different selections also pose challenges for younger readers. With each selection, students meet new vocabulary, new subjects, new characters—in short, new challenges. To help with difficult selections, the Reading Workshop presented here attempts to give you some tools to use with students during the reading process. At each step in the process—before they read, during their reading, and after their reading—you can help them succeed. This Reading Workshop can serve as a handy toolkit of strategies to use as needed.

This workshop has 3 parts:

• **Before Reading**

• **During Reading**

• **After Reading**

Within each part, reading strategies are explained and then followed by a do-it-yourself blackline master for you to adapt to individual *Daybook* lessons.

Before Reading

Before students open their *Daybooks*, your **goals** for helping students before they read are:

1. **to introduce key vocabulary**

2. **to build readiness and anticipation**

3. **to set the purpose for reading**

Among the better **strategies** for accomplishing these goals are:

➤ **Word or concept webs**

➤ **Vocabulary inventory**

➤ **Anticipation guides**

➤ **Think-pair-and-share**

Word   or   Concept   Web

What Is It?

A word or concept web can build a common background before students read. By writing the key word or concept in the center of a web and then brainstorming with the class or in small groups, all students can pool their common knowledge of a subject. Webs often work best in building background for animals, things, or concepts.

How to Introduce It

Either in small groups of 4-6 or as a whole class, hand out copies of the web diagram. Have students write the name of the animal, thing, or concept in the middle circle. Then brainstorm with students to answer some key questions about it.

- What does it look like?
- Where does it live or where do you see it?
- What are some examples of it?
- When do you see it?
- What do you think about it?
- How does it feel?

What It Looks Like

A word or concept web looks something like this once it is completed.

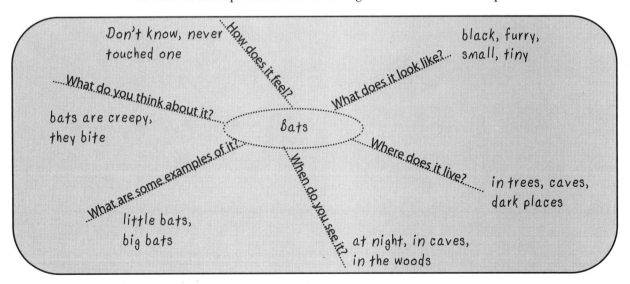

What to Look Out For

Remember that the goal of introducing a subject or idea in a word web is to build background. The exercise should be brief, involving a number of students, but not strive to be comprehensive. What matters is that students have a frame of reference as they begin reading and their minds are activated.

WORD WEB

Selection:

Author:

Write the name of the place, animal, or idea in the center circle. Then answer the questions around it.

What does it look like?

What are some examples of it?

...How does it feel?

When do you see it?

Where does it live?

What do you think about it?

Vocabulary Inventory

What Is It?

A vocabulary inventory gives you an understanding of how familiar students are with the vocabulary of a selection. Quick and easy, the inventory can be a great way to begin a lesson with challenging words, as well as a way to start students thinking about the selection, because the words can suggest the subject and be the starting point for making predictions. You make one by choosing ten words that are important to the selection.

How to Introduce It

Explain to students that you want to find out how familiar they are with some of the words in the selection. Be sure to say that this is not a test. Students will not be graded on the results. The purpose is to start students thinking about some of the words from the selection and what the selection may be about.

What It Looks Like

A vocabulary inventory looks something like this:

VOCABULARY INVENTORY

Ellen Tebbits

By Beverly Cleary

Pages 58-60

Look carefully at each word below. Then mark whether you know the word (+), whether it seems familiar (?), or whether you don't know the word at all (0).

+ I Know This Word

? Seems Familiar

0 Don't Know This Word

1. _____ scampered	6. _____ relieved
2. _____ lonely	7. _____ neighborhood
3. _____ furniture	8. _____ scraggly
4. _____ autumn	9. _____ scuff
5. _____ slippers	10. _____ anxiously

Now make a prediction. What do you think this selection will be about?

_____

_____

What to Look Out For

A vocabulary inventory will give you an idea if students can handle the vocabulary in the selection. If students are not familiar with more than half of the words, chances are the selection will pose strong reading challenges for them. Begin the lesson by using the **Vocabulary Warm-up** in the *Teacher's Guide*. If students are familiar with most of the words, preteaching vocabulary probably is not necessary.

VOCABULARY INVENTORY

Selection:

Author:

Look carefully at each word below. Then mark whether you know the word (+), whether it seems familiar (?), or whether you don't know the word at all (0).

$+$ Know This Word

$?$ Seems Familiar

0 Don't Know This Word

1. _____ ....

2. _____ ....

3. _____ ....

4. _____ ....

5. _____ ....

6. _____ ....

7. _____ ....

8. _____ ....

9. _____ ....

10. _____ ....

Now make a prediction. What do you think this selection will be about?

....

....

....

....

A n t i c i p a t i o n   G u i d e

What Is It?

An anticipation guide serves two purposes: it helps motivate students to want to read a selection and it builds some background about the selection before students begin reading. As a result, it becomes a powerful tool in your arsenal for creating reading readiness in your students. To make an anticipation guide, write 3–5 statements about the subject of the story or article.

How to Introduce It

Ask students to form small groups of 4-6 or work through the activity as a whole class. Tell students that, before they read, you want to find out what they already know about the subject of this next selection. Then hand out copies of the anticipation guide that you create from the blackline master on the next page.

Have students write whether they agree or disagree with each statement. Then, after recording their answers, ask students to share them with their classmates. Tell students that there are no right or wrong answers, but encourage them to discuss with each other places where their answers are different from others in the group.

What It Looks Like

An anticipation guide looks something like this once it is prepared.

Read each statement. Circle whether you agree or disagree. Then discuss your answers with a partner.

Agree   **Disagree**   1. Rabbits can have magic powers.

Agree   **Disagree**   2. No rabbit can change itself into a nail.

Agree   **Disagree**   3. If you were changed into a nail, you could never change back to normal again.

What to Look Out For

The idea behind an anticipation guide is to build background for students and motivation for what they are about to read. Encourage students to form questions, not argue about who is right and who is wrong. Have students share information they know and end by making predictions about what they think will happen. Then, after they finished reading, have students come back to see if they still hold the same opinions that they did at the beginning.

ANTICIPATION GUIDE

Selection:

Author:

Circle whether you agree or disagree with each statement. Compare your answers with a partner. Talk about what you agreed and disagreed about. Then, write a prediction of what you think this selection will be about.

Before Reading   **After Reading**

Agree Disagree 1. . . . . **Agree Disagree**

. . . .

. . . .

Agree Disagree 2. . . . . **Agree Disagree**

. . . .

. . . .

Agree Disagree 3. . . . . **Agree Disagree**

. . . .

. . . .

Agree Disagree 4. . . . . **Agree Disagree**

. . . .

. . . .

Agree Disagree 5. . . . . **Agree Disagree**

. . . .

. . . .

What do you think this selection will be about?

Then, after you are finished reading, come back and answer each statement again. Did any of your answers change? Why?

Think-Pair-and-Share

What Is It?

A Think-Pair-and-Share activity introduces a selection in a fun, interactive way, gently leading reluctant readers into the act of reading. It gives students some background about a selection and piques interest in what will happen.

How to Introduce It

If time permits, ask students to form small groups of 4-6. If possible, put each sentence on a separate strip of paper. Give each student in the group one sentence, and ask him or her to read it aloud to the others. Tell students that their job is to decide in what order the sentences appear in the selection and what the selection is about.

What It Looks Like

Here is an example of a Think-Pair-and-Share activity.

Think-Pair-and-Share

Read each quote below from the story. Put the sentences in the order in which you think they appear in the selection.

_____ 1. "TURN ON WATER. WET MAGIC FRECKLE REMOVER AND RUB INTO FACE."

_____ 2. "Then he took out the magic marker and decorated his whole face and neck with blue dots."

_____ 3. "Andrew had to use it four times to get his freckles off."

_____ 4. "'Andrew,' Miss Kelly said. 'How would you like to use my secret formula for removing freckles?'"

_____ 5. "He opened his desk drawer and looked for a brown magic marker. All he could find was a blue one."

What do you think this story is about?

What to Look Out For

Having students work in groups for Think-Pair-and-Share activities can become noisy, because students are reading the sentences from the story and discussing them. Try to keep students focused. The idea is to help students construct some idea what the story might be and to generate interest in reading the story.

THINK-PAIR-AND-SHARE

Selection:

Author:

Read each sentence to the others in your group. Then put the sentences in the order in which you think they appear in the selection.

1.

2.

3.

4.

5.

What do you think this story is about?

During Reading

While students are reading in their *Daybook*, the primary **goals** are:

1. **to build active reading and involvement**

2. **to increase comprehension**

Among the best **strategies** for accomplishing these goals are:

➢ **Double-entry journals**

➢ **Retelling**

➢ **Using graphic organizers**

- **story stars**

- **beginning, middle, and end organizers**

- **sequence organizers**

- **timelines**

- **cause-and-effect organizers**

Across the country, teachers have numerous ways of improving comprehension. Students need not know ALL of the strategies available. Strive instead to introduce a few KEY strategies that students can use again and again. Students need to know a few good comprehension strategies, but also know how and when to use them.

Try to introduce your students to these comprehension strategies over the year.

Double-Entry Journal

What Is It?

A Double-Entry Journal is a way to help students look closely at passages in the text. Often called a response journal, a quote or sentence from a selection is written in the lefthand column, and then students respond to it by writing their reactions in the righthand column. It builds students' ability to comprehend and interpret text.

How to Introduce It

Tell students that you will show them a way to get more from what they are reading. Write a quote from a text on the board and ask students to do the same in a notebook. Then write your thoughts or response to the quote, and ask students to do the same. Then discuss your response and explain why you wrote that with the class. Ask student volunteers to share their responses.

What It Looks Like

Here is an example of what a Double-Entry Journal looks like. (Because this technique is just being introduced in *Daybook* 3, quotes are provided for students, as well as prompts and a sample response to encourage their response.)

Comparison	Question
Life is a broken-winged bird That cannot fly.	How is a life without dreams like a broken-winged bird?
	Without dreams, a person is crippled in life.
Life is a barren field Frozen with snow.	How is a life without dreams like a frozen field?
Black is me Black is *the* color	What attitude about being black is the poet expressing?
Black **is boldness**.	What is the poet suggesting about the history of black people?

What to Look Out For

Double-Entry Journals can be used at almost any grade and are especially helpful in getting students to look closely at poetry. But students often have a difficult time choosing good passages from the selection on their own and may need guidance in which passages to select. The goal is for them to select meaningful passages that lend themselves to interpretation.

DOUBLE-ENTRY JOURNAL

Selection:

Author:

Write a quote from the story or poem in the lefthand column below. In the column next to it, write your thoughts and feelings about the quote. Then write two or more quotes from the story and your response to them.

Quote	My Thoughts and Feelings
1.	
2.	
3.	
4.	

Retelling

What Is It?

A retelling is a "telling again" of the story or article in the student's own words. Just as in conversation when, to show you understand, you might say, "What I hear you saying is . . .," retelling gives students a chance to put the message in their own words. The act of processing what they comprehend and translating it into words of their own helps students understand—and remember.

How to Introduce It

Tell students that you want to help them put what they read into their own words. Explain that, by retelling what they have read, they will comprehend more of what they are reading.

What It Looks Like

Often retelling is simply done orally. You ask, "What did you learn?" or "What has happened so far?" In written form, a retelling can take a number of different forms.

EXAMPLE 1

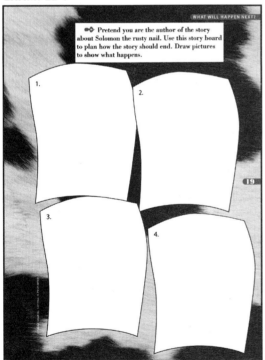

EXAMPLE 2

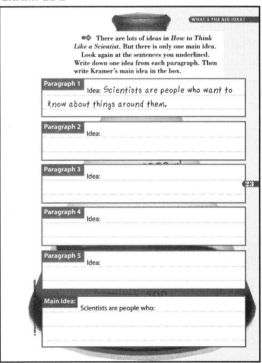

What to Look Out For

Students may not give perfect summaries in their initial retellings. Look instead for evidence that they are processing the information and putting it in their own words. By reading over what they have retold, students will themselves find ways their retellings can be improved. More than the final product, what's important is the greater comprehension the activity of retelling yields.

RETELLING

Selection:

Author:

Write down one idea from each paragraph or the 4 big ideas you remember. Put the ideas in the order in which they occurred.

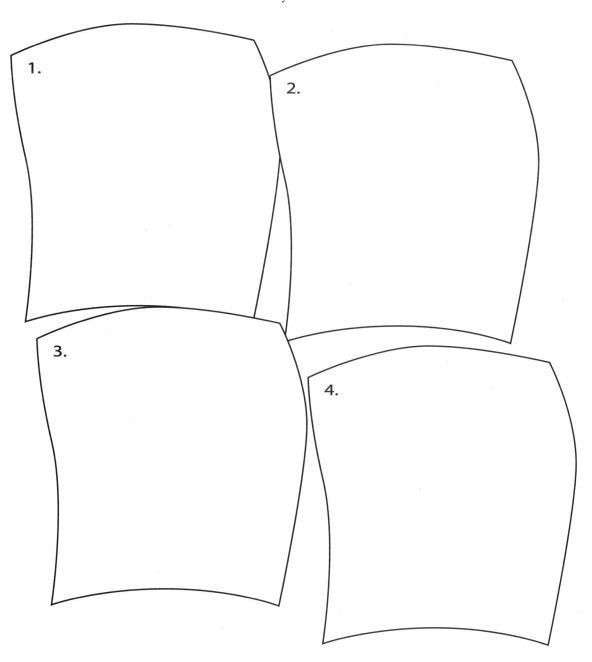

1.

2.

3.

4.

RETELLING

Selection:

Author:

Write down one idea from each paragraph or the 4-5 ideas you remember. Then write what you think is the main idea or biggest idea overall.

Paragraph 1 Idea:

Paragraph 2 Idea:

Paragraph 3 Idea:

Paragraph 4 Idea:

Paragraph 5 Idea:

Main Idea:

Graphic Organizers

What Is It?

A graphic organizer is a way to help students visualize information they are reading. Sequence, cause and effect, plot, characters, timelines—in short, almost all of the abstract ideas that come from reading can be organized and visualized better by learning how to use graphic organizers.

How to Introduce It

Explain that an organizer can help students collect and sort through all of the information they are receiving as they read. Explain too that different organizers can be helpful for different kinds of writing. For stories or fiction, the organizers called character maps, plot charts, and storyboards generally work best. For nonfiction, suggest that students use timelines, webs, cause-effect, and Venn diagrams.

What It Looks Like

Here is an example of one kind of graphic organizer.

Character Map

What he says:	How others feel about him:

Bobby

How he feels:	What I think about him:

What to Look Out For

Students will need to become familiar with a number of different graphic organizers and be shown which ones work best with which kinds of writing. Using the organizer tends to be the easy part. The difficulty for students is to know which type of organizer to use. You can help students learn which graphic organizer to use by introducing a limited number initially and then discussing which one might work best in different situations.

Graphic Organizer:
STORY STAR

Write down the answer to each question after reading the story.

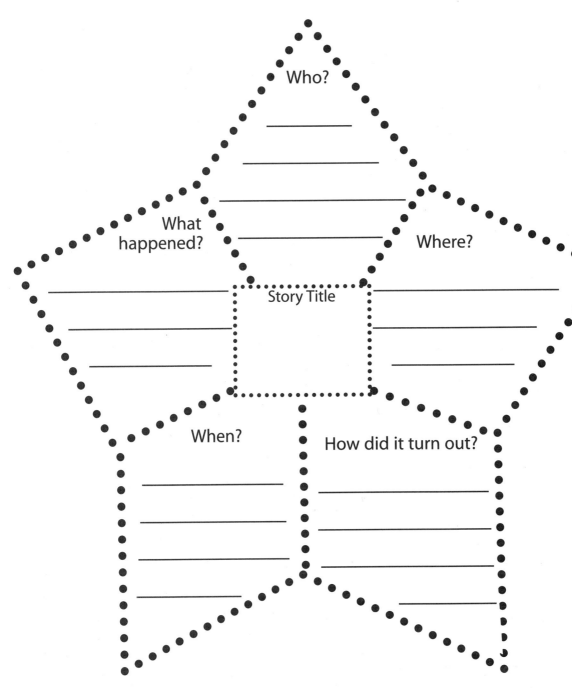

Who?

What happened?

Where?

Story Title

When?

How did it turn out?

Graphic Organizer:
TIMELINE

Selection:

Author:

Write the event that happens first in the column Time/Date on the left.
Beside it, write what happened. Write down each major event or occurrence.

Time/Date	Events

Graphic Organizer:
STORYBOARD

Selection:

Author:

Sketch four memorable scenes or events from the story. Next to each sketch, write a brief description of what happens.

1.

2.

3.

4.

Graphic Organizer:
MAIN IDEA AND DETAILS

Selection:

Author:

Write down one detail from each paragraph or the 4-5 details you can remember about the subject. Then write what you think is the overall main idea of the selection.

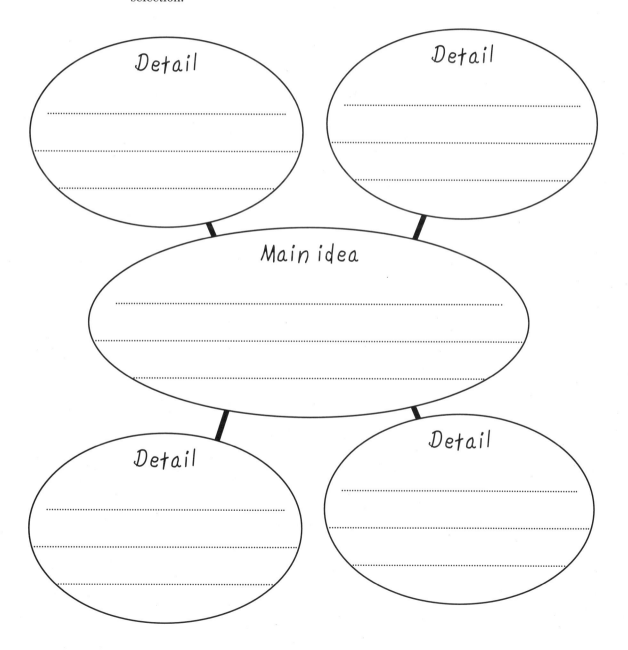

Graphic Organizer:
VENN DIAGRAM

Selection:

Author:

Use this Venn diagram to show how two characters or things are alike and different. Write the name of one thing you are comparing on each line. Write what is special or different about each thing in the outside part of the circles (#1 and #2). In the center, write how the two things or characters are similar (#3).

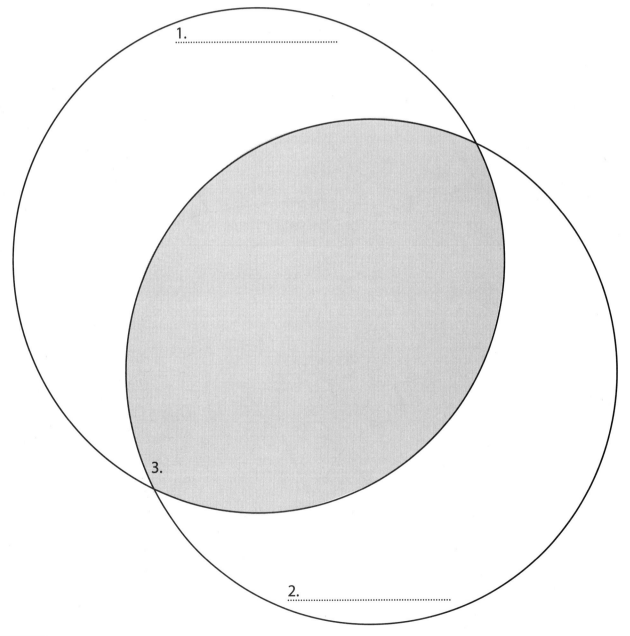

1.

3.

2.

Name:

Graphic Organizer:
PLOT CHART

Selection:

Author:

Use this plot chart to show the major events in the story. Begin with the first event in the story. Write it at the bottom beside Event 1. Then list the other events leading up to the climax, when the problem of the story is resolved.

Write the problem and its solution in the boxes at the bottom of the page.

Peak Event:

Event 4

Event 3

Event 2

Event 1

Problem

Solution

After Reading

After students are finished reading in their *Daybook*s, the primary **goals** are:

1. **to reread to increase comprehension even more**
2. **to make the reading their own**
3. **to remember or retain what is read**

Among the best **strategies** for accomplishing these goals are:

➤ **Rereading with a purpose**
➤ **Summarizing**
➤ **Organizing what you learned**
   - **charts (for nonfiction)**
   - **main idea and detail charts**
   - **cause-effect charts**
   - **sequence organizers**

Readers comprehend at different rates, and they comprehend different things from a selection. By rereading with a purpose, any reader can go back and find the information (about a character, story, subject) that they need.

Creating a summary or graphic organizer is another way for a reader to collect what he or she has learned. It is also a product, a way for a reader to work through and process the information, which is vital for retention and recalling the information later.

Encourage your students to reread, but with a purpose. Good readers go back into a text all of the time to gather more information or confirm a detail that they only partially remember. After reading a selection, help students get in the habit of rereading by using the strategies above for collecting and retaining what they read.

Reading with a Purpose

What Is It?

By asking questions before reading or making predictions while reading, students set a purpose for their reading. This gives a reason for the activity of reading. They want to find out something. Too often students read without any purpose. When asked, they respond that they are reading a selection because they were told to read it. Students need to learn how to set a purpose for themselves before they read. The purpose helps make them more active readers and will help them get more from what they read.

How to Introduce It

Help students set a simple purpose before they read any selection. In the *Daybook*s, the response strategy (or active reading strategy) sets the purpose for reading. Students are told what they should mark, underline, highlight, or circle—in other words, what to look for.

Point out the response strategies in the lessons to students. Tell them that the strategies signal what they should look for in the selection as they read.

Then, after an initial reading, ask students to double back and look for the details or specific information noted in the response strategy. Most of the time marking the text and reading with comprehension will tax the ability of most students. Encourage students to mark other details as they reread.

What It Looks Like

Here is an example of one kind of activity that requires students to go back into the text and reread to find details about causes and effects.

Causes	Effects
	Paul Revere's dog got out.
	A lady gave Paul Revere's friend her petticoat.
Paul Revere sent his dog back home with a note to his wife.	
	Paul Revere and his friends rowed quietly past the English transport on the Charles River.

What to Look Out For

Students will find rereading hard work. Encourage students as they reread, pointing out to them that expert readers are expert *rereaders*. Many students will think that they "didn't get it," when in fact rereading is normal—and necessary.

Reading with a Purpose:
ASKING QUESTIONS

Selection:

Author:

Before and as you read, write down questions that you want to know more about. Then, reread the selection to find answers to your questions. Write your answers in the middle column. In the last column, write the evidence from the selection that explains how you know.

Question	My Answer	How Do I Know?

Reading with a Purpose:
PREDICTIONS

Selection:

Author:

While you are reading, stop a few times and write down your predictions. Note the page in column one and your prediction in column two. Then, reread the selection once you have finished and note what really happened.

page number	I predicted . . .	What really happened . . .

Summarizing

What Is It?

A summary is a retelling of the important parts of a selection. For nonfiction, a summary tells the main idea and important details about it. For fiction, a summary recounts the major events in the story line.

How to Introduce It

Help students see what a summary is by using graphic organizers. Tell students that they will need to use an organizer like a Story String for stories or fiction. It helps them record events in the order they happen—that is, chronological order. Tell students they will need to use a **Main Idea and Detail** organizer for nonfiction selections. It helps them note specific details about a subject and decide what is the larger, main idea about the subject.

What It Looks Like

Here is an example of one kind of activity that requires students to go back into the text and reread to find details about causes and effects.

Subject			
Detail #1	Detail #2	Detail #3	Detail #4
Main Idea			

What to Look Out For

Students find it difficult to distinguish the main idea from the supporting details. Be sure to model sorting out the main idea from the smaller details for students at least once. Students will also need help matching the appropriate organizer to the kind of text they are reading, so you may need to choose the appropriate organizer for them the first few times.

Summarizing:
STORY STRING

Selection:

Author:

After reading, go back through the story one more time. Write down the key events that occur. Put them in the order in which they happen.

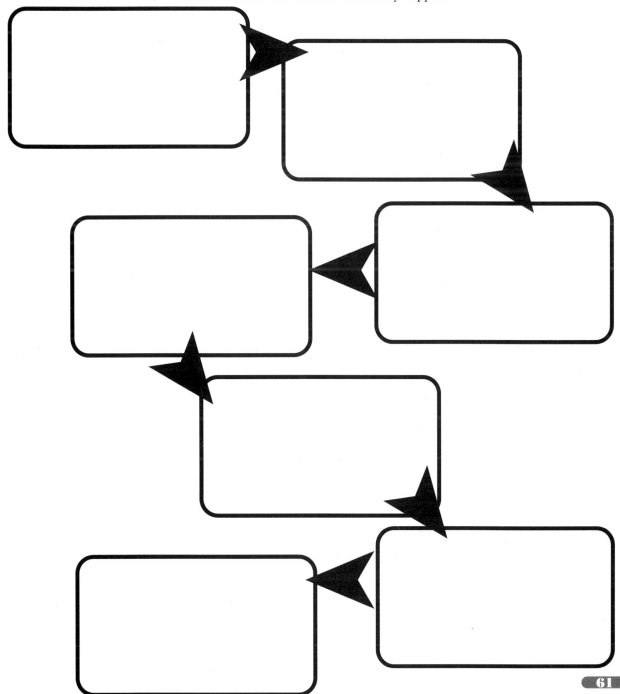

Summarizing:
MAIN IDEA AND DETAILS

Selection:

Author:

After you finish reading, look back over the selection and the highlighting you made. First list four supporting details you learned about the subject. Then, decide what the author says about the subject. Write that as the main idea.

Summary

Main Idea:

Supporting Details:

1.

2.

3.

4.

Organizing What You Learned

What Is It?

Organizing what you learned simply means taking time after reading to collect and organize the information. Quite often students stop reading with the last word in a selection. Helping students collect and organize what they have learned will show them a way to get the most out of the time they invest in reading.

How to Introduce It

Help students understand that reading is a process, not an act. Explain that, once students reach the end of a selection, they have more to do. Now they need to collect what they have learned. By taking notes, filling out a cause-and-effect chart, or creating a web diagram, they can get more from what they read and remember it better.

What It Looks Like

Here is one chart from *Daybook* 3 that collects what students learned about elephants:

Facts about Elephants
Eating habits:
Size:
Where they live:
Leader of the herd:
Young male elephants:

What to Look Out For

Students will probably not see why they have to do even more work after they finish reading. Help them see that, by collecting what they learned, they will remember more of what they read.

Name: _____

Organizing Fiction:
CHARACTER MAP

Selection: _____

Author: _____

After you finish reading fiction, take a minute to go back over the selection. Use the character map below to organize what you have learned about the main character. First, write the character's name in the center. Then fill in each box.

What the character says:	What others say about the character:

How the character looks:	How I feel about the character:

Organizing Fiction:
STORYCARDS

Selection: _____

Author: _____

After you finish reading a story, spend some time to go back over the selection. Use the storycards below to organize what happened. Fill in information about the author, title, characters, setting, and plot.

Storycard

Author

Title

Characters

Setting

Plot

Organizing Fiction:
PLOT CHART

Selection:

Author:

After you finish reading, an easy way to keep track of what happened is to describe what happened in the Beginning, Middle, and End of a story. Use the plot chart below to organize what happened. Write 2 things that happen at the beginning, 2 that happen in the middle of the story, and 2 things that happen at the end.

Plot Chart

#1	#2

#3	#4

#5	#6

Name:

Organizing Nonfiction:
CHARTS

Selection:

Author:

Write the names of specific things you learned about (countries, animals, types of things) in the column on the left. Across the top, write the names of general categories (for example, what animals eat, where they live, and so on). Then reread the selection, filling in the chart.

Specific details	General categories			

Name: _____

Organizing Nonfiction:
CAUSE AND EFFECT

Selection: _____

Author: _____

Reread the selection and use the chart below to help you organize the causes and effects. Write the causes you find in the lefthand boxes. In the righthand boxes, write the effects that result from those causes.

Causes and Effects

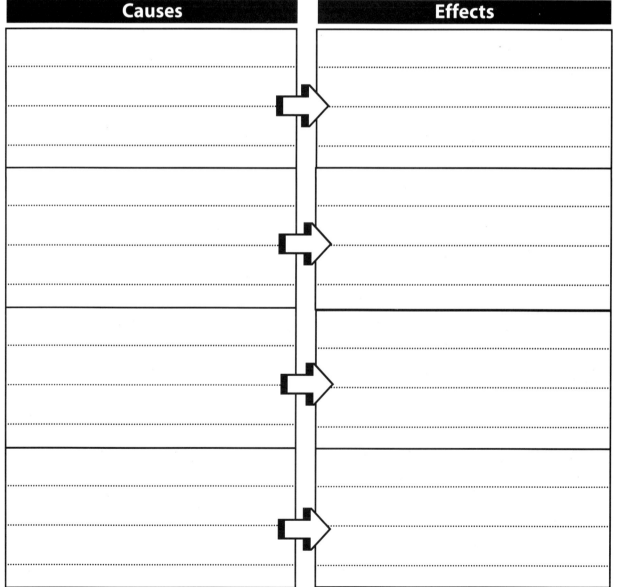

Causes	Effects

LESSON
RESOURCES

ACTIVE READING

For use with page 9

Unit Overview

In this unit, students learn how to mark up a text, underline, highlight, predict, question, and visualize. The purpose of these initial lessons is to start students marking in the *Daybook* and writing in the Response Notes. The active reading skills introduced in these first lessons will be practiced throughout the *Daybook*, so students do not need mastery of active reading before progressing out of this unit. The idea of the introductory unit is to start students on the road toward becoming active readers.

Reading the Art

Ask students to look at the art in the opener. In small groups of 3 or 4, have students discuss these questions:

- What do they see in the artwork?
- What things do the characters appear to be holding?
- What do the black lines in the artwork suggest?
- Why is this art a good choice to introduce a unit on *Active Reading?*

ACTIVE READING

L i t e r a t u r e   F o c u s

Lesson	Literature
1. Mark Up the Text	**Dick King-Smith,** from *A Mouse Called Wolf* This selection is about a young mouse who has a fancy name to make up for his small size.
2. Predict	**Dick King-Smith,** from *A Mouse Called Wolf* In this second part of the story, the mother mouse named Mary plays the piano at night.
3. Question	**Dick King-Smith,** from *A Mouse Called Wolf* In the next part of the story, the mother uses some music by Mozart to help make a cozy nest for her new babies.
4. Visualize	**Dick King-Smith,** from *A Mouse Called Wolf* In this conclusion, the mother mouse Mary names her thirteenth pup Wolfgang Amadeus Mouse.
5. Apply the Strategies	**Douglas Florian,** from *A Fire-Breathing Dragon* In this fun and fanciful poem, the poet describes what it would be like to have a dragon for a pet.

R e a d i n g   F o c u s

Lesson	Reading Skill
1. Mark Up the Text	mark, underline, and highlight parts of a text
2. Predict	use what you know and clues from a story to figure out what will happen next
3. Question	ask questions about the plot, setting, and characters as you read
4. Visualize	draw or sketch the pictures you see in your mind as you read
5. Apply the Strategies	use active reading strategies of marking, visualizing, predicting

Mark Up the Text

Before Reading

FOCUS
You will enjoy and understand more of what you read by reading actively.

The introductory unit walks students through becoming an active reader. Each introductory mini-lesson shows one way to respond to literature. In this first introductory lesson, students learn how to mark up a text.

BUILDING BACKGROUND

Explain to students that sometimes they may want to keep several ideas in mind as they read. Being an active reader means doing something as one reads. Marking up the text helps them to identify important passages, words, or sentences they want to remember. Writing margin notes helps them keep track of questions or responses to what they are reading. Marked-up text makes it easier to go back and find specific places in the writing later, if needed. It is also a way to stay focused on what they are reading.

Reading the Introduction

Read through the first paragraph with students. Tell them that as they interact with the text in this *Daybook* in different ways that they will be more involved, active readers. Remind students that they cannot mark up the other textbooks that belong to the school.

Reading the Selection

Read *A Mouse Called Wolf* by Dick King-Smith, stopping at the bottom of the page. Ask students:
➤ What types of sample responses do you see on the page?
➤ Why do you think "Wolfgang Amadeus Mouse" and "thirteen" are circled?
➤ What sentence is underlined, and why?
➤ What types of written comments do you see in the Response Notes?

Point out to students that they will be asked to write different types of comments in the Response Notes throughout this book. Their notes will sometimes help them to identify key parts of the selection and remember more of what they read.

Remind students that they can review this page as a model for the kinds of responses they might have.

Predict

B e f o r e R e a d i n g

In this second introductory lesson, students learn about predicting what will happen in a story.

BUILDING BACKGROUND

Explain to students that active readers learn to predict what will happen next in a story. A prediction can be related to a character's future actions or to the story line as a whole. Tell students that they will be asked to make predictions in many lessons in this *Daybook*. Sometimes they will underline the sentence clues related to the prediction, and at other times they will write their predictions as questions or comments in the Response Notes. Each lesson will give students instructions on how to mark up the text. With each prediction, students will be asked to give evidence from the text to support their prediction.

R e a d i n g t h e I n t r o d u c t i o n

Have students read the introductory paragraph. Ask them why making predictions is such a good way to get involved in a story.

R e a d i n g t h e S e l e c t i o n

Read *A Mouse Called Wolf,* stopping at the bottom of the page. Point out to students the example shown on the page. Ask students:
➤ What prediction did the reader make?
➤ Do you agree or disagree with the prediction? Why or why not?
➤ What predictions do you have from reading this selection? Try phrasing a prediction as a question and as a comment.
➤ What clues did you use to support your prediction?

Point out to students that some, but not necessarily all, of the prediction questions they have will be answered as they continue to read. But whether or not their predictions turn out to be correct, predictions keep readers interested in reading. Remind students that they can return to this page at any time in the book to see how to write any prediction comments in the Response Notes.

Question

B e f o r e   R e a d i n g

In this third introductory lesson, students learn about questioning as still another way to be an active reader.

BUILDING BACKGROUND

Explain to students that sometimes they will have questions as they read. The questions may relate to plot, setting, a word they don't know, or a character's actions. In this *Daybook*, students will be asked to record different types of questions. Asking questions is a good way to stay focused on the reading, because it provides motivation for reading on to find out the answers. This lesson models the response strategy of asking questions as you read.

R e a d i n g   t h e   I n t r o d u c t i o n

Read through the first paragraph with students. Ask students:
➤ Can you think of any other questions you sometimes ask as you read?

Tell them that in this *Daybook* they will be asked to record their questions about some of the selections. Remind students that questions can begin with *Who, What, Where, When, Why,* and *How.* Point out the examples in the Response Notes.

R e a d i n g   t h e   S e l e c t i o n

Read this segment of *A Mouse Called Wolf* by Dick King-Smith, stopping at the bottom of the page. Ask students:
➤ What questions did this reader have?
➤ What new questions do you have, based on the reading?

As a whole class, challenge students to think of one question that begins with *Who, What, Where, When, Why,* and *How.*
   Point out to students that their questions will help them stay focused as they read. They can record their questions in their Response Notes throughout this book. Their questions will stimulate their interest in the selection and will help them to complete exercises related to the reading.

Visualize

Before Reading

In this fourth introductory lesson, students learn about the importance of visualizing as another way to be an active reader.

BUILDING BACKGROUND

Explain to students that words are simply strings of letters until they are put together in words, phrases, sentences, and paragraphs that enable readers to form visual pictures of what is being said. The better the writing, the easier it is for readers to visualize the setting, characters, or plot. This mini-lesson models for students how to record what they visualize about the selection in their *Daybooks* as they read.

Reading the Introduction

Read through the opening paragraph with students. Explain that not only will they write in their *Daybooks*, but they will also be asked to include sketches and drawings as well. Visualizing the text is another way of being an active reader. Tell students that recording those images helps them remember, because they will be mentally adding to the pictures as they continue to read.

Reading the Selection

Read the final segment of *A Mouse Called Wolf,* stopping at the bottom of the page. Point out to students the sketch in the margin. Ask students:
➤ What image did this reader record in the Response Notes?
➤ Does this image match a picture you have in your mind? Why or why not?
➤ What other places in the text can you visualize clearly?
➤ How can you record those images in sketches or drawings?

Encourage students to identify one new place in the selection they can easily imagine. Ask them to draw or sketch a visual picture. Remind students that making visual notes is not an art assignment. Point out that the purpose of recording notes in a visual form is simply to keep the image alive for them and help them to remember, not to show their artistic talent.

Apply the Strategies

B e f o r e   R e a d i n g

> *In this last introductory lesson, students practice using at least two different ways of marking up and responding to a new selection.*

BUILDING BACKGROUND

Explain to students that it's time to use the strategies they learned in this introduction in responding to a new selection, *A Fire-Breathing Dragon.* Explain again that, in this *Daybook*, students will get lots of practice in responding to pieces of writing in different ways. In this mini-lesson, students are asked to use at least two of the response strategies discussed in this introduction. Review the four strategies mentioned and why each one is important in being an active reader.
• marking and highlighting
• predicting
• questioning
• visualizing

R e a d i n g   t h e   I n t r o d u c t i o n

Read through the opening paragraph with students. Explain that they will mark up the text and record their thoughts, questions, and comments about the poem in the Response Notes. Encourage students to go back and review the examples included for each one if needed.

R e a d i n g   t h e   S e l e c t i o n

Read *A Fire-Breathing Dragon* by Douglas Florian. Discuss these questions with students to help them get started:
➤ What words, phrases, sentences, or ideas represent key ideas to keep track of?
➤ What predictions do you have about this poem?
➤ What questions do you have about the characters, setting, vocabulary words, or meaning of this poem?
➤ What visual images of this poem can you keep track of by sketching or drawing the images?

Encourage students to read the poem several times as they make margin notes and highlight the text as desired. When they are done, allow time for students to share ways in which they marked up the text differently. Tell students that they can now call themselves "active readers." In this *Daybook*, they will be active readers as they read and respond to every selection.

Unit One:
READING WELL

For use with page 15

Unit Overview

In this unit, students learn the basics of how to approach a reading. They learn to predict what will happen next, find the main idea, and identify point of view. Explain to students that the skills they will learn about in this unit are basic approaches they will use with many pieces of writing. Take time to work with students until they understand that these skills—predicting what will happen next, finding the main idea, and identifying point of view—are the foundation of "reading well."

Reading the Art

Be sure students take a moment to "read" the artwork. Have them study the images as they answer these questions:

- What do you see?
- How would you describe this piece of art?
- What words can you find?
- What ideas does it give you about how to "read well"?

READING WELL

Literature Focus

Lesson	Literature
1. What Will Happen Next?	**William Steig**, from *Solomon the Rusty Nail*
	In this piece of fiction, Solomon, the rabbit, turns into a rusty nail.
2. What's the Big Idea?	**Stephen Kramer,** from *How to Think Like a Scientist*
	This nonfiction piece discusses what kind of people scientists are and what types of questions they ask.
3. My Side of the Story	as told to **Jon Scieszka**, from *The True Story of the Three Little Pigs by A. Wolf*
	The point of view of this familiar fairy tale changes as A. Wolf finally tells his side of the story of his adventures with the three little pigs.

Reading Focus

Lesson	Reading Skill
1. What Will Happen Next?	As you read, ask yourself: What do I think will happen next?
2. What's the Big Idea?	When you read, look for the most important idea. This is called the main idea.
3. My Side of the Story	When the point of view changes, the story changes too.

Writing Focus

Lesson	Writing Assignment
1. What Will Happen Next?	Write an ending for *Solomon the Rusty Nail* based on the readers' predictions and clues from the story.
2. What's the Big Idea?	Write a paragraph describing an observation of something of interest.
3. My Side of the Story	Rewrite a fairy tale using some details from the original version and some made-up details of your own.

What Will Happen Next?

Before Reading

FOCUS

As you read, ask yourself: What do I think will happen next?

In this lesson, students read part of a story and learn to make predictions as they read.

BUILDING BACKGROUND

Vocabulary Warm-up

rabbit	*nail*	*rusty*	*junk*	*dared*

Be sure students understand the words above. Try a **Vocabulary Quiz Show** to help all the students in class learn these words that are essential to the selection. Write the words on a 3 x 5 file card. Then write a definition for each word on five other cards. Pass out the cards to 10 different students in class. Ask one student to begin by saying one of the words. Have the student who has the meaning for the word read it aloud in class. Continue in this way until you are comfortable that all of the students are familiar with the words.

Prereading Strategy

If necessary, build even more background for the selection by using an **Anticipation Guide** to start students thinking.

1. Agree   Disagree   Rabbits can have magic powers.
2. Agree   Disagree   No rabbit can change itself into a nail.
3. Agree   Disagree   If you were changed into a nail, you could never change back again to normal.

Reading the Selection

RESPONSE STRATEGY

Students are asked to write their predictions in the Response Notes. Look for students to write something like this:

Sample Response:

I think he will change into a nail and can't change back.

Encourage students to write at least one guess about what they think will happen to Solomon the rabbit.

CRITICAL READING SKILL

The lesson encourages students to make predictions. Point out to students that predictions are really just their ideas about what they think will happen. Get students started by asking some helpful questions:

➤ What will happen to Solomon?
➤ What happens once he becomes a rusty nail?

REREADING

After students have finished reading, encourage them to go back over the selection. Ask them whether the prediction they made turned out to be right. Ask them to find the part in the text that tells them whether their prediction was or was not correct.

Writing

Do students' story endings:

✓ tell a story in a clear order?

✓ show creativity?

✓ give a clear ending to the story of Solomon?

In this lesson, students write an alternative ending to the story of **Solomon the Rusty Nail.**

As an initial response, students predict what will happen to Solomon. Encourage students to give clues from the text to support their predictions.

Sample Response:

I predict Solomon will change back into a rabbit. He changed into a nail real easy and can change back.

I predict he will keep his power a secret. He might be scared to try his power. The story says "he dared."

STORYBOARD

Encourage students to use the storyboard on page 19 to plan an ending for the story of *Solomon the Rusty Nail.* Use the examples below as possibilities or models to spur students' creativity.

ALTERNATE STORY ENDING

Help students come up with creative endings to their versions of the story *Solomon the Rusty Nail.* One possible example is as follows:

Sample Response:

Solomon was a rabbit again. He tried his powers one more time. He went "poof," and changed back into a nail. Then he tried to become a rabbit again, but he forgot how to do it. He tried and tried. Finally, he got lucky and changed back. Then he hopped over to the garden to eat.

WRITING REMINDERS

Remind students that when writing their ending:

✓ Clearly indent the first sentence in their paragraph.

✓ Check that each sentence begins with a capital letter and ends with a period, question mark, or exclamation point.

What's the Big Idea?

Before Reading

FOCUS

When you read, look for the most important idea. This is called the main idea.

In this lesson, students focus on looking for the main idea as they read.

BUILDING BACKGROUND

Vocabulary Warm-up

    scientists   meadowlarks   gravity   explanations   instruments

To help students understand the words above, find these words in the selection and look at the **Context Clues** around the words.

1. <u>Scientists</u> are people who are curious. They want to know about things around them. *(The word is defined by the context.)*

2. Some scientists study birds. They might ask the question, "Why do <u>meadowlarks</u> sing?" *(The word* birds *is used earlier as a synonym of* meadowlark.*)*

3. "How does <u>gravity</u> work?" *(The context is not completely clear but* work *suggests it is a force of some kind.)*

4. Scientists try to find patterns in things. They look for <u>explanations</u> for patterns in the things around us. *(The context suggests that* explanations *are things—or reasons—that tell about* patterns.*)*

5. Scientists often use <u>instruments</u> to help them make observations. *(The next few sentences suggest that* instruments *help us "measure" and "observe" things we can't through our senses.)*

Prereading Strategy

To help activate students' prior knowledge, create a **Word Web** around the word *scientist.* Work with students to identify:

What is a scientist like?   (scientist)   What does a scientist do?

How does a scientist look?   Where does a scientist work?

Reading the Selection

RESPONSE STRATEGY

Students are asked to underline the main ideas they find.

    Sample Response:

<u>Scientists ...are always asking questions and trying to answer them.</u>

Encourage students to underline at least 2 or 3 sentences throughout the selection.

CRITICAL READING SKILL

The lesson asks students to find the main idea. Sorting out the important ideas from the details is a difficult skill for some students. One technique that might help is to ask students to stop after each paragraph and ask themselves, "What is it all about?"

REREADING

After students have read the selection, encourage them to go back and reread the selection, underlining just one idea in each paragraph. If necessary, ask them to underline only the important words in each paragraph.

Writing

In this lesson, students are asked to observe something like a scientist does and to write their most important observation, and then some details.

ONE THING

As a first response to the literature, students recall one thing they learned.

Sample Response:

One thing I learned is that scientists ask questions.

MAIN IDEA OF A PARAGRAPH

Students are asked to come up with the main idea for each paragraph.

Sample Response:

1. Scientists...are always asking questions and trying to answer them.
2. They ask a lot of questions.
3. Scientists try to find patterns.
4. Scientists learn by observing and measuring things.
5. Scientists use instruments, or machines.

Main Idea: Scientists are people who ask questions and try to answer them.

OBSERVATIONS

Help students come up with creative objects to observe. If necessary, spend a moment brainstorming.

Sample Response:

Outside My Window

• cars speeding by, going in a hurry
• dark black road, looking shiny from the rain
• gray sky
• white buds on trees

PARAGRAPH

Students' paragraphs about what they observed will vary. Check to be sure they started with a main idea.

Sample Response:

Outside My Window

• Main Idea: Gloomy clouds and rain made everything look gray.

The sky was gray. The dark, black road was shiny with rain. Cars sped by, going fast. Everything looked cold and dark today, even the white buds on the trees.

WRITING REMINDERS

Remind students to:

✔ Clearly indent the first sentence in their paragraph.

✔ Check that each sentence begins with a capital letter and ends with a period, question mark, or exclamation point.

✔ Read back over their writing to be sure they spelled each word correctly.

3 My Side of the Story

Before Reading

FOCUS

When the point of view changes, the story changes too.

In this lesson, students learn to identify differences in point of view.

BUILDING BACKGROUND

Vocabulary Warm-up

sneeze   granny   itch   snuffed   doornail

Be sure students understand the words above. Try a **Vocabulary Quiz Show** to help students learn these words that are important to understanding the story. Write each word on a 3 X 5 file card. Then write a definition for each word on five other cards. Pass out the cards to 10 different students in class. Ask one student to begin by saying one of the words. Have the student who has the meaning for the word read it aloud.

Prereading Strategy

Give students more introduction to the selection by **Previewing** the selection as a group activity. To begin, ask students to read the first four paragraphs of the story. Then ask them to answer these four questions, based on their initial reading.

1. How do you know from the beginning that the wolf has a different point of view? *(He says that the whole Big Bad Wolf thing is all wrong.)*
2. How does he refer to his granny? *(He refers to her as his dear old granny.)*
3. What excuse does he give for going to the pig's house? *(He needed to borrow a cup of sugar to make his granny a birthday cake.)*
4. How do you think the sneeze will enter into the story? *(The wolf might say that he accidentally sneezed and knocked down the pig's straw house.)*

Reading the Selection

RESPONSE STRATEGY

Students are asked to write what they think really happened in the Response Notes. Look for responses like this if students circle the sentence "The real story is about a sneeze and a cup of sugar."

Sample Response:

The real story is about a big bad wolf who blew down the three little pigs' houses.

Encourage students to identify two or three places in the story that differ from the original version.

CRITICAL READING SKILL

This lesson helps students to learn about how point of view influences the telling of any story—even events in history and in their own lives. Help students to identify discrepancies between the two retellings of the "Three Little Pigs" by asking: "Is this true? What happened in the original version of the story?" Some students will need to review the sequence of events in the real story.

REREADING

After students have finished reading the selection, ask them to go back and review the places they circled in the text. Ask them to complete their Response Notes and tell why each circled sentence differs from the original version of the story.

Writing

QUICK ASSESS

Do students' new fairy tales:

✔ have a new title that reflects who is telling the story?

✔ tell the story from the identified character's point of view?

✔ show creativity?

In this lesson, students rewrite a fairy tale from a different point of view.

HOW DO YOU FEEL?

As a first response, students express their opinions about A. Wolf.

Sample Response:

I think A. Wolf isn't so bad after I hear his story.

WHAT REALLY HAPPENED

Encourage students to begin by circling each answer as True or False and then to write what really happened for the statements they marked False. Students will arrive at different answers, depending on how they think about A. Wolf's statement. Give students a chance to discuss their answers. .

Sample Response:

1. The wolf went to the pig's house because he wanted to eat the little pig.
2. The wolf said, "Little pig, little pig, let me come in."
3. The wolf huffed and puffed and blew the pig's house in.
4. The pig's straw house didn't fall down, the wolf blew it down and then he ate the pig.

CHOOSE ANOTHER FAIRY TALE

Help students to identify other characters who could tell the story of their choice. Remind them that the character could be another person or it could be an animal.

Sample Response:

In Cinderella, one of the stepsisters would tell the story.
The ball would still happen.
The stepsisters would be pretty and wouldn't be mean to Cinderella.

REWRITE A FAIRY TALE

Students may want to rewrite the fairy tale that they chose in the previous activity.

Sample Response:

The Darling Sisters
Once upon a time there were two beautiful sisters who had a mean stepsister named Cinderella. She caused the poor sisters nothing but trouble.

WRITING REMINDERS

Remind students to:

✔ Indent the first sentence in their paragraphs.

✔ Check to see that each sentence begins with a capital letter and ends with a period, question mark, or exclamation point.

✔ Read back over their writing to make sure they spelled each word correctly.

For use with page 31

U n i t   O v e r v i e w

In this unit, students learn about elements of fiction. They find out more about a character, visualize the setting of a story, and explore the element of plot. Explain to students that character, setting, and plot are the main elements of any piece of fiction. Reading a piece of fiction "well" involves paying attention to these elements, keeping track of questions, and sometimes making notes to refer back to when needed regarding plot or setting. Tell students that in fiction, writers take great care to embed important details about character, setting, and plot into the writing. These details provide clues to enable careful readers that help them untangle the meaning in stories.

R e a d i n g   t h e   A r t

The art on this page presents the elements of fiction. Ask students:

• What 3 main elements of fiction do you see?

• What is the setting and plot?

• Who is the main character shown?

L i t e r a t u r e   F o c u s

Lesson	Literature
1. Character Clues	**Judy Blume**, from *Freckle Juice* This excerpt from a fiction story focuses on an imaginative boy named Andrew who goes to school with blue freckles.
2. Where Am I?	**Jean Van Leeuwen**, from *Two Girls in Sister Dresses* This fiction excerpt describes the beach in a vivid way for readers.
3. What's Happening Here?	**Susana Sanromán**, *Señora Regañona* A child who is afraid of the dark finds an imaginative way to deal with her fear.

R e a d i n g   F o c u s

Lesson	Reading Skill
1. Character Clues	As you read, look for character clues. Pay attention to what the characters say and do.
2. Where Am I?	When you read a book or story, look for clues about setting.
3. What's Happening Here?	Plot is what happens in the beginning, middle, and end of a story.

W r i t i n g   F o c u s

Lesson	Writing Assignment
1. Character Clues	Write a journal entry about the day Andrew put blue dots on his face, using information from the story and what you imagine Andrew might think and feel.
2. Where Am I?	Draw a picture of the perfect day that shows where and when it takes place.
3. What's Happening Here?	Write a book review of *Señora Regañona* that describes what happened and what you liked and didn't like.

1 Character Clues

Before Reading

In this lesson, students use what characters say and do to find out more about the characters.

BUILDING BACKGROUND

Vocabulary Warm-up

To make sure that students understand the five words below, ask them to complete the **Cloze Sentences** below. To begin, have students read each word aloud. Ask for a student volunteer to read a sentence with the correct answer.

> reflection   decorated   freckles   chattering   formula

1. It is hard to see a clear _____ of your face in a mirror that is fogged up.
2. Carlos _____ the walls of his room with science fiction posters and drawings.
3. "Please stop talking," asked the music teacher. "Your _____ makes it hard to focus on the music."
4. Tristan's grandma told her a story about how she came to have so many "magic" _____ on her face.
5. Soap and water is a good _____ to use to remove dirt from your hands.

Prereading Strategy

To help increase students' background for the selection, try this **Think-Pair-and-Share** activity. Ask students to explain what each sentence tells you about Andrew. Then ask them to put them in the order they probably occur in the story and to predict what this story is about.
1. "Then he took out the magic marker and decorated his whole face and neck with blue dots."
2. "I grew freckles, Miss Kelly. That's what!"
3. "He couldn't wait to see what was in the package. Could there really be such a thing as freckle remover?"
4. Miss Kelly took a deep breath. "I see," she said.

Reading the Selection

RESPONSE STRATEGY

Students are asked to make predictions about Andrew in the Response Notes.

Sample Response:

I think that kids will laugh at Andrew when he comes to school with his face covered with blue dots.

CRITICAL READING SKILL

In this lesson, students are asked to focus on what they learn about Andrew, based on what he says and does. Stimulate students' curiosity by asking some questions:
➤ Why do you think Andrew wanted to grow blue freckles?
➤ How does Miss Kelly help Andrew?

REREADING

After students finish reading the selection, have them go back and reread their predictions. How many turned out to be right? Ask students to check the text they underlined to see whether it helps them support their predictions.

Writing

In this lesson, students write a journal entry for Andrew, imagining how he felt and what he thought on the day he put blue dots on his face.

A BOY LIKE ANDREW

Students begin to respond to the selection by telling their feelings about the character of Andrew.

Sample Response:

I think Andrew sounds goofy and lonely.

LOOKING BACK

This activity helps students to focus on Andrew's actions and words. Encourage students to reread the story carefully to find out exactly what Andrew did and said.

Sample Response:

Andrew followed the directions. He used the secret formula four times. Luckily, it removed his blue freckles!

JOURNAL ENTRY

Explain that the notes students have taken on Andrew can now become raw material to expand on Andrew's character as they write from his point of view. Encourage students to be creative. Some students may include drawings as well as words in their entry.

Sample Response:

Today was fun. Lucky for me that Miss Kelly had magic freckle remover. I wonder what would happen if I could shrink myself to six inches tall? How would Miss Kelly help me then? I may have to test it out soon!

WRITING REMINDERS

As students write their journal entries, remind them to:

✔ Write in first-person voice.

✔ Be creative in imagining what Andrew might do and say.

✔ Check to see that each sentence begins with a capital letter and ends with a period, question mark, or exclamation point.

Where Am I?

Before Reading

FOCUS

When you read a book or story, look for clues about setting.

In this lesson, students learn to gather information about the setting of a story.

BUILDING BACKGROUND

Vocabulary Warm-up

To give students help with some words from this selection, use this **Matching Definitions** activity. To begin, write these two columns on the board. Ask students to draw a line between the word in the left column and its definition in the right column. For added practice, ask students to think of a sentence for each word.

1. *overlooking* — large fortresses or houses made of sand
2. *whisper* — low, muttered, hard-to-understand sounds or words
3. *sand castles* — impressions of the foot left on a soft surface, such as sand
4. *footprints* — to speak softly in a hushed tone
5. *murmurs* — rising above, looking down on from above

Prereading Strategy

Use this **Anticipation Guide** to give students some background on the selection.

1. Agree Disagree Usually there is little to see at the beach.
2. Agree Disagree At beaches, you can see only water, sand, and the sky.
3. Agree Disagree The waves at the ocean are usually the same all year round.

Reading the Selection

RESPONSE STRATEGY

Students are asked to write questions that relate to when and where the story takes place. Students will write something like this:

Sample Response:

Where does Jennifer live?

What does she see and hear at the beach?

Encourage students to write at least two or three questions.

CRITICAL READING SKILL

Point out the places in the story that answer their questions and give information about the setting. Suggest students ask these questions.

➤ Does this sentence tell me about a place, such as a room or a geographic location? If so, that is a clue about *where* the story takes place.

➤ Does this sentence tell me about a year, an age, or a time of day? If so, that is a clue about *when* the story takes place.

REREADING

After students have finished reading the selection, ask them to go back and add any new places they find that tell *where* the story takes place. Ask students to review their Response Notes to see if there are any more questions they might add.

W r i t i n g

QUICK ASSESS

Do students' drawings:

✔ show where their days took place?

✔ give details about when their days took place?

✔ communicate why their days were so special?

In this lesson, students write a description of a wonderful day they experienced that includes information about the setting of their special days.

WHERE AND WHEN

As an initial response, students recall the setting.

Sample Response:

The story takes place in the ocean.
It takes place in the morning.

MY WONDERFUL DAY

This activity helps students to think about details related to the setting of their special days as they make notes.

Sample Response:

Where were you? fishing with my uncle on a lake in Minnesota
When were you there? last August
Who was with you? my cousin Andy
What were you doing? fishing and camping out
What made the day so special? I caught a fish.

DRAWING A PICTURE

Explain to students that they will be using the notes they made about their special days to help them as they create a drawing of their days.

Sample Response:

WRITING REMINDERS

As students complete their star frame entries, remind them to:

✔ Make notes about each of the five questions.

✔ Give enough information so that someone else can picture their day.

✔ Be creative in the details they choose.

3 What's Happening Here?

Before Reading

FOCUS

Plot is what happens in the beginning, middle, and end of a story.

In this lesson, students explore the element of plot as they identify the plot and then write a review of the story.

BUILDING BACKGROUND

Vocabulary Warm-up

To make sure that students understand these vocabulary words, have them complete the **Cloze Sentences** below. Have students read each word aloud. Ask for a student to read the first sentence with the correct word added.

    dreadful   dare   shone   starry   floated

1. Don't you _____ leave the kitchen until you have cleaned up!
2. The moon _____ down, lighting up the town in a beautiful orange-yellow glow.
3. The balloon _____ silently over the rooftops and finally disappeared from sight.
4. The movie had a _____ plot and an even worse ending.
5. The kids created a _____ night on their bedroom walls with stick-on stars.

Prereading Strategy

Give students more introduction to this selection by **Previewing** it as a group activity. Ask students to read the first two paragraphs of the story. Then ask them to answer these three questions, based on their initial reading.
1. Who is Señora Regañona? *(The author refers to the night as a creature named Señora Regañona.)*
2. What does the author do to try to keep this dreadful creature away? *(She puts a light under her covers, thinking the light will drive it away.)*
3. What problem did the light cause? *(It keeps the author awake, which gets her wondering what Señora Regañona does up there in the dark.)*

Reading the Selection

RESPONSE STRATEGY

Encourage students to ask two or three plot-related questions in their Response Notes. Look for questions that anticipate what will come next as the plot develops.
   Sample Response:
How will the author try to deal with Señora Regañona?

CRITICAL READING SKILL

This lesson helps students see how the plot of a story develops and keeps the story flowing from beginning to end by asking: What is happening now? *(The girl puts a light under her covers at night to keep Señora Regañona away.)*
Help students to anticipate the plot as it develops by asking: What might happen next? *(The girl will play with Señora Regañona every night.)*

    Encourage students to identify the plot as it develops and then to ask themselves what questions they will have as a result of the action that has just taken place.

REREADING

When students finish reading the selection, ask them to go back and review their questions. How many of their questions were answered as the plot developed? Lead a whole-class discussion that includes which ones weren't answered, and why.

Writing

In this lesson, students identify what happens in a story from beginning to end and then practice explaining the plot in their own words in the form of a book review.

SURPRISE

As a first response, students note what surprised them in the selection.

Sample Response:

I was surprised she became Señora Regañona's friend.

WHAT HAPPENS NEXT?

Encourage students to begin by reading over the story as they consider what happens next. Then they will write the plot of this story in order, using the boxes provided. Remind students that if they need more boxes, they can add more on another piece of paper.

Sample Response:

She puts a light under her covers to scare away Señora Regañona.

She forgets her light and falls asleep.

She flies out into the night sky.

She finds Señora Regañona and plays with her.

She floats over the houses with her new friend.

BOOK REVIEW

Encourage students to describe what happened in the story.

Sample Response:

Señora Regañona is a good book. It tells how a girl learned not to be afraid. She was afraid of the dark, but then she met a make-believe friend.

I liked the story because the girl was no longer afraid of the dark.

WRITING REMINDERS

Remind students to:

✓ Check to see that each sentence begins with a capital letter and ends with a period, question mark, or exclamation point.

✓ Indent the first sentence in their reviews.

✓ Read back over their writing to make sure they spelled each word correctly.

Unit Overview

In this unit, students learn about language through poetry. They listen for rhyme and rhythm, learn to identify and appreciate word choices, and use context clues to follow a plot in a poem as it develops. Explain to students that in poetry, especially, few words are wasted. Poets make every word count. Picking up clues from language not only adds information but also enjoyment to reading poetry and other writing. Give students time to begin to relish the richness of language in the selections in this unit at the same time you encourage them to look for rhyme and rhythm, word choices, and context clues in other fiction books they read.

Reading the Art

Ask students to look carefully at the art on this page. Then have them discuss the following questions as a whole-class activity:

• How does this image give you a clue about the content of this unit?

• What do the words add to the meaning of the drawing?

• What is the feeling of this drawing?

• How does the placement of the words on the page add to the effect?

UNDERSTANDING LANGUAGE

L i t e r a t u r e   F o c u s

Lesson	Literature
1. Listening to a Poem	**Shel Silverstein,** "Homework Machine"
	This humorous poem describes a machine that starts out to be the perfect invention.
2. Word Magic	**Aileen Fisher,** "Cricket Jackets"
	In this poem, readers learn how cricket deals with a pinchy, too-small jacket.
3. What's the Word?	**Jack Prelutsky,** "I'm an Amiable Dragon" and "The Multilingual Mynah Bird"
	These playful poems about a dragon and a mynah bird point out how context clues can be used to figure out the meaning of new words in a piece of writing.

R e a d i n g   F o c u s

Lesson	Reading Skill
1. Listening to a Poem	Rhythm and rhyme make poems enjoyable to read.
2. Word Magic	Sometimes writers choose words in order to help readers form pictures in their minds.
3. What's the Word?	Look for clues when you come to words you don't know.

W r i t i n g   F o c u s

Lesson	Writing Assignment
1. Listening to a Poem	Write a poem that has rhythm and rhyme similar to Shel Silverstein's.
2. Word Magic	Write a paragraph about an insect using words from the word bank that help to describe why it is interesting or special.
3. What's the Word?	Think of a made-up word and then use it in a paragraph with plenty of context clues to help readers figure out the meaning of the word.

Listening to a Poem

B e f o r e   R e a d i n g

FOCUS

Rhythm and rhyme make poems enjoyable to read.

In the lesson, students learn to identify the rhythm and rhyme in a poem by Shel Silverstein and then write their own poem.

BUILDING BACKGROUND

Vocabulary Warm-up

Make sure students read and understand the words that are underlined below using **Context Clues** to help them. Ask students to read these sentences and then tell what each underlined word means. Suggest that they read all three items completely to help them understand the meaning of each word in context.

machine   contraption   switch

1. "The Homework <u>Machine</u>, oh the Homework Machine,..."
2. "Most perfect <u>contraption</u> that's ever been seen."
3. "Snap on the <u>switch</u>, and in ten seconds' time, Your homework comes out, quick and clean as can be."

Prereading Strategy

Build more background for the selection using an **Anticipation Guide.** Ask students to read the three statements below and then read to find whether they agree or disagree with each statement.

1. Agree   Disagree   The goal of a Homework Machine is to save students time.
2. Agree   Disagree   A Homework Machine probably does a really good job.
3. Agree   Disagree   The writer is perfectly serious about inventing a Homework Machine.

R e a d i n g   t h e   S e l e c t i o n

RESPONSE STRATEGY

Students are asked to identify the rhyming words in the Response Notes. They are also asked to mark the places where the rhythm changes. Students will write something like this:

Sample Response:

"Machine" and "seen" rhyme.

Starting with line 7, the rhythm changes.

Encourage students to identify all the rhyming words and to notice how the rhyming structure changes in the last half of the poem.

CRITICAL READING SKILL

This lesson helps students to identify the rhythm and rhyme in a poem. Help them by asking:

➤ How does the line length help you to determine when the rhythm changes?
➤ How does the overall speed of the poem change in the last three lines?

Some or all students will benefit from reading the poem softly aloud to themselves in order to hear the subtle changes in rhythm and rhyme.

REREADING

After students finish reading the selection, read the poem aloud and ask them to listen for subtle changes in the last four lines. What happens? Ask students to check their Response Notes. Is this where they heard a change in rhythm when they read the poem to themselves?

W r i t i n g

QUICK ASSESS

Do students' poems:

✔ describe their machines?

✔ include rhyming words?

✔ include changes in rhythm that help to describe changes that happen in the poems?

In this lesson, students attempt to write a poem of their own.

BEST PART

Students respond to what they liked in the poem.

Sample Response:

I liked the idea of a thing to do my homework.

RHYTHM AND FEELING

Students are asked to mark where the rhythm and feeling change.

Sample Response:

At first the child is happy. Then he thinks, "Oh, no, it doesn't work."

INVENT A MACHINE

In this first activity, students think about a machine they would like to invent. Encourage them to brainstorm ideas for their machines by following Steps 1-3.

Sample Response:

Step 1: My machine washes and dries the dishes.

Step 2: My machine gets off stuck-on egg and spaghetti sauce. It also does not leave any drips on the glasses.

Step 3: grind, bump, chug, splash, splosh

MACHINE POEM

Explain to students that they will use their notes from the previous activity, Invent a Machine, to write a poem about their invention. Encourage them to think about the rhythm and rhyme in their poems. Will something unexpected happen, and how might that be reflected in the rhythm of the poem?

Sample Response:

Answers will vary, but will resemble the following:

Dishwasher

The dishwasher machine,
Oh the dishwasher machine
The most perfect invention
anyone has seen.
Just put in the dishes
and turn it on.
It grinds and bumps,
chugs, splashes, and goes splosh,
but the dishes come out clean.
Try it. You'll see what I mean.

WRITING REMINDERS

As students write their poems, remind them to:

✔ Check to see that their poems describe their machines, what they do, and how they look and sound.

✔ Think about what might happen to the machines and how any unexpected changes might affect the rhythm and rhyme.

✔ Read back over their writing to make sure they spelled each word correctly.

Word Magic

Before Reading

FOCUS

Sometimes writers choose words in order to help readers form pictures in their minds.

In this lesson, students identify descriptive words in a poem.

BUILDING BACKGROUND

Vocabulary Warm-up

cricket   jacket   pinchy   bracket   vigor

Be sure students can pronounce all of the words above. Try a **Vocabulary Quiz Show** to help students learn these words that are important in the poem. Write each word on a 3 x 5 card. Then write a definition for each word on five other cards. Distribute the cards to different students in class. Begin by asking one student to say one of the words. Then have the student holding the card with the meaning of the word read the card aloud. Continue until you are satisfied that all students are familiar with these words.

Prereading Strategy

Introduce the selection further by **Previewing** the selection as a whole-class activity. To begin, ask students to look over the whole poem. Then ask them to answer these questions, based on their initial reading:
1. What is this poem about? *(crickets)*
2. What problem does the cricket have? *(The cricket's jacket doesn't fit right.)*
3. How does the cricket solve his problem? *(The cricket cracks off his jacket and grows a new, bigger one.)*

Reading the Selection

RESPONSE STRATEGY

Students are asked to read a poem and to circle the words that help them to picture the cricket—that is, the descriptive words. In the Response Notes, students are asked to sketch one of the word pictures they circled. Encourage students to draw something. The intent here is to help students start to visualize words and images in the poem.

Sample Response: ➔

CRITICAL READING SKILL

This lesson helps students to understand the importance of choosing descriptive words when writing. Help students to reflect on this point by asking the whole class to share some of the words they circled. Then consider these questions:
➤ Why did the poet choose this word?
➤ What other words could she have used?
➤ What image does the word bring to mind?

REREADING

After students have finished reading the selection, ask them to review the words they circled. Encourage students to go back over the poem and circle other descriptive words they might have missed the first time through the poem. Ask students to find one or two descriptive words in each stanza. While rereading, students can also draw or sketch other parts of the poem.

Writing

In this lesson, students identify important descriptive words in a poem and then write descriptive paragraphs using words from their word banks.

MY INSECT

Encourage students to take their time in identifying an insect. When they begin to create word banks of descriptive words for their insects, students will want to use words that help to describe what it feels like to see, touch, and hear their chosen insects. Give students a chance to share some of their words.

Sample Response:

Insect: Bee, because he's fast and makes a neat noise.
Chosen words: striped, fuzzy, round, fat, buzzing, hungry

INSECT PARAGRAPH

Students next write a paragraph about the insect they chose. Remind them that they should refer to their word banks as they write, incorporating these words into their writing so that readers can vividly picture their insect.

Sample Response:

Spiders can be large or small, cute or ugly. The spider I saw on the wall this morning was large and black. He dropped down right by my backpack and scared me. He was fast, but not fast enough.

WRITING REMINDERS

Remind students to:

➤ Indent the first sentence in their paragraphs.

➤ Check to see that each sentence begins with a capital letter and ends with a period, question mark, or exclamation point.

➤ Read back over their writing to make sure they spelled each word correctly.

3 What's the Word?

B e f o r e   R e a d i n g

FOCUS

Look for clues when you come to words you don't know.

In this lesson, students practice using context clues to figure out the meaning of a word.

BUILDING BACKGROUND

Vocabulary Warm-up

To make sure that students fully understand the words in these poems, have students complete the **Cloze Sentences** below.

Ask for a student volunteer to read a sentence with the correct word added. Have students practice making up new sentences using these words.

> mynah   warble   squawk   Portuguese   invents

1. _____ is a language spoken by people in Portugal and in other countries.
2. She saw the newspaper headlines: "Girl _____ room-cleaning machine!"
3. The _____ of the excited bird was pretty, but hard to listen to all night long.
4. A sudden _____ from the henhouse told Lucy that the chickens were in trouble.
5. The _____ bird, with its bright yellow bill and feet, comes from Asia.

Prereading Strategy

To help increase students' background to these poems, use this **Think-Pair-and-Share** activity. Ask students to explain what each sentence tells you about the mynah bird.

1. "Birds are known to cheep and chirp/ and sing and warble, peep and purp,/ and some can only squeak and squawk,/ but the mynah bird is able to talk." *(The mynah bird can do a lot more than other birds, because it can talk.)*

2. "He can talk to you in Japanese,/ Italian, French and Portuguese;/ and even Russian and Chinese/ the mynah bird will learn with ease." *(The mynah bird can learn many different languages.)*

3. "The multilingual mynah bird/ can say most any word he's heard,/ and sometimes he invents a few...." *(The mynah bird can mimic speech and make up new words.)*

R e a d i n g   t h e   S e l e c t i o n

RESPONSE STRATEGY

Students are asked to use context clues to figure out what the word *multilingual* means by circling words or phrases in the poem that help them.

Sample Response:

"...the mynah bird is able to talk" or "He can talk to you in Japanese...."

Encourage students to reread the poem and find one phrase in each of the first four stanzas that provides clues about the meaning of the word *multilingual.*

CRITICAL READING SKILL

In this lesson, students are asked to focus on figuring out the meaning of a new word, *multilingual,* using context clues. Get students started by asking them:

➤ What important words do you see around the word *multilingual?*
➤ How does the poem say the mynah bird differs from other birds?

REREADING

After students finish reading the poem, have them go back and reread the poem. Encourage students to circle other words that tell them what *multilingual* means. Then ask them to do one last reading, and circle any context clues missed.

W r i t i n g

In this lesson, students learn to figure out the meaning of a word using context clues.

QUICK ASSESS
Do students' new paragraphs:

✓ have a made-up word?

✓ provide adequate context clues to figure out the meaning of the new word?

✓ show creativity?

ENJOY
Students' preferences for which poem they enjoyed are entirely personal. Encourage them to give reasons for their responses.

Sample Response:

I enjoyed "The Amiable Dragon" the most. It is short <u>and</u> funny. That's why I like it the best.

MULTILINGUAL
Help students find context clues, not just nearby words. One way would be to ask students to circle the two most important words in each line. Then ask, "What do these suggest *multilingual* might mean?"

Sample Response

cheep, chirp, squeak, squawk, talk, Japanese, French, Portuguese
Multilingual means being able to talk a lot and make many different sounds.

DON'T BE GLUMPFY!
This activity helps students to discern the meaning of a made-up word using context clues. Encourage students to reread the paragraph several times to find out what the little brother does that makes him so glumpfy. Then they can circle the words that provide clues and write their definitions in the space provided.

Sample Response:

"...an hour to eat his breakfast."
"...at least ten minutes tying his shoes!"
"...walks to school like a snail."
Definition: Glumpfy means slow.

MAKING UP A WORD
In this activity, students write a paragraph that contains a made-up word. By providing context clues to help a classmate figure out the meaning of the made-up word, students can demonstrate they understand the concept of "context" clues.

Sample Response:

fling-flong

My fling-flong flies on my bike. It blows in the breeze. It flaps in the wind. No one has a fling-flong quite like mine.

WRITING REMINDERS
As students write their paragraphs, remind them to:

✓ Check to see that each sentence begins with a capital letter and ends with a period, question mark, or exclamation point.

✓ Indent the first sentence in their paragraphs.

✓ Read back over their writing to make sure they have spelled each word correctly.

Unit   Overview

In this unit, students study Beverly Cleary's writing to learn more about character development, elements of style, and how personal experiences are woven into works of realistic fiction. Explain to students that when authors base their characters, setting, and plot on aspects of their own lives and life experiences, the writing often seems richer and more real.

Reading   the   Art

Have students study the words and drawing on this page. Remind them to read all the words, too. Then have them discuss these questions as a whole-class activity:

- What things do you see in this picture?
- What is the artist trying to show?
- What do the words tell you about the picture?
- What does this drawing suggest will be in this chapter?

READING AUTHORS

L i t e r a t u r e   F o c u s

Lesson	Literature
1. Finding Out About Characters	**Beverly Cleary,** from *Ellen Tebbits*
	This excerpt from Cleary's widely read story of Ellen, a third-grade girl, illustrates Cleary's skill in creating vivid characters that seem real to readers.
2. How an Author Writes	**Beverly Cleary,** from *Henry Huggins*
	In this excerpt from Cleary's first published story, she includes many interesting details and words that make Henry's character and adventure with a dog come alive for readers.
3. Writing About Real Life	**Beverly Cleary,** from *My Own Two Feet*
	In this excerpt from Cleary's autobiography, she discusses how she gets ideas for her writing from real-life events, people, and places from her past.

R e a d i n g   F o c u s

Lesson	Reading Skill
1. Finding Out About Characters	When you read, think about how characters look and act and what their lives are like.
2. How an Author Writes	Part of an author's style is the way he or she uses details to paint a picture in the reader's mind.
3. Writing About Real Life	Writers use their own experiences to create realistic characters, settings, and situations in stories.

W r i t i n g   F o c u s

Lesson	Writing Assignment
1. Finding Out About Characters	Write a character sketch of Ellen, using information gleaned from the excerpt about what she looks like, her family, friends, and interests.
2. How an Author Writes	Describe your afternoon schedule one day during the week, choosing words and details to help create a picture of each activity.
3. Writing About Real Life	Write a description of your neighborhood, using some real-life details and some new made-up ones.

Finding Out About Characters

Before Reading

FOCUS

When you read, think about how characters look and act and what their lives are like.

In this lesson, students learn how readers get information about characters.

BUILDING BACKGROUND

Vocabulary Warm-up

To help students learn these words, have them complete this **Matching Definitions** exercise. Write the words and the definitions in two columns on the board. Ask students to match them by drawing a line between the word in the left column and its definition in the right column. Ask students to give a sentence for each word.

1. *scuff*   with uneasiness or a sense of worry
2. *scraggly*   freed from worry
3. *anxiously*   hurried; ran playfully
4. *relieved*   shuffle; to walk without lifting up your feet
5. *scampered*   messy, unkempt

Prereading Strategy

Build more background before reading the selection by creating a **Word Web** around Ellen Tebbits. Ask students to read the first three paragraphs to find information to help answer these questions:

What does Ellen look like?

(Ellen Tebbits)

What is her family like?

What does she like to do?

What is she doing at the beginning of this selection?

Reading the Selection

RESPONSE STRATEGY

Students are asked to mark with a star in their Response Notes the places that tell what Ellen looks like, what her friends and family are like, and what she likes to do.

Sample Response:

Ellen: "*Ellen was a thin little girl, with dark hair and brown eyes.*"
What her friends and family are like: "*She had no brothers or sisters and, since Nancy Jane had moved away from next door, there was no one her own age living on Tillamook Street.*"
What she likes to do: "*...because she spent so much time reading and twisting a lock of hair around her finger as she read.*"

CRITICAL READING SKILL

This lesson helps students to see how an author develops characters in a story. Remind students that they can focus on one of the three questions at a time as they read. Discuss with students other possible questions they could ask to learn about a character.

REREADING

After students finish reading the selection, ask them to review the parts they underlined or starred in the margins. For each place marked, have them identify whether the passage answers
➤ what she looks like and likes to do
➤ what her friends and family are like

Writing

QUICK ASSESS
Do students' new paragraphs:

✓ tell what Ellen was like?

✓ paint a picture of the character, Ellen Tebbitts?

In this lesson, students create their own character sketch of Ellen.

WHAT ABOUT ELLEN TEBBITS?

The initial response activity encourages students to express their feelings about literature. Be supportive of their answers.

Sample Response:

I wonder what her secret was and why she didn't have a best friend.

ELLEN TEBBITS CHART

In this activity, students work through a series of questions about Ellen Tebbits. Encourage students to read over their Response Notes and any starring or underlining in the selection before they begin. Explain that they don't have to write the text word for word, but rather just make notes on the chart.

Sample Response:

What is Ellen's family like? *no brothers or sisters, parents don't allow her to have a pet, her mother likes a clean house*

What kinds of friends does Ellen have? *Ellen has lots of friends at school but she didn't have a best friend in the neighborhood.*

What does Ellen like to do? *ballet, read, play with friends*

CHARACTER SKETCH

In this activity, students use their notes about Ellen to write a character sketch. Remind students that they will put all the information gleaned from the selection into a new paragraph that is all their own. Encourage students to be creative.

Sample Response:

Ellen was plain and thin. She had brown hair. She didn't have any brothers and sisters, and she lived on Tillamook Street. Ellen also didn't have a best friend, but she loved dancing.

WRITING REMINDERS

As students write their character sketches, remind them to:

✓ Indent the first sentence in their paragraphs.

✓ Check to see that each sentence begins with a capital letter and ends with a period, question mark, or exclamation point.

✓ Read back over their writing to make sure they have spelled each word correctly.

How an Author Writes

B e f o r e | R e a d i n g

FOCUS

Part of an author's style is the way he or she uses details to paint a picture in the reader's mind.

In this lesson, students learn to identify interesting words and details that make up an author's style.

BUILDING BACKGROUND

Vocabulary Warm-up

scrubbing   tonsils   poster   drugstore   slot

Help students become familiar with the words above with a **Vocabulary Quiz Show.** Write each word on a 3 X 5 file card. Then write a definition for each word on five other cards. Pass out the cards to 10 different students in class. Ask students to begin by saying one of the words out loud. Have the student who has the card with the meaning of the word read it aloud. Continue until you are satisfied that all students are familiar with these words.

Prereading Strategy

Provide students with more introduction to the selection by **Previewing** the selection as a whole-class activity. To begin, ask students to read the first page of the story. Then answer these questions based on their initial reading:
1. Who is this story about? *(a boy named Henry Huggins)*
2. What do you learn about how Henry looks? *(His hair is like a scrubbing brush and he has most of his grown-up teeth.)*
3. What does Henry think of as "exciting" things that have happened to him? *(having his tonsils out and falling out of a tree)*

R e a d i n g   t h e   S e l e c t i o n

RESPONSE STRATEGY

Students are asked to underline interesting words and descriptions in the selection.
   Sample Response:
hair looked like a scrubbing brush, tonsils out when he was six, breaking his arm falling out of a cherry tree

CRITICAL READING SKILL

This lesson helps students to identify some of the specific words and details that add richness and interest to a piece of writing. Help students to become aware of these words by asking:
➤ What words or details do you especially like in the first paragraph?
➤ What descriptions help you to form a picture of what Henry Huggins looks like?

REREADING

After students finish reading the selection, ask them to go back over the selection and review the places they underlined. Remind them that they can write additional comments in their Response Notes. As they read the selection again, tell them to look for places where they can really *picture* the person, place, or thing being described.

Writing

In this lesson, students create their own after-school schedule.

QUICK ASSESS

Do students' sentences:

✔ contain interesting word choices?

✔ use descriptive details to help paint a picture?

✔ show creativity?

DRAWING A PICTURE

Tell students that good descriptions and details in a piece of writing help the reader to form a picture of what is being described. Encourage them to choose a detail from the selection that helps them to form a clear mental picture and then to draw it in the space provided.

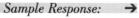 *Sample Response:* →

ADDING INTEREST TO A SENTENCE

Explain to students that they can add descriptive details to an existing sentence to make it more interesting. Have them begin by reading the example and the new sentence. Then ask them to brainstorm some words and details they could add to make the sentence more interesting.

Sample Response:

splash, waves, drops, clear
Henry liked to see the clear drops of the pool water when he splashed.
loud, mean, unhappy, angry, barking dog
The loud, mean bus driver was as cranky as an angry, barking dog.
cool, chocolate, dripping, cone
The cool, dripping chocolate ice cream in a cone was the best I have ever had.

MY AFTER-SCHOOL SCHEDULE

In this activity, students are to write interesting descriptive sentences about what they do at different times during one day of the week. Explain to students that, as with the Henry Huggins selection, any sentence can be made more or less interesting depending on the choice of words. Students can start by listing the things they do during each hour between 4:00 and 8:00 p.m. Then they can use their notes to create lively, interesting sentences that will allow readers to picture each activity.

Sample Response:

4:00 p.m. On Thursdays my school clothes fly across my room. I have only five minutes tops to race in the door, drop my piano lesson music, change clothes, grab my bike, and head to soccer practice. My new solo is running through my head as I ride.

WRITING REMINDERS

Remind students to:

✔ Check to see that each sentence begins with a capital letter and ends with a period, question mark, or exclamation point.

✔ Read back over their writing to make sure they spelled each word correctly.

Writing About Real Life

Before Reading

FOCUS

Writers use their own experiences to create realistic characters, settings, and situations in stories.

In this lesson, students learn about realistic fiction and how the writing, even though it is made up, seems real.

BUILDING BACKGROUND

Vocabulary Warm-up

To help students to become familiar with these words before they read the selection, have them complete this **Matching Definitions** activity. Write these five words and the definitions in two columns on the board. Ask students to match them by drawing a line between the word in the left column and its definition in the right column. For added practice, ask students to think of a sentence for each word.

1. *embroidering*   motivated; influenced by
2. *scooters*   a vehicle on rails that transports people in cities
3. *advent*   children's foot-operated vehicles
4. *inspired*   forming detailed decorative designs and stitches with needlework
5. *streetcar*   coming; arrival

Prereading Strategy

To help increase students' readiness for this selection, use this **Think-Pair-and-Share** activity. Read the sentences to students or write them on the board. Ask students which sentence comes first, which second, and so forth. Then ask students what they think the selection will be about.

1. "... so I named the dog Spareribs and continued the story. ..."
2. "Where Henry's name came from I do not know. It was just there."
3. "When I came to the skinny dog who found Henry, I needed a name."

Reading the Selection

RESPONSE STRATEGY

Students are asked to picture the neighborhood that Cleary describes and to draw sketches of what they see. Students may choose to draw a sketch of the Yakima neighborhood, the dog, or another image of their choosing. Encourage students to draw two or three sketches of their favorite parts of this selection.

CRITICAL READING SKILL

In this lesson, students focus on the connection between Beverly Cleary's writing and her own growing up as a way to write vivid realistic fiction. Ask several students to share the first passage they underlined and then to describe in detail exactly what they picture in their minds. After hearing each student's description, ask the class:

➤ What details were part of the picture that this student envisioned in his or her mind?
➤ Does the description you heard contain details that were <u>not</u> part of Cleary's description? If so, what were they?

   Point out that good descriptions help us create pictures in our mind that often are more than the actual words on the page. Our minds fill in the details, sometimes from *our* own experiences.

REREADING

After students finish reading the selection, have them go back over the selection again, looking for the description that was most vivid or interesting. Ask them to write in their Response Notes why they liked this description the best.

W r i t i n g

In this lesson, students learn to create a picture of the neighborhood that Cleary describes and then to draw a scene or a map.

QUICK ASSESS

Do students' paragraphs:

✓ contain ideas from their notes?

✓ contain both true and made-up details?

✓ create a vivid picture of the neighborhoods they are describing?

SURPRISES

Encourage students' responses to what surprised them in the selection. The purpose is to get students to articulate their feelings.

Sample Response:

I was surprised that she named a dog after some leftover spareribs she had in the refrigerator.

CLEARY'S NEIGHBORHOOD

In this activity, students are asked to draw a scene or a map of the neighborhood Cleary describes. Encourage students to reread the selection as many times as they want in order to glean further details and pictures that will become part of their drawings or maps.

Sample Response: →

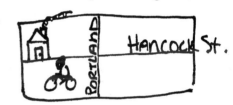

MY OWN NEIGHBORHOOD

Explain to students that they will now use their own experiences and neighborhoods as the basis for their own writing. They will begin by making some notes about what their neighborhoods look like, children that are a part of the neighborhood, and things that happen there.

Sample Response:

What my neighborhood looks like: lots of tall buildings, apartment houses, little stores

Children in my neighborhood: kids playing basketball, riding on bikes

Things that happen: cars honk, dogs go by, friends come out to play

Encourage students to read over their notes, close their eyes as they picture their own neighborhood, and then try to add more vivid details of all kinds.

NEIGHBORHOOD STORY

In this activity, explain to students that they will use their notes from the previous activity to write the beginning of a story in which they describe their own neighborhoods. Remind students that they should feel free to make up new details to add to the parts that are true in their writing, just as Beverly Cleary did in hers.

Sample Response:

A New Neighbor

One day the boys from the neighborhood rang the doorbell. It was late at night. But Matt and his brother had news. They had a new baby brother, who was just born.

WRITING REMINDERS

As students write the beginning of their stories, remind them to:

✓ Indent the first sentence in their paragraphs.

✓ Check to see that each sentence begins with a capital letter and ends with a period, question mark, or exclamation point.

✓ Read back over their writing to make sure they spelled each word correctly.

READING WELL

U n i t   O v e r v i e w

In this unit students learn more about how to read well. Students learn about an author's purpose, how to identify the main idea and details in a piece of writing, and how prior knowledge can help them understand and interpret writing.

R e a d i n g   t h e   A r t

Have students look closely at the illustration on this page. Then have them discuss these questions as a whole-group activity:

- What is the boy doing in this picture?
- Why do you think he has a key? What is he opening?
- What is popping out of the pages, and what does it represent?
- How would you sum up the meaning of this drawing in one sentence?

L i t e r a t u r e   F o c u s

Lesson	Literature
1. Why an Author Writes	**Arnold Lobel,** from *Fables*
	Two of Lobel's *Fables*, "The Hen and the Apple Tree" and "King Lion and the Beetle," highlight an author's purpose—to teach, to entertain, or a combination of the two.
2. What's It All About?	**Judy Hawes,** from *Fireflies in the Night*
	In this selection, Hawes recalls summers spent watching fireflies with her grandparents.
3. Using What You Know	**Ellen Schecter,** from *Real Live Monsters*!
	Schecter includes many interesting details in this nonfiction selection about the giant bird-eating spider.

R e a d i n g   F o c u s

Lesson	Reading Skill
1. Why an Author Writes	As you read, ask yourself, "Why did the author write this?"
2. What's It All About?	When you read, look for the most important idea.
3. Using What You Know	Before you read, ask yourself: What do I already know about this subject? What do I want to know?

W r i t i n g   F o c u s

Lesson	Writing Assignment
1. Why an Author Writes	Write a list of questions to ask Arnold Lobel about his purpose in writing and the book, *Fables*.
2. What's It All About?	Write a paragraph on a topic of your choice, beginning with the main idea and then adding details about that idea.
3. Using What You Know	Write a paragraph about the giant bird-eating spider, using your K-W-L chart as a guide.

Why an Author Writes

Before Reading

FOCUS

As you read, ask yourself, "Why did the author write this?"

In this lesson, students learn that an author's purpose for writing is to teach, to entertain, or a combination of both.

BUILDING BACKGROUND

Vocabulary Warm-up

Make sure students understand the words that are underlined below. Read the sentence and ask students to use **Context Clues** to help them with the meaning of each underlined word.

bark   quiver   noble   subjects

1. "Hen, come outside and rest your back against the <u>bark</u> of my trunk." *(Trunk explains the* bark *is part of a tree.)*
2. "The tree began to <u>quiver</u> and shake. All of its leaves quickly dropped off." *(Shake is a synonym of* quiver.*)*
3. "'What a beautiful and <u>noble</u> creature I am,' he said." *(Beautiful helps explain what* noble *means.)*
4. "'I will go forth to show my devoted <u>subjects</u> that their leader is every inch a king!'" *(King and* leader *suggest that* subjects *are under them.)*

Prereading Strategy

If desired, build more background for the selection using an **Anticipation Guide.**

1. Agree   Disagree   Hens are usually afraid of wolves.
2. Agree   Disagree   Wolves can usually outsmart hens.

"King Lion and the Beetle"

3. Agree   Disagree   Kings are usually nice people and kind to everyone.
4. Agree   Disagree   A beetle is a small bug.

Reading the Selection

RESPONSE STRATEGY

Students are asked to focus on the author's purpose by identifying any parts of the two fables that entertain and those parts that teach a lesson. Students will write something like this:

Sample Response:

"'The Hen and the Apple Tree' entertains until the very end, when the moral of the fable teaches a lesson."

CRITICAL READING SKILL

Help students to focus on places in the fables where Lobel entertains and where he teaches. Ask the class to read aloud passages that exemplify each purpose. Ask students:

➤ Which story is the most entertaining?
➤ Which one has a lesson you like the best?

REREADING

After students finish reading the selections, help them to consider these fables again by asking:

➤ Why do you think each fable combines entertaining and teaching?

W r i t i n g

In this lesson, students create a series of questions to ask Arnold Lobel.

STORIES

As an initial response, students give their own opinions about the fables. Their opinions of the fables will vary.

Sample Response:

I liked the one about the king because he learned a lesson. Don't be bossy.

AUTHOR'S PURPOSE CHART

In this activity, students describe the author's purpose and what they learned for each of the two stories.

Sample Response:

"The Hen and the Apple Tree"

Purpose: to entertain and teach

What I Learned: That it is better to be myself, because when I try to be something I'm not, I look silly.

"King Lion and the Beetle"

Purpose: to entertain and teach

What I Learned: You should be good to everyone and not think too much of yourself.

ASK ARNOLD LOBEL

In this activity, students write four interview questions to ask Arnold Lobel about these fables. Remind students that the more they read and think about the fables, the better the questions they will be able to ask.

Sample Response:

Why do you write fables?

What is the best fable you ever wrote?

What is the name of your latest book?

Will you be writing more fables or just stories?

WRITING REMINDERS

Remind students to:

✔ Start each question with a capital letter.

✔ End each question with a question mark.

✔ Read back over their writing to make sure they spelled each word correctly.

What's It All About?

B e f o r e   R e a d i n g

FOCUS

When you read, look for the most important idea.

In this lesson students learn to identify the main idea and details in a selection.

BUILDING BACKGROUND

Vocabulary Warm-up

To help students become familiar with the words in the selection, have them complete this **Matching Definitions** activity. Write these five words and the definitions in two columns on the board. Ask students to match them by drawing a line between the word in the left column and its definition in the right column. For added practice, ask students to think of a sentence for each word.

1. *fireflies*   a protective case for a light with transparent openings
2. *beetles*   vertical, erect
3. *punched*   any number of insects that have two pairs of wings
4. *lantern*   members of the beetle family that produce a bright, soft light
5. *upright*   pounded, pierced

Prereading Strategy

To help students gain more background for this selection, create a **Word Web** around the word *fireflies*. Ask students to suggest answers to these questions for their word web:

What other name are fireflies called?   fireflies   What do fireflies look like?

When do you see fireflies?   Where do you find them?

R e a d i n g   t h e   S e l e c t i o n

RESPONSE STRATEGY

Students are asked to circle the main idea in the passage and highlight or underline the details they find about that main idea. The important part is for students to underline details about the main idea.

Sample Response:

Main idea: Why I like fireflies
Details: "When I visit my grandfather in the summertime, we sit outdoors after supper and watch them." "Grandmother likes to watch fireflies too. She calls them lightning bugs. They look like little dancing stars." "Fireflies are easy to catch."

CRITICAL READING SKILL

This lesson helps students to see how an author develops an idea by supporting it with interesting details. Remind students that usually almost every sentence adds more detail.

➤ What new information did I learn about fireflies from this paragraph?
➤ Where does the author get her detailed information about fireflies?

REREADING

After students finish reading the selection, ask them to review the details that they underlined. Then ask them to reread the selection to see if they missed any details. For each place marked in the text, have students ask:

➤Does this add a new piece of information to the main idea, "Why I like fireflies"?

Writing

In this lesson, students write their own paragraphs after outlining the main idea and the details they will include.

WHAT DID YOU LEARN?

As an initial response, students recall one or two things they learned about fireflies. Their answers will vary.

Sample Response:

I learned that fireflies have two sets of wings.

ORGANIZER

To model how to separate the main idea from details, students complete an organizer, separating the main idea (fireflies) from the details.

Sample Response:

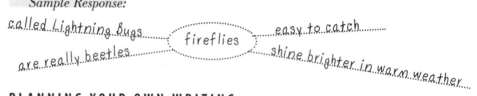

called Lightning Bugs   fireflies   easy to catch

are really beetles   shine brighter in warm weather

PLANNING YOUR OWN WRITING

In this activity, students fill in a chart to plan their own paragraph. Students create a topic, a main idea, and four supporting details. Discuss with students that a topic is general, while a main idea is a *thought* or *feeling* they associated with a topic.

Sample Response:

Topic: My dog
Main idea: Why my dog is my best friend
Details:
• He wakes me up for school.
• He loves me even when I am in a bad mood.
• He waits by the door for me to come home for school.
• He likes to play catch.

WRITE A PARAGRAPH

In this activity, students use their planners as the basis for writing paragraphs on their topics. Encourage students to add other details as they write interesting paragraphs on their topics.

Sample Response:

Don't get me wrong. I have a lot of friends, friends I play with after school and friends in my neighborhood. But when it comes to best friends, I have to say it's Casey, my five-year-old Golden Retriever.

WRITING REMINDERS

As students write their paragraphs, remind them to:

✓ Indent the first sentence in their paragraphs.

✓ Check to see that each sentence begins with a capital letter and ends with a period, question mark, or exclamation point.

✓ Read back over their writing to check their spelling.

3 Using What You Know

Before Reading

FOCUS

Before you read, ask yourself: What do I already know about this subject? What do I want to know?

In this lesson, students learn to use what they already know about the topic before they read.

BUILDING BACKGROUND

Vocabulary Warm-up

monster   poisonous   stabs   prey   fangs

To help students become familiar with the words from the selection, try the activity **Vocabulary Quiz Show.** Write each word on a 3 x 5 file card. Then write a definition for each word on five other cards. Pass out the cards to 10 different students in class. Ask students to begin by saying one of the words out loud. Have the student who has the card with the meaning of the word read it aloud.

Prereading Strategy

Use this **Think-Pair-and-Share** activity to help build background with students about spiders. Ask students to read these sentences and then answer the questions.
1. "It also catches and eats small birds."
2. "Then it sips up the insides."
3. "This giant eats insects, small lizards, and small snakes (even poisonous ones)."
4. "This giant stabs its prey with poison fangs up to one inch long."
➤ Which sentence appears first in the story? *(sentence number 3)*
➤ In what order do the other sentences appear? *(sentence number 1, then 3, then 2)*
➤ What new piece of information did you learn from these sentences? *(I didn't know that spiders could eat small birds!)*
➤ How are these spiders unlike other spiders you know? *(I've never seen a spider that had poison fangs one inch long.)*

Reading the Selection

RESPONSE STRATEGY

Students use their own questions to help focus their reading as they search for answers to questions in a K-W-L chart.

Sample Response:

What I Know: *Black widow spiders are poisonous.*
What I Want to Find Out: *How big is the monster spider?*

CRITICAL READING SKILL

In this lesson, students use what they know and their own questions to help focus their reading. Remind students to put a star by parts of the selection that answer their questions.

REREADING

After students finish reading the selection, ask them to review the places they starred. Then have students complete the third column of the chart, "What I Learned."

Writing

In this lesson, students use what they learned about the giant spider to write their own paragraphs.

FACT

Students can help share what they learned by sharing the weirdest fact about these giant spiders.

Sample Response:

The giant spider is so big it can even eat small birds.

SPIDER PARAGRAPH

Explain to students that they are to use what they learned about the giant spider to write a paragraph. Remind them to use their charts to help organize their thinking as they write.

Sample Response:

I learned that spiders can be very big. Some spiders are so big that they can even eat a small bird. The giant spider makes purring sounds like a cat. The spider stabs its food with fangs.

MORE QUESTIONS

In this activity, students reflect on questions that still remain on this topic, and where they might find the answers. Explain to students that the learning process goes on, and that as we gain more information, it also brings up new questions. Encourage students to list at least two questions they still have on the topic. Share students' questions with the whole class. Brainstorm as a class where they might find information to answer each question.

Sample Response:

"Where can I see this spider in person? Is it in a zoo somewhere?" Possible ways to find out the answer to this question might include: school or public library research, the Internet, the local zoo or science center, or talking to a person at a local college or university.

WRITING REMINDERS

Remind students to:

✓ Read back over their writing to make sure they spelled each word correctly.

✓ Check to see that each sentence begins with a capital letter.

✓ Make sure they write complete sentences.

Unit Overview

In this unit, students read nonfiction writing in order to learn about summarizing, following the order of events, and getting information from graphic aids. Explain to students that you can learn a lot about people, places, and events from reading nonfiction. Some nonfiction is presented in a story form to help the reader actually feel that he or she is part of the event or period of time in history. Knowing the skills taught in this chapter will help students get more out of reading nonfiction.

Reading the Art

Ask students to "read" the illustration on this page. Then have them discuss these questions as a whole-class activity:

- What is this girl using to gain information?
- What subject does she seem to be studying?
- How can each visual aid on this page help her with her topic?
- What other visual aids can you think of that might also help her?

Literature Focus

Lesson	Literature
1. Sum It Up	**Robert Bateman,** from *Safari* This description of elephants tells how they look and how they live.
2. Tracking the Order of Events	**David A. Adler,** from *A Picture Book of Helen Keller* This excerpt from the book tells how Helen came to meet her teacher, Anne Sullivan, and the importance of what she learned.
3. Reading Maps, Charts, and Graphs	**Steve Jenkins,** from *Hottest, Coldest, Highest, Deepest* This geography excerpt includes information about some of the hottest and coldest places on earth.

Reading Focus

Lesson	Reading Skill
1. Sum It Up	A summary tells the most important ideas.
2. Tracking the Order of Events	Understanding sequence helps you keep track of events.
3. Reading Maps, Charts, and Graphs	When you read nonfiction, use the graphic aids to help you picture ideas.

Writing Focus

Lesson	Writing Assignment
1. Sum It Up	Write a summary of a selection about elephants that tells only the most important information.
2. Tracking the Order of Events	Describe a familiar activity using words such as "first," "next," etc.
3. Reading Maps, Charts, and Graphs	Create a graph that compares the height of several friends.

Sum It Up

Before Reading

FOCUS
A summary tells the most important ideas.

In this lesson, students read to find and learn about the most important ideas in a passage about elephants.

BUILDING BACKGROUND

Vocabulary Warm-up
To make sure that students know and understand the words in this selection, use **Context Clues** to find the meaning. Have students read these sentences and then tell what each underlined word means. Ask students: What other words in the sentence help you to understand the meaning?

forage   munching   matriarch   creases   roam

1. "Elephants like to <u>forage</u> in forests where they can eat juicy young leaves and twigs from the treetops."
2. "You can hear them breaking off branches and <u>munching</u>."
3. "The leader of an elephant herd is always the oldest female, known as the <u>matriarch</u>."
4. "The face of one of these wise, old female elephants makes me think of a map. The <u>creases</u> and wrinkles are like the mountains and rivers."
5. "Young male elephants do not live with the females and calves. Instead, they <u>roam</u> together in small groups."

Prereading Strategy
Give students more introduction to the selection by **Previewing** it. Ask students to read the first three paragraphs of the story. Then discuss the following questions:
1. What do you learn about what elephants like to eat? *(Elephants like to eat the young leaves and twigs from the tops of the trees.)*
2. What do you learn about why elephants don't stay in one place for long? *(Because they need to eat constantly, they are always on the move, looking for food.)*
3. What do you learn about when elephants decide to stop for a time? *(They stop to cool down whenever they find water.)*

Reading the Selection

RESPONSE STRATEGY
Students are asked to underline the three or four most important ideas in this selection. Encourage students to choose ideas in separate paragraphs.
Sample Response:
Idea 1 - Elephants like to forage in forests where they can eat juicy young leaves and twigs from the treetops.

CRITICAL READING SKILL
This lesson helps students to identify the most important ideas in a piece of writing. Help students become aware of the most important ideas by asking themselves these questions as they read each paragraph:
➤ What is the main idea of this paragraph?
➤ Is this a big, important idea or a small detail?

REREADING
After students finish reading the selection, ask them to read the selection once more. Have them review the places they underlined. Do these still seem to be the three or four most important ideas? If not, encourage students to make changes.

W r i t i n g

QUICK ASSESS

Do students' paragraphs:

✓ summarize the most important information?

✓ use their notes from the Facts About Elephants page?

In this lesson, students write a summary of a selection about elephants.

MOST INTERESTING FACT

As an initial response to the selection, students recall one fact. The intent here is to develop a habit of recalling information from what students read.

Sample Response:

I liked that the leader is a girl elephant. Girls rule!

FACTS ABOUT ELEPHANTS

In this activity, students write down notes on elephants from their reading. By walking through the selection to find this information, students will collect all of the details needed to write a good summary.

Sample Response:

Early habits: They eat juicy young leaves and twigs from trees.

Size: Elephants are the largest land animals.

Where they live: Elephants live in Africa. They are always on the move.

Leader of the herd: The oldest female elephant is the leader.

Young male elephants: The young male elephants roam around by themselves.

SUMMARY

Students write a summary about elephants using the information gathered in the previous activity.

Sample Response:

Elephants are the largest animals in Africa. The oldest female elephant leads the herd. They eat leaves and twigs. Elephants roam all the time and look for food and water. The young male elephants do not live with the other elephants.

WRITING REMINDERS

Remind students to:

✓ Check to see that each sentence begins with a capital letter and ends with a period, question mark, or exclamation point.

✓ Make sure they checked the spelling of each word.

✓ Check to see that each sentence is a complete sentence.

Tracking the Order of Events

B e f o r e   R e a d i n g

FOCUS

Understanding sequence helps you keep track of events.

In this lesson, students use word clues to follow the sequence of events in a selection.

BUILDING BACKGROUND

Vocabulary Warm-up

To make sure that students understand words in this selection, complete the **Cloze Sentences** that follow. To begin, have students read each word aloud. Ask for a student volunteer to read a sentence with the correct word added.

    deaf   manners   soul   patterns   Braille

1. If you learn _____, you will be able to read the writing that many people who are blind can read.
2. The _____ of dots helped Helen to read many words.
3. Helen Keller was born blind and _____.
4. Helen's _____, or spirit, felt full of joy and hope when she began to learn words.
5. You will be considered polite if you have good _____ when speaking to people.

Prereading Strategy

To build more background for the selection, create a **Word Web** around blindness. If necessary, ask students to skim the selection quickly before beginning.

What is it like? — *blindness* — *Who has it?*

What do blind people do? — *How do blind people live?*

R e a d i n g   t h e   S e l e c t i o n

RESPONSE STRATEGY

Students are asked to circle words that give clues to the sequence of events. Help students to find the first few words, such as *then* and *later*. Encourage students to identify additional words that give clues about the sequence of events in a story.

Sample Response:

Then, March 3, 1887, First, Now, Many years later

CRITICAL READING SKILL

This lesson helps students to identify specific words that help them know that a story is being told in sequence. Explain to students that asking these questions as they read along will help them to think about the sequence of the story:

➤What happens *first*?
➤What is happening *now*?
➤What will happen *next*?

Encourage students to make some notes about the questions in their Response Notes.

REREADING

After students have finished reading the selection, ask them to go back and review the words they underlined in the text. Have them read the text one more time and add any additional words they find that give clues about the sequence of events. Then, have students work with a partner to explain the sequence, based on the words they underlined.

W r i t i n g

In this lesson, students create a sequence chart of the selection they read and then write about a process of their own.

HELEN KELLER SEQUENCE CHART

In this activity, students use their underlined words to help identify the sequence of events to place in order in the chart. Encourage students to refer to their Response Notes.

Sample Response:

On March 3, 1887, Helen first met Anne Sullivan.

First, Anne Sullivan taught Helen proper manners.

One day Anne and Helen passed a water pump. Anne taught Helen how to spell "water."

Many years later Helen wrote that learning to spell "water" gave her soul hope.

Soon, Anne Sullivan taught Helen how to read by feeling patterns of dots, called Braille.

MY OWN ACTIVITY

In this activity, students practice writing about their own activity. Have them begin by selecting an activity. Encourage them to review the list of words that signal sequence. Then have them describe what they do in order, using words like *then* and *next* to show the sequence. Ask students to underline the words in their writing that show the sequence.

Sample Response:

To make a peanut butter and jelly sandwich, you <u>first</u> get out the bread. <u>Next</u>, you find the peanut butter and jelly in the refrigerator. <u>Next</u> you put on the peanut butter with a knife. <u>After that</u>, you put the jelly on. <u>Then</u> you cut the sandwich in half.

WRITING REMINDERS

As students complete their writing, remind them to:

✔ Indent the first sentence in their paragraphs.

✔ Check to see that each sentence begins with a capital letter and ends with a period, question mark, or exclamation point.

✔ Read back over their writing to make sure they have spelled each word correctly.

3 Reading Maps, Charts, and Graphs

Before Reading

FOCUS

When you read nonfiction, use the graphic aids to help you picture ideas.

In this lesson, students learn to read graphic aids as a source of information.

BUILDING VOCABULARY

Vocabulary Warm-up

area   freshwater   peak   sea level   temperature

Make sure that students understand the above terms by using a **Vocabulary Quiz Show.** Write each word on a 3 X 5 file card. Then write a definition for each word on five other cards. Pass out the cards to 10 students in class. Ask students to begin by saying one of the words out loud. Have the student who has the card with the meaning of the word read it aloud. Continue until you are satisfied that all students are familiar with these words.

Prereading Strategy

If desired, build more background for the selection using an **Anticipation Guide.** Tell students to read the three statements below and then read the selection to find whether they agree or disagree with each statement.

1. Agree   Disagree   Graphic aids include maps, graphs, and pictures.
2. Agree   Disagree   Graphics give you little information and are used because they look good.
3. Agree   Disagree   A map only tells you the same thing that the text tells.

Reading the Selection

RESPONSE STRATEGY

In this lesson, students learn to get information from graphic aids, such as maps, charts, and graphs. In the Response Notes, have students identify which type of graphic aid they are using to get information.

Encourage students to analyze how each type of graphic aid is effective in presenting a specific type of information and what kind of information it gives.

CRITICAL READING SKILL

In this lesson, students glean information from graphic aids. Explain that graphics need to be read, just like text. Graphic aids can sometimes dramatically compare two items in a way that words alone cannot do as effectively. They can also create visual representations that enable the reader to see information. As students read this selection, suggest that they ask themselves these questions as they read:
➤ What information did I learn from this graphic aid?
➤ How does this graphic aid present information in a way that is more effective than words alone?

REREADING

After students finish reading the selection, ask them to go back and review each graphic aid. Which one did they find the most effective, and why? Did any of the graphic aids introduce new questions? Take the time to listen to new questions students have.

Writing

QUICK ASSESS
Do students' bar graphs:

✔ present the information requested?

✔ look neat?

✔ help the reader accurately picture the information?

In this lesson, students research and prepare new graphic information in the form of a chart.

RECORD-BREAKING PLACES

As an initial response, students give their opinion about which place they might like to see.

Sample Response:

I want to see Death Valley.

READING GRAPHIC AIDS

In this activity, students practice reading the information presented in the graphic aids in the selection and then record it. Encourage students to look carefully at each of the graphic aids in order to read and interpret the information correctly.

Sample Response:

Four rivers are larger than the United States.

The Nile River runs through Egypt, Sudan, Ethiopia, Uganda, and Zaire.

Mt. Everest is in the country of Nepal.

The hottest temperature ever recorded is 134.6°F in Death Valley, CA.

Room temperature is 66°F.

The coldest temperature ever was 129°F below zero. Freezing water is 32°F.

CREATE A GRAPH

Students here collect the heights of people in their family or several of their friends. Then they create a bar graph that shows this information in a graphic.

Ask students: Why is this bar graph a more effective way to present the information than simply listing the height of each person?

Sample Response: →

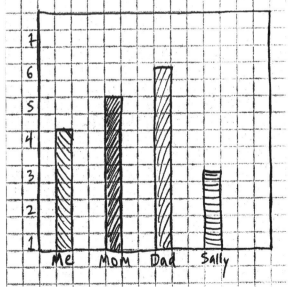

WRITING REMINDERS

As students create their graphs, remind them to:

✔ Collect information from two or more family members.

✔ Record the data they collect accurately on the graph.

✔ Neatly fill in the bars.

U n i t O v e r v i e w

In this unit students learn more about the importance of language. Sometimes writers choose words that make readers feel as though they are really experiencing what is on the page. Here students learn how adding sensory details, similes, and personification helps readers to more vividly picture—or experience—a piece of writing. Explain to students that such writing awakens readers' senses and makes reading more pleasurable. The writing is also easier to remember, because often the details are linked to something in the reader's own experiences.

R e a d i n g t h e A r t

Ask students to look closely at the art on this page. Then have them discuss the following questions as a whole-class activity:

- What is being described in this drawing?
- What words are shown?
- What senses are linked to the descriptive words?
- How would you finish the simile on this page? Why do you think the illustrator chose this simile?

UNDERSTANDING LANGUAGE

Literature Focus

Lesson	Literature
1. Hey, Reader—Are Your Senses Awake?	**Carolyn Lesser**, "The Crystal Bear" This poem presents many sense-related images of the life of the Arctic bear.
2. Understanding Similes	**Margot Theis Raven**, from *Angels in the Dust* Margot Raven writes vividly of the time in Oklahoma when the winds wouldn't stop blowing.
3. When Animals Talk	**Byrd Baylor**, from *Desert Voices* Byrd Baylor creates a poem like a riddle, so the reader can guess whose voice is personified.

Reading Focus

Lesson	Reading Skill
1. Hey, Reader—Are Your Senses Awake?	Sensory details help the reader imagine what the writer describes.
2. Understanding Similes	Similes make meaning clear by showing how one thing is like another.
3. When Animals Talk	Writers make stories come to life by giving animals and objects human qualities.

Writing Focus

Lesson	Writing Assignment
1. Hey, Reader—Are Your Senses Awake?	Write a short paragraph describing an animal of your choice that uses sensory details to make the paragraph interesting.
2. Understanding Similes	Write a short description of a familiar person or place, using at least one simile in the description.
3. When Animals Talk	Write a short paragraph describing yourself as an animal.

Hey, Reader—Are Your Senses Awake?

Before Reading

FOCUS

Sensory details help the reader imagine what the writer describes.

In this lesson, students learn how sensory details help the reader vividly experience a character or setting in the way the author does.

BUILDING BACKGROUND

Vocabulary Warm-up

To help familiarize students with these words before reading the selection, have them complete this **Matching Definitions** exercise. Write the words and definitions below in two columns on the board. Ask students to match them by drawing a line between the word in the left column and its definition in the right column. For added practice, ask students to think of a sentence for each word.

1. *crystal* — awaken from sleep
2. *veils* — very fat
3. *fringy* — transparent, colorless
4. *rouse* — things that hide or obscure like a curtain or covering of cloth
5. *blubbery* — resembling a border of short, straight, or twisted strips hanging from raveled or cut edges

Prereading Strategy

Continue students' preparation for this lesson by **Previewing** the selection as a whole-class activity. To begin, ask students to read the first page of the poem. Then ask them to answer these questions, based on their initial reading:

1. Where does this kind of bear live? *(in the Arctic)*
2. What kind of bear is it? *(a polar bear; she calls him a crystal bear, because he is white and transparent like the Arctic ice)*
3. What is happening in this part of the poem? *(The bear is going to sleep for the winter.)*

Reading the Selection

RESPONSE STRATEGY

Students read the poem and circle any words that help them to see, feel, hear, or smell the world of the great crystal bear. Point out the sample responses, "I see fringy paws" and "I feel cold snow" in the Response Notes. Ask students to write similar sentences in their Response Notes that help them to link the sensory details they circle to specific senses. Suggest that students identify at least five sensory details.

CRITICAL READING SKILL

This lesson helps students to identify sensory details in a piece of writing. Tell students that asking this question as they read can help them to pull the sensory details out of the text:

➤Can I *see* this detail? *touch* it? *hear* it? *smell* it?

For example, in the line "As you pad through the storm wind,....", the word *pad* lets you *see* and *feel* how the bear moves. Encourage students to ask the above question to themselves as they read each line of the poem.

REREADING

Have students reread the poem, circling any sensory words they might have missed the first time through. Have students indicate which sense they use with each detail. For example, for "cold snow" students would indicate that they can *feel* the detail.

W r i t i n g

In this lesson, students make notes in the form of sensory details about the animal, and write a paragraph using those details.

CRYSTAL BEAR DRAWING

In this activity, students use the details they identified in the poem to create visual images of the bear.
Sample Response: →

ANIMAL DESCRIPTION

In this activity, students choose their own animals and complete charts of sensory details about them. Complete a chart for one animal as a whole-class activity before students begin to work on their own. Encourage students to close their eyes and picture their animals before they begin to write. Suggest that they brainstorm as many words as they can for each category.

Sample Response:

Kind of Animal: long-haired cat
Feels like: fur like puffs of cotton or a cloud, whiskers like broomstraws, velvet pads
Sounds like: purring and meowing
Smells like: my blanket and the outdoors
Feels like: silk, smooth, and furry

ANIMAL PARAGRAPH

In this activity, students use the details recorded in the previous activity to write paragraphs describing an animal. Begin by asking students to review their lists of sensory details. Remind them that they don't have to use every word they listed. Instead, encourage them to use the best, most vivid details.

Sample Response:

I share my room with a huge, gray and white puff of cotton that reminds me of a cloud. She is my best friend. She lets me bury my face in her soft, silky, smooth fur when I'm sad. She even lets me brush her beautiful, long fur. She talks to me by purring and meowing. She's my cat Snowy.

WRITING REMINDERS

Remind students to:

✓ Indent the first sentence in their paragraphs.

✓ Check to see that each sentence begins with a capital letter and ends with a period, question mark, or exclamation point.

✓ Read back over their writing to make sure they spelled each word correctly.

Understanding Similes

B e f o r e   R e a d i n g

FOCUS
Similes make meaning clear by showing how one thing is like another.

In this lesson, students learn to identify similes as a way of describing one thing by relating it to something else.

BUILDING BACKGROUND

Vocabulary Warm-up

To familiarize students with the vocabulary in this selection, use **Context Clues** to find the meaning.

> grit   scorching   drought   Panhandle   withered

1. "The farm was on the <u>Panhandle</u> plains of Oklahoma. That's where the land reaches out straight as a handshake, like the end of a pot." *("Like the end of a pot" describes Panhandle.)*
2. "Great dust storms came blowing. They came with the <u>drought</u> that took hold of the land. No rain fell for a long, long time." *(The last sentence defines drought.)*
3. "Mean new winds came blowing, too, <u>scorching</u> hot and stiff as a dragon's breath." *(Hot is a synonym of scorching.)*
4. "They <u>withered</u> our corn. They withered our wheat. They baked our land bone-dry until it looked as cracked and old as Mama's white milk pitcher." *(Dry and cracked define withered.)*
5. "…dirt came right through the cracks in our little brown house….It covered our faces with sandy <u>grit</u> as we slept…." *(Sandy is a synonym of grit.)*

Prereading Strategy

Build more background for the selection by asking students to create a **Word Web**.

What was the storm like?
strong, hot winds; no rain

What might it feel like?
It made people's faces feel gritty.

(Dust Storm)

What might be the effects of the storm?
No crops could grow; the dust covered everything in the house, including their pillows.

R e a d i n g   t h e   S e l e c t i o n

RESPONSE STRATEGY

Students are asked to highlight all the similes they can find in the selection and then to write what is being compared in their Response Notes. Encourage students to look for the words *as* and *like* as clues. Then, after they have identified the similes, they can go back and write what is being compared.

Sample Response:
<u>I lived on a wheat farm, as flat as a breadboard.</u> Response Notes: wheat farm/breadboard

CRITICAL READING SKILL

In this lesson, students are asked to identify similes. Get students started by asking:
➤ How does comparing *eyes* to *dinnerplates* help a reader? [It suggests their size.]
➤ How does comparing a *face* to a *balloon* help? [It suggests its size and shape.]

REREADING

After students finish reading the selection, re-read the selection, looking for the words *like* or *as*. These words will help them find the similes.

W r i t i n g

In this lesson, students learn to create similes of their own.

QUICK ASSESS

Do students' paragraphs:

✓ describe a person or place?

✓ contain at least one simile?

✓ create a clear image of the person or place?

OKLAHOMA DUST STORMS

As a first response, students draw to help visualize the storms in Oklahoma.

Sample Response: ➔

REREAD PAGE 114

Have students look closely at the simile "wind like dragon's breath." By analyzing one or two similes closely, students can see how they compare two things.

Sample Response:

The wind was hot, like dragon's breath. It made the corn and land dry.

CREATING SIMILES

This activity gives students practice in creating their own similes. Encourage students to envision the objects before completing the sentences. Give students time to share their similes with the class.

Sample Response:

1. The horse ran like a deer.
2. The old man's hands were as rough as cracked leather.
3. The wind was as cold as ice.
4. The boy was as tall as the corn.

PLACE DESCRIPTION

In this activity, students write descriptions of people or places familiar to them and use at least one simile in their description.

Sample Response:

The quilt on my bed is as old as my grandma. My great-grandma made it for her when she was born, and my grandma is now ninety-two. She says she is as old as the hills, but to me she is ageless, like an angel who has always been in my life.

WRITING REMINDERS

As students write their paragraphs, remind them to:

✓ Indent the first sentence in their paragraphs.

✓ Check to see that each sentence begins with a capital letter and ends with a period, question mark, or exclamation point.

✓ Read back over their writing to check their spelling.

3 When Animals Talk

Before Reading

FOCUS

Writers make stories come to life by giving animals and objects human qualities.

In this lesson, students learn about personification, or the attributing of human characteristics to nonhuman things.

BUILDING BACKGROUND

Vocabulary Warm-up

To help students with the poem's vocabulary, ask them to complete these **Cloze Sentences.** To begin, ask a volunteer to read a sentence with the correct vocabulary word added. Have students make up new sentences using these words for other students to complete.

| mysteries | clings | shedding | tenderness | fangs |

1. He treated his children with great _____ and respect.
2. He _____ with desperation to the idea that he is always right.
3. When the dog showed his _____, everyone quickly left the party.
4. The cat was _____, which made everyone sneeze.
5. Little _____ and other surprises make life interesting.

Prereading Strategy

To build more background for this selection, use an **Anticipation Guide** to help students begin to focus on the reading.
1. Agree   Disagree   Not much happens in a desert.
2. Agree   Disagree   A poem called "Desert Voices" will be about how the desert talks.
3. Agree   Disagree   An animal has nothing in common with the sun.

Reading the Selection

RESPONSE STRATEGY

Students are asked to read each stanza of the poem and then to record their predictions about who is speaking in their Response Notes. Explain to students that, like a series of clues in a riddle, they will gain more information to help them as the poem unfolds.

Sample Response:

Stanza 1: Maybe it's a worm or a slug.

As they read each stanza, encourage students to use information from previous stanzas when making their predictions. Encourage students to make more than one prediction at different points in the poem.

CRITICAL READING SKILL

In this lesson, students read a strong example of personification. Ask students what human characteristics they find in the poem.
➤ How is this thing or animal like me?
➤ Why does the poem use the pronoun *I*?

REREADING

After students have finished reading the selection, ask them to go back and reread the poem one more time. Did students find new clues that help them with their predictions? Did they find any other ways this animal has human characteristics?

Writing

QUICK ASSESS

Do students' paragraphs:

✓ use first-person voice?

✓ include at least four special things about their animals?

✓ give an animal or object human qualities?

In this lesson, students write their own animal paragraphs that use personification.

KIND OF ANIMAL

As a first response, students give their opinions about what kind of animal is speaking and how they know.

Sample Response:

I think it is a snake. The poem mentions fangs, and snakes have fangs.

A SPECIAL ANIMAL

In this activity, students picture themselves as an animal and then list four things that are special about them. Remind students to write in first-person voice.

Sample Response:

I'm smarter than the person who feeds me.

I can hear better than people.

I am the best dog in the block.

I am stronger and braver than that family cat Puffy.

GUESS THE ANIMAL

In this activity, students use their notes from the previous activity to write a paragraph. Remind them that in personification the animal talks and acts like people. This means that they must write in first-person voice.

Sample Response:

I'm a lot smarter than Ellen, the lady who feeds me. The bones she gives me I take away and put in a safe spot. Then she gives me more. The other dogs on the block stay away from me, because I'm bigger than them. That cat Puffy also knows I'm stronger and braver than her.

WRITING REMINDERS

As students complete their paragraphs, remind them to:

✓ Make sure they have written in first-person voice.

✓ Indent the first sentence in their paragraphs.

✓ Read back over their writing to check their spelling.

U n i t   O v e r v i e w

In this unit, students learn about the people and stories that influenced Patricia McKissack. They learn about the importance of interesting characters, more about an author's purpose, and explore the richness of language through studying how characters talk. Explain to students that Patricia McKissack's writing provides an interesting lens through which to learn more about how authors use their own personal experiences with language in their own writing.

Ask students to think about these questions as they read:

- What kinds of stories influenced her as a child?
- What kinds of stories, characters, and colorful language are a part of your personal history that might be woven into a story?
- What makes the language of her characters so colorful?

R e a d i n g   t h e   A r t

Ask students to study the art on this page. Then have them discuss it as a small-group or as a whole-class activity:

- What does this art show?
- What do you think these two characters are talking about?
- Who do you think these characters might be?
- What would they be saying?

Lead students to the conclusion that one character is telling a child a story.

Literature Focus

Lesson	Literature
1. Characters Make the Story	**Patricia McKissack**, "Monday," from *Ma Dear* This short excerpt highlights the day-to-day relationship between a widowed mother and her young son.
2. What's My Purpose?	**Patricia McKissack**, *Ma Dear* McKissack discusses her reasons for writing *Ma Dear* in the "Author Note" from the book.
3. An Author's Language	**Patricia McKissack**, from *Mirandy and Brother Wind* This excerpt is packed full of wonderful images and sensory details about Brother Wind and Mirandy, who is determined to dance with him.

Reading Focus

Lesson	Reading Skill
1. Characters Make the Story	Interesting characters talk, act, and feel like real people.
2. What's My Purpose?	When you know a writer's purpose, it can help you make sense of what you read.
3. An Author's Language	Good writers make their characters sound like real people.

Writing Focus

Lesson	Writing Assignment
1. Characters Make the Story	Write a journal entry in the voice of one of the two characters.
2. What's My Purpose?	Write a tribute to a special person.
3. An Author's Language	Write a conversation between you and your friend.

Characters Make the Story

B e f o r e   R e a d i n g

FOCUS

Interesting characters talk, act, and feel like real people.

In this lesson, students learn how strong characters make a story interesting to readers.

BUILDING BACKGROUND

Vocabulary Warm-up

| clothespins | chafed | soldier | sword | mantel |

To help students become familiar with the words in this selection, try starting class with a **Vocabulary Quiz Show.** Write each word on a 3 X 5 file card. Then write a definition for each word on five other cards. Pass out the cards to 10 different students in class. Ask students to begin by saying one of the words out loud. Have the student who has the card with the meaning of the word read it aloud.

Prereading Strategy

Use this **Think-Pair-and-Share** activity to get students ready to read this selection. Ask students to read these sentences and then predict what the selection will be about. Then ask students which sentence appears in the story first, which one second, and so on. Then ask students to begin the lesson.

1. "At day's end, when the last sweet-smelling piece has been taken off the line and folded, Ma Dear rests in her rocking chair."
2. "Then she rolls up her sleeves and scrubs each piece on her rub board."
3. "First, Ma Dear heats water in the big kettle and pours it into several tubs."
4. "She's so tired, yet she holds out her arms."

R e a d i n g   t h e   S e l e c t i o n

RESPONSE STRATEGY

Explain to students that strong, well-drawn characters make us curious. We want to know more about them and what they might do or say next. Sometimes, they even remind us of ourselves. In this lesson, students underline places in the text that give them information about the characters. Then they write down any questions and comments about Ma Dear and David Earl in their Response Notes.

Sample Response:

Underlined text: blue apron

Ma Dear must wash and cook. Is she a mother? Is David Earl her son?

CRITICAL READING SKILL

In this lesson, students pay attention to what they learn about two characters, Ma Dear and David Earl. Help focus their reading by asking:

➤ What do you learn about these characters?

➤ What kinds of things do they say?

Encourage students to think about these questions as they read the selection.

REREADING

After students finish reading the selection, have them go back and reread the selection, looking for parts that tell about the characters. Have students underline these parts and write their comments in the Response Notes.

Writing

In this lesson, students write a journal entry from one character's point of view.

QUICK ASSESS

Do students' paragraphs:

✔ talk in first-person from their character's point of view?

✔ reflect one of the characters?

MA DEAR
Help students brainstorm words to describe Ma Dear.
  Sample Response:
hard-working, gentle, tired, happy

DAVID EARL
Help students brainstorm words to describe David Earl.
  Sample Response:
helpful, young, happy, sleepy, small

PICTURE THIS
In this activity, students create sketches of the face of one of the characters. Encourage students to read back over their underlined text as the basis for their sketches.
  Sample Response: ➜

A DAY IN THE LIFE
In this activity, students think about what a character might say in a journal entry of the day that just ended. Encourage students to reflect upon the character's personality, feelings, and dreams, based on what they know. Tell them to try to *hear* the character speaking, and then write it down on paper.
  Sample Response:
I don't know what I would do without David Earl. I wish his father were alive to see him. I can't believe that a year has passed since I got the news of his death. The future seemed to stop at that moment. It was only our baby that kept me going. I'm glad he is old enough to know the story of his father by heart.

WRITING REMINDERS
Remind students to:
✔ Write in the first-person and use the pronoun *I*.
✔ Read back over their writing to make sure they spelled each word correctly.
✔ Indent the first sentence in their journal entry.

What's My Purpose?

B e f o r e   R e a d i n g

FOCUS

When you know a writer's purpose, it can help you make sense of what you read.

In this lesson, students read to discover an author's purpose for writing.

BUILDING BACKGROUND

Vocabulary Warm-up

To help students get ready for this selection, use this **Matching Definitions** activity. Write the five words below and their definitions in two columns on the board. Ask students to match them by drawing a line between the word in the right column and its definition in the left column. For added practice, ask students to think of a sentence for each word.

1. *rural*   small pieces of wood used to start a fire
2. *appliances*   people who cook and clean for a living
3. *tribute*   the country; outside a city
4. *domestic workers*   equipment, including electric irons, washing machines, etc.
5. *kindling*   honor, appreciation, recognition, respect

Prereading Strategy

If desired, build more background for the selection by creating a **Word Web** about *great-grandmothers*. Encourage students to suggest words that describe great-grandmothers they have known or heard about.

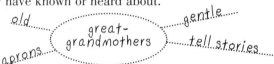

R e a d i n g   t h e   S e l e c t i o n

RESPONSE STRATEGY

Students are asked to highlight at least two places in the text that help them understand the author's purpose in writing *Ma Dear*.

Sample Response:

Those memories inspired me to write this story....

CRITICAL READING SKILL

This lesson helps students to identify an author's purpose in writing. The following questions are helpful to ask as students read this selection:

➤ What made McKissack think of her great-grandmother?
➤ How does McKissack describe her? Did she like her?
➤ What words or phrases help you know how she felt about her?

REREADING

After students finish reading the selection, ask them to review their underlined text and margin notes. For each place have them identify whether the passage relating to the author's purpose: gives information, tells a story, shares thoughts and feelings, convinces the reader.

Writing

In this lesson, students write tributes to a person who is special to them.

MA DEAR

As an initial response, students tell why the apron was special to Patricia McKissack and her purpose in writing.

Sample Response:

The apron makes her think of her great-grandma, who was special to her. Patricia McKissack's purpose was to remember her great-grandma.

PLAN A TRIBUTE

In this activity, students think of special people they want to honor. Encourage students to take their time in thinking of the people who are special to them. Ask them why these people are important. They may also select special objects that remind them of the people they chose.

Sample Response:

Special person: My grandfather

Reasons: He taught me how to ice fish and how to make maple syrup in the winter.

Special object: He gave me his carving knife, which is very special to me.

WRITE A TRIBUTE

In this activity, students write tributes to people who are special to them. Encourage students to re-read McKissack's tribute before they begin to write. Explain to students that a tribute is a way of honoring people and remembering them.

Sample Response:

He would wake me up early. I thought it was too early at the time. But since it was my grandfather, I would shuffle out of bed and put on my warmest clothes. Then I would follow him down the path to the snowy lake. There he would share with me all his best ice-fishing secrets.

Remind students that they do not need to use all their notes in their final piece of writing.

WRITING REMINDERS

As students write their tributes, remind them to:

✓ Indent the first sentence in the paragraphs.

✓ Check to see that each sentence begins with a capital letter and ends with a period, question mark, or exclamation point.

✓ Read back over their writing to check their spelling.

3 An Author's Language

Before Reading

In this lesson, students study the richness of language and how different characters talk.

FOCUS

Good writers make their characters sound like real people.

BUILDING BACKGROUND

Vocabulary Warm-up

Before beginning the selection, make sure students understand the words below. Use a **Context Clues** activity to help them.

bidding   cakewalk   shackles   wheeling   capture

1. "Mirandy set out to <u>capture</u> Brother Wind." *(The word* get *or* "go after" *could be substituted for* capture *in the sentence.)*
2. "'There's an old saying that whoever catch the Wind can make him do their <u>bidding</u>.'" *(Make him* suggests bidding *means* will.)
3. "'I'm goin' to,' say Mirandy. And she danced around the room, dipping, swinging, turning, <u>wheeling</u>." *(Danced, dipping, and* swinging *suggest the meaning.)*
4. "'This is my first <u>cakewalk</u>. And I'm gon' dance with the Wind!'" *(Dance is a description of* cakewalk.)
5. "'Can't nobody put <u>shackles</u> on Brother Wind, chile. He be special. He be free.'" *(The word* free *is an antonym of* shackles.)

Prereading Strategy

Give students more introduction to the selection by **Previewing** it as a whole class. Ask students to read the first four paragraphs and then answer these three questions:

1. What time of year is it? *(It's spring.)*
2. Who is Brother Wind? *(He is a fancy person who wears a silvery cape that swooshes behind him. He might also just be the Wind personified.)*
3. What does Mirandy want? *(She wants Brother Wind to be her partner at the cakewalk.)*

Reading the Selection

RESPONSE STRATEGY

As an active reading strategy, students circle the words and phrases they especially like. They mark any words or phrases they don't understand with a question mark.

Sample Response:

<u>There's an old saying that whoever catch the Wind can make him do their bidding.</u>** <u>Can't nobody put shackles on Brother Wind, chile. He be special. He be free.</u>**

CRITICAL READING SKILL

This lesson helps students to appreciate the way characters talk. Ask students:
➤ What do you like best about how these characters talk?
➤ How do the ways the characters talk add to the enjoyment of the writing?

REREADING

After students finish reading the selection, ask them to go back and review their circled words in the text. Ask them to circle any other interesting words they find on re-reading the selection. Ask them to take turns sharing their circled words.

Writing

QUICK ASSESS
Do students'
conversations:

✓ contain natural-
sounding dialogue
between friends?

✓ use some lively
words and expressions?

In this lesson, students practice writing a natural conversation with one of their friends.

DESCRIPTION OF BROTHER WIND
In this activity, students choose their favorite descriptions of Brother Wind and then illustrate them. Encourage students to read over their circled words to help them choose their descriptions.

Sample Response:
high steppin', dressed in his finest, trailing that long, silvery cape

REWRITING SENTENCES
Students are to rewrite sentences from the selection. Remind them to find the sentence in the text and read the whole paragraph in order to get any context clues that might help them.

Sample Response:
Grandmother Beesley thought about it.
"You can't stop the wind, child."
"I'm going to get him," she would say, turning around and around in the yard.

HOW DO YOU TALK?
In this activity, students make a list of some words and phrases they use when talking with their friends. Ask students to brainstorm long enough lists from which they can choose the best examples. Have students share some examples aloud with the class.

Sample Response:
cool, awright, no way, like

CONVERSATION WITH A FRIEND
In this activity, students take the word lists they brainstormed and write a conversation between two or more friends. Remind them to refer to their lists in the previous activity for ideas.

Sample Response:
"I have this like cool idea. Let's walk down to the music store and check out the new guitars they got in."
"Awright! This chore list is history! There's no way I'm stayin indoors anymore on a day like this. We're outa here!"

WRITING REMINDERS
As students write their conversations, remind them to:
✓ Indent the first sentence in each paragraph.

✓ Use quotation marks around the words used in conversations.

✓ Remember to start a new paragraph each time someone else speaks.

Skill	Teacher's Guide	Student Edition
Anticipation Guide	80, 90, 96, 112,	124, 132
Ask Questions	80	16
Ask Questions	92, 104, 112, 116	42, 58, 76, 87
Author's Purpose	112, 138	76, 129
Author's Style	106, 140	63, 133
Character	88, 104, 136	32, 58, 124
Cloze Sentences	88, 92, 100, 122,	132
Context Clues	82, 96, 112, 120,	130, 140
Context Clues	100	52
Graphic Aids	124	100
Highlight	82, 90, 130, 138	21, 37, 113, 129
Main Idea	82, 114	21, 82
Mark Clues	100	52
Mark Up the Text	84, 96, 114, 120, 122, 136, 140	26, 46, 82, 92, 96, 124, 133
Matching Definitions	90, 104, 108, 114,	128, 138
Personification	132	118
Plot	92	42
Point of View	84	26
Predict	80, 88, 132	16, 32, 118
Previewing	84, 92, 98, 106,	120, 128, 140
Prior Knowledge	116	87
Realistic Fiction	108	70
Rhyme and Rhythm	96	46
Sensory Details	128	108
Sequence	122	96
Setting	90	37
Simile	130	113
Summarize	120	92
Think-Pair-and-Share	88, 100, 108, 116,	136
Underline	106	63
Visualize	98, 108, 124, 128	49, 70, 100, 108
Vocabulary Quiz Show	80, 84, 98, 106,	116, 124, 136
Word Choice	98	49
Word Web	82, 104, 114, 122,	130, 138